D1743276

IN A FAR PLACE

LIZ HARRIS

HEYWOOD PRESS

PROLOGUE

**A**bove London
    June, 1960

PETER PULLED his seat belt tight, flattened his forehead against the aeroplane window and stared out into the blackness beneath him.

Every pinpoint of light was a house, a shop, a factory, hospital or school—all of the places he'd be finding in the city in which they were about to live again.

His heart beat fast in anticipation.

He was almost home.

Home. The place he'd been dreaming about for the ten long years that he and his parents had lived in Ladakh, a high mountain plateau beyond the Himalayas, where every aspect of life had been a struggle.

Home. Where he'd be able to walk up to people, talk to them and know that they understood him. Where he'd be able to turn on a tap and fill a glass with water, have a bath whenever he felt like it, use a proper toilet and not a hole in the floor, touch a switch on the wall and fill the room with electric light, go to the shops and buy anything he wanted, meet girls he could talk to.

He could hardly contain his impatience to return to the life his parents had snatched from him when he'd been a mere six years old.

He stared fixedly through the window, his gaze on the ground.

As the plane started to sink towards the bright lights, he turned in excitement to his mother and father.

His mother squeezed his hand.

On the other side of his mother, his father sat immobile, looking at the back of the seat in front of him, his face impassive.

His mother was as thrilled as he was, he knew. She, too, had longed to return to England.

But not his father.

His father had hated having to accept what he described as defeat. He'd wanted to stay in their small stone house on the plateau and continue his struggle to win the trust of people who'd steadfastly rejected them throughout the ten years they'd been in Ladakh.

He turned back to the window.

The ground raced up to meet him.

He caught his breath and waited to feel the glorious moment the plane touched England. Seconds later, the wheels on the landing gear grazed the tarmac, bounced a couple of times and settled.

With a deep sigh of contentment, he slumped back.

He was home at last.

From now on, life was going to be perfect.

1

Seven years later

B irmingham
   November, 1967

HIS WHITE COAT FLAPPING OPEN, Peter Henderson hurried along the corridor, the medical school behind him, the hospital in front of him. Clutching his stethoscope and file to his chest, he glanced at his watch.

Damn! He should never have stayed on after the lecture. He'd lost all track of time and now looked like missing the start of the consultant's afternoon round.

Someone would cover for him if his absence was spotted, he was sure, but since the consultant would've already heard every excuse in the book, and probably more than once, it was bound to be a black mark against him. Damn, again.

His head down, he walked more quickly.

CLAIRE MEREDITH GRIPPED her bag tightly and headed as fast as she dared in the direction of the corridor linking the hospital with the medical school.

Hastily, she pushed aside her short navy-blue woollen cape and glanced down at the Smiths watch pinned to the bib of her starched apron. She groaned inwardly. Mary was bound to be at the canal by now, and would be wondering where she was.

It must be the first time in her life she'd been grateful for having to wear regulation black lace-up shoes, she thought wryly. It meant she'd be able to go at a half-run once she'd got through the medical school.

Thank goodness one of the student nurses in her set had told her about a shortcut to the canal through the medical school. If she'd gone the long way round, she'd have been far too late for any sort of walk, no matter how short, before their next lesson.

She rounded the corner of the hospital wing. The corridor entrance lay ahead of her. Clasping the ends of her cape with one hand, and her bag with the other, she speeded up.

AT EXACTLY THE SAME MOMENT, they reached the middle of the corridor and crashed headlong into each other.

'What the!' Peter exclaimed, dropping his file.

'Ouch!' Claire cried. Her bag slipped from her hand and landed on the wooden floor, its contents spilling out.

Each faced the other, momentarily stunned.

'You okay?' he asked.

'I think so.' She touched her head, and winced. 'Yes, I'm sure I am. I doubt I'll have more than a bruise.' She took a step back and scowled at him. 'But it's no thanks to you. You should've been looking where you were going.'

'And so should you,' he said bluntly. 'And for the record, I'm fine, too. Thanks for asking.'

He knelt down, pushed everything back into her bag, picked it up and also his file, stood up and handed her the bag.

'Thank you,' she said shortly.

'You're sure you're all right?' he asked.

'I said I was, didn't I? And if you get out of my way, I'll prove it. I'm late enough as it is.'

'I'd be delighted.' He stepped sharply to one side.

Giving him a final glare, she continued along the corridor to the medical school.

WHAT A SHAME that someone as pretty as that should be so bad-tempered, he thought as he started walking again.

She'd been every bit as much at fault as he, and it wouldn't have hurt her to have said so. Instead, she'd been rude and unreasonable, and shown herself to have the fiery temper that famously went with red hair.

Well, glorious though her hair may be, there was nothing glorious about her attitude, and he very much hoped he never saw her again.

WHO DID he think he was, bumping into her like that and expecting her to take the blame?

In the split second before they'd collided, she'd realised he was heading straight for her—he'd been looking at the ground, not ahead of him—but she hadn't had time to get out of his way. And then he'd refused to admit it was his fault!

That was typical of a medic, or so she'd heard. Everyone said they were full of self-importance, and he was obviously no exception to the rule. What a waste of a good-looking man.

AT THE SAME MOMENT, both reached the end of the passage. Their steps faltered. On a sudden impulse, each glanced back along the corridor, and for a fleeting instant, their eyes met across the distance.

Then they turned away and continued towards their destinations.

 *week later*

HE MUST BE MAD, Peter thought as he left the medical school and headed for the bridge that spanned the canal separating the hospital and school from the red-brick buildings of the university.

Increasingly during the past week, the face of the red-headed girl had sprung into his mind. Yet it wasn't as if he'd even liked her! Yes, she was pretty—very pretty, in fact—and yes, she had striking hair, but she didn't seem to have anything else going for her. Important things such as reasonableness and fairness.

Nevertheless, since the day they'd bumped into each other, he'd found himself keeping an eye out for her.

Not that he'd had any success, and that surprised him. The plainness of her nurses' cap showed she was on the Preliminary Training Scheme. This meant she must be living and studying in Nuffield House, just across the road from the hospital, so he would've expected to see her around the place. But not so.

Nor had he seen her in the hospital canteen, even though he'd started bypassing the doctors' section and having his coffee in the main part, where the PTS nurses sometimes sat.

And there'd hadn't been any sign of her in the Union Bar on the evenings when he'd gone across to the university with some of the other medics.

But he'd stopped short at going to parties where he'd be likely to find trainee nurses.

He'd partied enough since starting medical school to know that although he now found it easier to think of things to say to people than when he'd first returned to England, he'd never truly enjoy that sort of social situation.

And when his parents had given him a second-hand Lambretta halfway through his third year, he'd started heading for the countryside in any free time he had—occasionally with one of the other medics, but more often than not on his own—and he'd more or less given up on parties.

To resume doing something he didn't really like, in order to meet someone who'd come across as self-righteous and unreasonable... He shook himself in despair. He needed his head examining for even thinking about her!

When he got to Hudson's, he'd buy the book he'd forgotten the last time he was there, grab a coffee in the refectory, which was next to the bookshop, and then return to the hospital. And he wouldn't allow himself to spare that nurse another thought.

.   .   .

THE RED-HEADED nurse was the first person Peter saw when he entered the refectory. She was reading at a table in front of the metal-framed window, a cup in front of her and a Hudson's bag on one of the other chairs.

That's a stroke of luck, he thought. If the table next to hers was still empty by the time he'd got his coffee, he'd grab it, start up a conversation, and if she was as rude as he remembered, he'd get her out of his system once and for all.

Finally, he reached the front of the queue, ordered a black coffee, hastily paid the woman behind the bar and made a beeline for the table. Thinking quickly, he chose the chair from which if he glanced to his left he'd see her face, and he sat down and opened his book.

Now for an opening line, he thought. And it had better be fast, before she left.

The obvious thing would be to call across that they'd bumped into each other the week before. But it wasn't the greatest opening gambit. She'd know he hadn't forgotten her, for a start, and while that might be true, he'd rather not spell it out.

His gaze fell on the sugar bowl in front of him, and inspiration struck. He pushed the bowl as far as possible from her table, and leaned towards her.

'Excuse me.'

She looked up from her book.

He saw her give a start of recognition.

'I don't suppose you've any sugar?' His voice was full of apology. 'My bowl's empty.' He paused, and then let his expression change into one of surprise. 'I believe we've met before.'

'If you mean that you collided into me, then, yes, I think we have. But I don't bear grudges,' she added, 'so you're welcome to my sugar.' She reached across to the bowl.

'A better idea,' he said swiftly. 'Rather than put you at risk of further injury by lifting such a heavy container, why don't I join you?'

She hesitated a moment, and then shrugged. 'If you like. But despite your best efforts, I was hardly injured the first time we met.'

He'd go through with this now as he'd started, he thought standing up, but his second impression was shaping up to be pretty much like his first, and he wouldn't be going out of his way to speak to her again.

'Suppose we call it an accident and leave it at that?' he suggested, moving his things to her table and taking the seat opposite her.

She nodded. 'Fair enough.'

Reaching across to the sugar bowl, he picked up the scent of flowers.

'You smell nice,' he remarked, putting two lumps of sugar into his cup.

She pulled a face. 'You don't, I'm afraid.'

He grinned ruefully. 'I'd forgotten I must stink of formaldehyde. We've just had Pathology and the formalin sticks to your hands, your hair, your clothes—you can't wash it off. The first and second floors of the medical school reek of it! And as for my wardrobe, it smells like a mortuary. It's a constant reminder of where I don't want my patients to end up.'

'Don't worry; it doesn't bother me.'

'Then not only was I lucky to be next to a table with sugar, but also where there was someone who lacked a strongly developed sense of smell,' he said cheerfully.

'Ah, but you were unlucky to pick a table with an empty bowl in the first place, and one that was next to someone you'd crashed into the week before. That rather balances things, doesn't it?'

He glanced at her sharply, but it was amusement that flickered in her dark-brown eyes flecked with gold, and he felt himself relax.

Those eyes really were striking with her red hair, he thought. He gave a short cough. 'We were in too much of a rush to swap names when we met, so perhaps we should make up for it now. I'm Peter—Peter Henderson.'

'And I'm Claire Meredith.'

'That's a nice name. It suits you. Let me guess—you're in the PTS?'

'Don't think you're getting brownie points for that guess,' she said drily. 'The uniform's a weeny bit of a clue.'

He smiled. 'How're you liking nursing so far?'

'Well, it's early days, but I've a feeing I'm going to like it a lot. So far, we've been learning how to give blanket baths, injections, feed patients, and so on. I'm now dying to be let loose on a live patient. Oops! Perhaps I could've chosen a better word than dying,' she added with a giggle.

'When will that fatal day happen—if I may continue the theme?'

'By all means. After our twelve weeks of PTS,' she continued, 'we begin three years of three months on the wards followed by three months in a block. The block's the classroom bit.' She paused. 'What about you? What year are you in?'

'The fourth. It's a five-year course. Or six, if you include the year between graduating and registering as a doctor. But we've only been on the wards for a month. Before that, we had eighteen months pre-clinical, followed by eighteen months clinical. Given the way we've been bumping into each other,' he added, 'I'm sure it won't be long before we encounter each other on a ward. If you spot me about to cut open the wrong end of a patient...'

'Don't think I'd fly to your rescue,' she said lightly. 'I'm afraid I'd have to let you do the deed—we lowly nurses aren't allowed to speak to doctors and consultants, not unless they've spoken to us first.'

'I hereby give you permission to speak to me any time you want,' he said with mock solemnity.

'Thank you, kind sir,' she said, inclining her head in feigned gratitude.

They smiled at each other across the table, and then each picked up their cup at the same moment.

'Do you come from around here?' she asked, putting her cup back on the table.

He shook his head. 'Nope, from London. At least, that's where I live now, but I've lived longer outside London than in it. And you?'

'We live in Hereford. Mother's got a flat there.' She glanced at her watch. 'Gosh, look at the time—I must go!' She downed the last of her coffee, slid her book into the Hudson's bag and stood up. 'I'm meeting my friends in the clinical room. We're going to practise blanket baths. We've got a test soon and I'm useless at them.'

He rose to his feet. 'I ought to leave, too. Now that I've bought the book I need, I should use it.'

They started moving away. As they did so, Claire glanced down at the table where Peter had first been sitting. She stopped abruptly.

He followed her gaze to the sugar bowl, which was full to the brim. 'It was all I could think of,' he said with a slight shrug.

She looked at him in surprise. 'To do what?'

'To wipe the slate clean after clumsily bumping into you.'

'Aha! I think I've just had a weird sort of apology.' Laughter played across her lips.

'If that's what it takes to get you to go out with me, then you have.' He cleared his throat. 'When we're free on a Saturday evening, my friends and I usually go for a Chinese. I don't suppose you'd like to come along next Saturday? If I promise to take a long bath first and spray myself with exotic cologne?'

She hesitated. 'Okay. But only if you leave off the cologne,' she added with a smile.

'It's a deal. I'll collect you from in front of Nuffield House at six thirty, if that's all right. I assume that's where you live.'

She nodded. 'I must be back by ten thirty, though—Matron's very strict.'

'No problem. But be warned—your carriage will be an ancient Lambretta. Or if you prefer it,' he said quickly, 'we can take the bus.'

'The Lambretta sounds fun. I've never been on the back of a scooter before.' She looked at her watch again. 'I really have to get off.'

'Till Saturday, then.'

He gave her a slight wave, and she hurried away.

Well, contrary to what he'd first thought, his first impression had been well and truly wiped out, he realised as he trailed after her towards the exit. Saturday couldn't come quickly enough.

THOROUGHLY IRRITATED, Claire hung up the telephone and headed for her room. Once again, her mother had managed to destroy her good mood within minutes. She'd no idea why on earth she'd been so stupid as to ring home.

Or actually, she had.

When she'd got back to Nuffield House from the refectory that morning, adrenalin streaking through her, eager to describe in detail for Mary her meeting with Peter, she'd been massively disappointed when Mary had failed to turn up to the blanket bath practice, and was nowhere to be seen afterwards.

Desperate to talk to someone, and not being especially close to anyone else in her set, her mother had sprung to her mind, and she'd promptly dialled home.

In a matter of moments, she'd regretted it.

The second she'd heard the frigid politeness in her mother's voice, she'd mentally seen her mother, rigid in her walnut-framed armchair, her back ramrod straight, her face set in an expression of disapproval, and her excitement had started to evaporate.

She and her mother had never been close, not even after her father's death, not in the way of some mothers and daughters. Grace Meredith was a woman of strong opinions, and not given to displays of emotion.

What warmth and sunshine there'd been in Claire's early years had come from her father, a kind, gentle man, who was some years older than her mother, and they'd died with him.

The three of them had lived in a house outside Hereford, but not long after Claire's father's death, Grace had found an elegant flat in a sought-after part of the city, not far from an excellent school, and she and Claire had moved there, living side by side in harmony, each hugging to herself her privacy.

Despite her mother's remoteness, Claire's life had been happy enough.

She didn't mind that her mother wasn't warm and demonstrative—it was just the way she was. Claire was sure she was loved, and that was what mattered. And she had everything she needed: her mother provided her with all her material needs, and when she was with her close friends from school, she was able to give rein to her innate liveliness and sense of fun.

It was true that it would've been more pleasant to have been brought up in a less austere home, one in which a child could relax and be playful, but she'd always seemed to know that one day she'd live in such a home. When she married, she'd have lots of children, and she'd surround them with the warmth of family life.

When the time had come for her to decide upon a career, an idea that had been hovering in the back of her mind since her father's illness burst forth, and she realised that she very much wanted to become a nurse.

Never for one moment did she think that her mother would object to her choice. After all, when Claire had been sixteen, and in the kitchen preparing the tea one afternoon, she'd heard her mother tell the three friends who'd come to visit, that her daughter was working voluntarily as a nurse in the Hereford County Hospital during her school holidays. She'd heard the pride in her mother's voice.

She'd every reason, therefore, to be confident that her mother would be delighted for her.

She couldn't have been more wrong.

At the word nurse, her mother's face had gone white, and her skin had tightened in anger. Ill-advised was how she'd described Claire's decision, and very stupid.

While nursing in a voluntary capacity for a few weeks in the holidays was praiseworthy, it was a menial job that was most unsuitable as a career. If one could even call it a career. It wasn't for a girl from a good family.

That a daughter of hers should even contemplate a life of drudgery was an acute disappointment.

Helping sick people get well was hardly drudgery, Claire had countered, trembling in shocked surprise.

With the education she'd had, her mother had continued, her voice ice-cold, Claire should be aspiring to a career that commanded respect from others. One that would enable her to meet people of standing.

Fresh opportunities for girls were opening up yearly, and Claire, with her background and qualifications, was well placed to take advantage of them. She might even obtain a position that allowed her to travel abroad with her work.

She'd absolutely no desire to go abroad for anything other than a holiday, Claire had said, struggling to hold back tears of frustration and disappointment. She loved living in England and would hate to live anywhere else.

In the weeks that had followed, Claire had proved unable to make her mother see beyond the bedpan element in nursing, and eventually, by unspoken agreement, they'd laid the subject to rest in the stony silence that paved the space between them.

Claire went ahead and applied to prospective nursing schools with the support of her teachers and friends, but without that of her mother.

And not even when she was able to tell her mother that she'd been accepted by the Queen Elizabeth School of Nursing in Birmingham, one of the best training schools in the country, and one of the few that required 'A' level qualifications, did Grace relent.

She agreed to support Claire financially, but no more than that.

When the form explaining her financial situation as a student arrived, and Claire read the details of the allowance she'd receive and of the expenditure she'd have to meet as a student nurse, she saw that her mother's displeasure had underpinned her every commitment.

She would receive the minimum allowance, and not a penny more. After they'd taken out for food and accommodation, she'd be left with six pounds only for the whole month.

Her letter in her hand, she'd stood in disbelief in front of her mother, a question in her eyes.

Claire had grown up in relative ease, her mother had told her in clipped tones, and the sooner she realised the consequences of her decision, the better.

By undertaking a low-paid job, she would never be able to provide herself with a fraction of the comfort she'd so far been lucky enough to take for granted, and she should not expect anyone else to do so for her. Each person must stand on their own two feet.

Furthermore, she'd added, it would be an unkindness for one person to prevent another from facing the reality of their situation. Not when there was still time to reconsider.

So this was an attempt to make her come to her senses, as her mother would put it, Claire railed accusingly. Her father would have been furious at her mother's tightness with the money he'd earned, and with her willingness to see Claire live in straitened circumstances in the hope that it would dissuade her from what he was sure to have seen as a worthwhile job.

Her father probably *would* have indulged her in a way that she was not prepared to do, her mother had agreed. But in his heart, he'd have been as unhappy as she to see Claire embarking upon what he, too, considered to be a low-status career.

He might well have kept his disappointment to himself, but he loved Claire and had wanted the best for her, and he, too, would have considered nursing to be a long way from the best.

Knowing there was nothing more she could say, Claire had walked away from her mother, and, to take her mind off her mother's coldness, had begun the preparations for her move to Birmingham. Not once did she ask for her mother's help, nor share with her the excitement that was building within her.

When the time came for Claire to leave Hereford, she picked up her suitcase and walked steadily towards the front door, determined not to look back. She'd say a terse goodbye from the doorway, and shut the door behind her. Her mother deserved no more than that.

But before she could reach the door, something within her forced her feet to stop. As if glued to the floor, her suitcase still in her hand, she turned and looked across the room at her mother.

Grace was sitting in her wing armchair, her back to Claire, waiting in stillness to be alone for the first time for many years.

In the harsh late-morning light, her mother suddenly seemed very frail, Claire thought in momentary shock, and looked older than her years.

A wave of affection for her mother engulfed her, taking her completely by surprise, and she dropped her suitcase, went impulsively to her mother, bent down and kissed her on her cheek.

As she started to straighten up, her mother caught her

by the arm and stared intently into her face, her lips quivering. 'Whatever you may think, Claire, I love you and I do wish you well.'

A lump in her throat, Claire swallowed hard. 'I know you do,' she said quietly.

The desolation in her mother's pale-grey eyes, so unexpected, and the emotion that lay in their depths, had stayed with Claire in the weeks that had followed, and deep down she knew that those last words from her mother had come from her heart.

But upon hearing her mother's chilly response to her friendly greeting that afternoon, the desire to share that had impelled Claire to ring home, intending to tell her mother in passing that she'd be going out on Saturday with a man she'd initially disliked, but who'd turned out to be very pleasant, had dissolved before their conversation had been more than a few minutes old.

3

The following Saturday, late morning

PETER BENT over his A4 block of lined paper, crossed out the couple of paragraphs he'd written and started again. *The classification and adequate description of bacteria necessitates knowledge of their morphologic, biochemical, physiological, and genetic characteristics*, he wrote.

His hand came to a stop. He stared at the sheet of paper in front of him.

Claire's face stared back at him.

He shut his Bacteriology textbook with force, put down his pen and leaned back. It was no good, he just couldn't concentrate. A page of crossing out and one line of writing was all he had to show for a whole morning's work. No matter how hard he tried to focus on his essay, all he could think about was that evening, and seeing Claire again.

He locked his hands behind his head, leaned further back and stared at the watercolour on the wall in front of his desk. His mother had given it to him, knowing it was the one he liked best out of all the watercolours she'd done during their ten years in Ladakh.

Increasingly since he'd been back in England, he'd been drawn to that picture and to the memories it held. And to the sense of freedom it symbolised.

His mother had succeeded in capturing with her brush the openness of the area, and its beauty—a beauty he hadn't appreciated when he lived there.

His gaze travelled across her depiction of the stone-strewn lilac-grey plateau that stretched away from the house where they used to live, its barrenness given life by intermittent patches of greenery and the occasional cluster of wild flowers.

Beyond the plateau, purple mountains pierced the azure sky with their snow-tipped peaks—peaks he remembered as lilac-pink in the dawn, blazing white at noon, and burnished gold at the setting of the sun.

So vivid was the picture that he could almost smell the intoxicating fragrance of the wild flowers and hear the marmots whistling to each other from their hiding places in the rose-purple haze of the mountains. Every time he looked at the painting, something deep within him stirred.

It was the view he'd had every time he'd stepped out of the small stone house that the Mission had given them. For all the years that he'd lived there, however, his gaze had been on England, and he'd been longing to return.

It had taken him by surprise, therefore, that at some point during the past few years, he'd begun to miss Ladakh.

It wasn't that he'd ever want to live there again—he

wouldn't. But he missed the freedom he'd had, and the sheer beauty of the emptiness that had surrounded him.

Thinking about it, though, it had been inevitable that he'd look back with nostalgia on the life he'd had there.

By returning at sixteen, he'd instantly had to get down to a huge amount of studying, firstly to catch up with the subjects his mother hadn't been able to teach him, and then to win a place at a medical school. And for the past three years as a medic he'd been bogged down under the heavy workload thrown at them by their lecturers and professors.

It was bound to contrast negatively with the relative freedom he'd had in Ladakh.

Not that he resented having to study all the time—he didn't. Once he was registered as a doctor, he'd have a great deal of choice over where he worked and what he did, and to have such a choice was worth any amount of sacrifice.

And if he were truly honest with himself, there hadn't been that much sacrifice involved.

The high hopes he'd had when his plane had landed had disintegrated rapidly.

Growing up in a place where everyday life was centred on the need to be able to survive in harsh conditions, with his parents as his only companions, plus the one Ladakhi boy in the neighbouring village who'd come to be able to speak English, had been no preparation for meeting people of his own age.

And when faced with his peers, all of whom seemed familiar with modern dances, pop music, the latest films, the fashions, what had been going on in the world—subjects he knew nothing about—he'd struggled to think of things to say.

Everything had become much easier once he'd started at

Birmingham Medical School. He liked his fellow students, and their shared interest in medicine gave them a common ground. But he'd finally come to accept that his early years had left him with a legacy he'd never completely shake.

As time had passed, he'd begun to feel that something was missing from his life; namely, a girlfriend.

Consequently, he'd worked out how to fit his studies around the hours he spent on the wards and in lectures in a way that left him some time for himself, and he'd started dating. So far, though, he hadn't met anyone he was keen on seeing more than once or twice.

Until that week.

As he'd watched Claire leave the refectory, his every instinct had told him that he might just have found that missing something.

If things went well at the Chinese that evening, and he'd a feeling they would, there'd be other things they could do with his fellow medics, or even better, by themselves. He might not have a lot of spare money, but he had the Lambretta, and that gave him a freedom of movement.

He unlocked his hands, straightened up and glanced at the small clock on the corner of his desk. Only a few more hours to go.

He pushed back his chair and stood up.

Clearly he wasn't going to be able to think about anything other than Claire for the rest of the day so he might as well accept that, and abandon any attempt at working, go downstairs and get a corned beef sandwich.

He could pick up some leaflets about local places of interest at the same time, and look through them while he ate. It'd kill time, if nothing else.

Checking in the rear pocket of his jeans to make sure he

had sufficient money, he went across the room and opened the door.

I wonder what Claire's doing now, he thought as he closed the door behind him.

CLAIRE STOOD in front of the full-length mirror fixed to the outside of her wardrobe door, a pair of jeans in one hand and tailored trousers in the other. First she held the jeans in front of her, and then the trousers.

'What d'you think, Mary? Shall I wear my new jeans and look studenty, or go for a slightly smarter look? A skirt's out of the question as we'll be on a scooter. My blue shirt will go with both.'

She turned towards Mary, who was sitting on the bed, leaning back against the wall. 'Which would you choose if you were me?'

'The jeans,' Mary said, eyeing them both. 'A Chinese is casual, and it's not like it's just the two of you. You don't want him to think you've spent most of the day getting ready. There's such a thing as not looking too keen. Even if you are,' she added, with a sly smile.

'I'm not.'

'Yes, you are.'

Claire lowered the clothes. 'Honestly, Mary, how could I be? The first time we met, he was in the wrong and wouldn't admit it, and the second was for the length of a coffee. It takes more than five minutes to undo a bad first impression and learn what a person's like inside, you know.'

'Forget about the inside! From the way you've described the outside, five minutes was more than enough. What was it you said—tall, rugged-looking, fair hair, deep blue eyes, broad shoulders? I'll bet that at the first glimpse of his *biceps brachii,* you stood there, tongue hanging out, and drooling. And all without him saying a word.'

Claire burst out laughing. 'Idiot!' She dropped the jeans and shirt on to the back of her wooden desk chair, opened her wardrobe and hung up the trousers.

'Fair enough; he *is* attractive, and, to my great surprise, I enjoyed talking to him. He came across as a nice guy, and not at all like the medical bods who are horribly full of themselves.' She closed the wardrobe door. 'But it's no more than that.'

'Just be careful, and I don't mean about crossing the road. And be back on time tonight. Another second year's been caught sneaking in late and Matron's on the warpath.'

Claire gave her a mock salute. 'Aye, aye, Cap'n!'

Mary tucked her legs under her. 'Try your shirt with the jeans, just to be sure they look right. I'll do your nails before you go, if you like.'

Claire pulled off her skinny rib dress and slipped into her jeans and pale blue denim shirt.

'My face won't know what's hit it tonight,' she said, buttoning up her shirt. 'After not being able to wear make-up all week, I can't wait to wear mascara and eyeliner, and my new pink lipstick. I won't bother with my nails, though, thanks all the same. It's not worth it—I'd have to remove the varnish before class on Monday.'

Leaving the top two buttons undone, she turned to Mary. 'Do they go together?'

'Indeed, they do. One look at each other and you'll forget all about the chow mein.'

Claire grimaced. 'Anything but that! I've had Vesta chow mein every week since I got here. Whatever I eat tonight, it won't be that.' She piled her hair on to the top of her head, turned sideways and glanced over her shoulder into the mirror.

'No,' she said, letting her hair fall again to her shoulders in a tumble of curls. 'It's just about long enough to put up, but I'll leave it loose. I need a change from the pinned-back, off-your-collar look.'

'Your meeting with Peter is the most exciting thing to have happened so far since we got here.'

'Not so!' Claire exclaimed, feigning shock. 'You've forgotten about the hospital's first ever batch of plastic disposable syringes and single-use needles. And the rapture on Sister's face as she gazed down at them.'

Mary laughed. 'You're right; silly me!' She uncurled herself and stood up. 'I must go. I want to get to the shop before it closes as I'll need to eat something before the party tonight. I doubt there'll be anything more than wine and crisps, and maybe not even crisps.'

'I hope you have a good time, and meet someone really nice.'

'I'll do my best. You'll get a full report tomorrow, and I'll want one from you, too.'

A moment later, the door clicked shut behind Mary.

Claire took off her jeans and shirt, arranged them on her bed, and then looked around the room in indecision. She paused when she reached her lecture notes on the desk. She really ought to write them up, after all she had the time.

She took a couple of steps towards the desk, and stopped. The notes would have to wait. With a stomach full of butterflies at the thought of the evening ahead, she just couldn't be bothered.

She'd have a bath before the Saturday night queue built up, and then find something light to read until it was time to get dressed.

She went over to her bedroom door, unhooked her quilted dressing gown and put it on. Then she took her toilet bag from the cupboard next to the washbasin in the corner of the room, opened her bedroom door and went out.

I wonder what Peter's doing at this moment, she thought as she pulled the door shut behind her.

4

Saturday evening

'MEET MY MATE, ALEX,' Peter said, indicating a tall, dark-haired man who'd moved swiftly to the chair on the other side of Claire while the rest of the group were spreading out around the table for ten, scraping chairs against the floor as they decided noisily where to sit. 'Fiona's with him.'

He smiled at the blonde girl who'd just sat down on the opposite side of the round table from Claire.

'If Peter doesn't mind, I'll sit next to you, Claire,' Alex said with a broad smile. 'But fear not, I promise not to say you'll be a rose between two thorns—that'd be far too corny.'

Peter laughed. 'Well restrained, Alex. Here, Claire; let me.' And he pulled out her chair, and then both he and Alex sat down.

While the others were settling, Claire glanced around

the small restaurant, at the plain walls and white cotton tablecloths, and at the candle burning in a tiny red glass jar in the centre of each table.

'I like it here,' she told Peter. 'I can't wait to try the food —I've never been to a Chinese restaurant before. My knowledge of Chinese food is limited to Vesta.'

'Not you, too! I alternate between their Chinese and Indian. Depending on my mood, it's either chow mein or beef curry.'

A waiter approached the table carrying a couple of bowls of prawn crackers, which he put in the middle of the table. He returned a moment later with menus.

The man on the other side of Peter leaned forward in front of Peter. 'Peter's not yet introduced us,' he called to Claire. 'He obviously wants to keep you to himself. I'm Mike.'

'I'm pleased to meet you, Mike,' she said with a smile. 'I'm Claire.'

He nodded to her and sat back in his seat.

'Right, you lot,' Alex said, raising his voice to be heard above the laughter and conversation. 'Shall we do the usual —each order a dish, and then all dive in? And fill up with rice? That'll keep it cheap and cheerful. Is everyone okay with that?'

There was a chorus of agreement.

'We need to order fairly sharpish,' Peter added. 'Claire has to be back by ten thirty.'

Alex nodded. 'Don't worry; there's plenty of time.'

The talking died down while they looked through the menu.

After a moment or two, Fiona lowered hers. 'You must be in the nurses' home, Claire,' she said.

'I suppose the curfew was a giveaway. What about you?'

'I'm in University House.'

'That's for both men and women, isn't it?'

'That's right,' Fiona said, her smile widening. 'Until recently, it was women only, which would've been ghastly. I struck lucky getting the only mixed-sex hall. Having said that, I'm thinking about moving into digs—perhaps in Bourneville, which isn't far away. Alex is keen on the idea. But I'm not sure—there're pros and cons with both.'

'You're lucky to have a choice. We can't move into our own accommodation until we've done at least one year, and then only if our parents write and say we can.'

Fiona pulled a face. 'I'd hate to be that restricted.'

'What's your subject, Fiona?' Peter asked. 'I've forgotten.'

'English.'

'Are you planning on being a teacher?' he asked.

'Not likely! I've no intention of having my hands permanently covered in chalk dust.' She held up an elegantly manicured hand. 'Whatever I do, it won't be that.'

'It must be fun, being able to sit and read all day,' Claire remarked.

'That side of it's all right. It'd be better, though, if we didn't have to write down what we thought of what we'd read. That part's a bore.'

They all laughed.

'What d'you think of nursing so far?' Fiona asked.

'I like it. And I'll like it even more when I've mastered the art of making a bed.'

'Bed!' Alex exclaimed, putting his menu down. 'Did I hear someone suggesting bed? And so early in the evening, too!'

Claire giggled.

Fiona glanced across the table at Alex. 'Don't you wish?' she said archly.

He gave her a half-smile, and then turned to Claire. 'I've a bed in my room that's not been made for a week. It's desperate for the ministrations of a hand that knows what it's doing. How about it, Nurse Claire?'

'I'm afraid you'd fall asleep in your chair while you waited for me to finish,' she said cheerfully. 'My fastest time so far is twenty-five minutes, and that was for a bed which ended up with a lopsided look, a crooked counterpane and a bottom sheet with wrinkles in it!'

He grinned at her. 'It's nice of you to offer, but I think I'll pass.'

'The waiter's coming, Claire,' Peter said. 'Have you decided what you want?'

She closed her menu. 'You order for us both. As long as it's not chow mein, I don't mind what I have.'

'Okay, you lot. Let's have some hush—it's time to order,' Alex called to the table. 'Each of you shout out the dish you want when the waiter comes round.' He turned to the waiter, who was hovering behind him. 'We'll have four lots of fried rice and two of boiled for a start.'

The waiter wrote that down, and then moved slowly around the table, making a note of the orders.

'Here, have a prawn cracker,' Peter said when the waiter had taken the orders to the kitchen. Claire took a couple, and he put the bowl down and turned towards her. 'Now let's forget about everyone else, and pick up where we left off.'

'Excuse my back,' she said, smiling at Alex, and she slid round in her chair to face Peter. 'If I remember rightly, you'd just said you'd lived longer outside London than in it, but you didn't say where you'd been.'

'We were in Ladakh. It's an Indian province north of the Himalayas, which has a border with Tibet. We were so high up that there was virtually no rain, only melt-snow water. It wasn't exactly the easiest place to live. My parents are missionaries, which is why we were there. But they've a mission closer to home now—in Walthamstow.'

'How long were you in Ladakh?'

'Almost ten years. From six to sixteen.'

'That's a long time. Did you like living there?'

'Like Fiona said a moment ago about something else, there were pros and cons. A big con was that it didn't equip me for life in England. One person only in the area spoke English—a boy of my age called Kalden.'

'How did he come to know English if no one else did?'

'My parents taught him in return for him teaching them how to make mud bricks, grow vegetables with next to no water, make food from the few plants that'd grow in stony soil, make the butter tea that stops your lips from cracking —how to survive, basically.'

'It sounds a hard life.'

He nodded. 'It was. So, with only Kalden to talk to, apart from my folks, when I came back to England, I hadn't a clue what to say to people my age. And it was even worse when I went out with a girl.'

'I'm not surprised.'

'For example,' he went on. 'On one truly desperate occasion, I heard myself telling my date that the Ladakhi people collected animal dung, and made it into pats that they dried in the sun and used as fuel. We were in a Wimpy Bar at the time, eating hamburgers.'

She threw back her head and laughed.

'You should've seen the expression on her face,' he said, grinning. 'She immediately stopped eating. We both laughed about it, but the evening couldn't end fast enough as far as I was concerned, and she didn't seem any keener on prolonging the agony. We said the speediest goodnight ever, and went our separate ways.'

'Well, you're easy enough to talk to now so you've clearly made up for lost time.'

'It was a challenge, but I love challenges.'

'You obviously don't have any brothers or sisters, so we can tick that off the getting-to-know-you list.'

'What about you?'

She shook her head. 'No, there's just me.'

'And you come from Hereford, you said.'

She nodded. 'We used to live outside the town, but my father died when I was fifteen, and Mother and I moved into a flat in the centre of the city.'

'What Hereford's like? I don't know it at all.'

'It's a cathedral city in a beautiful county. The country-side is stunning. If you like walking, and I do, it's a great place to grow up.'

'I enjoy walking, too. Which is fortunate—there wasn't much else for a boy to do on a mountain plateau.'

'It's me again.' Alex's voice came from the other side of Claire. She turned slightly towards him. 'It occurred to me that since I'm one of Peter's closest friends, we could be seeing a lot of each other in the future, Claire, so you really ought to know something about me, and not just something about my friend here.'

He grinned at Peter, and then his eyes returned to Claire.

'I need not tell you about my personal charm, of course —you'll be able to see that easily enough for yourself—but I could tell you about my abilities.'

Claire glanced at Peter and giggled.

'Tough luck, Alex,' Peter said, resting his forearm on the back of Claire's chair. 'Riveting though your account of your brilliance would've been, the waiters are here with our food.

So unless you plan to hold forth with your mouth full,
which wouldn't be the best of looks—'

'God forbid!' Alex exclaimed. His mock horror
embraced both Claire and Peter. 'Regretfully for you, Claire,
you're going to have to live in ignorance for a little longer.'

'I'll try to bear up,' she said gravely, and turned back to
the table as the waiters began putting dishes on to the circle
of hot plates in the centre.

'Time to dig in, I think,' Mike announced when the
waiters moved away. He picked up the serving spoon closest
to him, and began ladling fried rice on to his plate.

Peter dropped his arm and moved back to give Claire
room.

Taking the lead from Mike, she leaned forward and took
a spoonful of boiled rice. Sensing Peter's gaze on the side of
her face, she paused, her hand still on the spoon, and
looked back at him.

Their eyes met.

'You're really beautiful, Claire,' he said quietly. 'I'm so
glad I crashed into you. I might not have met you if I hadn't.'

She flushed. 'And I'm glad I wasn't looking where I was
going, either.'

A slow smile spread across his face, and he put two
spring rolls on his plate.

BENEATH A VELVET black sky that was punctured by a myriad
of sparkling shards of silver, they made their way slowly
along the road that ran between the hospital and Nuffield
House, Peter pushing the Lambretta, and Claire walking
beside him.

'I heard Mike say he was going to the Union Bar with
Fiona and Alex, and some of the others,' she said as they

reached the nurses' home. 'If you want to join them, I can go in now. I don't have to wait for the curfew.'

'I don't want,' he said. He balanced the Lambretta against one of the brick posts flanking the entrance, and stared down into her upturned face. 'I want to stay with you until the moment when you absolutely have to go through the front door. If that's all right with you.'

'It's very all right.'

'That's good. I don't want the evening to end a moment before it has to.'

'Nor me.'

Standing in the column of amber light that fell from the lamp atop the brick post, each gazed into the face of the other.

'I don't really know the etiquette for when a first date ends and you very much want to see that person again, such as how long you should leave it before you ask for another date,' Peter said at last.

'I've never needed to know till now. I know only that I won't be able to walk away from you until you've promised to meet me again very soon. Tomorrow morning wouldn't be too soon for me.'

5

M *onday morning*

'PETER!'

Peter stopped halfway up the steps leading to the Medical School, and turned to wait for Alex.

'You're up early today, Alex,' he remarked in surprise, as they continued up the steps together. 'It's not like you to make Pharmacology on a Monday morning.'

'There's a first for everything,' Alex said with a grin. 'It was a good night on Saturday, wasn't it?' he added as they went through the entrance and across the hall in the direction of the lecture theatre. 'I hope Claire enjoyed herself and didn't find us a bit too much.'

'She did. At least, I think she did.'

'She's quite a looker, that bird of yours, and she's got a bit about her. Lucky for you I didn't see her first or you wouldn't have been in with a chance, mate.'

Peter laughed. 'Your Fiona might've had something to say about that! I'd watch out—I dread to think what she might do with the formidable points of her shoes. And as for her nails...' He audibly sucked in his breath and shook his head.

'They *are* somewhat fearful, aren't they? However, I doubt she'll be my Fiona much longer. I feel that old familiar boredom creeping in.' Alex exaggerated a yawn.

'Already!' Peter exclaimed. 'You can't have been with her for more than a month or two. But why am I surprised? I should be used to your rapid turnover by now.'

'Love 'em and leave 'em, that's my motto. But I suppose I ought to be starting to look for someone who'll stop me being so fickle, like you've done.'

'I wouldn't say you were fickle. You're just chopping and changing a bit, finding out what you want. There's nothing wrong with that.'

'That's one way of putting it.' Alex threw him a quick glance. 'And what about you—what do *you* want? No, let me guess. A cottage with roses outside, and Claire and a bunch of kids inside.'

Peter pulled a face. 'No way! It's wide-open spaces for me, and I'm sure Claire feels the same. She loves the countryside and walking, and she's the sort of person to want some excitement in life. We can always do the cottage thing much later on.'

'So what're you going to do when you've registered?'

'God knows! I haven't a clue whether to be a GP or work in a hospital, or whether to live in the wilds of Britain or go abroad. If I had to put money on it, I'd say I'll end up in a hospital somewhere abroad. Being a GP smacks of that dreaded cottage. All I *do* know is that although I've only just met Claire, she's the one for me, and wherever I go and whatever I do, I want it to be with her.'

'Fortunately, we're not far from the Queen Elizabeth so there are lots of sick buckets to hand,' Alex said drily.

Peter laughed. 'Well, you did ask.'

They reached the lecture theatre and pushed the door open.

'I suppose if I'm being honest,' Alex said as they went inside, 'I'd like another year or two of freedom before I meet my Claire. With all the little nurses eager to bag themselves a doctor, it's like working in a sweetshop, and I'm not quite ready to stop gorging myself.'

'I wouldn't count on having that time! You know what they say about the best laid plans.'

'Yeah, well,' Alex said. 'That's something you'd better take note of, too. If you don't, you might find that you've kissed goodbye to the freedom you're always on about.'

With a knowing look at Peter, Alex slid on to the tiered bench closest to him.

CLAIRE STEPPED HASTILY into her short-sleeved purple and white check dress, swiftly did it up and fastened her starched white collar in the front with a stud.

After twisting herself to check in the mirror that the seams of her black stockings were poker straight, she pinned her fob watch to one of her breast pockets, put her pen and scissors into the other, and slipped into her black shoes.

There was a knock at the door. It opened, and Mary's head appeared in the gap. 'Are you ready?'

'Just about,' Claire said, speedily tying her laces.

'Let's go, then, or we'll be late.' Mary's face disappeared.

'Hang on, I'm coming.' Claire grabbed her lever arch file, and sped after Mary.

'I suppose Nutrition's what we called Domestic Science at school,' Mary said as they hurried along the corridor towards the classrooms. 'If it's what we've already done, it could be boring.'

'Then we'll just have to think of something that isn't so boring.'

Mary raised an eyebrow. 'Don't you mean someone who isn't so boring?'

'Spot on,' Claire said happily. 'Talking of Peter, I'm going to dash across to the hospital canteen in the tea break in case he's been able to get there. Why don't you come with me? You might meet someone interesting.'

'Maybe I will. After all,' Mary said, her tone of voice studiedly casual, 'Keith might be there.'

'Keith who?' Claire stopped abruptly and stared at Mary. 'Why, you dark horse!' she exclaimed, as realisation dawned. 'You've met someone. Why didn't you tell me?'

'You've been so full of Peter since Saturday that I thought I'd let you grind to a halt before mentioning Keith. And anyway, I'd never have got a word in edgeways.'

'Oh, God, have I been that bad? I have, haven't I? I've not even asked how the party went. Some friend, I am.' Claire groaned loudly, and they started walking briskly again.

Mary laughed. 'It's okay. I didn't mind. If I had done, I'd have broken into one of your hymns of praise to Peter and insisted that you listen to me.'

'Go ahead. I'm listening now.'

'Not to me, you won't be—we're there,' Mary said with a giggle. 'It's Sister's voice you'll be hearing for the rest of the morning, and maybe Peter's.'

'Darn, so we are.' Claire stared at the door in front of her

in annoyance. 'And if we don't go in at once, we'll be in trouble.' She put her hand on the door handle. 'We'll find somewhere away from the others at lunch, and then I want the
complete lowdown on Keith.'

'HE'S NOT AS good-looking as Peter sounds, but he's got a
nice face. He's got brown hair and brown eyes. Not mousy
brown like mine, but a nice dark brown,' Mary said, cutting
off a chunk of her pie. 'I liked him and I think he liked me.
He said he wanted to see me again, so he must've done.'

'Is he at the University or Medical School?'

'Neither. He works in the hospital in one of the haema-
tology labs. Has done for about five years.'

'I wonder if Peter knows him. The medics and lab tech-
nicians are bound to see each other around the place.'

'It's possible, but not very likely,' Mary said. 'When we
were talking, I said that my friend was out with a group of
fourth year medics. And that you'd been invited by someone
called Peter.'

'And what did he say?'

'That there were lots of Peters, and that medics tended to
keep to themselves.'

'Even if he didn't know Peter, he'd probably know Alex.
Alex is very lively in a loud sort of way, but he seems nice.
Peter's not as loud. He likes being out in the countryside.'

'Not your run of the mill medic, then.'

'Not at all. He's different—nice different, not weird
different. And he's really easy to talk to. Oh, my God!' Claire
clutched her head, her face crestfallen. 'I've got us talking
about Peter again, haven't I? And you're meant to be telling
me about Keith. Sorry!' She looked apologetically at Mary.

'You're forgiven,' Mary said with a laugh.

'I'm not going to say another word. Tell me about Keith. How did you get talking? Did someone introduce you?'

'No, no one. I met him just after I got to the party. As soon as I arrived, I did the usual thing—put the bottle I'd brought on the table with all the other bottles, poured myself a glass of red wine from an open bottle and moved away.

Just as I did so, someone knocked my arm. I don't know who it was, and it doesn't matter, anyway. The wine went all over the man next to me. He turned around and saw me standing there, looking horrified, an empty glass in my hand. Then he pulled the back of his white T-shirt round to the front, and we saw this big red stain spreading across it.'

'Was he mad at you?'

'Not a bit of it—he was really nice about it.'

'Peter would've been, too. Oops! I wasn't going to mention him again today.' Claire put her hand to her mouth. 'So what happened next?' she asked, her voice muffled behind her hand.

'We started talking and didn't stop all evening. He's really nice.'

Claire dropped her hand. 'And?'

'And we're going to meet up on Wednesday afternoon in the hospital staff canteen.' Mary beamed at Claire. 'I told him we sometimes went there on Wednesdays after we'd finished our classes for the day. He was going to try to get there today, too.'

'He sounds keen.' Claire narrowed her eyes and studied Mary intently. 'And so do you.'

'Put it this way, I was keen enough to tell my mother about him when I phoned home yesterday. I've never mentioned a boy to her before.'

'I bet she was excited.'

'She was dead quiet at first, but as soon as she'd got the answer to the all-important question, she was really chuffed.'

Claire wrinkled her brow. 'What all-important question?'

'Is he Catholic, of course. And he is, so that's perfect. But it's early days—we've only just met. I'm not getting carried away merely because we got on well for an evening.'

'Where does he come from?'

'The other side of Birmingham. But he's not really a townie sort of person. Ideally, he'd like to live out in the country somewhere. Like Peter might want to do. You said he likes the countryside, so he might want to work there. It's okay; you've got my permission to mention him again,' she added with a smile.

'Perhaps he will. But I don't really know him well enough to say for sure.'

There was a movement at the tables near them as the other nurses in their set started standing up. Mary glanced at her watch. 'We must go, too. It's almost time for the afternoon lecture.'

'I can't wait to meet Keith,' Claire said, getting up. 'It'd be great if he and Peter got on well.'

'When we get to know them better—*if* we get to know them better—perhaps the four of us can go out somewhere,' Mary said as they headed for the exit. 'Maybe to the cinema, or bowling. If we can all get the same time off, that is. Once the PTS ends, we won't have our evenings and weekends free any longer so it'll be harder to make plans. At least it will be for you, me and Peter. But not for Keith—he works regular hours.'

'What you said about Peter's got me thinking,' Claire remarked as they trailed behind the line of student nurses returning to the classroom. 'I wonder what he *will* do when he finishes—live in a town or move to the country.'

'Which would you prefer?'

'Oh, the country any day. I can just see myself in a cottage surrounded by roses, baking bread while several miniature Peters play on the floor around me.'

She laughed happily.

6

E *arly December*

THE SKY WAS steel-grey as they emerged from the cinema.

'Gosh, it's cold.' Claire's breath was a column of ivory mist in front of her face. Shivering, she clapped her hands together to warm them and stamped her feet on the ground. 'I bet it snows tonight,' she said, tucking her arm into Peter's. 'Come on, or we'll freeze to death.'

Bowing their heads against the chill evening air, they set off along the street at a brisk pace. Their feet crunched noisily on a pavement sheened with glittering frost as they hurried past shops and cafés that were gaudy with strings of Christmas lights and garlands of brightly coloured tinsel, their windows frequently bordered with artificial snow.

As they were passing a small, brightly lit café, the door opened and a couple of men stepped out on to the street.

With them came a rush of warm air and the strains of 'Hey Jude'.

Peter stopped walking. 'What about a coffee? That'll heat you up. We could go there.' He indicated the café. 'At least we wouldn't be forced to listen to "White Christmas" yet again—you can have too much of a good thing.'

'Good idea. After all, I don't have to be back for a while. That's the best thing about the early showing.'

'You grab a table,' he said as they went into the café, 'and I'll get the drinks.'

She made for an empty table between the radiator and the window, sat down and slipped off her coat. A few minutes later, Peter joined her, carrying two cups. He sat down and pushed one of the coffees across to her. 'So, did you like the film?' he asked as he unbuttoned his coat.

'Yes, I did. The little boy who played Oliver was ever so sweet. But I preferred *Rosemary's Baby*.'

'Me, too. *Oliver* was a bit too sugary for me.'

She took a sip of her drink. 'Thanks for the coffee, Peter —it's doing the trick. You know, I do feel guilty about you paying for so much. Fair enough if you were working, but you're not: you're a student like me.'

'It's what I want to do. And anyway, I'm not quite as broke as you. I don't know how you manage on so little.'

She warmed her hands around the cup. 'You get used to it. And fortunately, you can have a good time without spending too much. Like the darts match last night. It was great fun, even though our team lost.'

Peter grinned. 'That man's face when your dart missed his ear by inches! I thought we were going to have to give him mouth-to-mouth.'

Claire giggled. 'I told Alex and Mike that I'd never played before, but they said not to worry, that it was just a matter of relaxing, throwing the dart in the direction of the board, and trying to hit something.'

'Well, you almost did! Unfortunately, it wasn't the board!'

She giggled again. 'His ear *did* have a close shave, didn't it?' She paused. 'I hope we're going to be able to carry on like this in the future—you know, playing darts, ten-pin bowling, going to the cinema, having a coffee together and so on,' she said, a sudden hesitancy creeping into her voice. 'After the dreaded exams, I'll be on the medical wards, and it won't be as easy to meet.'

'I don't want to stop seeing you just because your hours are changing, and I'm hoping you feel the same.'

The deep blue eyes that gazed at her were filled with hope.

She caught her breath, and a sudden warmth coursed through her.

'Oh, I do!' she said in a rush, spilling her coffee as she put her cup speedily back on the saucer. She blushed and pulled an apologetic face. 'That sounded a bit keen, didn't it? Mary would've scolded me if she'd been here.'

He took her hands in his. 'Well, I'm glad she isn't. I like it being just you and me.'

'Me, too.'

'If only I didn't have to go to Walthamstow next week-end,' he said miserably, 'your last free weekend for God knows how long. But it's my mother's birthday on Sunday and I promised to go home for that. I've not seen them since the summer and I can tell they're looking forward to my visit. A phone call's not the same.'

'I suppose I ought to visit my mother, too, although I can think of a million things I'd rather do.'

'Surely she can't be that bad? After all, she gave birth to

you, and look at you.' He straightened up and released her hands. 'You must meet my folks as soon as we can arrange it, and I'd like to meet your mother.'

'We'll do Mother in the spring, maybe. Winter's not the best time.'

'If you say so.' He paused. 'What *is* it about your mother, Claire? It's pretty obvious you aren't close, and it's clear you don't want me to meet her. I know she doesn't give you much money, but that's all you've ever really said.'

She shrugged dismissively. 'There's not much more *to* say. My home wasn't a warm home—not like yours sounds —and that was because of Mother. Dad was quite a bit older than her. He was a kind, gentle man, who had a string of greengrocery shops, but Mother's a very different sort of person.

Basically, she's a snob. She's very anti me being a nurse because she thinks it's a low-grade job. Drudgery is how she describes it. To be fair to her, though, I know she loves me in her way, and genuinely wants what she thinks will make me happy. It's just that we don't agree about what that is.'

'What did she want you to do?'

'Just about anything other than be a nurse! She was always pushing secretarial work because of the opportunities it could lead to.' She pulled a face. 'But I'd hate to be stuck in an office all day. That's not me at all.'

'Nor me. It sounds horrendous! You and I are obviously two of a kind.' He smiled broadly at her. 'I'm glad you held your ground—if you hadn't, we wouldn't have met, and that doesn't bear thinking about.' He hesitated. 'And there's no other reason why you don't want me to see her, is there? It's not that you think I'm moving too fast?'

'Of course not. You must know by now how I feel about you,' she added with an awkward laugh.

Their eyes met. Each smiled slowly at the other, and then they looked back at their drinks.

'I've had an idea!' he said suddenly. 'Come with me next weekend. My parents are dying to meet you—they've said so several times. We've a spare room so it'll be easy enough for you to stay.'

'It's kind of you to ask, but I ought to start revising, and your parents are bound to want you to themselves.'

He grinned at her. 'So that's decided then; you're coming.' She opened her mouth. 'And before you say anything,' he went on quickly, 'it really isn't going to be any trouble.'

'You must check with your parents first. I would like to meet them, though. And it'd be great to be with you for my last weekend before I start on the wards. I'll be on for eight days at a time.'

'But you're off for a straight four days afterwards, and I intend to make the most of them. We'll go off on the scooter, or snatch a coffee in the canteen if I'm stuck in the hospital, or pay a late night visit to Mr Egg for a fix of egg and chips. We won't waste a minute.'

'I do hope it works out like that.'

'It has to,' he said quietly. 'You're everything to me, Claire.'

A hot glow crept through her body and settled in the pit of her stomach. 'And you are to me.'

Their gaze met across the table, and held.

A draught of cold air burst into the café.

Claire glanced over Peter's shoulder towards the open door. 'You know what you said about liking it being just us...?'

'So this is where you got to!' Alex's voice boomed across the room.

Peter looked round and saw Alex coming towards him, followed by Mike and two girls. He turned back to Claire in visible irritation. 'Sorry,' he mouthed.

'We saw you in the cinema,' Alex said, clapping Peter on the back as the four of them pushed past him to the next table, 'but you were too busy in the back row to see us.' He looked from Peter to Claire, an expression of benign amusement on his face.

She went red.

'Ignore Alex,' Peter told her with a smile.

'I think you'll find that's not so easily done, my friend,' Alex said cheerfully. 'Is it, Claire?'

'I'm sorry. Did you say something, Alex?' Claire said lightly.

Alex laughed.

'What have you been up to, then?' Peter asked. 'The film ended a while ago.'

'We grabbed a bite to eat, and were on our way back when Mike saw you through the window.' He glanced at Mike and the girls. 'We might as well have a coffee now that we're here. What about you, Claire?' he asked. 'Do you want another whatever it is you've been drinking?'

Peter cut in. 'It might be running things a bit close to Claire's curfew.'

'Peter's right,' she said. 'But thanks for the offer.'

'Pity. I was planning to explain how to avoid your dart ricocheting off the board and into the beer of an unsuspecting punter,' Alex remarked sagely.

She giggled. 'That was so embarrassing. Naturally, I'm disappointed at having to miss a much-needed lesson, especially as I couldn't have had a better teacher than someone who failed to hit the opening double until the game was virtually over, but we really must go.'

He grinned at her. 'Yes, to miss the double for so long really took some doing. But as you've obviously spotted, it was deliberate. I didn't want to unnerve you by revealing too soon the extent of my skill.'

'Well, your ploy certainly worked,' she said with a laugh.

'We'll be off, then.' Peter stood up, followed by Claire.

'You know, I think we'll skip coffee and get off now, too,' Alex said, glancing at the other three as he stood up. 'It's getting late, and we can have coffee, or something stronger, when we get back to our rooms.'

'See you tomorrow,' Peter said, and he grabbed Claire's hand, and hurried them out of the café.

'You could've gone with them, you know,' she remarked, linking her arm in his as they walked quickly along the street. 'I can get back by myself.'

'They're good fun, but I'd rather spend time with you than with them.'

'Right answer,' she said.

He put his arm round her shoulders. 'Let's talk about next weekend, when it'll be just us—no Alex, no Mike, no other nurses or medics.'

'I can't wait,' she said. She moved closer to him, slid her arm round his chest, reached up and kissed him lightly on the cheek.

He stopped walking and hugged her tightly. 'Nor me.'

ALEX PULLED the café door shut behind them. 'Let's go,' he said, and set off briskly. Mike hurried after him and caught him up. The two girls trailed behind.

'Peter's certainly come out of his shell,' Mike said, walking fast to keep up with Alex. 'It seems no time at all since you were teasing him for saying something dumb.

D'you remember when he learnt the hit parade, like it was another subject to swat up on?'

'Yes, the awkward, tongue-tied Peter is now definitely a thing of the past. His success with the lovely Claire saw off the last of it.'

'D'you think they're having it off?'

From behind them, one of the girls exclaimed in rebuke, and then giggled.

Alex shook his head. 'Not our Peter. And certainly not Claire. Much too soon for him to have suggested she drop 'em, and for her to have done so. Nope, it'll still be about respect—he'll be pathetically anxious to prove he respects her, and she'll be lapping it up. Not for them a hot and hasty fumble behind the nurses' home, her regulation knickers around her ankles.'

Mike glanced at Alex in surprise. 'I thought you liked Peter. I know you used to tease him, but in a friendly way.'

'Don't get me wrong—I *do* like him,' Alex said hastily. 'He's not the sort of friend I'd normally choose—he's a bit outdoorsy for me—but he seems a genuinely nice guy. No, that was envy speaking. Peter's a good mate, but it doesn't stop me from finding Claire a bit of all right.

My fantasy of the moment is seeing that amazing hair splayed out on the pillow next to me. Not that I'd seriously want to go down that path,' he added. 'It'd be a bit too virginal for my taste. Give me a woman who knows what she's doing. I expect you'll be relieved to hear that, ladies,' he called over his shoulder to the two girls.

They giggled again.

He exchanged a grin with Mike, and then turned again to the road ahead.

'No,' he said, as if to himself. 'Peter's welcome to her.'

7

W*althamstow*
     The following Saturday

THE EARLY AFTERNOON sky was clear blue above the uneven line of roofs that were deep grey interspersed with the occasional burst of terracotta-red. Icicles hung from beneath metal gutters, sparkling like bejewelled stilettos as they dripped into the brightness of the day.

Having had to wait no more than five minutes for each of the two lifts that had brought them south from Birmingham, they'd reached Walthamstow unexpectedly quickly. Not wanting to descend on his parents too early, they decided to take advantage of the crisp, bright day and have a look at the town.

Their coats pulled tightly around them, they walked through residential streets that were lined on both sides with tired grey stone houses, the small front gardens of which were bordered by low railings or hedge-high thickets of skeletal thorn.

On the stretches of pavement touched by the wintry sun, the frost had lifted, but there was ice on the puddles that had yet to feel the warmth of its rays, and the ice cracked loudly beneath their shoes as it shattered like fragments of broken glass.

When they came out into the main shopping area, they paused and stared around at the concrete conglomeration of shops, cafés, pubs, launderettes and bookmakers that flanked the pavements on both sides of a seemingly endless stream of traffic.

'It seems even busier than it used to be,' Peter said, and they began to stroll along the pavement, stopping from time to time to look in a shop window.

By the time they reached the Dominion Cinema, the afternoon light had started to drain away and cold was nipping at their fingers.

Peter glanced at his watch. 'Woolworths isn't far from here. I suggest we go there—if you're not too cold, that is—and then go to the house. We'll have left it long enough.'

'D'you want to get something in Woolworths, then?' she asked as they resumed walking.

'Yes—raspberry fondants,' he said with a grin. 'They're my favourites—I like the red coconutty centre. When we first arrived back in England, I couldn't get enough of them, they were so different from anything I'd had before. On one occasion, I even took them to school for an Art class. But sadly, I don't have a fraction of my mother's talent for drawing, and my still life ended up looking like a bunch of red amoebae.'

She laughed.

'What are your favourite sweets from the past?' he asked.

'Spangles, I think. I haven't had them for ages. I used to love them.'

'Then Spangles for you, it is. After that, we'll go down the high street, and past the stalls. You've got to see them— it'll be getting dark by then, and they'll look magical. Most have paraffin-powered hurricane lamps, which give out an unearthly yellowy light. You can actually hear them hissing as you walk past. After that, we'll get off to my folks.'

'YOU'VE GONE to so much trouble, Mrs Henderson,' Claire said, finishing the last of her roast beef. 'That was really delicious.'

'I'm glad you enjoyed it, Claire. As I've already said, Christopher and I are delighted to meet you at last. Peter talks about you every time he telephones.'

'Thanks, Mum!' he exclaimed in feigned indignation. 'Here I am, trying to play hard to get... ' He smiled at Claire, and she beamed back at him.

Christopher Henderson shook his head in mock amazement. 'And I thought it was only girls who played hard to get. Things have obviously changed since my day.'

'Indeed they have, Dad. They finished the ark and escaped the flood.'

'Anyone for apple pie,' Margaret asked, standing up and leaning across the small table to take Claire's plate.

'That sounds lovely.' Claire picked up the china vegetable tureen in front of her and started to rise.

'No, you don't, Claire. Sit down—you're our guest,' Margaret said quickly. 'Peter will help me; won't you, Peter?'

'As long as I don't have to wear a frilly pinny. Now that really would destroy my image.'

As he took the tureen from Claire, his hands brushed

hers. They exchanged a quick smile, and then he followed his mother through to the narrow kitchen.

Claire sat down again.

'On the rare occasions we have guests, we eat in the front room, but we thought we'd treat you like family,' Christopher said, as Peter and Margaret went backwards and forwards, clearing the plates and dishes from the table. 'It's cramped in here, but cosier.'

The sound of running water was heard in the kitchen, and of dishes clattering against the sink. Claire made a move to get up.

Christopher put out his hand to stop her. 'You heard what Margaret said—sit.'

'But I can hear them washing up. I ought to give a hand.'

'There's no need. Treat today as a holiday,' he said with a smile. 'You won't have many weekends off in the future from what Peter tells us. Make the most of this one.'

'Thank you, then.'

Sitting back in her chair, she glanced around the room, at the dark blue and red patterned carpet, at the once-white anaglypta wallpaper, at the electric fire with its teak wood surround, at the glass bowl filled with apples and oranges that stood on the top of an oak sideboard next to a cluster of photographs.

'It's very pleasant in here.' She nodded towards the photographs. 'Are they of Ladakh? Peter told me you used to live there.'

'Unfortunately, no. We didn't take any photos. I wish we had—it would've been nice to have had a few. Mind you, Margaret did a number of watercolours so we can always look at those—not that we often do. Personally, I find it a little painful. I hadn't wanted to leave the place. I don't know if Peter told you that.'

She nodded. 'Yes, he did.'

'Apart from Margaret's paintings, the only things we brought back were a book on the Ladakhi language and a wooden butter dish. But ten years is a long time to spend in a place, and it'll always be in our heads, and in our hearts, too. Even in Peter's,' he added. 'More so than he realises, I rather think.'

'He mentions his life there quite a bit.'

'That doesn't surprise me. None of us found it easy to settle back here. I was prepared for that as I hadn't wanted to return, but I think Margaret and Peter were quite taken aback to find themselves missing a number of things about Ladakh. For a long time, we all had one foot in Ladakh and one in England. And maybe still do, to a certain extent.'

A bolt of alarm shot through her, and she straightened up.

'After all, the past makes everyone into what they are today, and what they'll be in the future,' he went on. 'It colours the way we think about everything.'

'You don't think he'd ever want go back, do you? Perhaps be a doctor there?'

He shook his head. 'I can't see that happening. From the worried look on your face, I take it you've no interest in going there.'

'Not really. I don't want to live anywhere but England. Holidays are one thing, but living abroad another.'

He nodded reassuringly. 'Well, you needn't worry—I'm sure he won't go back. Deep down, he won't have forgotten the many things he didn't like about living there, and how unwelcome the people made us feel. They wouldn't even let us teach their children, they mistrusted us so.

And just as they've got monks and *lamas* for their spiritual needs—not that we tried to push our beliefs at them—

each village has an *amchi* for its medical needs. English doctors wouldn't be any more welcome than missionaries, and I can't see that changing. Or certainly not for some time.'

She felt herself start to relax.

'What's more, he's remarked several times since we got back that returning to a place is never what you think it'll be,' he added, pouring them both a glass of water. 'He'll have been talking about coming back to England, of course, but the same would hold true about returning to Ladakh.'

'I've certainly never felt he was hankering to go back there again.'

'I'm sure he isn't. Of course, that doesn't mean he'd never want to live overseas again. I did wonder when we were first back, and he was obviously very restless, if the idea of moving to another country wouldn't one day exercise a strong pull. That at some point in the future, he might jump on a plane and go somewhere very different from here, somewhere more exciting.'

'More exciting,' she echoed hollowly.

'I *used* to think that, but since he met you,' he said, smiling broadly at her, 'he's been a different man. You've done wonders for him, Claire.'

Relief flooded through her. 'I'm so glad you think so.'

'I do. And so does Margaret.'

'Did I hear my name?' Margaret called from the kitchen. 'We won't be a minute.'

'And what about you?' Christopher said, sitting back. 'You come from Hereford, I believe.'

'That's right. My mother's got a beautiful flat in the heart of the city. It's just the two of us—my father died of cancer a few years ago.'

'I'm sorry to hear that. Was it your father's illness that inspired you to be a nurse?'

'Probably. I was the one who looked after him at home. Mother's awful at anything like that. I'd been thinking about either teaching or nursing, and Dad being ill probably made me come down on the side of nursing.'

'Your mother must be very proud of you. It's a worthwhile profession, and one with a future—we'll always need our nurses.'

She pulled a face. 'Unfortunately, my mother doesn't agree.'

He raised his eyebrows. 'I take it she's in rude health.'

'Yes, she is. She prides herself on being very fit. An apple a day and all that.'

'I wouldn't wish her ill, or anyone else for that matter, but you may find her attitude changes if she's ever in need of nursing herself. And it comes to us all at some point.'

'Well, I don't envy the nurse who'd have to look after her!' she said wryly. 'She'd be a diabolical patient—she'd boss the nurses and consultants around and treat the hospital as a hotel.'

He laughed.

'Peter's told me about the Mission,' she said, 'and how you help homeless people and those down on their luck. It's a fantastic thing to do.'

'Help like that's very needed in an area like this. But you'll see it for yourself tomorrow. Peter said you're going to walk up to his old school in the morning, have a look around and then join us at the Mission for Margaret's birthday lunch. I know you won't be able to stay long as you've got to get back, but next time you come—and I hope there'll be a next time—we'll show you around properly.'

'What's this about the Mission?' Margaret said, coming

up to the table, a large Pyrex pie dish between her oven gloves. Peter followed with a pile of four small glass bowls and a jug of custard.

'I was telling Claire that we hope she'll come again.'

'Christopher's right, Claire. You'll always be welcome.' She put the dish in the centre of the table and started spooning the pie into the first of the bowls. 'I'm sorry we took so long, but the pie wasn't quite ready so we attacked the washing up while waiting.'

'So you thought I might jump on a plane and take off, did you, Dad?' Peter said, sitting down and passing a bowl to his father.

'Ah, you heard what I said, did you?'

'It was hard not to, given the absence of a door between the parlour and kitchen.'

'You'd seemed so lost after we got back, so, yes, at one point I did think you might have a stab at living somewhere else.'

'What, and leave you both to get old on your own!'

Christopher glanced at Margaret and smiled. 'In our line of work, we'll never be alone.'

'Be that as it may, I won't be going anywhere. This is the first time I've felt truly home since getting back, and I like the way it feels. I couldn't be happier.'

He looked across the table at Claire, and smiled at her.

8

L ater that evening

PETER LAY in bed on his back, his hands behind his head, and stared up into the darkness. The air was chill, its sharpness raw against his face.

The ticking of his small travel clock on the bedside table sounded loud in the still of the night.

With a sigh, he glanced across at the clock's illuminated face. Only three o'clock, he thought wearily, and he looked back up at the ceiling. A mere fifteen minutes since he'd last checked the time.

Well, at least he was consistent, he thought. He'd been in bed since eleven o'clock and he'd looked at the time every fifteen minutes since then. Never had a night crawled by so slowly.

Claire had come up ahead of him. She'd left him and his parents in the parlour at ten thirty, gone up to collect her wash things and returned in a quilted dressing gown with flowers on. Blushing, she'd hurried through the kitchen to the narrow bathroom, and after a quick wash, had come out all pink and glowing, said goodnight and had gone up to her room.

A moment of madness had almost come over him when he'd seen her emerge from the bathroom ready for bed, looking so lovely, and so sexy, and he'd felt a sudden urge to fling his arms around her and hold her tightly against him.

How he'd held himself back, he didn't know.

But he had.

He'd forced himself to stay in his chair and be satisfied with a "Sleep well." Any emotional display on his part was bound to have embarrassed his parents, and also Claire, and he wouldn't have wanted to do that for the world—he loved her far too much to do anything that would make her feel uncomfortable. And he might have felt pretty awkward about it, too, in the morning.

He glanced at the wall that separated them.

Hopefully, his "Sleep well" had done the trick for her and she was out for the count. But unfortunately for him, he'd never felt further from sleep than he did at that moment.

After Claire had said goodnight, he'd deliberately stayed downstairs for a while, talking to his parents—he'd be hard pushed to say about what—until he decided that a suitable amount of time had lapsed between hearing her bedroom door close and going up to his room.

He'd then hastily washed, said goodnight to his parents and gone upstairs after her.

Well, not after her as such, much as he would've liked to have done so, but to his bedroom, which was next to hers. Trying not to think of her lying there, so close to him, he'd got into bed, closed his eyes and waited for sleep. Four hours later, he was still waiting.

He must've been mad to think that he'd ever be able to go to sleep, knowing that she was on the other side of the wall, a few feet only away from him. What man would be able to fall asleep knowing that?

He turned to face the wall that separated him from Claire.

How would she be lying, he wondered? Would she be curled up in a ball on her side, a temptation for someone to wrap her in his arms and draw her close? Or would she be lying on her back, her legs stretched out in front of her, as if waiting?

Would she be asleep now, or might she be lying awake, thinking about him, just as he was lying awake, thinking about her, wishing she was in bed with him, wanting her so badly that it hurt?

When the time came that they could lie in each other's arms all night, his life would be complete. He'd ask for nothing else. He'd told his parents earlier that he couldn't imagine being happier than he now was, but that hadn't been strictly true—he *could* imagine being even happier: he'd achieve perfect happiness on the day he slept with Claire.

He'd long known that there was nothing he wanted more than to spend the rest of his life with her.

And the great stroke of luck in falling for someone like Claire was that he'd no longer be limited to dreaming about living a life that gave him the kind of freedom he'd known in his childhood—he'd actually be able to live that life.

Their careers were a perfect combination. With him a doctor and her a nurse, they'd always be in demand—not only in England, but in other countries, too. It meant that if they decided to travel before settling down and starting a family, they could do so. They could stay in England or go to the other side of the world—they could go anywhere they wanted.

But all that was for the future. For the present, having Claire lying so close to him, wearing so little, but being unable to touch her, was driving him mad.

His body taut, he rolled on to his back again.

The idea of slipping next door and sliding into her bed was so tempting, but he absolutely mustn't. What would she think of him if he did?

At the very least, she'd think he didn't respect her. Whatever happened, he mustn't jeopardise their happiness together.

They both knew the risks two people took when they threw caution to the winds, and he wasn't about to pressure her into sleeping with him, desperate though he was. He would go at *her* pace, not his, no matter how difficult that may be.

But the thought of being in bed with Claire, her lying beneath him—his body hardened.

Turning sharply on to his side, with his back to the wall between them, he found a piece of cold sheet on which to lie. Please, Claire, he whispered into his pillow, please don't make me wait too long.

I WONDER if Peter's asleep, she thought, looking up at the ceiling. It'd be nice to think that one of us was.

She reached across for her clock, held it close to her face and saw that it was just past three fifteen. She returned the clock to the bedside table, and sighed. It was hard to remember when a night had seemed longer.

Rolling on to her side, she stared at the wall that separated her room from Peter's.

It felt really funny knowing he was as near to her as he was, but that it was impossible to go to him.

Perhaps funny was the wrong word, she mused. Knowing that Peter was so close that he could probably hear her breathing if he was awake, was the reason why she couldn't sleep, and there was nothing funny about that.

Impossible wasn't the right word, either. If she wanted to creep into his bedroom, she could. From the expression in his eyes whenever he looked at her, she was pretty sure that he'd throw back the covers readily enough.

But she'd no intention of doing that: she'd heard far too many dire stories of what happened to girls who went all the way with their boyfriends before they were married. As a nurse, she'd be able to protect herself better than some of those girls, but there was still a risk.

And quite apart from the chance she'd be taking, what would Peter think of her if she suddenly rolled up at his bedroom door, clad only in a flimsy nightie? Men had a name for women like that, she knew.

Peter had always behaved like the perfect gentleman, even though she'd sensed that with the slightest encouragement, he would've happily abandoned his self-restraint. She'd felt the evidence of his feelings for her in their every close embrace, and her body had made its own response.

So much so that on several recent occasions, she'd come very close to giving him the encouragement he was obviously waiting for, but had pulled back at the last moment, frightened at the thought of the risk she'd be taking, and fearful that he might lose respect for her.

But it was natural they were longing to go the whole way

—she loved him and he loved her. There'd be something wrong if they weren't.

She rolled on to her back again and stared up at the ceiling. She needed to be careful, though. Her feelings for Peter had almost got the better of her earlier on, and she'd come horribly close to doing something that could have embarrassed them all.

She'd heard him come up the stairs not long after she'd got into bed.

She'd waylay him on the landing, she'd thought in sudden glee, and she'd jumped out of bed and gone quickly across to the door, eager to see him tousle-haired and in pyjamas.

Smiling in anticipation, she'd started turning the handle, and then stopped.

Caution and common sense had prevailed, and with great reluctance she'd released the handle and returned to bed.

He might not have wanted her to see him in his dressing gown, she'd told herself as she slid back beneath the covers. But worse than that, his parents could've been right behind him!

She could just imagine what they'd have thought if they'd seen her, clearly ready for bed, flinging herself physically on top of their son. A nervous giggle escaped her. One thing was sure, she'd never have been able to look them in the eye at breakfast.

So she'd stayed where she was and Peter's door had clicked shut behind him.

She turned her head to look at the wall between them, and imagined him on the other side. She wondered if he slept on his side or on his back. She knew she'd find out one day. And hopefully, that day wouldn't be too far away.

When Peter had told his parents how happy he felt, her spirits had soared and she'd felt that day come a giant step closer. She could just see them married, with a small house somewhere, probably in the country, and lots of children.

Not necessarily the cottage surrounded by roses that she and Mary always joked about—that wouldn't be Peter's style —but it'd be a lovely friendly house, nevertheless, in a way that her parents' house had never been.

As for the children—well, she couldn't wait to get started on making them.

The blood rose to her face and she rolled on to her side, her back to the wall between them. If she couldn't see the wall, she might forget how close he was and have a better chance of falling asleep.

She closed her eyes.

Please, please, Peter, she breathed into the cold night. Don't leave it much longer to make a move.

9

Hereford
    End of January, 1968

'YOU STAY WHERE YOU ARE, PETER,' Claire said, going across to the nest of mahogany tables in the corner of the room. She came back with two, and placed one next to each of the upholstered armchairs on which she and Peter were sitting.

'I'll get the tea,' she told her mother, who was sitting in her wing armchair, her hands clasped together in her lap.

'You'll find everything set out,' Grace Meredith told her. 'It's just a matter of heating the water.'

A few minutes later, Claire returned with a tray on which there were three floral bone china cups, a silver teapot and jug of boiling water, a milk jug, sugar bowl, and a plate of biscuits.

She put the tray on the walnut dining table, poured out the tea, and put a cup on each of the side tables. Then she offered the plate of biscuits to Peter. He took one, and she put the plate down on the side table next to her mother, and took a biscuit for herself.

'I've left them there so you'll be able to help yourself, Mother,' she said, going back to her chair and sitting down. 'There's more tea if anyone wants it.'

'You should know by now that I don't eat between meals, Claire. I don't believe in spoiling one's appetite. I suggest you put the plate next to your friend.' Grace gave Peter a thin smile.

'Thanks, Claire,' he said, glancing up at her as she moved the biscuits to his table. She gave him a quick smile, stood the tray against the side of her chair and made as if to sit down.

'Would you be good enough to return the tray to the kitchen, please, Claire?' Grace asked. 'The carpet's still fairly new, and I'd hate any drops of tea to discolour it.

The flat isn't so large that a second walk to and from the kitchen could be considered excessively demanding. And I'm sure that any doctor would advocate as much exercise as possible. Isn't that so, Peter?' The thin smile appeared again.

'Indeed, it is, Mrs Meredith.' He looked around him. 'If you don't mind me saying so, your flat is lovely. It's very elegant.'

The smile widened. 'Thank you, Peter. The pace of life outside being as it is, I wanted an environment inside that was both tranquil and pleasing to the eye.'

'Well, you've certainly achieved that,' he said with a slight nod.

'How kind of you.' She took a sip of her tea, and replaced the cup on the saucer. 'So tell me about yourself, Peter. Claire's mentioned you on the rare occasions she's tele-phoned, and I understand you're training to be a doctor.'

He nodded. 'That's right. I'm in the fourth year of a five-year course. At the end of that, you're qualified, but there's a further year of graduate training before full registration. There's no organised teaching in that last year, though. We spend six months in Medicine, and the last six in Surgery at an approved hospital.'

'What a very long period of study,' she remarked.

'It is, but there's masses to learn. You don't want to make too many mistakes on the job,' he added with a laugh.

'Indeed not.' The trace of a smile flickered across Grace's lips. 'And you're enjoying the course?'

'Very much so. The certainty of science really appeals to me. It's so different from the uncertainty of faith.'

'Your parents must be proud of you. It's a worthwhile career for them to be able to tell their friends about.'

'I hope they are. Just as I'm proud of my parents.'

Grace cocked her head slightly to the side. 'May I ask why? While it's pleasant to hear of a child being proud of a parent, it's not that usual.'

'They're missionaries,' Claire cut in.

'Missionaries!' Grace exclaimed in surprise. 'You didn't tell me that, Claire. You mean they're in Africa?'

'It's possible to be a missionary a little closer to home than that, Mother. They live in Walthamstow.'

'Walthamstow! I've heard of it, of course, but I've never been there. I rarely go to London. However, if I *had* gone there, I doubt I would have visited Walthamstow. It's a less than salubrious part of London, I believe. And your parents live there, you say, Peter?'

'That's right. And it's because it's less than salubrious that they do. We haven't always lived there, though. For the ten years before that, we lived in Ladakh.'

'Ladakh!'

'It's north of the Himalayas, Mother. Does that sound more missionary-like to you?'

'Thank you, Claire,' Grace said coldly. She turned back to Peter, raised a hand to the hair rolled in a tight coil on the back of her head, and then returned her hand to her lap. 'I now understand your earlier reference to faith, Peter. What an unusual childhood you must have had.'

'I suppose I did. But it's only now that I'm aware of it. I was too young when we lived there to appreciate the cultural differences. But I was old enough to remember something of the life I'd left behind, and I spent most of my time there wishing I was back in England.

As for the ways in which the Ladakhi people coped with their harsh conditions and the lack of rain, their kindness to each other, the beauty of the place—all that rather escaped me at the time. Now it's too late, I wish I'd taken more notice of it.'

'Do you intend to go back there?'

He shook his head. 'No way. For a start, I've virtually forgotten the language. I'm not a linguist, not like the boy I was friendly with there. He learnt to speak English quite well, but I never mastered Ladakhi. And if a doctor can't talk to his patients, he'd be of limited use.

And I'm not a great believer in going back to places, anyway. They're never as you remember them. It's always much better to go somewhere new.'

Grace nodded. 'That sounds very wise.' She glanced at Claire, and then back at Peter. 'I understand you met Claire at the hospital.'

'That's right. We literally bumped into each other, and then came across each other again in the refectory, and bingo.'

He smiled warmly at Claire, and she at him.

Grace glanced from one face to the other. She ran her hand slowly along the scroll arm of her chair. 'And do your parents intend to stay in Walthamstow, Peter?'

'They'll stay for as long as they're needed. If they're needed somewhere else more urgently, they'll be sent there.'

'And what sort of things do they do for the people in Walthamstow?'

'Just about everything. They try to see that everyone has the necessities of life. They help with heating, see that families have sufficient blankets, provide free breakfasts, serve hot lunches and dinners for next to nothing or even for free.

They make sure people have the medical help they need, and find places in refuges, if necessary. Also, they try to arrange summer holidays for the children of poor families. Basically, they try to improve the lives of people who can't improve their lives for themselves.'

'I sometimes wonder if much charitable action isn't misguided,' Grace said slowly. 'After all, if people like your parents are doing all those things, is there anything left for a person to do for himself? One can so easily slide into a dependency upon others and cease to make an effort oneself.'

Claire glanced anxiously at Peter.

He leaned forward towards Grace. 'It's a view I've heard many times before, and so have my parents. Their reply would be that homelessness, or needing help with warmth and food, can be caused by different things. Many of those they help have had appalling experiences as children.

And there are others with little academic ability, or with mental problems. People like that will always need outside help as they'll never be able to manage on their own.'

'Quite so. I'm aware that not everyone has led an easy life from the outset, and that not everyone is of equal intelligence, but you're talking about the extremes. I'm sure there are those in the middle, who, if they had to, would strive on their own behalf, but because it's all done for them, lose the impetus to do so.'

'That's one way of looking at it, but it's not my parents' way. They see people in desperate need of help, and they give them that help.'

He shrugged his shoulders. 'Everyone's different. There are those who turn their backs on the misfortunes of others, and there are those who try to help in some way, perhaps by giving a small amount of money or some of their time. My parents are unusual in that they've given up their lives, in effect, for others. And I'm proud that they're the people they are.'

Grace inclined her head slightly. 'And I'm sure they're equally proud of you. May I ask whether you're planning to become a missionary, too? Obviously not in Ladakh—you've said that you've no wish to return there—but there must be other foreign places in which a doctor could be of service.'

He shook his head and sat back. 'I'm not cut from the same cloth, I'm afraid. I hope to be a good doctor and help people that way, but I want a life outside my work, and my parents don't really have that. I don't yet know what I'll do—maybe I'll end up a GP, or work in a hospital, or even do something I haven't yet thought of.'

'I see.' She smiled at him, and then turned towards Claire. 'And how are you getting on, Claire? You've hardly mentioned your studies on the very few occasions since September when you've contacted me.'

'You've a telephone, too, Mother,' Claire said lightly.

'As you've said on more than one occasion, your hours are unpredictable. It's easier for you to contact me when you have a moment to spare.'

'It's going well, I think. The days are long and tiring, but the things we're learning are really interesting.'

Her mother raised her eyebrows. 'Emptying bedpans is interesting?'

'Occasionally we do other interesting things, too. I was thinking more about those, such as wiping up vomit or cleaning up the sputum of elderly men.'

Peter burst out laughing.

Grace glanced at him, and then back at Claire. A smile ghosted across her lips. 'Indeed yes; that does sound interesting, Claire.'

'Good gracious, Mother. Did you make a sort of joke?' Claire asked in mock surprise. 'But enough about us, what have you been doing since I went to Birmingham?'

GRACE STOOD up and smoothed down her skirt. 'I've enjoyed your visit, Claire, and meeting you, Peter. I hope Claire will bring you to see me again before too long.'

'I hope so, too, Mrs Meredith. It's been a pleasure to meet you.'

Grace glanced at Claire. 'You heard what Peter said, Claire.'

'Now here's a thought for you, Mother: you could consider coming to see us. Birmingham's a straightforward drive from Hereford, and you could easily afford to hire a car and driver for the day.'

'It's certainly something to think about when the weather improves.' Grace offered Peter her hand, and he shook it. 'Perhaps next time you come you'll stay long enough to visit some of the attractions of Hereford, Peter. We've a beautiful cathedral, which dates from 1079. Its most famous treasure is a thirteenth century map of the medi-aeval world. I really do recommend you see it.'

'I'll remember that,' he said with a smile, and he opened the door and went out.

Claire kissed her mother on the cheek. 'It's been lovely seeing you today, Mother,' she said warmly. 'I promise not to leave it so long before coming again.'

Her mother nodded.

Claire turned to go after Peter, but Grace reached out, caught her arm and stared into her face. 'I hope you will always respect yourself, Claire,' she said. Colouring slightly, she dropped Claire's arm, and stepped back into her flat.

Claire gave an awkward laugh. 'Of course I will, Mother.' Then she turned and left the flat.

The door clicked closed behind her, and three locks snapped into place, one after the other.

'Mother likes to feel safe from any riff-raff who might get into the building,' Claire said as they crossed the landing to the staircase. 'Or ordinary people as you and I might say.'

He laughed. 'She's typical of a lot of her generation, but I quite enjoyed the visit. At the same time, I'm relieved we don't live on her doorstep.'

She nodded. 'Me, too. She was getting quite insistent about meeting you, so I finally thought what the hell.'

'Well, I'm glad you did—it makes me feel that we're more solid now, if you know what I mean.' He glanced up at the high-corniced ceiling above the stairs. 'It's certainly a wonderful building. Victorian or Edwardian, I'd guess. I don't really know one from the other, but this is genuinely old, whatever it is.'

'Like my mother's attitudes. For example, she refuses to recognise the difference between a State Registered Nurse and a State Enrolled Nurse. And you've seen her complete lack of interest in the poor and the needy. And as for sex! I think I've just had my first ever sex education lesson from her, if you can call it that.'

He looked at her in amusement. 'What did she say?'

'That I must be sure to respect myself. And judging by the colour she went, she wasn't hoping I'll always tell the truth or change my underwear regularly. It was clearly related to what we might get up to behind closed doors.'

'Well, I respect you, Claire.' He jumped down the last two stairs and turned to look up at her. 'And I would, even if we got up to the worst of your mother's fears. And that's the truth,' he added, suddenly serious.

She stood still and looked down at him. 'It's easy for you to say that,' she said quietly.

'I mean it, Claire. I love you. You know I do. You're the first thing I think about in the morning when I wake up, and you're the last thing I see at night before I fall asleep. There isn't a single minute in the day when I don't long for you to be at my side.'

'But—'

'But nothing. Nothing could ever change the way I feel about you. It's because I love you that I'm not trying to push you into doing something you don't want to do, no matter how much I want it. And I'm not going to say that it'd make me love you even more than I do now, as that'd be a lie—I couldn't love you any more than I do now.'

She stepped down to him. 'But if something went wrong —you hear such terrible things. I'd lose my job for a start.'

'You mustn't think like that.' He put his arm around her shoulders and they went out through the door and started walking along the road.

'We love each other, and we'd cope with anything that happened. But it's got to be right for you. I can wait. That the showers in Hall are often freezing cold is no bad thing. In fact, it's probably deliberate on their part.'

She stopped abruptly, put her hands to his face, brought his head down to hers, and kissed him hard. Then she drew back. 'I love you, Peter Henderson. I really do.'

For a long moment, each stared at the other.

Then Peter took her hand in his, and together they walked along the road in silence.

10

L *ater that evening*

'THANK GOODNESS THAT'S OVER,' Claire said, handing a cup of hot chocolate to Mary, who was sitting on Claire's bed.

She picked up her cup from her desk, sat down next to Mary, tucked her feet under her housecoat, and took a sip of her drink. 'Mother was just what I'd expected—all heart and generosity of spirit.'

Mary laughed. 'Was it really that ghastly?'

'Just about. But Peter handled the inquisition very well, I thought. He was amazingly calm when my mother all but blamed his parents for the fact that there are needy people in the world. Apparently, the only things preventing such people from taking a seat in Parliament or running a major company are Peter's parents and others like them.'

'Ouch.'

'Ouch, indeed. She didn't go quite as far as saying that as

she'd managed to get where she was by herself, so could every down and out if they'd only make the effort, but she came pretty close.'

'I can't wait to meet your mother—she sounds quite a character.'

Claire nodded. 'She is, but characters aren't always that pleasant to live with. And to crown it all, she gave me the first sex talk she's ever given me. She hauled me back as we were leaving and hissed that I should always respect myself. It was pretty obvious what she was talking about.'

'How embarrassing,' Mary said with a giggle.

'You can say that again! I didn't know where to look.'

'Did Peter hear her?'

'I don't think so, but I told him anyway.' She shifted her position on the bed so that she faced Mary. 'On that subject, I've been meaning to ask you something,' she said, a trace of awkwardness creeping into her voice.

'You're going red. I can guess what this is about.'

'It's just that you've been going out with Keith for a while now—for as long as Peter and me, in fact.' She paused.

'True. And?' Mary prompted.

'Do you ever think about... well, you know?' She felt herself going crimson.

Mary laughed. 'You're trying to ask if we've gone all the way, aren't you?'

Claire grimaced in embarrassment. 'Well, *have* you?'

'Not yet, but we will do soon.'

Claire hesitated. 'Aren't you worried about what he'll think of you afterwards?'

'That old chestnut! If I didn't know he loved me, I wouldn't even think about it. Why should it change anything? It'll just show how much I care about him. And anyway, it's what I want, too.'

'Suppose you got pregnant. You'd be kicked out at once. Student nurses can't even be married.'

'Obviously I'd prefer to get qualified first and have some time alone with Keith before we had children. But if they came along sooner, it wouldn't be the end of the world. We love each other and we'd work it out.'

Claire bit her lip and stared at the floor.

Mary lowered her voice. 'Men can use something, Claire. Or you could. There are devices you can use. I know it sounds unromantic and clinical, but if you want to do it with Peter—and I'm guessing you do from this conversation—and you don't want to get caught out, what choice have you got? And there's always the contraceptive pill.'

'But it's only for married women.'

'Tell your doctor you need it to regulate your periods. You wouldn't be the first to get it that way.'

'I hadn't thought of that!'

'Anyone can see you love Peter, and he loves you. Do you really want to spend the next two and a half years thinking about going to bed with him, but not doing anything about it? You'd start to dwell on the subject and that's unnatural. You'd turn into a bore, and no longer be fun to be with.

If you want to go all the way, do it. You know that if your precautions failed, Peter would marry you.'

'But I want him to marry me because he loves me, and not because he's doing the so-called decent thing. How would I know he'd have proposed if I hadn't got pregnant?'

Mary shrugged her shoulders. 'I'd never look at it like that. I'm sure we'll marry eventually, and if it ends up sooner rather than later, I'd try to complete my training later on. It might be possible by then. There've been loads of changes in nursing recently and we can't know what it'll be like in a few years' time.'

'Yes, that's a good point,' Claire said slowly. She paused. 'Has Keith proposed yet?'

Mary shook her head. 'Not in so many words, but it's sort of understood. And one other thing to think about. You say you wouldn't want Peter to marry you just because you were pregnant. Well, would you want him to marry you just because it was the only way to get you into bed? I know I wouldn't with Keith.'

'When you put it like that, no, I wouldn't, either.'

'So what's the alternative? Unless, of course, you and Peter are comfortable waiting for several years.'

Claire stared at her. 'He isn't, and nor am I.'

Mary gave her a broad smile. 'And that's my answer, too.'

MARY HAD MADE GOOD SENSE, Claire thought, sitting in her armchair, staring at the two empty cups on her desk as she tried to summon up the energy to cross the room and get into bed.

She and Peter loved each other, and that meant, as Mary had pointed out, that there was really nothing to fear. She'd take Mary's advice about the contraceptive pill, and then she and Peter would be able to relax about everything.

If despite everything, she *did* get pregnant, he'd obviously be disappointed at her having to give up the nursing course, but he was sure to be thrilled about becoming a father, even though it'd be sooner than planned.

She changed her position in the chair.

To be strictly accurate, though, they hadn't planned anything.

They'd never talked about having children, but she knew instinctively that he'd want them. She'd seen his patience with her mother, and his real affection for his parents. And being an only child as she was, who was bound to have been lonely at times in the past, as she had been, he was sure to want a number of children.

She stood up, and smiled inwardly.

How annoyed her mother would be if she knew that unwittingly that afternoon she'd started Claire on a train of thought that had led her in totally the opposite direction from the one she'd intended.

How ironic, she thought, and she was still smiling broadly as she went across to her bed.

11

E *nd of February*

THE AIR CHILL against their faces and the rutted track rock-hard beneath their feet, they struggled up one of the paths leading to the summit of Beacon Hill, Peter in front, Claire climbing more slowly behind him.

Every so often, she'd pause on the narrow path and stare at the woodland floor, a carpet of gold beneath the afternoon sun that streamed in slender columns between the gaunt trees.

Gossamer catkins hung from the leafless branches, dissolving into liquid gold against the shimmering backcloth of bright light.

After a moment or two absorbing the scene, she'd start to climb the track again.

Gradually, the trees thinned and the summit stood proud ahead of them. She saw Peter waiting for her at the foot of the short slope leading up to the crenelated stone wall surrounding the toposcope, and hurried up to him.

Together they walked to the castle-like structure and climbed the few steps to the metal plaque that indicated distance and direction.

'You're nuts,' she said as they walked. 'You went so fast that you can't have seen the flowers, and they're really lovely.'

'So's this,' he said as they reached the plaque and stood by the wall, gazing at the view, his arm around Claire's shoulders, her arm around his back.

The city centre lay sprawled out in front of them; to its left stood the hospital; the shadowy shapes of the South Staffordshire Pennines were visible beyond the city; to the north west lay the Black Country, and to the south east, the Forest of Arden could be seen on a clear day.

Claire's gaze moved across the wide panorama. 'It's all a bit too flat for me. I preferred the trees and flowers lower down. And I also like rolling hills, and fields with sheep and cattle grazing.'

He nodded. 'I like them, too, but not if they're just pretty chocolate-box scenes. That's not my thing. Being surrounded by emptiness is so much better. Give me wide horizons and a wilderness any day.'

'You and your emptiness,' she said with a laugh. 'A good thing about Birmingham is that although it's a busy city, you can easily escape to Cannon Hill Park, and that feels open, and to the Lickey Hills, like we've done today. What was it—thirty minutes on the Lambretta, and look at the walk we've had! We're lucky—we've got the best of both worlds.'

He glanced down at her in surprise. 'You wouldn't want to live here forever, though, would you?'

She shook her head. 'Certainly not!'

'Ideally, what would you prefer—to be in the country or in a town?'

She thought for a moment. 'I don't really know. It'd have to be somewhere I could get work, but definitely a much smaller place than Birmingham. What about you?'

'I don't know, either. I'd love to live in the middle of nowhere, but if I did, I'd almost certainly have to be a GP.'

'What's wrong with that?'

He shrugged. 'Well, you could certainly be surrounded by openness, but you'd see the same people, day in, day out, and that could get boring.'

She looked at him curiously. 'You've got two more years before you need to decide, but you sound as if you've already made up your mind.'

'I wouldn't go as far as that. It's just that the graduates registering as doctors this year are making their choices now, and it's got us all talking about what we'll do when *our* time comes. And with the first part of the Finals in June, it doesn't feel that far away.'

'What happens if they can't decide what to do?' she asked, struggling to quell her disappointment that he'd hadn't discussed his options with her.

'I suppose they'll stay on as housemen,' he said, his eyes on a silver airplane that was moving across the sky above them, leaving a thin white trail in its wake.

'So you're more against being a GP than for it?' she asked after a few minutes' silence. 'Is that right?'

'I haven't ruled anything out yet.' He looked down at her and smiled broadly. 'How could I? It's something we'll need to talk about together, isn't it? At least, I hope it is.'

Relief swept through her.

'But you're right, I think I'm unlikely to want to be a GP. It's not just the steady diet of the same people. It's that I wouldn't get to do much surgery, and that's the thing I like most. I can't really see myself giving up surgery for a job where the height of my week's excitement could be prescribing for athlete's foot.'

'I can understand that,' she said. 'Mind you, you might see the occasional verruca, too!' she added with a giggle.

He laughed. 'Good point! But to be honest, Mike and Alex have also rather put me off. Listening to them, you'd think a GP was no more than a failed specialist who'd no choice but to work in dire conditions. And a lot of other people seem to be saying the same.'

'So it looks like a hospital, then, does it?'

The distant barking of a dog broke into the quiet of the afternoon, and they heard the muffled sound of voices.

'I expect so. But there's no need to think about it today. We should be making the most of your last day of freedom for eight days.' The dog barked again, sounding closer. 'Shall we get off before we've got company? We've had the best part of the day, anyway.'

They turned from the view. Claire tucked her arm in Peter's and they went back down the stone steps, and down the grassy slope to the track that wound between the trees.

Walking one behind the other as the track narrowed, they reached the bottom of the hill and headed for the scooter.

'We'll pick up a takeaway on the way home, if you like,' he said, kicking the brake undone as he sat on the leather seat, waiting while she donned her helmet. 'It'll save going out for something later.'

'Good thinking.' She climbed on to the seat behind him, wrapped her arms around his chest, and leaned as close to him as she could.

· · ·

'WE TIMED THE WALK WELL, judging by the sky,' Peter said, hanging his jacket on a peg by his door. He turned back into the room, and stopped abruptly. His hands flew to his forehead. 'Damn! We forgot the takeaway. I've a couple of Vestas we could have, or we could go out for a proper meal. Whatever you prefer.'

'I'd rather eat here, thanks. If we go out, we'll only bump into someone we know.' She took off her jacket, threw it over the back of his desk chair, and sat down on his bed. 'Besides, it's getting colder.'

'How about a coffee, then? That'll raise your body temperature. Or wine? I got some for later on so that we could toast your move to men's surgical, but we could have some now.'

'Coffee sounds great, thanks. And the wine later.'

She leaned back against the wall and watched him switch on the kettle and open a jar of instant coffee. 'You're so lucky, being able to have women in your room,' she called to him. 'It'd be absolutely impossible to smuggle a man into our room, if we were so inclined.'

He paused and grinned at her from across the room. 'I rather think that having women in my room might prove too much even for me. But having one woman in my room, and a very special woman at that, well, that's a different matter.'

'I'm relieved to hear it!'

As soon as the coffees were ready, he brought them over to the bed, handed her one and sat down next to her. 'Some women stay overnight, you know,' he said. 'Obviously it's against the rules, but they just stay on after they should've left. They keep quiet and no one knows they're there.'

'I'd be scared of being caught.' She took a sip of her coffee.

'You're not caught if you're careful.' His drink in one

hand, he slid his free arm around her shoulders. 'And what about you? Are you so inclined?'

Clutching her mug with both hands, she looked at him questioningly. 'To do what?'

'To smuggle a man into your room.'

Blushing, she laughed. 'The thought may have crossed my mind on occasions.'

'Only on occasions?' He raised his eyebrows in feigned surprise. 'Am I being challenged to make you so inclined on every occasion, I wonder. If I am, I'd be happy to pick up the gauntlet.'

A tremor of nervousness shook her laughter, and she glanced at him.

Their eyes met, and locked. Their smiles slowly faded, and for a long moment, each stared at the other.

Then he took the mug of coffee from her hand, leaned across to his bedside table, placed both mugs on it, straightened up and turned to her.

Her heart raced.

'Coffee's not the only way to raise a person's body temperature, you know,' he said quietly. 'Just being near you raises mine, Claire.'

'I know what you mean,' she said, her voice shaking. 'I know what being near you does to me.' She raised her hand to his cheek and ran her palm very slowly down the side of his face.

He took hold of her hand and kissed the tips of her fingers, very slowly, one by one. Then he slid his arm around her back and pulled her close to him. She felt the strength in his arms, and the hard muscle of his chest.

A burst of desire shot through her, dragging the breath from her body.

He stared down into her face, his eyes darkening into a

deep blue intensity. She gazed back up at him, her heart thumping loudly in trepidation, her lips parting.

Goosebumps ran down her spine.

Then he leaned down and kissed her lightly on her forehead.

She put her hand to the side of his face and held him there, feeling his breath hot against her skin, her every nerve tingling. Her hand slipped to his chest, and they sat there, motionless.

Then abruptly he pulled away from her. Her hand fell to her lap.

'I love you, Claire,' he said, his voice breaking, 'so I'm not going to push you into anything, much as I want it. The moment's got to be right for you.' He made as if to get off the bed. 'And we mustn't take any risks. You know what I mean.'

She caught his arm. 'There wouldn't be a risk,' she said, blushing furiously. 'I've taken care of it. The moment's right, Peter. I love you, too.'

He glanced at the hand that was holding his arm, and then at her face, and she saw the hope that filled his eyes, and the love.

Taking his hand, she placed it on her sweater above her left breast. 'You won't need a stethoscope to tell you how fast my heart's beating,' she said, her voice trembling as she pressed his palm against her. 'I don't want to wait any longer.'

'Oh, Claire.' Her name was a long, low sigh full of love.

'So why today?' he asked, as they lay in his bed, his arm around her shoulders, her cheek against his bare chest. 'You must know how long I've been wanting this, so what was special about today?'

She ran her fingers through the coarse fair hair on his chest, and then pulled her hand back and tucked it under her chin. 'I suppose I couldn't bear to wait any longer. It's getting so hard to get time off together, and it'll get worse. And the thought of waiting till goodness knows when... . And then this afternoon... being here alone with you... with no takeaway to keep us busy.'

She glanced up at his face and giggled.

'Believe me, I've never been more delighted to have forgotten something. And to think I said earlier that we'd had the best part of the day.' He ran his fingers down her cheek. 'How wrong can a person be!'

'Not much wronger than that.'

'I love you, Claire Meredith, more than I can say.'

She slid her hand behind his head, pulled his face to hers and kissed him hard on the lips.

'What time did you say you were on tomorrow morning?' he murmured when she'd released him.

She groaned and lay back on the pillow, her auburn hair a tangle of curls that framed her face. 'Don't remind me— seven thirty.'

He rolled over on top of her, put an arm on either side of her body and gazed down at her. 'Since you're about to be let loose on men's surgical, I think the more you know about the male anatomy, the better. You want to impress Ward Sister, don't you?'

'Oh, absolutely! Teach on, maestro,' she said laughing. And instinctively, she wound her legs around his back.

12

As he made his way back to his hall after leaving Claire at the nurses' home, Peter realised that he was smiling at nothing.

And why not, he thought, smiling even more broadly into the darkness ahead—he couldn't imagine ever being happier than he was at that moment.

He loved Claire and Claire loved him, and that made him the luckiest man alive.

From the moment he'd met her, his world had changed —it had become better, so much better.

Looking back, he knew that he'd fallen for Claire that day in the refectory, and since then he'd been desperately hoping that she felt the same about him.

Now he knew for a fact that she did.

She would never have gone to bed with someone she didn't love and with whom she couldn't imagine sharing her life, any more than he would've slept with her unless he'd been certain that one day they'd marry. She wasn't the sort of woman you treated lightly.

With anyone else, he might have had strong misgivings

about tying himself up before he'd had time to spread his wings and enjoy his longed-for freedom, he mused as he crossed the road, but not with Claire.

Marrying the right person didn't mean giving up your freedom—it meant having someone with whom to share that freedom. Claire and he wanted the same things. With her at his side, his life was going to be so much more enjoyable.

He could see it now—both of them doing a job they loved, that brought them adventure and excitement in an amazing location. It might be in Britain; it might be overseas.

They obviously differed slightly in the sort of scenery they found beautiful, but all that was needed was a little give and take, so he couldn't see that posing a problem.

He thrust his hands deep into his pockets. He couldn't wait to get married, and start sleeping alongside Claire every night.

It was a real drag having to wait, but he'd be crazy not to get his degree, do his pre-registration year, and register before he married. And by then he'd know what he wanted to do, and where.

A long way off though that sounded, there wasn't a sensible alternative.

He'd heard far too many horror stories about the difficulties facing medics who'd married before they'd completed the course, who'd found themselves living in cramped conditions, often with children, while still studying. So there was no attraction in the idea of starting married life before he was fully qualified.

He wanted something better than that for them both, something more romantic. When he married Claire, everything must be perfect for her. She deserved nothing but the best.

And also there was *her* career to consider—student nurses weren't allowed to marry. She'd qualify in the year that he registered as a doctor. If they didn't wait till then, she'd be forced to leave the hospital, and that would make it even harder for them to meet than it already was. Neither of them would want that.

Fortunately, Claire didn't seem in any hurry to have children—she'd have already brought up the subject if she was.

She probably wanted, as he did, for them to have some time together after they married, when neither was studying and they were free to do whatever they wanted.

Obviously, if she got pregnant, they'd have to re-think things, but ideally it wouldn't happen until they'd been married for several years.

There was nothing to stop them getting secretly engaged, though, and he'd propose to her as soon as there was a romantic occasion on which to do so.

They'd have to keep it a secret from the hospital and the Medical School, but he wanted his friends to know how serious they were about each other. And he'd never been more serious.

Just the thought of Claire forever with him, of them travelling through life together...

He stood still and gazed up at the star-studded sky, his heart overflowing.

It was years since he'd stopped believing in the God his parents had told him about when he was little, but standing beneath the grandeur of the sky that night, with the scent of Claire on his body, and his skin still on fire from the touch of her fingers, he was closer to some sort of religious feeling than he'd ever been before.

. . .

IT WAS NO USE—SHE just couldn't get off to sleep. All she could think of was Peter.

She jumped out of bed, pulled open the curtains, leaned forward, put her elbows on the windowsill and rested her chin on her upturned hands.

The cold glass misted and she wiped it clear with a sweep of her forearm. Pressing her face against the pane, she tried to peer through her reflection into the night.

She was the luckiest woman alive, she thought gleefully. The man she loved with all her heart loved her as much as she loved him.

She'd long been certain about Peter's feelings for her, but now he'd confirmed it. He'd never have taken advantage of what she felt for him if he hadn't intended them to have a future together—he wasn't that kind of man. He had made a statement that day, just as she had.

She turned away from the chill night, closed the curtains, leaned back against the window and stared at her rumpled bed.

And if he were at her side right now, she'd willingly have made that statement again, she thought happily. But unfortunately he wasn't.

She looked around the room. The next two years were going to feel like an eternity. But much as she was dying to settle down with Peter, common sense told her they had to wait, agonising though that was going to be.

If only she'd chosen a different career, she thought in a moment of bleak despair. If she had, they could've married at once.

She shook her head—she'd only depress herself if she started thinking like that. They both wanted to do the jobs they were training for, so they'd have to be patient and endure the temporary difficulties that caused.

And anyway, she told herself sharply, rubbing her arms up and down to warm herself, she was jumping the gun—Peter hadn't yet mentioned marriage. For all she was certain he was going to, it was a little too soon to be thinking about a trousseau and children's names.

Having taken Mary's advice about the contraceptive pill, she and Peter had reduced the obvious risk of sleeping together, so there was no pressure to rush into marrying, if pressure was the right word.

It was infinitely better to wait until the time was right in terms of both of their careers. After all, until they'd both qualified, they weren't really in a position to marry and have children.

It meant that for the next two years, they'd just have to relax and enjoy the time they managed to snatch together.

She climbed back into her bed, pulled the blankets up to her chin and turned on her side to face the wall.

In her mind's eye, she saw Peter sitting across a kitchen table from her, a rack of toast and a jar of marmalade in the middle of the table.

A smile on her lips, she drifted slowly into oblivion.

13

Beginning of March

CLAIRE SWIFTLY ARRANGED her starched apron in front of her dress and tied its wide straps around her waist. Then she pulled up the apron bib, fastened it to the dress, slid two more kirby grips into her frilly hat, and hurried out of the locker room and up the stairs in the direction of the men's surgical ward.

Halfway up, she reached Mary.

'Talk about last minute,' Mary said as Claire kept pace with her, panting heavily. 'I was worried you'd be late.'

'Not half as worried as I was! And on our first morning, too.' She glanced at her fob watch. 'Oh, my God, Mary— we're already one minute late. Let's run.'

The reached the second floor in minutes, pushed open the outer swing doors, dashed through them, and stopped.

They glanced at the kitchen and side room on their

right, but both were empty. So was the Ward Sister's office on their left, and the two single side rooms and linen cupboards next to her office.

Shooting each other a nervous look, they went as quickly as they dared through the inner swing doors into the main ward, and anxiously scanned the line of six beds on either side of the room, looking for a nurse in the dark-blue uniform of a sister.

The bed curtains had been drawn back on all but one of the patients' beds, and a cleaner was wet-dusting around the beds, ensuring that all of their metal wheels pointed in the same direction.

A nurse was going from bed to bed with a metal trolley, and another was standing by one of the beds, shaking a thermometer.

An elderly man was shuffling through the ward, replacing the paper rubbish bag taped to the front of each bedside locker, and refilling the water jug on top of the locker.

With relief, they saw the Ward Sister at the far end of the ward, where a small television set stood under the window, facing a semi-circle of Draylon-covered armchairs, and they went swiftly towards her.

'I see you've finally arrived,' she said, glancing up from tidying the magazines on the low coffee table in front of the armchairs.

She picked up a clipboard from the table and straight-ened up. 'I pride myself on a well-run ward, and I insist on punctuality.' Her voice was acid. 'You're three minutes' late. There's no room in a busy ward for nurses who make a habit of being late. You'll be disciplined if it happens again.'

'Yes, Sister,' they chorused, their expressions meek.

'Your perm for today will be Nurse Brown. She'll do

wound inspection and dressings with you,' Sister continued. 'These are your patients.'

She handed the clipboard to Claire.

'Nurse Brown has indicated the names of the patients whose wounds you're going to inspect. You'll find masks and gowns in the bathroom.' She indicated the right-hand corner of the ward. 'When you've put them on, go straight to the sterilising room, which is next to the bathroom. Nurse Brown is already there, waiting for you.'

'Yes, Sister,' they said again in unison, and turned towards the bathroom.

'Every time I hear the word "perm", I think of a fuzzy head of hair and it makes me want to laugh,' Mary whispered as they hurried off.

'Me, too. But I fear that might have been our last laugh for the day.'

Having slipped a white gown over their uniform, put on a white cloth mask, the loop of which they slid behind their ears so that the mask covered their nose and mouth, they went quickly into the sterilising room.

'About time!' Nurse Brown said sharply. 'We should've started a while ago.' She pulled the dressing-trolley closer to her. 'I know you've set up trolleys in the PTS and medical, but a surgical ward's requirements are slightly different, so watch what I do very carefully. You'll do it by yourself for the next patient.'

She wiped the trolley with carbolic using a swab, and then threw the swab away. Picking up tongs, she used them to remove two large stainless-steel bowls with lids from a big metal steriliser that stood on legs by the wall, and placed the bowls on the top shelf of the trolley.

'The tongs are sterile, too, of course,' she said, opening up a metal drum, and with the tongs taking out two sterile green cloths, several cotton wool swabs and gauze dressings, all of which she put into one of the bowls.

From a smaller steriliser, also on legs, she took three pairs of forceps, a pair of scissors, and a small container into which she poured some alcohol, and placed them in the other bowl.

'You'll have noticed that everything in these two bowls has been sterilised,' she said, replacing the lids. 'I expect you've already been shown the new disposable sterile syringes.'

'Yes, Nurse Brown,' Claire volunteered.

Nurse Brown nodded. 'You won't yet appreciate what it means not having to sterilise every single syringe, tube and needle, but the volume of sterilised equipment needed for this one dressing-trolley alone should give you some idea. Fortunately, we're starting to get in other sterile supplies, as well.'

'So we won't need to do all this for much longer?' Claire said, indicating the two sterilisers.

Nurse Brown nodded. 'That's right. You're coming into nursing at an exciting time,' she said, her face devoid of any sign of excitement.

'That's lucky!' Mary exclaimed.

Nurse Brown frowned at her. 'Nevertheless, Nurse, at the moment we still sterilise most of the equipment ourselves, so we have to know how to do it.'

She reached up, took a bowl with a lid from the cupboard, and stood it on the bottom shelf of the trolley.

'None of this has to be sterile,' she said, placing a chest blanket and a tray filled with rolls of tape, bandages and safety pins next to the bowl. She stood upright. 'Do you think you can remember all that?'

'Yes, Nurse Brown,' both said quickly.

'Then we're almost ready to start our round,' she said. She paused. 'Is there anything else we should do first?'

Claire and Mary looked at each other and then at the trolley. Neither said anything.

Nurse Brown shook her head in a gesture of despair. 'We must put another two bowls and a complete set of instruments into the steriliser so that they'll be ready for use when we return,' she said with exaggerated patience.

'Only then can we go to the first patient on the list. He had an appendectomy five days ago, and I'm hoping to remove some of his stitches. Watch me closely because you're going to be doing the rest of the dressings by yourselves.'

CLAIRE PUSHED her empty plate away, leaned back in her chair, and sighed. She was desperate to shut her eyes, but afraid that if she did so, she'd fall asleep in an instant.

Her first morning in men's surgical had flown by in a flurry of tasks, and she was absolutely shattered. Much as she always enjoyed seeing Peter, for once she wasn't sorry not to be meeting him until the end of the week.

It was going to take every ounce of her energy to get through each day, and the envy she'd felt that morning for Mary who was having lunch with Keith, had long disappeared.

She felt her eyelids gradually close.

'Don't let me keep you awake.' Alex's voice sounded above her.

Her eyes sprung open. 'Alex!' she exclaimed, sliding upright in her chair. 'What're you doing here?'

He pulled out the chair opposite her, and sat down. 'Rescuing a lovely damsel in distress.'

She laughed. 'So why're you wasting your time with me? Go rescue her.'

'Because, lovely damsel, even from the other side of the room, I could see you were about to drop off. Peter told me you were starting on men's surgical today, and knowing the harridan in charge, I didn't think it a good idea for you to be late back to the ward, rubbing the sleepies from your eyes and looking well rested.'

She laughed. 'You really are an idiot, Alex, but a nice one, and I'm grateful to you. We were three minutes late this morning, and she said we'll be disciplined if we're late again.'

'Three minutes!' he exclaimed, and held up his hands in feigned horror. 'How much longer have you got left?'

She looked at her watch. 'Fifteen minutes at the most.'

He leaned forward and smiled. 'Then I'll do my best to keep you awake for those fifteen minutes.'

'Don't you have to get back?'

'Not yet. I ate in the doctors' canteen, but there was no one there I wanted to talk to so I left. I saw you on my way out and thought I'd come across for some lively conversation.'

'You're out of luck, I'm afraid. Nurse Brown drowned my last vestige of liveliness in carbolic.'

He grinned at her. 'I'll take my chances. So, what shall we talk about?'

'Your latest conquest, if you want. I've hardly seen anyone since we started on the wards so I'm really behind with the news.'

'Her name's Karen, and we've been together for about a month.'

Claire raised her eyebrows. 'A month, indeed. That's

pretty long for you. Are you in danger of being tamed, I wonder.'

He looked at her in amusement. 'Don't rule it out. The image of Karen bearing down on me with a whip is a somewhat appealing one. All the more so if she's wearing knee-high leather boots at the time.'

Claire laughed.

'She's not the type I usually go for,' he continued cheerfully. 'There's less slap on the face, and more between the ears. I think you'd like her. We should all go out at some point soon. Saturday at the Chinese has rather fallen off, but maybe the four of us could make an effort to get there again.'

'I'd like that. Is she at the University?'

He shook his head. 'No, she's a secretary, which means her hours are easier. But enough about me, how are things with you and Peter?'

'Absolutely fine. Not that we get much time together, and when we do, there's usually someone else around.'

'Ouch! I suspect that someone else is often me, and what's more, I've just suggested more of the same.'

'I'm not talking about you, Alex. You don't count,' she said quickly.

'Ouch again,' he said, assuming a mournful expression.

She laughed. 'You know what I mean. You're a really good friend and we always like seeing you. And I'd love us all to go out together. Really I would.'

'Okay, I'm mollified now. You know, I do sympathise, Claire,' he said, his voice suddenly serious. 'But in a couple of years, all this grabbing a moment together will end. You and Peter will be able to do whatever you want, and go wherever you want.'

'I can't wait,' she said, hugging herself. 'I can just see

Peter and me in a little house somewhere, surrounded by numerous children. It'll be blissful.'

He glanced at her sharply, surprise in his eyes.

Then he looked down at the Formica-topped table.

Some crystals of sugar had fallen from the bowl, and he pushed them meticulously into a heap with his thumb. 'I'm sure Peter's impatient for that, too,' he said.

'He is.' She beamed at him. 'Our dream is to live in a beautiful place, have lots of children, and be near somewhere open where we can go for long walks. But I'm rather jumping the gun, I'm afraid.' She laughed in sudden embarrassment. 'We're not even engaged.'

'I think it's a gun you can safely jump over. And it's a good dream.' He looked at his watch. 'I'm afraid you'd better get going if you don't want Sister to fasten you to her broomstick and fly you off to Matron.'

She stood up. 'Thanks so much for keeping me company, Alex. I feel much more alert now.'

'And thank *you* for helping me pass the time so pleasantly.'

She gave him a broad smile. 'Don't forget our Saturday date, will you? I'm looking forward to meeting Karen.'

He stared up into the dark brown eyes that sparkled from a lovely face framed by the tendrils of red hair that had escaped her hat. 'You can be sure I won't.'

With a little wave, she turned and hurried across the canteen towards the exit.

ALEX ROSE TO HIS FEET, and stood still, his eyes following Claire until she'd disappeared from sight.

Then he started to move slowly forward, threading his way between the tables, lost in thought.

14

April

'It looks pretty different from two months ago,' Claire said as they stood on the summit of Beacon Hill, and stared ahead at a Birmingham that sparkled in the sunlight that bounced off the windows and brought a rich golden glow to the wide expanse of concrete, brick and stone. 'It's amazing what a little sun can do.'

He nodded. 'It certainly is.'

'Did you see the bluebells lower down? They're a lovely purply-blue now. Silly question—once again, you charged right past them, your eyes on the track.'

'You're wrong. I did see them. Ask me a question and I'll prove it.'

'Okay. The clearings were full of bluebells and one other flower. What was it?'

'Haven't a clue. You'll have to tell me.'

'Wild garlic. The white flowers were hard to miss. And I'm surprised you didn't pick up the scent.' She looked around her and sighed with pleasure. 'I'm so glad we decided to come here today. Everything looks really beautiful now.'

He looked down at her. 'It's always beautiful where you are, Claire,' he said. He gave a loud groan. 'I'm sorry—that sounded like a very bad line from a B film.'

She laughed. 'Don't apologise! The thought behind it makes it forgivable.'

'In that case, I'll carry on.' Resting his forearm on the crenelated wall, he continued. 'Lovely as it is here, it's not nearly as lovely as you.' He paused. 'How does that sound?'

'Fine, but you can stop now. I'm starting to feel sick.'

'But I haven't got to the bit where I tell you that you're beautiful every minute of the day: morning, noon and night. There's never a time when you're not lovely. And when you're not funny and a pleasure to be with.'

'Now you'd really better stop. No one could ever think I'm lovely in the morning when I've just woken up and my hair is all over the place and I need to do my teeth. And nor when I'm bright red as I am now. You're crazy, Peter.'

She reached up and kissed him lightly on the lips.

He wrapped his arms around her, and pulled her to him.

'Crazy about you is right,' he said, and he kissed her hard on the mouth. 'But you're wrong about the morning. That's when you're at your loveliest. To be able to open my eyes and see you next to me, makes me the luckiest man alive.'

He hugged her tightly. 'Even after all these months, I can hardly believe that I'm the one who's got you. Thank goodness I saw you before anyone else could pounce on you. For a start, I can tell that Alex fancies you.'

'Now I know you really *are* crazy! Alex likes me as a person—I can sense that he does—but he goes for the ultra-sophisticated type. Slinky types in stilettos are Alex's thing. I'm much too down to earth for someone like him.'

'If you're what down to earth is like, men are mad to aim for the moon.'

'You smarmy creature!'

'It's not smarm if you're telling the truth,' he said with a grin. He paused. 'Joking apart, you know I love you so much that it hurts.'

'And I feel the same about you, Peter. I'm as mad about you as I was when we met. Perhaps even more so. In the middle of my work day, I often find myself standing still and thinking about you.'

'I hope that the tasks that bring me to mind aren't the action of sliding a bedpan beneath an elderly gentleman's rear end or injecting a horse-sized needle into a boil on a plump buttock,' he exclaimed with mock indignation.

'Darn! You must've been spying on me.'

They smiled at each other, and then he put his arm around her shoulders and they turned back to the view.

She pulled his arm more tightly around her, and rested her head against his shoulder.

'I wanted us to come back here today as the last time we were here, it ended up being an amazing day,' he said.

She heard a tinge of nervousness in his voice and glanced up at him in surprise.

He dropped his arm and turned to look her in the face. 'This seemed the perfect place to ask you something.'

Her mouth went dry.

'When we've finished studying, our lives will change. I want you to be part of my new life, wherever that is. I love you, Claire, and I know there'll never be a time when I don't love you. Without you, I'd be incomplete. Please say you'll marry me.'

She jumped up and down, clasping her hands together as if in prayer. 'Oh, yes, Peter, yes! Yes, yes, yes! Of course, I will.'

He flung his arms around her.

Laughing and crying at the same time, she leaned against his chest.

He buried his face in her hair. 'You could've had anyone, and yet you're willing to throw your lot in with me. I can hardly believe it.'

'Oh, Peter,' she whispered.

'I'll do everything I can to deserve you,' he went on fervently, 'and I'll never let you down, I promise. I'm going to spend the rest of my life showing you just what you mean to me.'

Her eyes glistening, she looked up at him with love.

'I promise,' he repeated, gazing down at her.

15

E *nd of June*

PETER PAID the bartender for two beers, and pushed one of the beers along the wooden counter to Alex.

'Cheers!' Alex said, picking up the glass. He leaned against the bar, took a swig of his beer, then wiped his mouth with the back of his hand. 'I sure needed that. Thank God the first part of the Finals is over. I really hope I don't have to re-sit any of the papers. Whatever I do in the future, it won't involve exams.'

'Apart from anything needed for registering, you mean.'

'Apart from anything needed for registration, that is,' Alex echoed. 'Look, that group's leaving. Let's grab their table. We'll need one for when the others get here.'

He slung his leather bag over his shoulder, picked up his glass, moved across to the table and sat down.

Peter followed him. 'Well spotted,' he said, sitting down

opposite Alex. 'And right by the darts' board, too, which is a bonus. Mike was saying he wanted a game. Your very good health.' He held up his glass, and then took a drink.

'And if it turns out to be otherwise, at least I'm in the right place and in the right company,' Alex remarked with a grin.

Peter laughed. He leaned back and stretched his legs out under the table. 'I wouldn't count on that—you should've seen the trouble I had inserting a stomach pump last week. I felt quite sorry for the poor patient.'

'In that case, I'll try not overdose on the booze. Anyway, why were you and Claire so determined to get us together tonight? Is it just an end of exam celebration or is it about something else?' He held up his left hand and studied the back of it.

'Yup, we're engaged. Have been since April, in fact, but we decided not to say anything till after the exams. We've obviously got to keep quiet about it as we don't want Claire to get chucked out, but we've decided to tell our closest friends.'

'You lucky dog. She's a stunner, mate. Congratulations.' Alex took another swig of his beer.

'Thanks, Alex. But you don't do too badly yourself. You've got a girl on your arm whenever you want one, and probably in other places, too.'

'Most definitely in those other places.' Alex gave him a knowing nod. 'I'm quite keen on Karen, but, if I'm honest, I don't feel about her as you clearly feel about Claire. Like I've said before, it's lucky for you that you saw Claire before I did. If you hadn't, you wouldn't have been in with a chance.'

'Your trouble is, you're too modest and self-effacing.'

'Ain't that the truth!'

Both laughed.

'Yes, Claire's well and truly taken,' Peter continued. 'But if you're honest with yourself, whatever you say about Karen, you'd shudder at the thought of settling down with just one person. You're never happier than when you're on the chase. It's once you've caught them that the rot sets in.' He smiled at Alex. 'Admit it. You know that's true.'

Alex frowned. 'Maybe it was a couple of years ago, but I'm not so sure it is now. I've been with Karen for several months and we're still going strong.'

Peter shook his head. 'I just don't see you as husband material.'

'There's a lot about me you don't know,' Alex said, a trace of irritation in his voice. 'When the time and the girl are right, I'll be as good a husband as anyone else.'

Peter glanced at him quickly. 'Sorry, pal. I shouldn't have said what I did. I'm sure you will. In fact, you'll be better than many as you'll have got your wild oats out of the way. If Karen proves to be the one for you, she'll be a lucky girl.'

Alex put his glass down on the table. 'Hm. Don't think I don't know you're humouring me. But believe me, a steady stream of women can pall, and the truth is, I'm starting to be a bit bored by it all.'

'Despite the advantages of being free, and working in a sweetie shop, which is how you once described it?'

Alex nodded and gave a slight smile. 'I did, didn't I? Sure there are advantages in living the way I do—I've no ties and I can do what I want, and with women able to get the pill more easily now, I don't need to worry too much about an unwelcome surprise. But nevertheless, I reckon I'll be settling down in a year or so.'

'If you're keen on Karen, why wait so long? She's a secretary, which puts you in a different position from Claire and me.'

Alex shrugged his shoulders. 'Having to study when you've just got married wouldn't be much fun. And we're going to be having even less time off in the future. When we're not in the hospital, we'll have to swot like mad for the final two parts of the exam. They're in only a year, after all.

And after that we'll be housemen, and on call for twenty-four hours a day, with just half a day off a week. It's far better to marry after registration.'

Peter nodded. 'That's what we think, too.'

'And Claire doesn't mind waiting two another years? Most women wouldn't be that patient.'

'Fortunately, Claire isn't most women. But also, there's her career to think about as well as mine. We can't marry till we're in a position to move away. Yes, the hospital allows married sisters these days, but not if they're married to doctors in the same hospital. Claire would be made to leave. I'd hate it if she had to work somewhere else, and so would she.'

Alex nodded. 'I'd forgotten about the problems it'd cause Claire. But to come back to the present and the two of you, I'm delighted for you both.'

'Thanks, Alex. I've asked to transfer to University House in October. Being mixed sex, it'll be easier.'

'Good thinking, mate.' Alex lifted his glass and took a drink.

'What were you two discussing a moment ago? We saw you deep in discussion when we came in,' Claire said, coming up to the table, with Mary at her side.

'Nothing much,' Peter said, standing up. 'What can I get you both?'

Claire glanced at Mary, who nodded. 'A Dubonnet and lemon for each of us, please.'

'Another beer, Alex?'

'Don't mind if I do,' Alex said, shuffling round to the middle of the leather banquette to make room for Claire and Mary.

'We saw Mike in the distance—he's on his way with the others,' Claire said, sliding in next to Alex. Mary sat down on the other side of her.

Alex leaned slightly in front of Claire. 'It's nice to see you again, Mary—we don't often see you in here.'

'I know. I can't remember the last time I came here. But I wanted to join in the celebration.' She glanced at Claire, and smiled.

Alex raised his eyebrows in exaggerated curiosity. 'Celebration? Celebration of what, may I ask?'

'Why, the end of the first part of the exams, of course,' Claire said lightly.

Alex raised his glass. 'Congratulations, Claire!' he said, and he emptied his glass.

'It's *your* exams that are over! I didn't mean that ours were.'

'Nor did I,' he said with a grin. 'I'm really pleased for you both—that's great news.'

'Trust Peter!' She glanced across to the bar where Peter was waiting to order the drinks. 'We were going to wait till everyone was here before saying anything. I should've guessed he'd tell you.'

'Is that so?' He glanced sideways at her. 'And you haven't told Mary, of course.'

'Touché,' Claire said, and laughed.

He tapped his shoulder. 'If ever anything goes wrong, that's the shoulder you must cry on. That's what friends are for.'

'Thanks, Alex. I'll remember that. But if you end up with a soggy shoulder, I'm sure it won't be down to me.'

. . .

So Claire and Peter were going to tie the knot in two years, were they, Alex thought in annoyance as he made his way back to his hall of residence, his hands thrust deep into his pockets.

Not that there was any reason why it should bother him —what they did was none of his business. And their engagement was hardly a surprise. Peter had been stupid about Claire from the minute he'd seen her, and she seemed to feel the same about him. A happy-ever-after ending had long been inevitable.

But it irked him that Peter had seen her first. By the time he'd met Claire, she was already so stuck on Peter that there hadn't been a hope in hell of anyone else getting a look in.

The chase, as Peter had put it, had been over before he, Alex, had even reached the starting post. And irrational though it was, he couldn't help seeing Claire as the one who'd got away.

And he didn't like feeling he'd missed out. Not one little bit.

Not about someone as striking as Claire, with that fabulous figure and those wonderful eyes and the sort of hair you longed to bury yourself in.

Damn Peter!

He didn't like losing at the best of times, and certainly not to someone who could be smugness itself on occasions. And who'd had the bloody cheek to tell him that he wasn't good husband material! What made Peter think he had the monopoly on good-husband ingredients, whatever they were?

Given the help Peter had needed in the early days, at the time when he couldn't string a coherent sentence together while talking to a woman, he should be grateful, not critical and disparaging.

It was true that Peter had developed into being good company, but he knew himself well enough to know that if they hadn't been thrown together by being in the same set, he was unlikely to have sought Peter's friendship.

On the face of it Peter was now just like him and his friends. But deep down, he sensed that Peter was different from them, and he couldn't see their friendship lasting once they'd left Birmingham.

And he wouldn't want it to, not if it meant having the marital bliss of Peter and Claire thrust regularly into his face.

He stopped walking, and frowned in puzzlement.

Why on earth was he so put out about Claire being with Peter?

She wasn't at all the sort of woman he normally went for, and she certainly wasn't the sort of woman he'd want as a permanent fixture in his life. God, no! Karen's style was much more to his taste, falling somewhere between the over-thin, over made-up women he used to date, and Claire with her natural beauty and homespun charms.

A date or two was all he'd ever have wanted with Claire, or however many dates it took to get her into bed.

He certainly wouldn't have wanted anything long-term and serious with her, so the fact that those few dates were never going to happen was hardly reason enough for him to feel so aggrieved, and to be so unable to let it go.

And yet he couldn't let go.

Even though, thinking some more about it, it was probably just as well that Peter *had* seen Claire before he did.

Although Peter had never exactly said that he and Claire were sleeping together, it was pretty obvious that they'd done the deed, and Claire wouldn't have been a pushover.

One or two dates, and a declaration of undying love, would never have been sufficient to get someone like Claire into bed, and Peter might well have been forced to propose in order to get her to open her legs.

And a proposal was further than he, Alex, would ever have gone.

So he could've ended up investing quite a bit of time and money in her pursuit, but fallen at the last hurdle.

No, it was better as things had turned out.

He resumed walking.

After all, his hang-up with Claire, which he'd sort of recognised fairly early on, wasn't about him fancying Claire as a person. It was that he'd known from the very start that he couldn't have her.

But actually—his steps faltered a moment—until she and Peter were married, there was no real reason why he *should* consider her out of bounds.

Seducing her would be quite a challenge, but Peter wasn't the only person who was drawn to challenges. And with Claire now more *au fait* with what to do in bed, thanks to her practice sessions with Peter, his victory would be infinitely more enjoyable.

Fate was on his side.

No one was going anywhere for at least two years, and that was sufficient time for him to prise open the potentially destructive gulf between Peter and Claire, a gulf of which neither principal player was yet aware.

But he was.

That they wanted very different things out of life was something he'd glimpsed when Peter had talked about the way in which he saw his future and Claire's in terms of the world out there, and then Claire had shared with him her very different vision for their life together.

That he might one day be able to benefit from this divergence of dreams had slid into the back of his mind, and settled there.

Now that he'd made a conscious decision to get Claire into his bed, and was armed with the knowledge he had, he was pretty sure that all he'd need to do was sit back and wait for the time to be right to intervene.

When that time came, he'd know it, and he'd be ready.

16

Two years later

J*uly, 1970*

CLAIRE LOOKED around the hospital staff canteen. Her eyes returned to Mary, and she smiled with pleasure.

'I'm so glad you're back, Mary. I really missed you when you were on your honeymoon—the place didn't feel the same. But I expect that you're less than pleased to be back.'

'You expect right. I had to force myself to come in today. I know it's a cliché, but we had such a wonderful time I didn't want it to end.'

'But it doesn't have to, does it? You and Keith can now live openly in his flat. Just think of it, no more holding your breath at night, hoping you'll not be heard.'

'True. But it won't be the flat for much longer. On my first days off, we're going to look for a house. Only a small one, mind you, but ideally with a little garden.'

'That sounds lovely.' A bolt of envy shot through her, and she pushed back the jealousy that rose in her throat. 'I know I've told you before, but your wedding was beautiful,' she said. 'Peter enjoyed it, too. Everyone was so happy, and your mum's lovely.'

'Amazingly, I enjoyed it enormously, and you know how terrified I'd been. But once the Mass started, it was fine. And the country hotel we went to for our honeymoon was perfect. It was only tiny, but it was run by a really friendly family, and was just what we needed after a hectic few weeks.' She paused. 'I'll give you the name if you want.'

Claire groaned audibly. 'I doubt we'll be needing a honeymoon hotel for some time yet. I know Peter's about to register as a doctor, but he's still undecided about working in a hospital or being a GP, so he's staying on as a houseman till he's made up his mind. I'm working here, too, so we can't get married.'

'I thought he wanted to be a surgeon.'

'He does. But he'd have to work in a hospital, and a fair sized one at that, which probably means living in a large town. He doesn't want that, and nor do I. We can't think about weddings until he knows what he'll be doing and where.'

'But now you're a registered nurse, why not get married quietly? If you were found out and told to leave, you'd easily get a job somewhere else. There're enough hospitals in the area, and good nurses are always in demand.'

'We thought of doing just that. But as Peter said, with the hours a houseman works, if I didn't work here, we'd never see each other. Alex was there at the time, and he said he knew of a couple of marriages that had recently broken up when they'd started working in different hospitals. He thought we should wait.'

'Well, I don't envy you. It must be really difficult, waiting so long.'

Claire pulled a face. 'Don't I know it! But it'd be even more difficult not to see him.'

Mary nodded. 'I can understand that.'

'And now that you're not living here,' Claire added wistfully, 'if I didn't work here, I'd see a lot less of you. So it's another reason why I'd be stupid to risk being thrown out.'

'It makes me even more pleased that Keith's not a doctor.' She hesitated. 'There's—'

'And because I don't have to plan a wedding,' Claire went on, 'I can put my energy to use elsewhere. I intend to go after any ward sister vacancies. Nothing ventured, et cetera.

If I'm successful, it'll boost our savings. As I want to stop the pill as soon as we're married, we might have children in the first year, so the more we've saved beforehand, the better.'

'You've obviously got it all worked out.'

'I have.' Claire nodded confidently. 'And if Peter's one of my housemen when I'm a sister, he'll stop by the ward office for coffee, like they all do, so there's a chance I'll see a great deal of him.'

She drew in a sudden sharp breath. 'I've just had an awful thought, Mary! Suppose we end up going after the same jobs?'

'We won't.' Mary blushed. 'I'm about two months pregnant.'

Claire's stomach lurched.

A lump lodged in her throat.

Swallowing hard, she jumped up, ran round the table

and hugged Mary. 'I'm so pleased for you. I know how much you want to be a mum. And Keith will be an excellent dad. I'm thrilled for you both.' She hugged her again.

'Mind your hat! It's gone skew whiff.' Laughing, Mary reached up to straighten Claire's hat.

'I'm really pleased for you,' Claire repeated, and sat down again. She put her hand to her stomach, and tried to still the strange feeling that swirled deep within her.

'I want to hear all your plans, down to the very last detail,' she said, her voice sounding strange to her ears. 'That explains the garden. When did you find out?'

'I rather thought I might be pregnant before I walked down the aisle, but I didn't go to the doctor till we got back from the honeymoon. I'd told Keith, of course, but no one else. He was really excited.'

'What did your mum say?'

Mary giggled. 'She doesn't know. We'll tell her in about a month, and then say the baby was premature.'

'When's it due?'

'February. Happily, the rhythm method worked for more than two years, and by the time it failed, it didn't really matter.'

'When are you telling the hospital?'

'When I start showing. I'd only tell them sooner if it looked as if something might be wrong and I had to take time off. And talking of time.' Mary glanced at her watch. 'Much as I'd like to carry on talking about babies and houses, we ought to get back to the ward.'

They stood up. 'At the risk of repeating myself, I couldn't be happier,' Claire said. 'Well, that's not quite true—I could. I'd be even happier if I was the one carrying a little Peter.'

'Well, it certainly isn't a little Peter,' Mary remarked in mock indignation.

Claire laughed. 'You know what I mean. It's funny, I'll be getting used to hearing myself called Sister—at least I hope I will—while you're getting used to hearing yourself called Mother.'

'That's true.' Mary's face reddened. 'I'm going to miss seeing you at work, Claire,' she blurted out, her voice shaking, 'and chatting like we do. Everything's going to change.'

'I'll miss you, too, but we'll always be friends. I know it won't be as easy to meet, but we'll manage. I'm truly happy for you, and also a weeny bit jealous. Just a bit.'

'Oh, Claire,' Mary said quietly.

'I know Peter and I have made the right decision,' Claire went on quickly, 'but I'd love to be married and expecting a baby. The first of many.' To her dismay, her voice broke. 'Look at us,' she said, pointing to her brimming eyes. 'We're a right pair.'

Mary put her arm round Claire's shoulders. 'I'm sure you're doing the right thing in waiting, Claire.'

Not trusting herself to speak, Claire nodded her agreement.

'Keith not being a doctor makes a huge difference.'

Claire nodded again, and wiped her eyes. 'You're right,' she said, a tremor in her voice. 'It's just that it's an emotional moment, learning your best friend's going to become a mother. And it's made me realise how much I'd love to be in the same position.'

'And you will be—just not as soon.'

Claire pulled out her handkerchief. 'You know, sometimes in the middle of the night, I wonder if perhaps there isn't more of my mother in me than I'd realised. She put getting married ahead of a career. I've always thought I was different, but at times now, I almost regret being a nurse. If

I'd done the secretarial course she suggested, Peter and I could be married by now.'

'But you'd be married to a different Peter,' Mary said with a smile. 'Since you live in Hereford, you're unlikely to have got a job here so you wouldn't have met him.'

'You know what I mean.'

'Like I said before—you'll have it all. Just not as soon. Nothing can stop it from happening—you're on the home stretch now.'

HER LEGS CURLED UNDER HER, Claire sat on Peter's bed, her back against the wall, and stared across the room at Peter. He was sitting at his desk, his head bent over his textbook. Her novel lay open on her lap, untouched.

'D'you want something to eat?' she asked when he pulled an A4 pad towards him and picked up his pen. 'I could make you an omelette.'

He glanced at her and smiled. 'That would be fantastic. I know we were going to take advantage of my half day off clashing with one of your free days and go out, but I've really got to check the details of the procedure I'm doing tomorrow morning. I'm quite nervous about it.'

'That's fine. I had a bite to eat when I saw Mary earlier. I'll go along to the kitchen.'

She didn't move.

He put down his pen and looked at her curiously. 'Is anything wrong? You've not seemed yourself all afternoon. Are you tired? You've had a lot of seven thirty mornings in a row, so you must be. We could always have fish and chips— a few minutes away from this won't hurt.' He indicated his book.

'Come on.' He scraped back his chair and stood up. 'Let's do that. It'll be good to get some fresh air.'

'Mary's having a baby,' Claire said, looking down at her book with unseeing eyes. She heard Peter sit down again, and she felt the touch of his eyes on her face. 'In February,' she added.

She stared fixedly at the page.

'I'm very pleased for them,' he said at last. 'But not in the least surprised. I didn't think they'd let the grass grow under their feet. They've been together for a while now.'

She looked up at him. 'For as long as *we* have. They met the day we went out for the first time. To the Chinese with Alex and the others. Mary spilt wine on Keith at a party that night.'

He nodded. 'I remember.' He paused. 'What do you want me to say, Claire?' he asked quietly. 'I may not be specialising in Psychology, but that doesn't mean to say I can't see the effect this is having on you. You'll miss living and working alongside Mary. Things are going to seem very different. I understand that.'

'You're wrong if you think I'm not pleased for them—I truly am.'

'I know you are. You're bound to be—you care about Mary. There's a but, though, isn't there?'

Her shoulders sagged. 'But it's made me realise how much I want to be married, too. To be married to you.'

He got up, swiftly crossed the room and sat down next to her. He put his arms around her. 'And you will be, I promise. As soon as we know what I'm going to do and where we'll be living, we can marry. The worst of the wait is behind us.'

'I know that. I'm being silly—just ignore me,' she said into his chest, her voice muffled.

'I could never ignore you.' He tightened his hold on her.

'But unlike them, if we married, we'd see less of each other, not more. And my priority is to see as much of you as I can.' He stopped abruptly, then dropped his arms. 'No, it isn't.'

Jerking her head up in alarm, she stared at him.

He was looking down at her, a slight frown on his face. 'Of course, it isn't.'

She felt the blood drain from her face. 'What d'you mean?' She couldn't stop herself trembling.

'I'm being really selfish, making what *I* want my priority, when it shouldn't be. My priority should be to make you happy. That's the most important thing. And if making you happy means marrying right now—well okay, let's do it! We can make it work.

We'll have a small wedding, do our best to keep it quiet, and delay the honeymoon. By the time they find out, if they do, it'll be too late to matter.'

A thrill of excitement shot through her, followed by a warmth that radiated from inner happiness.

Her eyes shining, she opened her mouth to speak.

Then she closed it again.

Slowly, her eyes traced the planes of his face, a turmoil of emotions fluttering within her. Then her mind cleared, and she was filled with a sense of peace.

'Thank you, Peter,' she said. 'You've made me very, very happy. I didn't realise how much I wanted you to suggest throwing caution to the winds, but now I do. It's probably been building up since Mary set the date for her wedding, and then when she told me about the baby, it poured fuel on a fire I didn't even know was smouldering.'

He took her face in his hands and brushed his lips across hers. 'That's a yes then, is it, lovely Claire?'

She heard the smile in his voice, could see the love in his eyes.

Very slowly, she shook her head. 'It's a no. Much as I want it, it's better to stick to our plan. If anything went wrong, I'd hardly see you, and I couldn't bear that.'

'I'm so lucky to have you,' he said, his voice a croak. 'There's no one in the world like you, Claire.'

She ran her fingers down his cheek. 'And I feel the same about you. I'll get the first ward sister's post I can, and that'll give you time to decide what to do. You don't want to get it wrong. Then, when we finally do get married, we can make as much noise about it as we want.'

'You'll never regret this,' he said quietly. 'I'll make very sure of that. You'll see.'

17

S *eptember*

STANDING IN HER LONG-SLEEVED, dark-blue dress, her starched white apron in place, Claire stared in the mirror. Well, at least she looked as if she knew what she was doing, even if she *was* panicking inside.

She glanced around the empty locker room and felt momentarily depressed—if only either Mary or Peter could have been there as moral support for her first time out as a ward night sister.

Not that it was their fault, she told herself quickly, turning back to the mirror.

Mary had wanted to come and see her off, but her pregnancy was taking its toll and by the time she'd finished her shift, she'd been visibly exhausted, and could never have hung on till after nine o'clock, what with such a long journey home.

And it wasn't Peter's fault, either. He was on call, and although right until the last minute, it had looked as if he'd be able to come, at the eleventh hour there'd been a nasty road accident and he'd been needed in theatre.

She turned sideways to look at her dress in profile in the mirror, and sighed. She was absolutely terrified, and looked it.

She knew she shouldn't be in such a state—they'd never have given her the post if they hadn't been certain she could do it.

But it wasn't just the extra responsibility that was daunting—it was also the thought of everyone shouting "Meredith's in blue" when she made her first appearance in the dark blue of a sister.

She'd always thought that new ward sisters must feel really self-conscious when that happened, and now she was about to learn if she'd been right.

She took a deep breath, and let it out slowly. It was the first night only that was going to be nerve-wracking. But she knew she was ready to take this step forward, and she'd soon settle into the work.

The night sister's job had been to get her to sister status, but she wanted to work in the day, and fully intended to go after the first day sister's post that came up after she'd done a suitable amount of time on nights.

By working in the day, she'd be more likely to see Peter. Although the housemen were on call at night, the night nurses did everything possible to avoid getting them up, knowing that the long hours they worked meant they needed all the rest they could get.

But until then, working nights wouldn't be too bad, especially as Peter had said he'd join her in her office for a late cup of tea whenever he could. And also, she was now entitled to a better room in the nurses' home.

Reaching into her locker, she took out the piece of starched muslin that was her sister's bonnet, shook it to let the two ribbons pinned inside the bonnet hang down, and then slipped it on to her head and tied the ribbons under her chin.

Glancing at her fob watch, she saw that it was almost nine o'clock—time for her to find out the section she'd been allocated.

She closed the locker door, took another deep breath and hurried out.

HER FIRST NIGHT had gone well, she thought in relief as she went into the sisters' canteen in the nurses' home to get her breakfast, and she'd actually enjoyed it.

As soon as she'd been given her section, she'd phoned the front-hall porter and told him the number of her beeper and the list of her wards in case he needed to contact her, and then she'd headed for her wards.

By eleven o'clock, when the phone calls from relatives started coming in, she'd found out the names of the sickest patients, and those who'd been in theatre, and had visited them and made notes on them.

Also she'd checked the wards with students in charge, and had supervised the dispensing of sleeping pills and other medication.

After she'd spoken to the relatives who'd telephoned, and again visited the patients who were very ill, she'd returned to her office for a cup of tea.

As she'd expected, there were already several housemen in there, leaning against the cupboards, drinking tea or coffee, but sadly, no Peter. One of the housemen had told her that he was still in theatre.

Swallowing her disappointment at not seeing him, she'd run through her patients' notes with the housemen, and had asked what they'd like the nurses to do if certain situations were to arise, to try to avoid disturbing them.

Once the housemen had gone to bed, she'd started the nurses on their dinner shifts and had done her first full round of the wards, but without letting any junior nurse follow her as she didn't yet know the patients well enough to be able to teach anyone anything.

She'd got back to her office at about three, and had just made tea and begun to sort out her notes when the door had opened.

'Alex!' she exclaimed in delight. 'What on earth are you doing here?'

He laughed. 'I thought I'd come and see how you were getting on. But if I'm in the way.' He glanced back at the door.

'You're not. It's great to see you. This is my first night on as a sister, you know.'

'So I hear. Peter told me you'd got a step up. And since one of my favourite fantasies is to have a sister, clad in her dark blue, standing astride me in commanding pose, I thought I ought to check you out, Sister.'

She laughed. 'People have been calling me Sister all night, but I keep looking over my shoulder, thinking they're talking to someone else. And as for that commanding pose, by the end of my shift, I won't even have the energy to sit up straight, let alone stand up!'

'I've a fantasy for that, too,' he said with a lazy grin. 'In that fantasy, Sister is lying on her back and I'm the one in commanding pose.'

'Now why doesn't that surprise me?'

Both laughed.

'Don't worry—you'll soon get used to bossing people about.' He indicated the kettle. 'Mind if I make a tea and join you?'

She started to get up.

'No, sit down. I can do this. I've actually mastered how to make a cup of tea. In fact, I'm more domesticated than you'd realise.'

'That's not saying much! But really, I'm ever so pleased you've dropped in. I'd been so nervous about tonight, and seeing a friendly face—not that they haven't all been friendly, but you know what I mean—it's driven away the last of my fears.'

He made his tea and brought it over to the table. 'I'm glad to have been of some use, then,' he said, sitting down opposite her. 'So, it's been okay, has it?'

'Yes, touch wood. I love the hospital at this time of night—with the lights dimmed in the wards, the corridors empty and the hospital waiting in silence for the morning.'

'You've forgotten the unearthly screams when the surgeons saw off limbs without administering anaesthetics,' Alex corrected her. 'I believe that's what Peter's engaged in right now.'

'Apart from those, of course. But you get so used to the ghastly wailing that you don't notice it after a bit.'

They smiled at each other.

He sat back in his seat. 'So, is being a night sister what you expected?'

'More or less. The things I've had to do—or rather supervise the students or juniors doing, in most cases— were pretty much what I'd do in the day. You know, a blocked tracheotomy tube, a leaking post-op wound, a plugged drip—nothing I couldn't handle.

But there's always the fear that something'll happen in the dead of night and you won't know what to do and the patient will die. You feel less alone in the day when there's so much going on and so many people around.'

'Perhaps dead of night isn't the best choice of expression,' Alex said in amusement. 'But to be serious, you don't need to worry about killing anyone—you're an outstanding nurse.'

'Flattery will get you everywhere,' she said with a tinge of embarrassment. 'You know, it's done me a world of good, you turning up like this. I've always hated the hour between three and four. It's about the only time in the night when I feel tired. After four, it all kicks off again, and you've no time to feel anything as you're so busy.'

'Well, I'm glad I'm keeping you awake. At least, I hope I am.'

'You are. It's great having you here to talk to. I have to be careful now what I say to the nurses as they're under me.'

He wagged his finger at her. 'Tut, tut. You really shouldn't talk about someone being under you. Remember my tendency to fantasise.'

'The same old Alex.'

'Am I that predictable?' He grinned at her.

'No, actually, you're not. For example, I'd never have predicted that you'd still be with Karen after two years.'

'I must admit that's a surprise to me, too.'

'Are we going to hear wedding bells in the near future?'

'Karen wants to know that, too,' he said. 'But *your* wedding bells are more interesting.'

'What bells?' she asked lightly.

'Point taken.' He sat back in his chair. 'Knowing the way

women think—and I confess I've been privy to many a female's thoughts in the wee small hours—I'm curious to know how Peter got you to agree to wait so long to tie the knot.

I could do with knowing that as Karen's starting to sound impatient. But if I'm out of line asking, you must tell me,' he added hastily.

'You're not. It's a fairly obvious question for anyone who knows we've been engaged for as long as we have. We just told a few friends, but I expect it's more widely known by now. But not by anyone in authority, I'm sure, or I'd have heard from them.'

'You're probably right about that.' He paused. 'So to go back to my question.'

She shrugged. 'It's just the way it is with our jobs and the hospital rules. But the situation won't last for ever. Peter must be closer to knowing what he wants to do, and in the meantime, I'm making the most of the wait—I've got my promotion and I'm saving up.'

'All that's true. But why do I feel it's your head talking, not your heart? My God!' His hand flew to his forehead in a theatrical gesture. 'I'm beginning to sound like a romance novel, and a bad one at that!'

She stared at him, a degree of surprise in her half-smile. 'If you're asking whether I wouldn't prefer to be married by now, well obviously I would. But I'd rather have things as they are than hardly ever see Peter.'

Alex sighed loudly. 'I envy Peter. He's a fortunate man that you're letting him take so long to make a decision.'

'Come off it,' she said with an awkward laugh. 'You're making me sound like a saint, and Peter sound as if he's done something wrong.

But if you think it's so unusual for a woman to wait for

that amount of time, why aren't you asking the same question about you and Karen? After all, you've been with her for almost as long as I've been with Peter.'

'Good point.'

'You're like a bird fighting against its wings being clipped, Alex. I suspect that it's because deep down, you'd hate to have what Peter and I want—a house, a bunch of kids and a garden. But at the same time, you don't want to lose Karen.'

'Like a bird, am I?' He raised his eyebrows. 'A majestic golden eagle at the very least, I hope. Not a common sparrow or starling.'

'Oh, definitely an eagle and a very attractive one at that.' She put her hand to her mouth and went red. 'Gosh, that sounded awful, coming from someone engaged to someone else. I didn't mean attractive to me.'

He grinned at her. 'From where I'm sitting, that sounded even more awful.'

'You know what I mean. I'm just making a bad job of saying that I can see why you're attractive to women. Objectively, I mean.'

'Hmm. Objectively is a controversial word, but I'm not sure—'

Her beeper sounded, and he stopped abruptly. She dialled the porter. 'I'm needed,' she said, replacing the receiver and standing up. 'It's a cancer patient.'

'Saved by the beeper, so to speak,' Alex said, rising to his feet. 'You get off—I'll rinse the cups.'

She went to the door, and then turned towards him. 'Thanks again for coming tonight, Alex. I've really enjoyed your company.'

He nodded to her. 'My pleasure.'

As she walked along the corridor, she seemed to feel

eyes on her back, but when she looked round, there was no one there. It must have been her imagination, she thought.

Turning back, she'd continued towards the sick patient.

SHE FINISHED HER BREAKFAST, loaded her plate and cup on to the trolley set aside for dirty dishes, and made her way across the canteen to the exit, deep in thought.

Alex clearly believed she was kidding herself about not minding that it was taking Peter so long to decide what to do. Had he been right, she wondered. Was she really inwardly peeved about the situation?

No, she wasn't, she decided, walking more briskly.

What Alex didn't know was that Peter had suggested they marry at once, and she'd said no. So waiting longer was *her* decision, not Peter's, and she didn't for one minute doubt that this was the right thing to do.

As Mary had said, the worst of the wait was behind them, and there was nothing ahead that could stop them from marrying.

18

T*he following evening*

'I'll put the darts back in their box and we'll take the weight off our pins, shall we?' Alex said. 'There's a table over there. You bring the drinks.'

Peter picked up the beers and went across to the table.

Alex returned the box to the shelf by the darts' board, and stood for a long moment, his hand on the shelf, excitement pulsing within him. Then, biting down on a strong desire to smile, he went and sat opposite Peter.

'Before I forget, it was nice of you to stop by and see Claire last night, or rather this morning,' Peter said, pushing Alex's beer towards him. 'I was gutted to be stuck in theatre.'

'A pleasure, mate. I had a few spare minutes and thought I'd stroll over and see how she was getting on. When you're nervous, a familiar face can be welcome.'

'It was. She'd got herself into quite a state, and your visit helped. I'll make sure I get there this evening. Working nights is going to be tough on her.'

'Look on the bright side,' Alex said with a grin. 'You work nights, too, don't you? I foresee many a steamy assignation over hot cocoa, followed by shenanigans in the sluice room.'

Peter smiled. 'I think we'll talk about a different sort of fusion—spinal fusion.

It's amazing that after we were discussing it yesterday, I had to do two of them today. In one of the cases, I fused the vertebrae with a bone graft taken from the pelvis, and in the other from the hip bone. Textbook operations, if I say so myself.'

'You'll have to say it yourself, mate—I was going to say something far more interesting.'

Peter settled back into his seat. 'Fire away, then!'

'I was talking to my uncle over the weekend and you'd be amazed at what that man's doing,' Alex said with studied casualness. He paused and took a swill of his beer.

'Okay, you've got my full attention.' Peter picked up his glass. 'Amaze me about this uncle of yours.'

'He's only emigrating to Australia!'

'To Australia! Why on earth?'

Alex shrugged. 'His marriage hasn't been great for a while, and he was thinking of calling it a day, clearing off and building a new life miles away. And Australia's as good a place as any, if not better than most.

He's a builder and he's heard there are lots of opportunities for builders over there. And all it costs to get there is ten pounds.'

'Ten pounds!' Peter put his beer on the table and stared at Alex. 'Good God, that's cheap!'

'That's what he thinks. You have to agree to work for the

Australian government for two years, but that's all. After that, you can go wherever you want and do whatever you want.'

Peter frowned. 'And it really is only ten pounds for a ticket?'

'That's right. Apparently, they need people to help build up the country, so they're subsidising their journey. My uncle's always been up for a challenge, and he thinks he'll find the freedom he wants in the wide open spaces of Australia.'

Peter sat back and whistled. He ran his hand slowly through his hair.

'To go to a place like Australia—now that really *would* be something. What an adventure.' His voice shook with admiration.

And envy, Alex thought in satisfaction.

Reining in any sign of the effect of his choice of words on Peter, Alex glanced up from his drink.

'Yup,' he said slowly, his eyes not leaving Peter's face. 'He hates being shut in. He's very much an outdoor type, which he'd have to be with the job he's got, and there're miles of red desert and bush land there—it's called the Outback—as well as mountains and sea.

He'll be able to choose exactly the sort of life he wants. He could play it safe in a town, or head for the mountains, or live a life of adventure in the Outback.' He shook his head in admiration. 'That's real freedom for you, mate.'

'If there's nothing here to keep him, why not go? I assume he hasn't got kids. Or has he?'

'None that he knows about.'

'That's certainly the way to do it—get settled there before children come along.' Peter picked up his beer again. 'Australia, indeed,' he said, and he shook his head in wonder. 'We'd better drink to your uncle and his big adventure.'

Alex held out his glass. 'Cheers!'

'Presumably,' Peter said, nursing his glass, 'if his wife wanted to give their marriage another go, he'd stay in England.'

'Not so. He's going whatever happens. From the moment he learned what was on offer there, he was determined to go. And when I last spoke to him, he said his wife might go with him. She was quite excited by the idea, which amazed him.'

'But it wouldn't be every woman's cup of tea.'

'True, but it obviously appeals to some. It's a chance to do something different with your life, something adventurous.' He paused imperceptibly. 'In fact, I found myself quite tempted by the idea.'

Peter stared at him in surprise. 'Are you serious?'

'Put it this way, I've not ruled it out. Like you, I haven't yet applied for a post in England, and I'm now going to wait and see what my uncle says when he gets there. I'm sure they'd take me if I applied—they're bound to need doctors.

I don't know about the two-year work thing, though. But as we're earning, and we've virtually no time to spend our money, I could pay for my passage myself and look for a job when I got there. Let's say I'm interested enough to check it out.'

'I would imagine that your way with women, and your dedication to an activity that would rapidly increase Australia's population, would place you at the top of their list.'

Alex laughed. 'Then I'd better drink this down, get off and get some practice in.'

'Mind you,' Peter said, finishing his drink and standing

up, 'living in another country isn't necessarily all it's cracked up to be. I've done it so I know.'

Alex rose to his feet and together they started walking towards the exit.

'But you were very young at the time. It's different at our age,' Alex said casually. 'As I've heard you say, it was only when you looked back that you appreciated the beauty of Ladakh's emptiness.'

'That's true. I spent the whole time there wishing I was back in England. But I can see now how great it was to live in such a place. I just wish I'd realised it at the time. Never again will I spend so much time regretting what I haven't got that I blind myself to all the things I *have* got.'

'You've got a lot in common with my uncle. Like you, he's always banging on about miles of nothingness.' Alex paused. 'Would you go back to Ladakh?'

Peter shook his head. 'Nope. That ship has long sailed. While I'd like to see Kalden again, we wouldn't have anything to say to each other as our lives are so different, and have been for years.

And it was too cold for me for most of the year. If I go anywhere, it'll be somewhere that's hot for at least six months.'

Reaching the exit, Peter paused. 'We're going in opposite directions now. Keep me posted about your uncle, won't you? I'm curious to hear how he's gets on.'

'You can be sure I will,' Alex said, and he gave him a broad smile.

THAT WENT WELL, Alex thought as he made his way towards the staircase that led to the locker room.

With Peter always on about challenges, it had been a fair

bet that his uncle's Australian plans would interest him, although he, Alex, shuddered at the very thought of going to such a place.

But he hadn't expected the idea to take hold as quickly as it obviously had.

He'd thought he'd be sowing a seed that would need to be watered several times before he saw any result. But not so. It was as if his uncle's plans had really tapped into Peter's hankering for a life of adventure.

Of course in his head, Peter was seeing himself striding into the unknown with Claire at his side, eager to share the great adventure. But from what Claire had said only hours earlier, she was eager for something entirely different.

Well, well.

Before that evening, he'd have predicted that Peter would go through life, boring on about excitement and adventure, but not doing a damn thing about it.

He'd have put money on him ending up playing it safe in the arms of his sexy Claire, and becoming a country GP with a small house and several kids.

Despite all his big talk, his life would be defined by a pair of slippers waiting for him inside the front door when he got home at night.

But it looked as if his prediction might have been wrong!

He'd clearly underestimated the strength with which Peter yearned for a life that was different from the norm, and that yearning was something that Claire should be shown.

And shown soon. Before she wasted any more of her life on Peter.

And since he was Claire's friend as well as Peter's, it was his duty, of course, to make every effort to open those lovely brown eyes to the truth.

His mood increasingly buoyant, he took the stairs to the locker room floor two at a time. Whatever else they turned out to be, the next few weeks were going to be high for their entertainment value.

The day before, he'd have bet on Peter and Claire marrying that year.

The day before, Claire had looked like the one who'd got away.

But that was the day before.

19

M *id-October*

'Hey, you guys. Before we head off for the morning briefing from our slave-driving registrars, I'd like to make a toast,' Alex said loudly. As he held up his cup, he glanced around at Peter and the other housemen gathered in Claire's office.

'Keep your voices down,' Claire hissed. 'It was sheer luck getting a day sister job this fast, and I'd hate to lose it as quickly. I've got to get off to the wards now, and I don't want to hear you all the way down the corridor. Understood?'

'Yes, Sister,' they chanted with exaggerated meekness.

Laughing, she tightened the ribbons under her chin and went to the door.

'So who or what are we toasting?' Mike asked as the door closed behind Claire.

Watching Peter out of the corner of his eye, Alex raised his cup a little higher. 'My uncle.'

He saw Peter look up with sudden interest.

'As we sit here,' Alex went on, 'labouring to restore people to good health so that they can continue their humdrum lives, my uncle has landed in Australia in search of excitement and adventure. That's the way a life should be lived.'

He smiled around the room. 'To Uncle Bob,' he said, and he waved his cup in the air and then downed his tea in one go.

'To Uncle Bob,' they chorused.

'So he's there now, is he?' Peter remarked a little later as he and Alex followed the others out of the office.

'He is, indeed,' said Alex, walking along the corridor with Peter.

'With his wife?'

'Yup—she's gone with him. The more she heard about the place, the keener she got. Not everyone's a mug like us, content to do the same thing day after day, year after year,' he added, making his voice a monotone.

Peter looked at him curiously. 'So, are you tempted to go? It sounded before as if you might be. I can see it being something Karen might go along with.'

'I'm seriously thinking about it. My uncle passed on brochures and things before he left and I'm going to contact Australia House for more information. When I've got everything together, perhaps you'd take a look at it and tell me what you think.'

'I'd like that.' He threw a wry glance at Alex. 'Who knows, *I* might even be tempted!'

'I rather doubt it,' Alex said. 'You and Claire seem to be heading for a life of cosy domesticity.'

'Nothing's decided yet.' Peter paused. 'And you say his wife's genuinely happy about going there?'

'So I believe. They used to fight like cats and dogs, but she obviously loves him and wants to give it a chance. A woman will go to the ends of the earth for the man she loves —at least that's what it tells you in books.'

'Then it must be true. Just like everything you read in the papers.'

Both laughed.

'But think about it, what woman wouldn't want to go there?' Alex continued. 'On the cover of every brochure, there's a rugged Australian squinting against the sun as he stands on a rocky outcrop at the edge of the Outback.'

He stopped walking, stood back and made a show of looking Peter up and down. 'In fact, with a bit of a tan, it could've been you on that rocky outcrop.'

'Then what am I waiting for—I must send for a visa at once!'

'No need. My uncle didn't need a visa or entry permit or whatever it's called. Everyone on the assisted passage gets a Document of Identity. They couldn't have made it easier. I presume it's the same if you fly and pay for your own ticket.

Personally, I wouldn't do six weeks on a boat—I'd want to get there sooner. And I'd want to be able to come back at once if I didn't like it.'

'You certainly seem to have given it a lot of thought. And it does sounds tempting.'

Alex heard with pleasure the envy that coloured Peter's voice.

'But I couldn't go because of Claire,' Peter remarked. shaking his head. 'She's an only child, and she'd never go miles away and leave her mother alone, even though they aren't exactly close.

I don't know Karen's situation, but if she decided not to go with you, or you didn't want to take her, I'm sure that for every good-looking Australian male, who's squinting in the sun, there's a similar female.'

'Can't say I've ever fancied a woman with a squint,' Alex said with a laugh.

'But seriously, mate,' he went on, 'Claire's not one of those people who'd want to live on her mother's doorstep. From what you've said, she hardly ever visits her.

And her mother's got money enough, by the sound of it, to visit Australia if she wants. And you could come back here and see her. If you moved there, you'd probably see her about as frequently, or infrequently, as you do now.'

Peter nodded. 'That's true.' They reached a side corridor and stopped. 'This is where I turn off,' he said. He hesitated. 'And as you say, if your uncle doesn't like it, he can always come back in two years' time.'

'That's right.' Alex glanced at his watch. 'I must go, too.' He put his hand into his pocket and pulled out a brochure. 'This is all I've got with me at the moment. Take it and let me know what you think. If I have a moment later today, I'll sort out some other pamphlets.'

Peter took his stethoscope out of his coat pocket, and put the brochure in its place. Then with a slight wave, he turned and walked quickly down the side corridor.

Alex stood and watched him until he was out of sight.

Then, a broad smile on his face, he turned and retraced his steps along the corridor and past the Ward Sister's office as he headed for the ward to which he'd been assigned that morning.

CLAIRE CARRIED two cups of coffee across the office, put one of the cups on the desk next to Peter and holding the other, sat down.

She glanced curiously at the glossy pages that Peter was poring over. 'What's that about?'

He looked up. 'Australia,' he said. 'It's really interesting.'

At the expression in his eyes, her breath caught in her throat.

He gave her a quick smile and looked back down.

'What's so interesting about Australia?' she asked a few minutes later. She heard the hint of strain in her voice, and gave a short cough.

He shook his head. 'Nothing really. Alex's uncle has gone there. That's all.'

'Come on, Peter. I was watching you as I made the coffee, and you were glued to the brochure.'

'It's just that Alex asked if I'd take a look at it and at some other information he'll give me later. He's thinking of going there and wants my advice.'

She forced a laugh. 'Trust Alex. He never ceases to surprise me. I wonder what Karen would say to leaving her family and friends.'

'I don't know if he's discussed it with her yet.'

'Well, sooner her than me.' She leaned across the desk and pushed his cup closer to him. 'Don't let your coffee get cold.'

He closed the brochure, pushed it aside and picked up his cup. 'I can read this later. I'm almost through it anyway. I'd rather hear what kind of morning you've had.'

'It's okay, Peter,' she said, forcing herself to sound unconcerned. 'You can read the rest now if you want to.' She pushed the brochure back to him.

'But I don't. I'd rather talk to you.' He sat back and smiled at her.

She shrugged her shoulders. 'It's up to you. Actually, it's been quite a sad morning. I'm losing a really nice patient who's got leukaemia. We've put her in a side ward and asked her family to come in.'

'Poor woman, and poor you. Losing a patient doesn't get any easier with time, does it?'

She shook her head. 'No, it doesn't. What about your morning?'

'It turned out all right, thanks to an amazing stroke of luck I had. Last night, they woke me up about a man who'd come off his motorbike and had fractured his femur as well as getting a lot of cuts and bruises. His leg needed traction so I decided to put it in a Thomas splint. But all I could think of was getting back to bed, and I rushed it. I was dead tired, but I know that's no excuse.'

'It *is* an excuse. You work ridiculous hours. No one can concentrate for that many hours at a stretch.'

'Well, anyway, I didn't measure his leg carefully enough and I put on the wrong size splint. Not only that, I put the cords through the pulley incorrectly. While I was back in my bed, that poor man was in agony.'

'What happened?'

'One of the nurses told me that at some point after I did it, the Night Sister spotted my mistake. She gave him a shot of morphia, changed the splint for one of the correct size, and fitted it into his groin, not on his thigh, which was where I'd put it. Then she ran the cords through the pulley as they should have been done, and weighted them.'

'Thank goodness she saw he was in pain.'

'You're telling me! Apart from helping the patient, she saved my bacon—I got full marks on the consultant's round that morning, and he's a difficult man to please. He praised everything I'd done, or, rather, everything the Night Sister had done, beaming at me all the time. I'm really grateful to her.'

'What perfect timing! The consultant might give you a reference.'

'Now that's a thought!' he said cheerfully.

His eyes strayed to the brochure.

'Oh, go ahead and finish reading it,' she said, nodding towards the brochure. 'I really don't mind. You're like a dog whose bone is just out of reach, and he's champing for it.'

'I'm not sure about being likened to a dog,' he said with a laugh. 'But if you really don't mind.'

He opened the brochure again.

Sipping her coffee, she watched him.

A few minutes later, he looked up. 'That's it. I can now tell Alex I've read the lot.'

'D'you think he's really serious about going there?'

'He seems to be.' He tapped the magazine. 'It's a big decision to make so I'm not surprised he wants to talk it through. And he's bound to have asked Mike what he thinks, and maybe some of the others, too.'

He sat back and locked his hands behind his head.

'It makes you think, though, doesn't it, what it'd be like to go to a new country like Australia? Life in the Outback must be about as different as you can get from life over here. You'd never be bored.'

Her stomach turned over, and she felt cold.

She slid upright in her chair, and stared at him. 'Are you serious?'

'No, not really.' He unlocked his hands, straightened up and shook his head. 'No, definitely not.' Then he hesitated. 'To be honest, I don't know.'

He glanced again at the brochure.

'Truthfully, I really don't know. I know I'd like to see the other information that Alex has got, and I know I'd like you to look at it with me.'

She put her cup down on the table. 'You're frightening me, Peter.'

'Well, I don't mean to.' He hesitated a moment. 'It's just that sometimes I feel I'd love to go somewhere new, somewhere I've never been before—just you and me. While we're young enough to do something exciting.'

He looked her in the eyes. 'But there's nothing to worry about, Claire. We'll always be together wherever we are—I'd never go anywhere you didn't want.'

'I see,' she said quietly, fingering the chain of her fob watch.

'I think that's why I've been finding it so hard to decide on a job—I just can't see myself doing the same thing in the same place for the rest of my life. And now reading about Australia and what it offers.'

He shook his head. 'You'd be part of a country where there's every kind of scenery, a country that's only just finding its feet. It's an exciting thought and it makes you think.'

'That's what thoughts are meant to do.' Her voice was shaky to her ears. 'You'd really throw all of this up for goodness knows what?'

Rubbing her arms to bring back some warmth into them, she glanced around her.

'No way! I like being a doctor, and that's what I'll be wherever I go.' He leaned across the desk, took one of her hands and smiled. 'I expect everyone has moments when they feel like escaping—that's why escapist books and films are so popular. But it doesn't mean they do it. Most don't.

But you must admit that what Alex's uncle has done is pretty interesting. And his wife must think so, too, as she's gone with him. It's given us another option to think about. But that's all it is.'

'Suppose they don't like it?'

'Then they'll come back. It's not a prison and they're not in chains.' He grinned at her. 'Those days have long gone.' He released her hand and picked up his cup again. 'Anyway, I thought it sounded quite an adventure.'

'Well, good luck to them. I hope they find what they're looking for. Me, I've already found what I want. All I want is here. I don't need to go to Australia for adventure.'

The smile he gave her didn't quite reach his eyes, she noticed.

'Obviously Alex can't say the same,' he said, finishing his drink and standing up, 'or he wouldn't be thinking of following his uncle.'

'What does his uncle do?'

'He's a builder.'

'There you are, then.' She gestured the point with her hands. 'It's easier for a builder to fit into the life of another country than it is a doctor.'

'Not if you go to a country where they speak the same language.'

'You'd soon get used to the scenery,' she said, 'so the novelty would wear off.'

'You may well be right, but we'd never know if we didn't try it. And as with Alex, if we didn't like it, we could come back.' He paused. 'Look, Claire; it's just an idea—no more than that. But have a look at Alex's brochure before I return it, won't you?'

'I don't want to. You can take it with you.' She stood up, her face pale. 'I don't want to look at anything at all about Australia. If Alex is thinking of going there, it's Karen he should be talking to, not you.'

'That's a fair point. There's no need to look so worried, you know,' he added gently. 'It's not as if I'm seriously considering emigrating, just because I'm reading up about it.'

Giving her a reassuring smile, he picked up the brochure, rolled it up and slipped it into the pocket of his white coat.

Her eyes went to his pocket.

He followed the direction of her gaze, and looked back at her. 'Like I said, you've nothing to worry about, Claire. As you won't read it, I'll give it back to Alex and wish him luck with whatever he decides to do. That's the last time I'll mention Australia.'

'You must do whatever you want with it.'

'What I want to do is return it.'

Relaxing slightly, she smiled at him. 'Okay then. But I suppose it's no bad thing that the subject of our future's come up again—it is time we got everything sorted.

You've been working in the hospital for a while, so you should know by now whether you want to get a post in a hospital somewhere else, or become a GP. It's time we began looking for jobs for both of us and a place to live, and also started planning our wedding.'

He nodded. 'You're right.'

'We've said we'll marry in Birmingham to be near all our friends, no matter where we go after that, so there's no reason not to fix a date and book the reception.'

He hesitated, and then smiled. 'You're right again. We'll talk about it when we next have half a day off at the same time.'

'Luckily, being the Ward Sister, I can make that happen,' she said cheerfully. 'A couple of nurses owe me a favour, so one of them can swap with me, if necessary. It means we can meet next week and set a date. And you can tell me if you're going for a hospital post or into a GP practice.'

He nodded. 'Sounds good to me.' He started towards the office door, stopped and looked back at her.

'I do love you, Claire,' he said quietly. 'Maybe I don't say that often enough as we've been together so long. But I love you from the bottom of my heart, and I can't wait for you to be Mrs Henderson.'

She gave him a wide smile. 'And I love you, too, Peter. Like you, I can't wait to start our married life together.'

And she cleared her throat in an attempt to remove from her voice any suggestion of lingering anxiety.

20

H er heart beating fast in a panic that refused to subside, Claire made her way towards the furthest of her wards.

From the moment she'd seen the expression in Peter's eyes when he'd looked up from the information about Australia, she'd been filled by a sense of foreboding she couldn't shake.

And nothing he'd said had helped—she'd heard his words, but she'd seen his face.

It wasn't as if she honestly believed he'd plan their future without taking account of her wishes; he wouldn't do that. And it wasn't as if she seriously thought he'd pressure her into something she didn't want; he wasn't like that.

But the moment he'd mentioned Australia, she'd felt a sudden, horrible premonition that nothing was ever going to be the same again.

If only Alex had never told Peter about his wretched uncle.

That Peter had once had a restless streak inside him, she'd known. It was hardly surprising, given his unusual childhood. But she'd thought him long over any desire to go overseas in search of adventure, and so had his parents.

But that look in his eyes!

In that one moment, she'd known deep down that both she and his parents had been wrong. And that had hurt like mad.

Hurt? Her brow furrowed. Yes, she'd felt hurt. But why?

All he'd done was show an interest in something that Alex was thinking of doing. An interest—no more than that. And he'd made it clear that whatever he did, he'd be doing it with her. So there was no reason why she should feel hurt.

But she did.

Her steps speeded up.

She'd find Alex as soon as she'd finished her shift.

By now, Mike and the others were likely to have told him that going to Australia was a mad idea, and with the negatives they would've listed, he could easily have concluded that pulling up roots and travelling to the other side of the world wasn't for him.

He was a sociable man, a party animal, a sophisticated man who liked his creature comforts—not someone who'd enjoy leaping into the unknown, possibly on his own, into a country still in the stage of development.

She'd ask Alex to tell Peter that he'd changed his mind about going. And if he hadn't yet changed his mind, he could tell Peter, anyway, that he probably had.

Alex owed her that.

He should never have given Peter that brochure.

He'd known Peter for long enough to realise that there was a real risk of him being drawn to the idea of Australia. And if Alex had given it a minute's thought, he'd have omitted Peter from the list of those he consulted.

She'd done what she could to bring Peter back down to

earth by pushing him to decide about his job—the first time she'd ever done so—hoping that when he'd made his choice, he'd be so busy, and so excited at the idea of moving to a place they didn't know, that he wouldn't waste any more thoughts on Australia.

Also, she'd be armed with possible dates for their wedding when she met him the following week, and with some suggestions about churches and places where they could hold their reception. Mary would help her with those.

When they'd worked out the details, they'd run their ideas past their parents, and if there weren't any problems, and if the cost was right for her mother, who was insisting on paying, they could go ahead and book everything.

Reached her ward, she pushed open the outer swing doors and walked in.

Yes, it was time to pin everything down.

IT WAS BOUND to have been a shock for Claire, Peter thought as he hurried along the white-walled corridor towards his section.

The mention of Australia had come out of the blue for her, and by letting his excitement show so clearly in his face, he'd disquieted her.

He'd give anything to be able to wind the clock back, and introduce the subject of Australia in a less blunt way.

Nevertheless, her reaction had taken him somewhat aback.

As he'd worked through the brochure, and seen photos of the wide vistas of Australia, it had hit him with force, for the first time for a very long time, how much he wanted to live in a place that was totally different from England.

The strength of his emotion had quite shaken him, and in fact, he was still shaking.

And Claire's attitude had shaken him, too.

It had never occurred to him that she'd dismiss the idea outright, without even looking at what Australia had to offer. It was obviously an automatic reaction to the degree of interest he'd shown, but she shouldn't have been so worried.

He'd said often enough that whatever they did in the future, it would be a joint decision. She should know him well enough by now to know that he'd keep to his word.

Hopefully, when she'd got over her initial shock, she'd give some serious thought as to what it would be like to try living somewhere else. If she did, she was sure to start feeling as excited as he about the idea of Australia.

And it *was* still only an idea—not a decision.

All the same, it wouldn't hurt to find out about flights— he'd prefer to buy their tickets rather than be obliged to stay there for two years. And he might as well get the necessary application forms from Australia House, where Alex said he'd got his.

They could even fill in the forms, send them in and see if they'd be accepted.

It wouldn't commit them to anything, and it could stop them from getting carried away about something they wouldn't be allowed to do.

But if it were to prove possible…

It wasn't just his career that would benefit—it was Claire's, too.

Being a nurse, she'd probably work in a hospital till they had children, and that meant she'd treat a whole range of cases that were very different from the ones she'd have treated in England.

Every environment threw up its own diseases and problems, and that in itself would prove interesting and challenging. And it would be a useful experience to say she'd had if they ever decided to come back home.

So far in her life, Claire had lived only in Hereford and Birmingham. She didn't want to stay in the Birmingham area, and had said many a time that she wouldn't want to live too close to her mother, which ruled out the vicinity of Hereford.

So they'd be moving to somewhere that was new to her, anyway.

That somewhere might just as well be Australia.

He patted his pocket to make sure the brochure was still there.

He'd make a point of seeing Alex later that day, take a look at the rest of his material, and ask how far he'd got with his thinking.

It could well be that Alex had come up with some drawbacks that rendered the idea impossible, and if so, it'd be better to know them before he spoke to Claire again.

And if there weren't any downsides, he'd fill in the forms as soon as they arrived.

He reached his section, glanced again at the brochure, and then headed to meet up with his consultant.

21

T *he following week*

THE AFTERNOON SPARKLED as the colours of autumn broke out everywhere.

Making their way up the steep track, Peter and Claire left in the valley behind them a sleepy church, a small café and a cluster of red-brick cottages, the walls and gardens of which were home to many a late-flowering rose.

Higher and higher they walked, the silence between them laden with consciousness.

Gradually, the track narrowed, and Claire hung back to let Peter lead the way between a tangle of dusk-green hedgerows, their arching stems rendered bare by the loss of blackberries that had either shrivelled and dropped to the ground, or fallen prey to pickers and wild birds.

Every so often, a patch of vibrant colour from the last of

the red campion flowers burst forth through the banks of yellowing blackthorn leaves.

As they neared the top of the slope, the hedgerows thinned. An upturned log spanned the grassy knoll that was visible ahead of them, and wanting a few moments in which to catch their breath, they went and sat on it.

Side by side, they stared without speaking across a profusion of gorse to the distant folding hills which lay before them—an undulating carpet of burnished beech woods, of crimson, bronze, russet and gold, that swept across the horizon like an all-consuming fire.

Above them, the sky was a brilliant blue.

'I love the autumn,' Claire said, breaking the silence that felt increasingly awkward. 'I love the way the leaves turn every imaginable shade of brown and gold. It's so beautiful.'

Peter nodded. 'Yes, it is. Good old Lambretta! Once again, it's served us well. Sadly, the poor old thing's on its last legs, though, but rather than replace it, I'm going to have some driving lessons. In fact, the first one's tomorrow.

You never know when you might need to drive. And when I've learnt, I'll teach you. That makes sense, don't you think?'

'It's a really good idea.'

'That's decided, then. But as far as today goes, are you ready to go back?'

She nodded. 'I think we've gone far enough. We could stop at the café we passed on the way up, and have a coffee. When we're sitting down, it'll be easier to talk. It's time we talked, don't you think?'

.   .   .

'It's lucky they still had a table, with so many people taking advantage of the good weather,' Peter said. He leaned back and smiled at her.

A trace of nervousness hovered at the edge of his smile, she noticed.

She picked up her teaspoon, stirred her hot chocolate with vigour, and glanced around the café.

'It's crowded all right. It's funny to think we might well see these people again one day, but next time they could be in Casualty or in a hospital bed.'

He looked at her curiously. 'Doesn't it ever bother you that the future seems all mapped out, that the only surprise will be whether they come in with a broken toe or something more serious?'

'No, not really.' She heard a sharp note creep into her voice. 'That's life, isn't it? And in a way, I rather like the stability it suggests.'

'It's not life for some people. It isn't for Alex's uncle, for a start.'

'I presume that's the Australia one?'

'That's right.'

She stared hard at him. 'You've not yet told me what Alex said when you returned his brochure. Or what you said to him. I looked for him later that day, but he'd already gone, and I still haven't seen him. He's not even stopped by the ward, which is unusual.'

'He's dropped the idea of going.'

Her heart leapt. She felt herself start to relax. 'What made him decide that?'

Peter shook his head. 'I don't really know. Cold feet, generally, I think. You were right—it was never going to be an Alex thing.'

'And is it a Peter thing? You're not going to say it is, are you?' She held her breath, her heart thumping unevenly.

He glanced at her. 'There's no such thing as a Peter thing. It's a Claire and Peter thing, or nothing.' She released her breath.

'To be honest, in answer to your question, I don't know,' he went on. She tensed. 'I'd more or less decided to be a surgeon in a not-too-large hospital, and then Alex told me about Australia.' He hesitated. 'I'm not going to lie to you; it's thrown me.'

'And?'

He picked up his coffee and took a sip. She saw that his hand was trembling.

'And I read everything else that Alex had, and I liked what I read. I'm sure you'd like it, too. And I've filled in the forms for Australia.'

He paused imperceptibly. 'I told them I was engaged to be married.'

Her heart thumped loudly. 'And you didn't think you should talk some more to me first? You think our short conversation in my office was sufficient for something as important as this?'

Her voice sounded shrill to her ears, but she couldn't help herself.

He slumped in his chair. 'I'm just finding out if we'd be able to go; that's all. Even if we can, we don't have to go any further with it. But I thought it worth checking out the situation.'

'There's no *we* about this, Peter.' She pushed her drink away from her and stood up.

'There's no point in discussing it further as the only voice you're hearing is yours. And there's certainly no point in talking about weddings while everything's still as up in the air as it is. So much for all the ideas I had.

We might as well go to the cinema. We'll make the matinée if we leave now.'

She pulled on her jacket and headed for the door.

MOONLIGHT SLID through the uneven gap between Claire's flimsy curtain and the wall, pouring silver across the bottom corner of her bed.

Motionless, she lay on her back, trying to block out the jumble of thoughts that had kept her from sleep for hour upon hour.

After everything Peter had said about them deciding their future together, he'd gone ahead and filled in the forms for Australia without discussing it further with her.

That had really hurt.

Her feelings were clearly irrelevant, and it was beginning to look as if he was so set on Australia, that he'd settle for England only if Australia turned him down.

Or maybe he wouldn't even do that!

Now that he'd got the bit between the teeth, if Australia didn't want him, he might well push ahead and look for somewhere else that would take them far away from the life and country she loved.

She'd never before realised how very differently they'd been seeing their future.

How long would it take, she wondered, before he realised how much he was upsetting her, and abandon the idea of leaving England.

And what if that never happened?

Closing her eyes, she longed for the mental peace that was carried on the back of sleep.

· · ·

PETER STARED AT THE WALL, trying in vain to blank out the hurt and misery that had sprung to Claire's eyes the moment he'd told her that he'd filled in the forms.

They'd gone to the cinema, but neither had paid any attention to the film—he'd been too aware of her misery, and was drowning too much in his own.

When the film had ended, on the pretext of tiredness and an early morning the following day, they'd decided to go back to their own rooms that night.

With silence hanging heavily between them, he'd walked Claire to Nuffield House, where they'd parted with the briefest of kisses.

Her unspoken words and her silent reproaches had followed him all the way back to University Hall.

Loving her now every bit as much as he'd loved her the day he met her, if not more so, the anguish he was causing her was tearing him apart, and he desperately wished that things could be different—that he was less keen on adventure, or that she was more so.

If only Alex had never mentioned his bloody uncle and Australia!

But he had.

And it had grown into something he wanted passionately for Claire and him. And he fervently hoped that she'd come to want it, too.

There was still time.

All he asked of her was that she kept an open mind, read everything he passed on to her and give some thought to what he was suggesting. After all, he'd made it clear that if she didn't like it, they could return.

Until she'd read up about the place, it was impossible to

take her refusal as her final word on the subject. How could anyone say they didn't want something they knew nothing about?

If she loved him as much as she said, at the very least she'd want to find out what it was that he wanted to do. It didn't make sense not to do that. What's more, it wasn't fair.

Of course, it might turn out that for some reason, their applications were refused, and the whole thing ended before it began. If so, it'd bring the matter to an abrupt halt and they'd just have to focus on what there was for them in England, or perhaps look somewhere else.

But wherever they were, it would be him and Claire together. That was the most important thing. And that she was happy. As long as he was with Claire, he'd be happy, too.

It was just that he very much hoped they were going to have that happiness in Australia.

22

F*our weeks later*

SHE OPENED the door and saw him standing there. He didn't have to speak; she could read the words in his eyes.

They stood looking at each other, neither moving.

'I've got the all clear for Australia,' he said at last. 'There's a future waiting for us there and I want us to give it a go. By flying there rather than going as ten-pound poms, it'll give us greater freedom. And I promise we'll come back if you hate it.'

She stared at him without speaking, her hand still on the door.

He ran his fingers through his hair.

'Please say something, Claire,' he urged. She heard the desperation in his voice. 'This is about us. About our future. I've deliberately kept away from you for a while to give you time to think.'

'It's about you, you mean,' she said bluntly, and she turned away. He followed her into the room and closed the door behind him.

'No, I don't,' he said. He dropped his leather bag on to her desk, put his hands on her shoulders and turned her to face him.

'Maybe it was too big a leap for Alex, but it's a leap the two of us could make together. I want us to do that. Just think of it, Claire,' he urged her, hope and excitement flowing from his eyes.

'Think of the life we could have; the sense of freedom; all the new things to discover. It'd make you want to leap out of bed in the morning.'

'And what if I won't go there?'

She noticed his slight hesitation.

'Then nor would I, of course. But I know you're fair and you'd never dismiss something like this out of hand, something I'd love to do. When you've read up about the place... Look, I've brought everything with me.' He indicated his bag. 'Read it with an open mind; that's all I ask.'

She glanced at the bag, but didn't move. 'You say things would be different there, Peter, but illness is illness—a broken leg is a broken leg. It'd be the same sort of work as you'd do here, with some snake bites thrown in for good measure.

And the weather would be hotter and drier. But that's about all. Except, of course, that we'd be miles from anyone we knew.'

'We'd make new friends. People do that all the time.'

'And we'd make new families, too, would we? Our parents aren't getting any younger. D'you think it's right to leave them to fend for themselves as their health declines? There's no one else to look after them when they can't look after themselves any longer. You'd be happy with that, would you?' she said, her voice rising.

He held out his hands in a gesture of despair. 'I honestly don't think it'll matter to them if we go. They love us, yes, but they don't need us.

My parents have given their lives to the Mission, and when the time comes, the Mission will take care of them. They're surrounded by people who love them.

I know they love me, but their work is their life, not me. I don't blame them for that; that's how it is, and I understand it.'

'My mother doesn't have any support like that.'

'But she's got money and she's very much a self-contained unit. She's perfectly pleasant to us, but even though she loves you, you're on the periphery of her life, not in the centre of it.

She genuinely believes that everyone should stand on their own two feet and not rely on others to help them, and she's not going to change overnight and decide to lean on you.'

'You don't know that for sure.'

'I as good as do. She's made it pretty clear. As she gets older, she'll dig deeper into her pocket and buy the care she needs. If you were around to visit, fine. But if you weren't, equally fine.

People like your mother derive their happiness from what they can do for themselves, and not from having a daughter dance attendance on them. So making her the reason to stay in England doesn't hold water.'

'You can't know what a person will be like when they're old.'

'Yes, I can. I've been on geriatric wards, just as you have. From talking to patients' families, I've come to realise that when people get old, they're just as they were when they were young, only more so. She'll be more independent rather than less.'

'I don't want to leave England, Peter,' she said flatly.

'Don't dismiss it just because it's not as safe, if you like, as our other options. Pease, don't do that, Claire.'

He opened his bag. 'At least read what I've got. You'll see it's a great place to bring up children, with plenty of sunshine, an outdoor life, lots of career opportunities. They'd be bound to love it.'

'You mean like you enjoyed being brought up in Ladakh? And I don't mean when you think about it now, looking back with rose-tinted glasses, but when you were actually there?'

He gestured helplessness, his hands held out, palms upwards. 'Be fair; that was different. I was old enough to remember my life in England, and what I had in Ladakh compared unfavourably.

Our children would be born in Australia so they wouldn't know what it was like to live somewhere else. And anyway, Australia's more like England than Ladakh was, but with masses more space and better weather than we have here.'

'And you think I'd want to go to the other side of the world for a bit more sunshine? And a bit more space?' Her voice spiked with incredulity. 'If you think that, you don't know me at all.'

'Of course, I don't think that,' he said, locking his fingers behind his head and staring at her in despair. 'You'd want to go because you wanted to try somewhere new, and because you know how much I want to go there. I'm sure we'd both love it. Please, think about it, Claire.'

She stepped back from him.

His hands fell to his sides.

'If you want space, Peter, we can move to the Highlands of Scotland or to parts of Wales or to the moors or to North Yorkshire or Northumberland. There are plenty of areas over here that'll give us the freedom and space you want—we don't have to go to Australia to find it.'

'I just want to try something totally different. Australia sounds more exciting. I don't know why, but it does.'

'And what if I didn't like it and you did?'

He stared at her, frowning slightly. 'Well, we'd come back, I suppose. You'd have given it a chance and you couldn't do fairer than that.' His face brightened a little. 'We could get married first and look on it as a honeymoon.'

'Every time you've talked about this, you've used the words exciting or excitement. You seem to think it's the only way to get excitement into your life.

The others in your intake don't seem to have the same problem as you. They must find their work challenging, different, even exciting, or they'd find another job. Why can't you be satisfied like they are?'

He gave a slight shrug of his shoulders. 'We're not all the same. I had a taste of something different when I was too young to enjoy it, and then I had several years in Walthamstow, a run-down, depressing area. And now Birmingham, a large, built-up city. I guess I want different again. That's me; I can't help it.'

'I see,' she said quietly.

'Please, Claire. I know you're upset because I jumped the gun with the forms, but don't let that turn you against the idea.'

'It's not that. It's that I love England. It's the country where I was born and I love living here. And I love you. I can't think of anything more thrilling, more exciting than settling down with you in a home of our own, having children, and doing the work we've been trained to do.

The reason I'm so upset is that being with me clearly isn't an equally thrilling and exciting prospect for you.'

He took her by the arms, desperation in his eyes. 'I love you, Claire, and you know that. I want everything you want. It's just that I want us to do it somewhere else. Surely we can take a little time out to follow a dream?'

'You're not hearing me, Peter. It's your dream, not mine.' Her eyes brimmed with tears. 'I dream of growing old with you in a place where we can see our family and friends. I'd miss Mary like mad if I was on the other side of the world, and I can't bear to think that I might never see her baby—a great unofficial godmother that'd make me! I don't need great empty spaces to feel fulfilled. I need you, only you.'

He hugged her tightly to him. 'And I need you, too.'

She stood, unmoving, in his arms. 'But obviously not enough.' She pulled herself free and looked him in the eyes. 'I don't want to go to Australia. And I don't need to read up about it to know that I never will.'

He stepped back from her, his face pale.

Tears rolled down her cheeks. 'You've got a restlessness inside you, Peter. If you stay here because of me, you'll come to hate me.

And if I pull up my roots and go with you, I'll always know that just being with me was not enough for you. I could come to hate you for that. What kind of choice is that?'

'We're discussing it, that's all,' he said bleakly.

'I don't think we are.' She wiped her cheeks with her hands. 'You're telling me what you're going to do. You'll go there without me, if I won't go. I'm right, aren't I?'

They stared at each other without speaking.

'I'm right, aren't I?' she repeated more loudly. 'You'll go by yourself if I refuse to go. Admit it.'

'Yes,' he said quietly. 'I didn't know it until this minute, but, yes, you're right. And you're right about the other thing, too—I don't think I'd ever be able to forgive you if we stayed here and didn't give it a go.'

She caught her breath.

Neither moved.

'Well, Peter, I'm afraid you'll be going alone,' she said, breaking the heavy silence. 'I think I've known deep down that it would come to this from the moment you looked up from that brochure.'

He reached for his bag and thrust the brochures back into it. 'People take up new challenges all the time, Claire—it doesn't mean they don't love their wives. But obviously in your narrow, small-minded world, it does.'

He shut his bag with an angry flourish.

'But it may do,' she snapped. 'What does it say about your feelings for me if you need something other than me to put excitement into your life? How d'you think that makes me feel?'

'And how d'you think it makes *me* feel that you won't seriously consider my suggestion, even though you know how much I want it? What's that telling me about your feelings for me? If you truly loved me, you'd follow me to the ends of the earth without hesitation.'

She gave a dismissive laugh. 'Rubbish. That's a cliché and you know it. It belongs inside the pages of books, but not outside.'

He picked up his bag. 'If I played chess, I'd say that sounded like stalemate.'

An icy tentacle wound through her body and clutched at her heart.

'So it's goodbye then,' she said, her mouth dry.

He shook his head. 'I'm not saying goodbye. I'll be going to Australia in about a month. I'll leave my flight details in your office at some point in the next few days, and I'll hope until the moment I enter the plane that you'll change your mind and come with me.

Whatever you think this says about my feelings for you, you're wrong. I love you with all my heart. I have done since the moment we met, and I always will. We belong together, not continents apart, and I'm going to pray you come to realise that before it's too late.'

He stretched out his hand and touched her cheek, which was wet with tears. 'I can't imagine us not being together. You're a part of me, and nothing can ever change that. Please come with me, Claire.'

His voice caught in his throat.

She took his hand from her cheek, kissed his palm and released his hand. Unable to speak, she turned away.

She heard him reach the door, open it, walk out and close it.

Numb, she stood alone in the middle of the room, and she was still standing there long after the light of day had died.

23

D*ecember*

STANDING in Terminal 3 of Heathrow Airport, amid the noise and bustle of building work taking place around him, Peter looked up at the departure board, searching for the number of the check-in desk for his flight to Sydney.

When he found the number, he turned and stared back at the doors he'd come through.

Every day for the past month, he'd listened for a knock on his door or for the sound of someone calling him to the telephone, certain that Claire would change her mind and decide to come with him after all.

But there'd been no word from her.

And yet, even now, so close to leaving, he couldn't stop himself from expecting to see her rush through the doorway towards him, a cluster of suitcases with her, laughing and apologising and telling him that she'd bought a ticket, too.

So he stood there, jostled on all sides by porters and travellers struggling with their luggage, with hope in his eyes, waiting.

But time passed and she wasn't among the people streaming through the doors, and gradually a sense of emptiness swelled within him, pushing out hope.

Finally, he turned away and looked back up at the departure board and at the future he would now have to accept he'd be walking into on his own. He found the number of his check-in desk, and then, his rucksack on his back and a suitcase in each of his hands, he headed across the hall.

Glancing to his left as he walked, he saw that he was passing a WH Smith. His steps slowed. He'd already got a couple of newspapers and a book, but it was going to be a very long flight, without anyone to talk to, and having something else to read might not be a bad idea. A magazine or two, maybe.

Veering to the left, he went into the shop.

The magazine shelves lay directly in front of him, and he went straight up to them and scanned the rows.

One cover stood out from the rest because of its colour. It had a wide, bright red band running across the top. The word 'aircraft', written in thick white letters, stood boldly out from the red background, and under it, in smaller letters, 'illustrated' was written in black. Beneath the heading, a colour photograph of an aeroplane took up most of the rest of the cover.

Not particularly interested in aircraft, he was about to look further along the row, but before he could do so, he caught sight of the words 'Australia's Royal Flying Doctor Service', which were written in a white rectangle below the aeroplane.

Curious, he took the magazine down from the shelf and saw that the article was one of the five main articles for that month.

The other articles didn't sound particularly interesting, being about different aircraft, so he flicked through the pages until he came to the article about the Flying Doctors. Australia was a land of violent contrasts, he read; a country of arid and lonely areas that tested the mettle of men.

His interest piqued, he bought the magazine, slipped his rucksack down his shoulder, tucked the magazine into one of its pockets, hoisted the rucksack back up, picked up his suitcases and continued to the check-in area.

BEFORE THE PLANE had even left British air space, he knew what he was going to do as soon as he reached Australia: he was going to do his utmost to join the Royal Flying Doctor Service.

He couldn't have found a job that sounded more perfect for him—it was as if it had been designed for him—and he couldn't wait for the plane to land so that he could get on with applying.

He'd fill in the application form as soon as he could, and enclose with it copies of the documents he'd sent to Australia House, and from then on he'd be keeping his fingers tightly crossed.

Only one thing could have made the moment he discovered his ideal job more perfect, and that was if Claire had been at his side. He desperately wished she were!

She would have been right behind him, knowing there could be nothing more worthwhile than to be part of a team that flew medical aid to people whose remoteness put them out of the reach of traditional forms of medical care, and who could die from something that could've easily been cured had an experienced practitioner been at hand.

But she wasn't there.

He was on his own, and his excitement and enthusiasm were tempered by his tremendous grief at her absence.

With difficulty, he pulled himself together and read through the article again. He'd be restricted to New South Wales or Queensland as they were the only two Australian States where the Service employed their own doctors. Apparently, the other States used doctors from their own medical service, or they called out local doctors for any emergencies.

He didn't know why but he didn't fancy Queensland—it looked a bit too lush and tropical for him from the pictures he'd seen—but New South Wales, with its miles of Outback, caught his imagination. And as he was flying into Sydney anyway, which was in New South Wales, things couldn't have worked out better.

He'd find himself a room in a boarding house in Sydney, and he'd write at once to the Flying Doctor Station in Broken Hill, which was apparently the headquarters for the State.

If they didn't have any posts going, he'd give Queensland a try, unless, of course, the people in Broken Hill thought they might have something coming up fairly soon, in which case he'd hang around and take a chance on getting that.

Oh, if only Claire could have seen that after all his dithering about a job, as soon as he'd come across the perfect one for him, he'd decided on it in a matter of moments. She'd have been amazed.

But it was something she wouldn't know.

Not having her physically at his side, hurt like mad.

But by getting a job that was right up his street, he'd be

taking the first step towards getting over her and thus freeing himself from the ever-present pain he'd lived with for the past four weeks.

He realised that it would take a lot more than that to bring back his peace of mind and fill the void that ached deep within him, but it would be a strong start.

n untouched cup of coffee in front of each of them, Claire stared at Alex across the desk of the ward office, her eyes red-rimmed.

'That's that, then,' she said flatly. 'He really has gone.'

His forehead creased in a frown of disbelief, Alex shook his head. 'Right until the last minute, I didn't think he'd actually do it. I thought that even if he got as far as the airport, he'd turn round and come back.'

Claire nodded. 'If I'm truly honest, so did I. But he didn't, did he? We know the plane's left and we know he's on the passenger list for the flight to Sydney.'

'I just don't understand it. You and Peter are made for each other. *I* can see that; everybody who knows you can see that. It's a crying shame that Peter couldn't see it, too.'

'People see what they want to see—Peter's no different.' She paused.

'It's down to you that he's gone, Alex. You gave him the idea in the first place,' she said, bitterness creeping into her voice. 'Telling him about your brave, adventurous uncle.

That started him off. And then giving him brochures about the place. There was no stopping him after that.'

'You've no idea how often I've blamed myself for that. It lost me a good mate.'

She stared at him in bewilderment. 'So why *did* you give him the brochures? You must've seen his interest as soon as you mentioned your uncle's plans. He wouldn't have hidden it from you. So why do something likely to build on it instead of letting it die a natural death?

You can't have needed his advice, or anyone else's for that matter, about whether or not to emigrate. Only *you* could decide that.'

He shook his head again. 'I'm not so sure about that. Your friends can often see you better than you can see yourself. I wanted an honest opinion from the people who knew me best as to whether they thought I had the right temperament. It wasn't only Peter I asked. I asked Mike and the others, too.'

'Well, it's a shame you didn't think twice when it came to Peter.'

'Come on, Claire. You can't really blame a few coloured brochures for what's happened. Everyone was interested in what Uncle Bob was doing, but no one else devoured everything they could about Australia, and hopped on to the next plane.'

'That's meant to make me feel better, is it?'

He gave her a wry smile. 'Of course not. I'm just pointing out that there's a big difference between being interested in where someone's gone, and deciding to go there yourself.

As far as I knew, you and Peter were getting married in the autumn, and I thought he'd take up a post as a surgeon in a town that was smaller and prettier than Birmingham, and that's where you'd go.'

'Did he tell you he'd written to Australia House for the application forms?'

'No, he didn't. He'd be afraid I'd tell you. I expect he wanted you to get used to the idea before he said anything that made it sound too final.'

'Well, it's certainly final now,' she said, her eyes filling with tears.

Alex pushed the box of tissues on her desk closer to her. 'I still can't believe he's gone without you. Believe me, I'm desperately sorry for the part I played in that.'

'Oh, it's not your fault, Alex.' She took a tissue and blew her nose. 'I'm just looking for someone to blame because I don't want to face the fact that Peter chose a country over me.'

'I'm sure it's more complex than that,' he said gently. 'He had a pretty weird childhood and that must count for something. Don't be too hard on him.'

'I'm sure his childhood comes into it, but it doesn't make me feel any better. Still, it's nice of you to put his case— you've been a really good friend to him. Perhaps unintentionally a better friend than I'd have liked,' she added, and she wiped her eyes again.

Alex leaned forward and helped himself to a biscuit from the plate between them, and then sat back in his chair.

'Once you've got over the immediate shock of what's happened, I think you'll see things a little more clearly, and you may feel better then.' He bit into the biscuit.

She frowned slightly. 'What d'you mean by that?'

He shrugged. 'It was just an expression.'

She sat upright in her chair. 'No, it wasn't. You knew what you were saying. What did you mean by it?'

He hesitated. 'Nothing, really.' He glanced at his watch. 'Good gracious, is that the time? I ought to be off.'

'Please, Alex.' She put her hand on his arm as he started to stand. 'I'm devastated that Peter's gone.' Her voice broke. 'And if you know anything you think might help, no matter how much it'd hurt me to hear it, then tell me. Please.'

He glanced at her face, and sat back down again. 'Okay; but don't shoot the messenger.'

He took a deep breath. 'I'm inclined to think that if Peter hadn't been drawn to the idea of Australia, he'd have gone for something else equally dramatic and adventurous. He was never going to settle down and lead the sort of life you wanted. Not when it came to it.'

He put his hand lightly on top of hers. 'And if you're truly honest with yourself, Claire, I think you know this, and that's part of the reason why you're so upset.'

She drew her breath in sharply, ready to deny it.

'No, don't say anything; just think about it,' he went on. 'There's no publicity leaflet in the world powerful enough to make a person act in a way that's completely out of character.

Peter craved what Australia offered. There had to be some danger attached to what he did, and some drama. And it had to give him the sense of freedom he was always on about.

Living and working in small-town England, having a house and kids—the things you wanted—would never have been enough. There, now I've said it.'

He released her hand, relaxed in his chair and stared at her.

She frowned more deeply. 'Are you saying you don't think he genuinely loved me?'

'Not a bit of it! I'm sure he loved you. He's never so much as glanced at another woman since the day he met you. The way he looked at you—that never changed over the years.

I've often envied him feeling the way he does. Fond as I am of Karen, I know I don't feel about her as Peter felt about you, and I'm sure still does.'

'Well, he can't have felt that strongly to have done what's he's done. Actions speak louder than looks or words.'

'Wanting to try living somewhere else doesn't mean he didn't love you. And from what he told me, he kept asking you to go with him, but you wouldn't.'

She bit her lip. 'I suppose that's true.'

'And think about this. If he'd tried to forget about Australia and had stayed here, living the life you wanted him to live, it almost certainly wouldn't have worked, and he'd have eventually left, anyway. That would've been even worse for you.'

'So I should thank you for putting the idea into his head, should I?' she said sharply. 'You're telling me now that you did me a favour: misery today rather than even greater misery tomorrow.'

He gave her a rueful smile. 'If it helps, take it out on me —that's what friends are for.' He picked up his cup and took a drink.

'Be honest with yourself, Claire,' he went on, putting the cup down again. 'Obviously you knew Peter better than I did, but I rather think that in your heart you know I'm right.'

She glared at him, and then her expression softened. 'I suppose I do. I can't really blame anyone else for the way Peter was. I saw only what I wanted to see.'

'You loved him, and love can be blind—it's as simple as that. Don't be too hard on yourself.'

'You're right about him, of course,' she said. 'He was always looking longingly at what he hadn't got. He used to say that when he lived in Ladakh he spent the whole of the time wishing he was back in England, but when he was back in England, he really missed what he'd had in Ladakh. Maybe he's the sort of person who can never be truly happy with what he has.'

'That could be true.'

'And in a way, his father tried to warn me this might happen, but I didn't want to hear it. But it must have always been in the background, and you're right, I think deep down I knew it.'

Her eyes watered again. She wiped away her tears with her fingers. Alex took a tissue from the box and handed it to her.

'How I'm going to get through the shift, I don't know,' she said, rubbing the tissue across her face. 'I ought to be in the ward right now, checking on the students. Heaven knows what they're getting up to.'

'You'll get through this, Claire, and I don't just mean the shift. You're strong.'

'But after being with Peter for so long ...' Her voice cracked.

'You'll get through this, I tell you,' he repeated firmly. He hesitated a moment. 'I know it's way too soon to think about it now, but at some point you'll meet someone who wants the same things as you, and who isn't convinced that the grass is greener on the other side. One day, Peter's name will come up in conversation, and you won't feel a thing. It'll happen; you'll see.'

He stretched out his arm, put a finger under her chin and made her look directly into his face. 'Trust Doctor Alex,' he said with mock gravity, and dropped his hand.

She gave him a wan smile. 'I know you're trying to help, but I'll never feel about anyone else the way I've felt about Peter since the day I met him.'

He stared at her thoughtfully. 'You know, maybe I

shouldn't say this,' he said at last. 'But I'm going to, never-theless. It's something for you to think about in the future. Once you've got over your resentment towards me, that is.'

'I don't resent you.'

'Yes, you do. You're still angry that the Australia thing originated with me.'

'Maybe I am. But only a bit. And that bit is fast being erased by seeing what a great friend you are. You're still arguing Peter's case to make me less critical of him, and you're trying to help me feel better.'

She paused. 'So what might I want to think about in the future?' she prompted.

'It's just that during the last year, I started to wonder if you felt as strongly about Peter as you'd originally felt about him.'

She opened her mouth to speak.

'No,' he cut in quickly. 'Don't say anything now. But later on, in a week or two maybe, when the immediate hurt has faded, give some thought to what I'm about to say.'

She wiped her hands swiftly across her cheeks. 'Now you've got me curious.'

'It's just that by the time a year group registers as doctors, fifty per cent have already got married. You met Peter more than three years ago, but he said you weren't making any attempt to push him into a permanent commitment.'

She stared at him, and frowned. 'What exactly are you trying to say?'

'Just that you might have had a subconscious reservation.'

'You're totally wrong. Yes, half an intake of medics are married by the time they register, but the other half aren't,' she said, her voice getting stronger.

'And we *did* make a permanent commitment to each other. An engagement is a legal contract: people can be sued for Breach of Promise. So if you're saying that because I didn't want to risk being sent to another hospital, I was unsure of my feelings for Peter, you're completely wrong.'

He grinned at her. 'Well, at least it's stopped you crying. I've a feeling you'll get through the day a bit better now.'

'Why you so-and-so! I'd never have thought of you as devious, but you are. And to be honest, I'm glad. I'm not going to say you've cheered me up—no one could do that today—but that much-needed kick has helped.'

He raised his eyebrows. 'Devious, am I? Hmm. Some of it was devious, I'll grant you, but there could be a grain of truth in it. And there might come a day when you're not quite so satisfied with the answer you've just given me.'

'I'm certain you're wrong.'

'Maybe; maybe not.' He sat back and ran his finger round the rim of his empty coffee cup.

'Do you want another coffee?' she asked.

'No, I'm fine, thanks. I really must get off. And talking of being off, when are your next free days?'

'I'm on for three more days, and then off for four.'

'So you'll be off on Saturday. A few of us have wangled some time off together and we're going to meet in the city centre and get a bite to eat. If you're still speaking to me after what I've just said, why don't you come along? The worst will be over by then, and having a meal with friends will be a good way to start the rest of your life.'

'I don't know—'

'I do. We'll pick you up from your flat at seven.'

'Won't Karen mind if I tag along?'

'It'll be Mike and me in the car—Karen's doing something else on Saturday. I'll be happy to collect you if you don't mind being seen in my ancient Morris Minor. Karen moans about it all the time.'

'Are you sure?'

'Of course I am. I'll need someone to help Mike push the banger up the hill, and you'll do very nicely, thank you.'

She gave him a watery smile. 'Okay, then. Thanks, Alex.'

He stood up. 'And now I really must get a move on.' He started to go to the door, and then stopped suddenly and turned to her.

'You need not wait till Saturday, you know, Claire. If at any point between now and then, you want to talk to someone other than your usual friends, remember I'm here. Mary's not around in the same way any longer.'

'Thanks again for being such a good friend to me, Alex, just as you were to Peter.'

He raised his hand in a slight wave and went out of the office.

She got up, adjusted her starched muslin cap, and looked around the office. Her eyes came to rest on the drawers in her desk. Moving forward, she opened the top drawer on the right.

Peter's face smiled up at her.

She picked up the photo and stood there, hugging it tightly to her chest.

Then she put the photo back in the drawer, face down, closed the drawer and walked out into the corridor.

 *week later*

'I LIKE THE ATMOSPHERE HERE,' Claire said, glancing round the small Italian restaurant when the waiter had gone to the kitchen with their order. 'What a shame the others couldn't get the time off.'

'I suppose I ought to own up,' Alex said with a wry smile. 'There were never going to be any others.'

She stared at him in amazement. 'Why not?'

'I figured you might still be feeling a bit jaded, and I thought it might help you to talk things through, and you wouldn't be able to if there were other people around.

But if I'd suggested you coming out on a Saturday night with just me, you'd have said no. It would have sounded too much like a date and you won't yet be ready to start dating again.'

'Wow, that's really thoughtful of you, Alex. I wouldn't have put you down as a sensitive type, but I was obviously wrong. To be honest, I almost cancelled this evening. The closer it got, the more I was dreading having to make light-hearted conversation, feeling the way I still do.'

He smiled with understanding. 'I thought that might be the case.' He leaned forward and took a bread stick. 'So what are your thoughts at the moment?'

'Pretty much the same as four days ago. No, that's not quite right. I've probably moved on a little, but only a little. Today's the first day I didn't wake up and find my pillow wet.'

'That's a definite step forward.' He paused as the waiter approached the table with a bottle of Chianti encased in raffia and started to pour them each a glass of the wine.

'Have you any idea about what you want to do in the future, whether you're going to stay on here or move away?' he asked when the waiter had moved away.

'Not really—it's still early days. And at the moment, I can't bear the thought of leaving a place that's so full of memories of Peter. Not yet, anyway.'

He picked up his glass and waited for her to pick up hers. 'Whatever you decide to do, cheers,' he said. 'To happier days.'

'I'll certainly drink to that—I must be awful company at the moment.' She clinked her glass with his, took a sip of wine and then put the glass down.

'To be honest, I haven't a clue what I'll do. But I think I'll probably move somewhere else, though Heaven knows where. It'll depend on the jobs that come up.'

'Even though you've got friends here? At a time like this, it's usually a good idea to be among friends.'

'I can see that. But while it's inevitable that I'm wallowing in thoughts of Peter at the moment—and I need to wallow for a bit longer—I won't always want to be surrounded by memories.

I don't think I'd want to live in a tiny country town on my own, but if a job came up in something medium-sized, I'd probably go after it. I'm no keener on living in a large town than Peter was, and we were always going to move away from here, just not as far away as Australia.'

'It beats me how Peter can want to live over there. Or anywhere other than England, for that matter. As soon as I gave serious thought to leaving the country, I knew I couldn't do it. I'd happily go abroad for a holiday, but no more than that. I like living here.'

She nodded. 'Me, too.'

'I'm still furious with myself for asking for Peter's advice. You've no idea how much I wish I could turn the clock back. I really miss him. He was a good mate.'

'There's no point in blaming yourself. As you said the other day, if it wasn't Australia, it would have been some-where else. It's not your fault that Peter is as he is.'

They paused while the waiter put a bowl of spaghetti Bolognese in front of each of them, and then grated Parmesan cheese on the top.

'Let's change the topic, shall we?' she said with an attempt at a smile. She picked up her fork. 'So what about you?'

He looked up from his food, and smiled back. 'Me?'

'Yes, what are *your* plans? D'you think you'll stay in Birmingham?'

'Definitely not. I only stayed on after registration to build up my experience and make sure I really did want to be a GP.'

'A GP!' she exclaimed. 'You? I don't believe it.' She burst out laughing.

He gave her a rueful grin. 'That's the response I've had from everyone.'

'Could it be that we all remember what you've said about GPs in the past?'

'You might be right. Nevertheless, I shall look for a practice in a town. Not in a large city like Birmingham—that'd be too frenetic—somewhere a bit smaller, where I'd have time to go fishing.'

'I didn't know you liked fishing!'

'I don't know if I do—so far I've only fished for women. But I might like it if I tried it.'

'Well, you're certainly full of surprises this evening.' She shook her head. 'But no, try as I might, I can't see you as a GP.'

He laughed. 'I won't ask you to explain why not. You've already got me down as devious. There's only so much a man wants to learn about how others see him.'

'Well then, I'll give you a positive to balance the negative: you're very good company, and you're nice. That's two positives, in fact.'

'Why, thank you, ma'am,' he drawled. 'Although I'm not sure I like being called nice. That sounds a bit dull. '

'In the state I'm in, talking to someone nice means a lot.'

'I'm delighted with the adjective, then. And I could say about you that you're good company, too.'

'Now that's carrying niceness too far! I've done nothing but weep and wail for the past few days, and I'd hardly be the life and soul of any party.'

'If I'd wanted a life and soul type, I'd have headed for a club in town, but I didn't. I can see you're sad, and it'd be strange if you weren't, but you *have* been good company—you always are.

What's more, even with a Kleenex in front of your nose, you're still very easy on the eye. We all thought Peter a lucky devil to have you.'

She flushed. 'To move on,' she said quickly, tucking the Kleenex up her sleeve. 'I've made my mind up about one thing—I'm going to learn to drive. Peter intended to teach me, but we never got started. I saved some money for our wedding, and I'm going to use it to buy a small car.'

'You can borrow mine, if you want. Peter did.'

'That's kind of you, but I'll really need to have my own. I want to be able to do things on the spur of the moment, and it'll give me more choice about where to work in the future.'

'That makes sense. Well, if you need any help with finding a car, let me know, and you can count on me sitting in with you whenever you want to get some practice, assuming I can free myself at the time.'

'That's really kind, but isn't it rather going above and beyond? You mustn't feel so guilty about Peter that you martyr yourself.'

He shrugged. 'I do feel guilty, but helping you isn't exactly a sacrifice. Like I said, I enjoy your company and have always done so.'

'Then, thank you. I may well take you up on your offer.'

'You mustn't hesitate to call on me until you're back on your feet and don't need a prop any longer,' he said, his voice taking on a serious note. 'That's an order.'

'Thanks, Alex,' she said quietly. 'I really appreciate it.'

'You don't have to thank me. It's the least I can do.'

She glanced at him across the table and smiled. 'You know, I already feel a whole lot better, thanks to you. I really do.'

· · ·

THE LIGHT in Claire's room went out.

Alex didn't move.

Half-hidden in the gloom that lay beyond the reach of the street lamp, he stood on the pavement, staring up at the now-black rectangle that was her window.

A glow of satisfaction deepened within him.

He felt as if he'd been waiting a long time to step out of Peter's shadow into the light of Claire's affection, but it looked as if his wait was almost over. There were signs that Claire was starting to see him as a person in his own right, and not just as Peter's friend, a pleasant waster.

Yes, the evening had definitely been much more successful than he'd dared hope.

The timing of everything couldn't have been better, with Karen giving him an ultimatum at about the time that Peter was leaving—they had to step things up a notch or split up. Without a moment's hesitation, he'd obviously gone with the splitting-up option.

And now, with Karen consigned to history, and Claire increasingly turning to him in her struggle to get over her loss, all he had to do was bide his time until her friendship and gratitude became something stronger, something very much stronger.

And it would become that, he was very sure.

In the past, he'd rationalised that Claire's attraction for him had been her unavailability, but with that no longer the case, he'd get that lovely body into his bed, and see if there was any more to his feelings than that.

And he was pretty sure there would be.

Elated, he turned away, crossed the road to his car and opened the door. Pausing a moment, his hand on the car door, he looked back up at Claire's window.

What a strange trio they would have seemed in the past

few months to any outsider who happened to see into their hearts: him with his eyes on Claire; Claire with her eyes on Peter, and Peter with his eyes on an unknown horizon.

26

C obar, New South Wales, Australia
Early January, 1971

THE MORNING HEAT was building up as the sun inched higher into the sky.

Grabbing his medical bag as an afterthought, Peter hurried out of the bungalow, climbed into the dark-green Land Rover that had been on the drive when he'd reached the house the evening before, shifted it into gear and headed down the short dirt track that led to Lerida Road.

At the end of the track, he glanced down at the instructions he'd found on the passenger seat, and turned left.

Settling into his seat, he drove slowly along the strip of bitumen that ran down the middle of the road, a ribbon of black asphalt bordered on either side by red, pebble-strewn dust.

Tinged with green from the sparse shrubs that hugged

the ground, the expanse of dust on both sides of the road was backed by intermittent trees.

The further he drove, the further back from the road the trees grew, pushed away, it seemed, by the widening stretch of red-green dust that lay between the bitumen and the trees.

By the time he reached the sign that pointed towards the airport, and turned right, the green vegetation bordering the road had drastically thinned, and it was the red of the dust that increasingly dominated the landscape.

A little further on, he saw a white fence in the distance.

That would be the metal perimeter of the airport grounds, he realised, and he felt the same surge of excitement that he'd felt the moment he'd read about the existence of a Flying Doctor Service—an excitement that had been swiftly drowned by his longing for Claire.

Slowing down, he rattled noisily over the metal cattle grid that spanned the open gateway in the fence, drove forward a short distance, and brought the four-wheel drive to an abrupt halt.

He switched off the engine, wound down the window, and wiped his forehead with the back of his hand. Leaning forward, he rested his forearms on the rim of the steering wheel, and stared around him.

On his left, a wire enclosure stood back from the road. Inside it, two aerial masts tapered upwards. Behind the wire mesh lay a vast red-ochre desert, its crimson earth interspersed with patches of green from the spinifex and mulga scrub that clung to life in the sun-baked soil.

There was not a house to be seen.

In the far distance, a row of eucalyptus trees was outlined against the horizon, dark shapes against the bright blue sky.

He sniffed the air, but there was only the faintest trace of eucalyptus. It was the slightly sweet smell of dry dust that stood out, and to his surprise, also a touch of lemon.

If only his Claire were here to share the moment with him, standing at his side on the threshold of an exciting new life, it would all be so perfect.

But she wasn't.

His excitement faded, and the pain of loss that had ached relentlessly since he'd left England, rose up and threatened to overwhelm him.

He took a deep breath and shook himself mentally. He mustn't think of Claire as *his* Claire. She was no longer his: she'd chosen to stay behind. She'd be getting on with the life she'd chosen over a life with him, and he must do the same.

With fierce determination, he pushed her image out of his mind, and turned to look to his right.

A short dirt track led from the road to a low white bungalow. He turned slightly towards it, and wondered for a moment if that could be the Flying Doctor Base Station, the building in which the Base Director lived and worked.

But there were no aerials near the house, and nothing to suggest it was the Base Station—no signs or anything—so he decided it probably wasn't.

He looked back at the road ahead, put the vehicle into gear and began to drive slowly forward, glancing to the right as he did so.

Telegraph poles lined the right-hand side of the road, which started curving gently to the right. Beyond the poles, there were eucalyptus and mulga trees, and other trees that might be the bimble box trees he'd read about.

Every so often, he glimpsed a small white house, standing in isolation.

A little way along the road, he came to another narrow dirt track that led off to the right, at the end of which there was a single building.

He slowed down and stared hard along the track. But again there were no visible radio masts, so he continued driving, and passed yet another track that ended in front of a bungalow that looked purely residential.

At the point where the road straightened out, he saw a wide dirt track leading off to the right, and at the far end of the track, a white bungalow with an aerial mast half-hidden behind it.

That must be it, he thought, his heart beating faster, and he turned on to the track and drove towards the bungalow. Pulling up a little way back from the entrance to the building, he sat and stared at the house.

A few steps led up to a wooden veranda and the front door. Shaded by a sloping corrugated-iron roof, the veranda ran along the side of the building, which appeared to be made of concrete, and round the back as far as he could see.

Above the entrance, a sign read, 'Royal Flying Doctor Service of Australia, Cobar Base, New South Wales'.

So this was really it, he thought, and he leaned back in his seat and smiled.

The front door opened and a slim young woman with dark hair piled on top of her head came out.

He promptly straightened up, wiped his forehead again with the back of his forearm, opened the door and jumped down from the Land Rover.

As he walked across the dusty yard to meet the woman, he ran the palms of his hands down the sides of his jeans.

The woman came towards him, a smile of welcome on her face.

He held out his hand to her.

'G'day,' she said, shaking his outstretched hand. 'Hot, isn't she?'

He grinned at her. 'This isn't just hot—it's more like the inside of a furnace.'

She laughed. 'You'll get used to it like I have. At least you'd better: it gets hotter than this. We're not yet far into the Australian summer—just wait till it hits you full force.'

He gave a low whistle.

She laughed again. 'Don't look so appalled. Like I say, you'll be used to it by then.' She glanced across the yard to the Land Rover. 'I see you got the car all right. You might want to put it under that old gum tree: it'll stay in the shade if you do.'

'You call that hunk of metal a car!' he exclaimed. 'It's a four-wheel drive at the very least.'

She shrugged. 'Everyone around here's got one. We all say car. We save our breath for what matters.'

'Fair enough.'

'While you're moving the car, I'll get you something to drink.' She turned towards the house. 'I've lemonade, or you could have a beer if it's not too early in the day for you. Have a beer if you want—you'll not be flying for a day or two.'

'Lemonade sounds good to me.'

'Or tea? You're British, after all. I could make you a bush tea. You put three or four eucalyptus leaves into a pot, take the top off and swing it in whole-arm circles from the knee upwards. Because of the centrifugal force, the water and leaves don't fly out. How does that sound?'

'Highly entertaining. But I think I'll pass.'

'Come on in when you've moved the car, then,' she said with a smile, and went back up the steps.

He drove the Land Rover into the shade, climbed out and ran up the steps and through the open doorway into the house. Finding himself in a small hall, he hesitated a moment.

Then, following the muffled sounds he could hear, he turned into the room on his right. It was a long, slightly dark room.

Hovering in the centre, he could hear the woman moving around in the room that led off the far end. He wondered whether he should sit down. But he decided he wouldn't, and went towards the room where the woman was.

It was the kitchen, he saw when he got closer—the corner units were visible through the open doorway.

'I take it you're the Base Director's wife,' he called.

The woman appeared at the door, a jug in her hand. 'What makes you think that?'

'Well, the sign in the front and the aerial mast behind the house suggest that this is his home. Also the fact that you were clearly expecting me.

After all, you didn't ask who I was, yet you made that comment about me flying. The radio apparatus over there helped, too.'

Smiling, he indicated the apparatus on the table next to the wall between the room and the entrance hall.

'Quite the detective, aren't you?' she said lightly. 'Why don't you sit on one of the chairs over there while I get the lemonade? You're sure you don't want a beer?'

'Quite sure, thanks.'

'Then hang on a tick; I'll be back in a minute.' She disappeared into the kitchen again.

He sat down on one of the two wooden-framed easy chairs that backed against the window and looked around the room.

In front of him, a low square wooden table stood on a

cream rug. At each end of the table, there was an easy chair at right angles to his. On the opposite side of the room, a divan bed covered with a cream and navy striped rug had been pushed against the wall, and a couple of navy cushions had been propped up on it.

A cluster of photos had been hung on the wall to the right of the divan. On the left of it, there were two full-length cream-coloured curtains that had been pulled across what he suspected might be an open doorway.

The only other pieces of furniture in the room were a small television set that stood between the divan and the kitchen, and the long table with the radio apparatus and telephone that he'd noticed on the way in. Two wooden chairs had been pushed in under the table.

'These buildings are surprisingly cool and they're termite proof,' the woman said, coming back into the room with a tray. 'And we're very fortunate—we've got an air-conditioner. It's powered by a thirty-two volt electrical generator, which also supplies the lighting.

To save electricity, I turn it off at night and on all but the hottest days. The smallish windows also help to keep the house cool.'

She put the tray on the table and sat down on one of the chairs at right angles to his.

'It's a very comfortable temperature in here,' he said, for something to say.

'Glad you think so. Just as well, as this place is pretty much like yours, except you've got an extra bedroom. You've got air-conditioning, too. Help yourself to a cake. They're called lamingtons. They're just squares of sponge cake covered in chocolate icing and coconut, but they're a sort of Aussie icon.'

She indicated the plate of cakes, and then took one of the glasses of lemonade and sat back.

'Like I say, help yourself. If you wait to be offered something, you'll have a long wait. We don't stand on ceremony around here. If you want more lemonade, there's plenty.'

'Thanks.' He leaned forward and picked up his glass and a cake. 'Talking of lemon, there was a smell of lemon in the air as I drove along. How come?'

'Lemon grass is one of the native grasses. All native grasses smell strongly, though perhaps not as strong as lemon grass. Aboriginal people used it as a natural fly repellent—there're flies everywhere out there, as you'll find out soon enough.'

'They're everywhere, even in England.' He finished his mouthful of cake. 'D'you mind me asking your name? I'd like to know who I'm talking to.'

'Not in the least. In fact, it'd be mighty difficult if you didn't know my name since we're going to be working together. I'm Susie Lentini. And you're Peter Henderson. It's bonzer to meet you, Peter.'

'You're obviously not Italian, despite your name. From your accent, I'd guess you were from England originally. You sound a bit Australian, but I can hear some English in there, too.'

'And you'd guess right. It was my husband, Marco, who was born in Italy. Whereabouts in England are you from?'

'Hard to say, really. London, I suppose. It's where I was born, but I've spent a relatively small amount of time there.' He leaned forward and helped himself to another lamington. 'You said not to stand on ceremony. You can see I'm taking you at your word.'

'Is that all you intend to say about where you come from? I thought men always liked talking about themselves, even if they pretended they didn't. If you stop at that, you'll be letting your sex down.'

He shook his head. 'Better that than talking about England. Not unless you want to see a grown man cry. It's too soon after leaving everyone.' He took another bite of his cake.

She glanced at him curiously over the rim of her glass. 'On the forms you sent, it said you're engaged,' she said after a few minutes.

'Wrong tense—*was* engaged. She decided to stay in England.' He saw a wave of sympathy cross her face.

'It's okay,' he said quickly. 'I chose to get on the plane, even though by then I'd realised she wasn't going to join me. I loved everything I read about Australia, it's beauty and the miles of emptiness, and I was determined to come, even if it had to be on my own. But like I say, I'm not ready to talk about it.'

'I understand.'

At the sympathy in her voice, he felt a lump come to his throat.

'But as for the emptiness you mentioned,' she said, 'it's not nearly as empty as it looks at first glance. Or as red. There are lots of oranges, greens and blues, too. There's a surprising amount of vegetation and the place is teeming with wild life. It's an intriguing place, the Outback.'

'I can well believe that,' he said. 'So tell me, what d'you do around here? They told me there was a Base Director and a pilot, and that both lived fairly close to the airport. You said we'll be working together. Are you the secretary, then, or the Base Director's wife and you help him out?'

'You're going to fit in here very well,' she said sharply. 'Cobar's a blokey town, and you've just shown that you've got a blokey set of mind.

A sheila belongs in a kitchen, and Australian men don't like her straying too far from her natural habitat. If she hasn't got any cooking, washing or cleaning to do, a little light secretarial might be permissible. But nothing more demanding than that.'

'Ouch. I'm guessing again—you're the Base Director. Or you might be the pilot, of course,' he added hastily.

'The apparatus tells you that this is the operator's station, and here I am, pouring lemonade and helping myself to biscuits, so I guess I must be the Base Director.'

'I'm sorry. It was crass of me to assume that the operator was a man. D'you think we could start again?'

She gave him a wide smile. 'Don't worry, Peter; you're not the first and I'm sure you won't be the last. Is it Peter or Pete, by the way?'

'Peter. I've never been a Pete.'

'Do you want to become one now?'

He thought for a moment, and then he shook his head. 'Nope, I don't think so. I've been a Peter for too long. If you called me Pete, I'd probably just ignore you, thinking you were talking to someone else, and I think I've already done more than enough to offend you for one day.'

'You'll find I've a thicker skin that that! Remember, I was married to an Italian. Marco was a typical Mediterranean man, with the same attitude towards women as heaps of Australian men, especially the ones outside the big towns. So like I say, I'm used to it.'

'Thanks, anyway.'

There was a slight pause. Each had a sip of their drink.

'I'm sorry I wasn't at the airport when you arrived,' Susie said, putting her glass back on the table. 'I'd intended to be there, but there was a small celebration in town that I had to go to. Who drove you to the house?'

'The van that was collecting medical supplies from the plane dropped me off on its way to the hospital. It was late by then, and had been a very long day. I was too tired to be any sort of company, so you did better not to come.'

'Good oh.' She put her glass back on the tray. 'If you're ready, I'll show you around the place. We'll leave the airport and Ned till tomorrow, though. Ned's your pilot.'

'You know what's best.'

'I'm not sure you're right about that, but it's better than your last assumption. We'll also go through your daily routine tomorrow. You've got to be able to take over from Brian in three days' time—he can't carry a double load for much longer.'

'Who's Brian?'

'Brian Bailey. The doctor in town. Your predecessor was flown to Sydney three days ago. We knew he had health issues, but his sudden deterioration took us by surprise. And him, too! That's why things moved as quickly as they did after Broken Hill got your application. With you able to come out at once, it wasn't worth getting a locum, so Brian's been doing the morning and afternoon clinics for us.'

'So he'll he coming here today?'

She shook her head. 'No, he does them from home. They're done over the radio, so you can do the same, or you can come here. It'll be up to you.

As well as the routine daily clinics, Brian's been covering any emergencies and also doing his own practice. But the townsfolk know how busy he's been, and they've been holding off going to him this week if they can.'

'If you fill me in tomorrow, I can start the day after.'

'You can have one more day than that. We'll go through everything here tomorrow, take a look at the airport and meet Ned. That's a day's work in itself.

Then the following day, we'll go first to the hospital, which luckily for us is this side of Cobar, and then I'll take you into town. I think you'll like it—it's got a bit about it. There's a lot of original nineteenth century architecture, if you're interested in that sort of thing.'

'I'm looking forward to seeing it.'

She nodded. 'I'll introduce you to one or two of the locals when we're there. Fortunately, there aren't many whackers in Cobar. And then—'

'Sorry, what's a whacker?'

'An idiot. Someone who talks drivel.'

'Thanks.'

'And then we'll have a bite to eat with Brian,' she went on, 'provided he's not out on a call. After that, I'll show you something of the surrounding area. It has a beauty all of its own. And then you'll be ready to begin.'

He grinned at her. 'Bring on the day.'

———

27

Susie pulled out a wooden chair, sat down in front of the radio, and indicated that Peter should sit next to her.

'I hope you slept well,' she said.

'I did, thanks. Like a log.'

'Good; we'll get down to business, then. I know you've already been plied with info about the Service, but I still need to run through the basics. Each of the seven Flying Doctor sections is different, and you have to know how our section works.'

'Okay.'

'We cover an area that's roughly the size of France. For safety reasons, we slightly overlap with Broken Hill, and with Charleville, which is in South Queensland.'

'That's a lot of ground!'

'Too right. And we do non-medical things, too, but I'll tell you about those later.'

'You're the boss.'

She laughed. 'That's pleasingly non-blokey. I can see

we're going to get on well. Right, we're on call for emergencies twenty-four hours a day.'

He let out a long breath. 'Wow. That's a long stretch.'

'It's not as bad as it sounds. We're closed from five in the evening to eight in the morning, and I've got an assistant, Maisie Allen. She lives in the town. She'll cover for me tomorrow when we go into Cobar.' She paused. 'Ask any questions as I go along, won't you?'

'I will, thanks.'

'Each outpost has a radio transmitter-receiver known as a transceiver, and it has its own call sign. Every drover, padre, regular traveller carries a small mobile transceiver. And so do we, whenever we go out.'

'What if it breaks down?'

'It shouldn't. We've got a radio-technician who travels around, keeping the transceivers ticking over.'

'What if someone needs help when the base is shut?'

'I live here so I pick up the call. If I'm away overnight, Maisie covers for me. If anyone needs help at night they stand in front of their station transceiver and blow a whistle that sets off an alarm here. It's a cheap, simple tin whistle, but it works.'

He nodded. 'The simplest things are often the best.'

'Too right. My base radio is connected by the landline phone to your house, the airport, and to Ned's house. He lives nearby. It means you can talk directly to the outposts from your home. You find out the symptoms, say what treatment's needed and decide if a visit's necessary. If it is, you can be there an hour or two after receiving the call.'

'It's incredible when you think about it.'

'You haven't heard the half yet. We also deal with telegrams—or radiograms, as they're called. They're radioed to and from the outposts after the medical calls. And then there are the galah sessions.'

'Galah sessions! What are they?'

'Gossip time. A galah's a kind of cockatoo. We also call a noisy idiot a galah. All the transceivers in the area are tuned into the base's wavelengths and frequencies, and twice a day, everyone can talk to everyone else. It's usually just the women, though, as the men tend to be outdoors. They talk about anything and everything. It's important for them keep in touch as some are very isolated.'

'What if there's a medical call while they're gossiping?'

'The call has priority, and they instantly stop talking. It's quite impressive when that happens.'

'It must be.'

'But there's a downside to open communication: there's no privacy. Everyone can hear what everyone else says.'

'Even their medical problems?'

'Yup.'

'Don't people feel uncomfortable about that?'

'They get over it. They have to if they want help.'

'What happens if I need to prescribe something?'

'Every outpost has a Standard Medical Chest with simple, easy-to-handle things in it. They've got some antibiotics, but basically only stable drugs that don't expire quickly, and in tablet and powder form rather than as liquids.'

'Suppose they take the wrong medication, or the wrong dose?'

'It's all clearly labelled. The dangerous drugs are marked 'Doctor's Orders Only'. And every item has a number as well as a name. For example, if you said Homatropine Oculets, a patient might mishear that, but if you said number fifty-three, they wouldn't.'

'But you said there was an overlap. What if you're called to a Queensland outpost?'

'The same numbers are used all over Australia.'

'It's obviously very well thought out.'

'It is. Also, there are two anatomical charts in the medical chest, one for the front of the body, one for the back. The body's divided into sections on each chart. The front is marked with numbers and the back with letters. It's easier for them to refer to the chart when you need more precise information.'

'While I wouldn't wish anyone ill, I can't wait to see this in practice.'

'You'll see it soon enough. The non-emergency patients go to our monthly clinics, and so do those who can't bring themselves to share their personal info with every woman for miles around. The monthly clinics are for routine matters and follow-up work, such as checking on diabetics, antenatals, patients with chronic heart disease, and so on.'

'It's great that people can get an early diagnosis.'

'It certainly is—it saves lives. And prevention's essential, too. You'll immunise kids against polio, smallpox and so on. And at your baby clinics, you'll advise expectant mothers about prenatal care. You don't do all this by yourself, by the way—one of the hospital nurses usually does the monthly clinic with you. They do their own rota and just turn up.'

'I can see I'll be covering a lot of ground. Literally and figuratively,' he added with a smile. 'Where are the clinics held?'

'Generally in the larger outposts.' She rubbed the back of her neck, and stood up. 'I think we'll stop for a bit,' she said, moving away from the radio table. 'We'll go through your daily routine next, but I expect you need a break first. D'you want coffee or some other drink?'

'I'm happy to carry on; it's all interesting stuff.'

'Well, *I'm* ready for a break, and I'm having a coffee. You can join me if you want or you can watch me drink.'

'When you put it like that, coffee sounds good.'

'In fact, I can run through your day's routine while we have coffee. You can start by coming into the kitchen with me, and seeing where everything's kept. We'll be taking it in turns to make the coffee. I'm only letting you off at the moment as you're new.'

'I'll remember my pinny next time I come,' he said, following her into the kitchen.

She glanced back at him and smiled. 'Good onya. Now you're talking.'

When she'd made the coffees and put them on a tray with a plate of biscuits, Peter picked up the tray, followed her back into the main room and put the tray down on the table.

'So what do you think of the house they've given you?' she asked, taking a biscuit and dunking it into her coffee. 'I know this is usually done with tea, but nobody's watching.'

'It's fine for my needs. I'll probably get a cushion or two to liven it up a bit, and maybe a rug. I might see something in town tomorrow. But tell me, how did you and your husband come to move to Cobar?'

'That's better left for another time—we must see Ned before he breaks for lunch.' She hesitated. 'Maybe we should both put our pasts in a box and leave them there.'

He nodded. 'I'll second that.'

'Okay, let's run through your normal day, then. Remember, an emergency takes precedence over your routine.'

He took a pad from his pocket and put it on his knee. 'Fire away.'

'Fire might not be the best choice of word,' she said lightly, 'given you've got the job on a trial basis.'

'There you go again,' he said with a theatrical sigh. 'You're just too literal for me.'

She smiled. 'I'll try to watch it in future. Right, you do two clinical sessions on the radio each day, one at eight in the morning, the other at four in the afternoon. If you're in the air at the time, you'll hold the clinic from the aircraft.'

'So I'll be on the air in the air.'

She laughed. 'That's the ticket. The clinic's a two-way thing: you'll ask after your patients, and people with medical problems call in and ask you for help. You use a question-and-answer technique.'

'I suppose we fit patient visits between the clinical sessions.'

'Correct. On average, not counting emergencies, you'll make about three or four flights a week. They'll mostly be to your monthly clinics, or sometimes to a doctor who wants a second opinion or something like that. A small town doctor working on his own is often glad of another opinion. Or he may be ill and need temporary cover.'

'Do you ever go on the aerial rounds yourself?'

'I have done, but not as a habit. I wouldn't leave the base unattended, and Maisie might not be able to be here. I've had a small amount of medical training which helps when I take the calls, but there's no need for me to go out with you.'

'That's a shame,' he said.

'Not a bit of it. We'll spend more than enough time with each other as it is. You'll be glad to have a break from seeing my face.'

He returned the gaze of the dark brown eyes that shone out from a vivacious face. 'I doubt that,' he said.

She moved slightly back in her chair and smoothed

down the skirt of her pale blue cotton dress. 'I wasn't fishing.'

'You wouldn't be—we're in the parched outback, aren't we?' Then he glanced at her in sudden anxiety, and frowned.

'I hope I didn't overstep the mark just now,' he said quickly, his voice full of apology. 'In England, everything's much more formal and hierarchical than it seems to be here. But maybe I'm taking Australian informality a little too far.' He paused. 'If I am, you'd tell me, wouldn't you?'

'You can count on it,' she said cheerfully. She put her coffee cup on the table, glanced at her watch and stood up. 'I think that's enough about your routine for today. You'll pick up everything else as you go along. Ned will have finished his daily by now.'

'His daily?'

'He gives the plane a once-over every day—you have to be able to leave at a moment's notice. The airport engineers give it a thorough check-out on a regular basis, too.

I suggest we go up to the airport now, I introduce you to Ned and then leave you both. When he's finished showing you around, come back and have a bite to eat. After that, you can practise the radio and telephone connection.'

'Sounds good,' he said, standing up. 'I could do with stretching my legs.'

'Me, too. Some days it's too hot to walk more than a very short distance, but this isn't one of them. Not that the airport's far from here—it's minutes away.

I'll just rinse the cups first. You don't leave dirty dishes lying around or you'll come home to flies like you've never seen. The bathroom's through there, if you want,' she added, pointing to the full-length cream curtains that hung next to the divan bed.

'Thanks,' he said, and headed off to the bathroom while Susie picked up the cups and went into the kitchen.

SUSIE STARTED towards the front door as soon as she saw Peter return, and he followed her out on to the veranda and down the steps.

Turning to the right at the bottom, she started to make her way past a group of stunted gum trees that rose up from the parched earth, ghostly spectres with their silver-white bark and leaves from which the green had been leached by the sun.

'Always watch where you're putting your feet,' she called over her shoulder, increasing to a brisk pace. 'There are things you wouldn't want to step on.'

'Don't worry, I will,' he said, his eyes riveted to the cracked earth. Speeding his steps, he caught her up and walked beside her. 'I've been to the reptile house in the zoo so I know all about Australia's venomous snakes. I've checked out what to do if I get a patient with a snake bite, but I've no wish to be that patient myself.'

'Very wise. If the grass comes up to your ankles, stamp hard with each step. The snakes will pick up the vibrations and clear off.'

Still keeping pace with her, he began to pound the ground with his every step. A fine red dust billowed up around them, gradually sinking down, and settling on their skin and their clothes, which took on a terracotta blush.

'You really only have to stamp hard when you're walking in grass, or it gets a bit dusty,' she said, trying to brush her dress down as she walked.

'Mind you, some people keep dust on their skin for protection when they're in the Outback. It prevents against sunburn. Also, you should watch out for spiny emex. Not so much here, but on open ground. They're really painful if you stand on them. Basically, it's just a matter of watching your step. Literally.' She threw him a quick smile.

'What are they?' he asked, with an anxious glance at the ground.

'Small round balls with three long pointed spines. They look a bit like those six-pointed metal pieces children pick up while bouncing a little ball. They're called three-cornered jacks in some parts of Australia for that reason.'

'Yup, I'll watch out for those, too,' he said.

They walked along in silence for a few minutes.

'I feel as if I've been here much longer than two days,' he remarked as they skirted a gum tree. 'You're very easy to talk to.'

She glanced at him. 'It's nice of you to say that, but it's not like we've been having a real conversation, is it?'

He stopped in his tracks and stared at her. 'So I dreamed we were talking all of yesterday and this morning, too, did I?'

She paused. 'Yes and no.' She started walking again, and he hurried after her. 'Yes, you were dreaming if you thought that was a conversation. We were talking all right—or rather, I was—but it wasn't a conversation: it was me telling you what you need to know.

You've a lot to learn and little time in which to learn it. But no, you weren't dreaming if you meant that we were exchanging words, because we were.'

'Are you always so blunt? I'm not complaining—in fact, I quite like it. It's just that it's different. In England, women aren't quite so open about what they're thinking. Or men for that matter.'

'Feel free to be equally open. It's the way we do things here.'

'I'll remember that.' He glanced at the gum tree they were approaching. 'Do you get koalas around here? They eat eucalyptus leaves, don't they?'

'That's right. But contrary to popular belief, it's not eucalyptus oil that makes them sleepy—it's that their diet's low in nutrition, and they've a low metabolic rate and body temperature. They've only got six hours of energy a day, so they conserve that by sleeping for up to twenty hours a day. There are not many around here, though.'

'About saying what's on your mind,' Peter said after a few minutes. 'I think I'll take you up on that. Every time you've mentioned Marco, you've said was, not is. D'you mind me asking if you're still together?'

She glanced quickly at him. 'You're determined to go home this evening, congratulating yourself on having had a proper conversation, aren't you?'

'To use one of your favourite expressions, too right.'

'Marco was killed in an accident,' she said abruptly. 'A silly accident.'

Peter stood still and stared at her. 'God, I'm so sorry, Susie. That never occurred to me.'

'Don't apologise,' she said, shaking her head. 'You'd no reason to think he'd be dead.'

'Was it recent, if I might ask?'

'Six months ago. But it belongs to the past, and we're locking the past in a box, aren't we?'

Her voice broke, and she started walking again.

'I'm so sorry,' he repeated, catching her up.

'I know,' she said, her eyes on the ground. 'Everyone is. It doesn't help, though.'

28

The late evening sun beat down with intensity.

In the shade of the airport building, Peter sat side by side with Ned Riley, each of them with a beer, both staring beyond the grey landing strip in front of them to the distant heat-hazed horizon, an illusion of shimmering glass that fused the crimson earth with the clear blue sky.

From time to time, a small green lizard would dart past them, stop suddenly, look back at them, its eyes bright with cunning, and then hie away at speed.

'That's some heat,' Peter murmured, taking a swig of his beer. 'Susie reminded me yesterday that your summer's only just begun and that it's going to get even hotter. I'm not complaining, mind you—I signed up for this; I'm just remarking.'

Ned nodded. 'You'll get used to it.'

'She said that, too.'

'She's a great gal. You'd have to go a long way to find another as good as Susie. It's a cryin' shame about Marco, even if you couldn't figure out what he was saying. He never really mastered the lingo.'

He paused. 'To be honest, I didn't take to the bloke, but that's neither here nor there. Susie's bin in a state since he was killed.'

'It can't be easy for her, being out here on her own. At least, I assume she's on her own now.'

'She is in the way you mean. There's no one else, and there wouldn't be. He's not been dead that long, and you can tell she's still hurtin'. She'd never say she was, but you can take it from me, she is.

Shame they didn't have any kids. Havin' kids would've given her somethin' else to think about. But she's got friends in town, and she and Maisie are good mates, even though Maisie's a right gasbag and can fair bash your ears. Don't know how Susie can stand it, but she obviously can.' He shook his head. 'Yeah, she's a good'un, is Susie.'

'That's what I thought. She's going to be very pleasant to work with.'

They sat in silence for a few minutes, staring at the view.

'Thanks for showing me around today, Ned. It's been really interesting.'

'You're welcome, mate. As you can see, the airport's small, but it's big enough for our needs.'

'It's amazing you've got an airport at all in a small town like this.'

'Too right, it is. It was built not long after the CSA mine re-opened. The mine's about eleven or twelve kilometres north-west of Cobar.'

'What do they mine?'

'Copper. Started in the late nineteenth century, but the mine had to close in the 1920s 'cos of an underground fire that ended up burning for sixteen years. They finally opened it again about four years ago. It's the most modern underground mine in the whole of Australia,' he added proudly.

'From the small bit of the town I've seen, the place looks quite prosperous. I expect the mine helped with that.'

Ned nodded. 'It did. We got the hospital, the high school, a swimming pool, and even a weather station after the mine re-opened.

But the big thing is our water supply—for the past five years or so, water's bin piped into town from the Burrendong Dam. Drought or no drought, Cobar's always got water now, even though the population's fair doubled since the mine started up again.'

'So was the mine the reason why the airport was built?'

Ned nodded again. 'That, and also 'cos the government was set on funding airports in remote areas. They had this thing about people being able to hook up with the cities. We'd already got a natural surface runway here, which went way back to the 1930s, I think it was, so Cobar got an airport, and not long after that, a Flying Doctor Service.'

'For my sake, I'm glad it did.'

Ned smiled broadly at him. 'Have another coldie, Pete. You can't beat a cold Melbourne Bitter on a hot day.'

'You've twisted my arm,' Peter said, taking the can that Ned held out to him.

Ned sat back and pulled the metal tag from his can. 'I could've shown you more today, but I reckon you've seen all you need before you take over from Brian. You've gone over the plane and seen what we carry and where it's kept, and that's the main thing.'

'The way they've used the internal space is really something.'

'As far as planes go, you won't find anything more reliable than the Beagle 206s. There's only two ambulance Beagles in the whole of New South Wales, and we've got one of them. And it's not just their engine, mate—their landing gear's the best, too, as it's built to airline standards. When you've had a gander at some of the strips we've gotta land on, you'll appreciate that.'

Peter smiled at Ned. 'For the moment, I'll have to take your word for it.'

'You're taking over the day after tomorrow, aren't you?'

'That's the plan. Susie's taking me into Cobar tomorrow. She's going to show me around, introduce me to one or two people, including Brian, I think, and then it'll be all stations ahead the following day.'

'Too right, it will! Out here, outposts are called stations as often as they're called outposts or homesteads.'

Peter grinned at him. 'So I'm already speaking the lingo and I didn't even know it. How's that for a speedy settling-in?'

'Impressive, mate; that's what it is. As for Brian, I reckon you two will hit it off. He's an easy bloke to get on with, a good guy all round.

There was a call-out last night, you know. We don't often get called out later than dusk, but a sick baby took a turn for the worse just after midnight. I suggested he take you on the call with him, but he reckoned you'd still be fair zonked, having just arrived, so we let you be.'

'Yup, I *was* fair zonked, as you put it, with so much happening so quickly, and I still am. But you must be, too, being disturbed in the night like that.'

Ned shrugged. 'It doesn't happen that often. But it's no sweat if I have to fly at night. We'd only do a night flight if the landing strip can be lit by flares and the patient's condition is very serious. But it's not a nine to five kind of job this, and I wouldn't want it if it was.'

'It must be quite dramatic, flying at night.'

Ned nodded. 'It can be tricky. There are few towns, so there's generally no light at night, and if there's no moon it's even more difficult. It's just you, your GPS and your instruments. That can be hairy if you've gotta land on a small airstrip.'

'It sounds it.'

'Like I say, it doesn't happen often. More usually, we reach the outpost's strip at dusk. Even at that time, though, we need flares. I remind them every time to face the lights into the wind as I come in to land, and not to face them towards me. You can't take anything for granted, no matter how many times you do a thing.'

'I can see that.'

'And you've got to watch for birds, too. Those fork-tailed kites can be a hazard, always soaring above, looking for carrion. And the wedge-tailed eagle is just as bad. That's the largest of the local birds of prey and goes after kangaroos and lambs.' He shook his head. 'Nope, you've gotta know what you're doing when you fly one of these.'

'How long've you been the pilot for this station?'

'Since it opened. I was seconded here for two years, but it's turned out to be the longest two years I've ever known,' he said with a smile.

'Susie didn't mention any other pilot but you. Are you the only one?'

'Yup. Some base control stations have extra pilots on call —it depends on the State and the size of the control station —but this isn't a large station and they have to keep costs down, so there's just me.'

'It's a free service, isn't it?'

'Sure is; and it's not cheap to run. There's the upkeep of planes, the equipment to be serviced and replaced, the salaries to be paid, and obviously the cost of fuel. It all comes from donations, subscriptions and things like that, so they don't have money to waste. I'm on call twenty-four hours a day, ready to leave at any hour, day or night. Bloody marvel I am, I'd say.'

Peter laughed. 'D'you find yourself hanging around a lot?'

'Sure, but that's all part of the job. You won't know till you've done your radio clinics if you need me to fly you somewhere. Some days you won't, and you won't have any emergency call-outs, either. And other days, we'll hardly be out of the air.' He shrugged. 'That's the job, Pete.'

'I take my hat off to you. It can't be easy, being your own navigator, servicing the plane and also refuelling it yourself. That's a lot of different skills.'

'Like I say, a bloody marvel.' Ned took another gulp of his beer and grinned. 'I know I'm kinda blowing my own trumpet, but that's the truth. Some days we'll fly mile after mile over flat country, looking for one small homestead, and there'll be virtually no landmarks––no special rocks, no strangely shaped trees.

It's easy to get lost in the Outback when you're on the ground, but believe me, mate, you can also get lost in it when you're in the air.'

'I believe you.'

'One homestead looks pretty much like any other from above. Fortunately for me, more and more stations have now got their name written on top of their roof, and that helps a lot. But they haven't all done that yet.'

'Being a pilot's a skilled job all right.'

Ned nodded. 'You should see me land in a strong cross

wind or on a makeshift strip that's soft from a sudden rainfall. And you can fly into bad dust storms in the dry season just as you can in the wet. Dust storms ain't fussy about the weather they come in.

You're right, cobber, it takes skill to do the job, and the ability to keep going for as long as you must. There's days when I'm on duty for far more hours than I can log.'

'I didn't know the half of it before. One day's never going to be the same as the next, but that's part of the job's appeal.'

'But don't think there's no routine. There is, just like with any other job. But unlike them other jobs, you can start a day having had one eye open for the whole of the night.'

'How come?'

Ned finished his beer and wiped his mouth with the back of his hand. 'We could be on stand-by all night, ready for a dawn take-off, and then at the last moment, the patient improves and the flight's called off. Other times, we make that dawn flight.'

He paused. 'You startin' to think about getting on that Beagle over there and heading straight back to pommie land?'

'You're forgetting, you're the pilot, not me. It's your call where we end up.'

They smiled at each other.

'That last Flying Doctor before you, Pete,' Ned said. 'He couldn't blow the froth off a glass of beer. You're gonna be fair dinkum, I can tell.'

'Thanks, Ned. And I'm pretty sure I've struck lucky in having you as my pilot. Cheers!' He inclined his can towards Ned, put it to his lips and downed the rest of his beer.

'More of the amber fluid, mate?' Ned asked, pointing to the cool box. 'Me, I can't drink any more as I'm on call, but you might as well go ahead while you can. In one more day, you'll be on call, too.'

'So this is where you guys are?' Susie appeared round the corner of the building.

'G'day again,' she said, coming across to them. She pulled up a chair and sat down on the other side of Peter.

Ned reached into the cool box and pulled out a can of beer. 'Have a cold tinny,' he said, holding it out to her.

She shook her head. 'Thanks, but no, thanks.' She smiled at them. 'I thought you might have reached the beer part of Peter's visit by now. When you've finished your drink, why don't both of you come across to the base station? I've made something to eat. It's nothing special, but it'll keep the wolf from the door.'

Ned shook his head. 'I'll pass on the meal, Susie, thanks all the same. I've had your cooking before. So far, I've always survived it, but I wouldn't want to tempt Fate.' He threw back his head and laughed.

She arched an amused smile at him. 'Your problem is, you've got so used to the stuff you cook all the time, you've lost any appreciation of really good food.'

He grinned at her. 'You don't say. And there was I, thinking that it was 'cos you ain't able to boil so much as an egg without burning it!

But much as I'd like to see if there's bin any improve-ment, I can't—I told my mates I'd see them in town when I'd clued up the doc. It's my turn to shout for the round, which is gonna give me the irrits as I'll have to stick to lemonade.'

Peter threw him a look of surprise. 'How can you go into town if you're on call?'

'Portable transceivers; that's how. They mean freedom for us, Pete. We can get calls from anywhere and make them from anywhere. And they're really easy to carry around.'

'What I said about transceivers probably got lost among everything else,' Susie said, standing up. 'But we all have them. We'll get off then, Ned, and leave you in peace to finish up here. We'll be in town tomorrow so I doubt we'll see you till the following day.'

'Will Pete be doin' the radio clinic from his place or the base?'

'The base to begin with, both morning and afternoon. He'll need several sessions with me there to help him before he goes it alone. It's one thing to know how to do a thing; it's quite another to do it by yourself.'

She turned to Peter. 'If you're ready, then, we'll go,' she said, and she started to walk towards the corner of the airport building.

Peter got up quickly, swallowed the last of his beer, thanked Ned and hurried after Susie.

She glanced at him in amusement. 'So it's Pete, is it,' she said. 'You know, I reckon Ned may have got it right. I think it was a Peter who left England, but it was a Pete who stepped off the plane.'

She stopped walking and held out her hand to him. 'Welcome to Australia, Pete.'

Peter pulled off his boots and picked up his canvas espadrilles. He banged them on the floor to check there weren't any scorpions or spiders inside, slipped his feet into them, sat down on the end of his bed, and looked around his room.

The man who'd lived in the house before him can't have been married, he thought, and he certainly hadn't been into house beautiful.

What he'd said to Susie about the place needing a cushion or two and a rug was absolutely right. Claire had used cushions to brighten their rooms in Birmingham, and he'd got used to something rather more pleasant than this to come home to.

But a bit of colour here and there was all it needed. He'd make a list of what he wanted, and ask Susie to build in time for him to go to a few shops in Cobar the following day. Maybe she'd even give him a hand; after all, she'd made the base station comfortable enough.

He yawned, lay back on the bed, stretched out his legs and clasped his hands together behind his head, and stared up at the fan on the ceiling.

Working with Susie was going to be fine. She seemed very pleasant and easy to be with, and she was good-looking, which always helped.

It was true she didn't have Claire's real loveliness, but she was striking in her own way. On the down side, she could be a bit forthright at times, but on the plus side, at least he'd always know what she was thinking.

Not like with Claire. He'd really got it wrong with Claire, seeing her as something she wasn't, thinking she'd want something she didn't.

Mentally, he pulled himself up. He was going to have to make a far greater effort to forget Claire—to forget how truly wonderful it had been to be with her. And he'd have to work much harder at not feeling so anguished that she'd chosen to let him go off alone. It hurt too much.

Admittedly, it was still early days, but letting himself give in to his misery at not being with her, wasn't helping him to move on. He'd need peace of mind if he was going to enjoy the next stage of his life—a life without Claire—and he'd only get that if he eliminated her entirely from his thoughts.

But how he was going to do that, he didn't know.

Yawning again, he looked at his watch. It was still relatively early, but it had been a long day in which he'd had a lot of information to absorb, and he felt more than ready to turn in. He decided to do just that, and he swung himself off the bed and stood up.

As he did so, out of the corner of his eye he caught sight of the flimsy blue air letters he'd bought in Sydney that were on the table next to his radio apparatus. He glanced at his bed, and hesitated.

As he'd drifted into sleep the night before, it had come to him with sudden clarity that there was one short message he absolutely had to send to England, but he'd fallen asleep before he could get up and write it.

But it wouldn't take more than a moment or two to write the message now, and if he did that, he could post it in Cobar. If he left it till the morning, he was bound to forget to do it in the rush to get out.

He went over to the table, sat down, took a pen from his shirt pocket, pulled one of the air letters towards him and started writing. A few minutes later, he leaned back against his chair and read to himself what he'd written.

DEAR ALEX,

I know we agreed we wouldn't contact each other after I'd left, and that I wouldn't send you or anyone else my address, as we all thought it would be much easier for me to make a fresh start if I wasn't continually being reminded of the people I'd left behind—the people I knew I was going to miss enormously.

I still think this was the right decision, but I can now see that I'd never be at ease if I didn't know that we could contact each other, should there ever be a need to do so.

That hit me the minute I saw Heathrow recede into the distance, and I bought some air letters as soon as I landed in Sydney. I couldn't write to you, though, until I had a permanent address.

I do have one now, and I have a job. I've been taken on by The Royal Flying Doctor Service in New South Wales, working out of their Cobar Station. I can't believe my luck, not only in finding a job so quickly, but in finding one that seems to have been tailor-made for me, and on the fringe of the Outback, too.

I obviously have your present address, but if you move, would you send me your new address? You'll find my address on this letter.

Now that I know that if you or anyone else ever wants to get in touch with me, they'll be able to do so, I can relax.

Keep my address to yourself, mate. But if there comes a time when you're sure I'd want you to pass it on, it'd be okay to do so. I trust you.

Cheers,

Peter

HE PRINTED his address under his name, folded the paper, sealed the sides, addressed it to Alex on the front, and wrote his address on the back of the letter.

As he put down his pen, he felt a massive rush of relief. At least one of his Birmingham friends would know where he was.

Unlike the other friends he'd made in Birmingham, Claire would always be able to contact his parents if she'd kept their address. Of course, she might not have done, but in that case, she could always contact them through the Mission, and she'd know that.

But contacting his parents would be as far as she'd get —she wouldn't be given his address, assuming she wanted it.

He'd written briefly to his parents from Sydney as soon as he'd been sent his address in Cobar so that they would know where he was, but he'd forbidden them ever to give his address to anyone—not without his permission.

He'd been determined to cut himself off from everyone other than his folks, and sending his address to Alex was going to be the only exception he allowed himself.

He went into the kitchen, propped up the letter against the kettle so that he'd see it first thing the following morning when he went in to make his coffee, which would ensure that he remembered to take it with him to Cobar, and then he turned and went back to his bedroom.

Standing in the doorway, he looked around the silent, empty room. His eyes lingered on the bed he'd have given anything to be sharing with Claire. The pain of not being with her sliced through him, and he felt a sudden over-whelming sense of aloneness.

He shook his head. He absolutely had to forget Claire. All that was over. It had been over the moment she'd chosen England over him.

He was never again going to hold her in his arms, hug her tight and feel her warmth spreading through him, and he was only prolonging his agony by allowing himself to wallow in what he'd lost.

But oh, how he missed her!

An image of Claire's laughing face forced itself into his mind, ramming into his consciousness the enormity of what he'd lost. Pressing his hands hard against his eyes, he tried in vain to push it back.

His throat constricted by grief, he spun round, ran back through the kitchen to the rear door, flung the door wide open and rushed outside.

Standing in the middle of the narrow veranda, his heart beating furiously, he shut his eyes, tilted his face to the sky, and drew his breath in long, deep gasps.

The immediacy of his pain gradually receded, leaving in its wake a bleak desolation.

Breathing more evenly, he opened his eyes, went up to the wooden railing, leaned against it, and stared across his yard to the desert that lay beyond, a vast continuum of red, broken only by the vivid green of the solitary trees that dotted the landscape.

The Outback was just as Susie had described it. A place with its own beauty, she'd said, or something like that.

And indeed, stretching out in front of him was a beautiful empty canvas upon which he could paint the rest of his life, and his every instinct told him that it would excite and fulfil him to do so.

He leaned against the wooden veranda post, and watched the sun sink slowly into the exhausted land, and the blue sky shatter into vivid streaks of flaming red, orange and yellow.

The isolated trees, at first dark silhouettes standing proud against the massive orb of burnished gold, blurred gradually into a drama of black, and were lost in the all-consuming band of lapis lazuli that crept inexorably across the wide sky.

A sense of peace filled him.

This was his home now, a home that stood on the brink of an unknown world, a world that offered challenge, excitement, variety and freedom.

It was a world for which he'd paid a great emotional price, one that he'd never expected to have to pay, but there was nothing about his decision he regretted.

Except Claire.

Losing Claire was something he was going to have to learn to live with. He would just have to take each day at a time, putting one foot in front of the other, until the time came that she no longer invaded his thoughts night and day.

He would never stop loving her—that much he knew—but if he didn't expect too much too soon, he'd one day be able to think about her without it hurting so very much.

Turning, he went slowly back into the house.

As he passed the kettle, he glanced at the letter.

Cutting himself off quite as completely as he'd originally

intended hadn't seemed such a great idea, after all, and he was confident that he'd done the right thing by sending his address to Alex.

If anyone would know what best to do in circumstances that might arise, that person was Alex.

'You'll not get a better view than the one we've just had. It's pretty flat around here for the most part, but as you saw, there are some rocky hills to the east and some wooded areas, and also a number of dry water courses,' Susie said as she led the way back to the car.

'I thought that seeing the sun set over Cobar would be a good way to end the day. You can see now where the name came from. The Aborigines who lived here before we did used to call the place *Kubbur*, which means Burnt Earth.'

'They certainly got it right. Funnily enough, Cobar's not that different from an English town. There's a mixture of old and new houses in both, and the houses stand in small gardens. Also, both have wide roads and tree-lined pavements. It's the colour of the earth that's different.'

'And the kangaroos, emus, echnidas, snakes, goannas and so on,' she added.

'On second thoughts, maybe they aren't so alike,' he said with a grin. 'You forgot wombats.'

'Not really, I didn't. It was a fluke we saw one today. Usually, you only see their burrows, which are like giant molehills, or you might see their cube-shaped dung. They don't come out till night to graze. They're very shy and if they think you've spotted them, they'll shoot back into their burrow.'

'That's interesting.' He glanced at her. 'Thanks for everything, Susie. The day's really flown by—I've learned a lot and enjoyed it enormously.'

'No worries.' They reached the car. 'I've enjoyed it, too,' she said, unlocking the door. 'It's been fun showing you around. I've obviously got friends in Cobar—Maisie and I are good mates, for a start—but it's been a while since I've gone out for the day with someone else.

Normally, my mates and I just get together for a galah session. I've not had a day like today since Marco died, and I was more ready for such a day than I realised.'

'I'm glad I've been of help, albeit unwittingly.' They climbed up into the car.

'You know,' he said, clicking his seat belt shut. 'It's sometimes easier to talk about things you feel deeply about to an outsider, which is what I am as I never met Marco. If you ever want to talk about him, feel free. Or, as Ned would say, you can bash my ear any time.'

She nodded. 'I'll remember that. But I think I'm past that time now. I hope so, anyway.'

'Just keep it in the back of your mind.'

'If you insist, Doc.' Her hands on the wheel, she looked across at him. 'You know, you really ought to see some of the other places around here, too. If you want, we can go further into the Outback one day, to Louth perhaps. It's a small village on the Darling River. There's a road from Cobar that goes straight there.'

'I'd like that a lot; thanks,' he said.

'Burke's also worth visiting,' she added. 'I bet you've heard of Burke. Or Back o' Bourke.'

He shook his head.

'That's what people often call the Outback. Burke's at the head of the River Darling so there are lots of billabongs there, as well as saltbush plains and mulga scrub. It's heaven for anyone who likes birdwatching. But it might be a bit far to go in one day.'

'I'll leave that for you to decide.'

He stared through the windscreen and smiled at nothing.

'Yes, it's been a really good day. People couldn't have been friendlier. I liked Brian a lot. It'll be a great help, him running through the sick patients' list with me before I do my first clinic tomorrow, and then sitting in with me.

Afterwards, he's going to take me through some of the admin things.'

'I can help you, too, you know!' she said sharply. 'There's not much I don't know about the patients—I've sat through enough radio clinics.'

He threw her a quick glance. 'I know that. But there're bound to be one or two medical things you might not know, and Brian will.'

'I suppose so.' Her voice was tinged with lingering annoyance.

'If I get a call-out tomorrow, can you come with me? I'd feel better if you were with me the first couple of times.'

'Brian is going with you if there's a call-out. And don't think I don't know what you're doing,' she added tartly.

'What d'you mean?'

'You think I'm angry with you, so you're trying to butter me up.'

He angled his head to look at her face. 'Is it working?'

She looked across at him, and laughed. 'I'm laughing so it must be. No, you're right about Cobar people,' she went on.

'With very few exceptions, they're a nice bunch. They were brilliant when Marco died. I'm lucky to have had the support I had. It wiped out any ideas about jumping on a plane for England.'

'I'm not surprised you decided to stay. What with the people and the scenery, this place seems to have everything. Above all, as soon as you get out of the town, it's got the sort of openness I love. I only wish Claire had been prepared to give it a chance.'

'That's the ex-fiancée, I presume.'

'You presume right. She didn't want to live anywhere but in England, and I wanted to come here. It isn't the sort of thing you can compromise about, so now she's in England and I'm over here, and she's free to date anyone she wants.' He hesitated. 'If I'm honest, the thought of her with someone else really hurts.'

'But you're free to date whoever you want, too.'

'It's much too soon for anything like that.'

'And she probably feels the same. Over here, women have it much easier than men as there are far more men around than women.'

She threw him a smile. 'But I don't think you need worry. When you're ready to paint the town red again, you won't have any problem getting a woman.'

'I suppose being a Flying Doctor *is* a glamorous-sounding job, and women go for that sort of thing.'

'There you go again! Women go for that sort of thing,' she mimicked. 'That's a bit of a generalisation, isn't it, and a bit of a put-down for women.'

He gave her a rueful smile. 'I guess it is. Sorry.'

'Anyway, I didn't exactly mean that.'

'I don't get you.'

'You want me to flatter you?'

His brow creased, and then cleared.

He gave an awkward laugh of embarrassment. 'Got you. It lets you off the flattery. Not that I've any ego left to flatter since Claire chose England over me. But I think we'd better change the subject.'

'What subject shall we go on to, then?'

'How about you? Tell me to mind my own business if you want. You're a good-looking woman surrounded by lots of men, and I wondered if you had anyone in your sights. You know what I mean.'

'Well, you've certainly stopped mincing your words—you're becoming more Aussie by the minute. No, there isn't; I'm not ready for anyone else yet. I'm still missing Marco.'

'I'm sorry. I shouldn't have asked that. I suppose six months isn't that long.'

'Too right, it isn't.'

They drove along in silence for a while.

'Can I buy you dinner tonight as a thank you for today?' he volunteered. 'Only if you want, though. You might have had enough of my company by now.'

'Tut, tut, Pete. Could that be the ego calling out for attention, the ego you don't have?'

He laughed. 'Not a bit of it. It's just that it's been a good day, and I thought it might be nice to end it by having a meal together. But if you don't want to...'

'No, that sounds okay. I'm getting too used to having dinner alone.' She paused. 'If you want, I could cook something.'

He shook his head. 'You made lunch yesterday. I enjoyed it, despite Ned's dire warnings,' he added with a wry grin.

'But let's eat out. Choose the place you like best of all. We'll end today in style.'

She smiled at him. 'Good thinking. We'll go to the hotel restaurant.'

AFTER DINNER, Susie dropped Peter off at his bungalow, drove back to the base station, parked her car next to Maisie's and went through the front door and into the sitting room.

'How ya going, Maisie?' she asked, tossing her bag on to the sofa. 'I'm sorry you've had to do a massive stint today. I owe you.'

Maisie shook her head. 'No, you don't. I was pleased to help out. And it's not as if we've been busy—there weren't any call-outs, and Brian did the clinics from town. I can read here just as well as at home. You were long overdue some time off, and I'm glad you enjoyed it.'

'Who said I enjoyed it?'

'Your face did. You look more relaxed than I've seen you look for ages. That new doctor's done you a world of good, and in two days only. I can't imagine what you'll look like after several months with him.'

'You're daft, that's what you are. It's not the doctor that's the tonic—it's having something to do. The last whacker we had here knew it all and I was always being sidelined. Until he got ill, that is.

Pete's different. Even though he's highly qualified, he doesn't hesitate to ask for advice. He's not coming across as another know-it-all. Or not so far, anyway.'

'So the happy look on your face is all about his mind, is it?'

'And that he can work as one of a team. That's very

important, too. I can tell that Ned likes him, and Ned's a really good judge of character, so that means something. No, I think it's going to be fun working with Pete. He's not up himself, and I'll enjoy having someone intelligent to talk to.'

'Charming!' Maisie exclaimed. She picked up one of the cushions from the sofa and threw it at Susie, who managed to duck in time.

'You should see your face.' Maisie giggled. 'It's a picture. Don't worry, I know what you mean.'

'And you know what I didn't mean. I can't believe I just did the very thing I was sniffy about Pete doing to me earlier today, which is saying something that could be taken as a put-down of the other person.'

'No worries, it's easily done. Especially when you're still thinking about Doctor Pete and his amazing brain.

It *is* just his brain we're talking about, isn't it? I've yet to meet him, but with the radio on this morning and the galah session in progress, I couldn't help overhearing the gossip. In fact, the moment you hit Cobar, the townswomen started yacking about him.'

'What were they saying?'

Maisie put her finger under her chin and screwed up her face in a thoughtful pose. 'Hmm. Funnily enough, I don't recall anyone mentioning how intelligent he looked.' She giggled.

'Okay, so what *did* they say?'

'Well, I know he's got fair hair, is tall, well built—neither too fat nor too thin—that he's very good-looking and has got piercing blue eyes. Oh, yes; and he fills his trousers well. They're kinda hoping to see him in shorts soon.'

She went into peals of laughter and made a move towards the front door.

'Poor Pete. I've a feeling there's going to be a record

attendance at his first few monthly clinics,' Susie said, pulling a face. She opened the front door and stood back to let Maisie go through.

Maisie went out on to the veranda, stopped and looked back at Susie. 'Get a good night's sleep. Something tells me you're gonna be flat out like a lizard drinking with an awful lot of requests for home visits tomorrow. I'll be here just before eight in the morning.'

'But you're not on tomorrow,' Susie said in surprise.

Maisie put her hand to her forehead, pushed her black curls away from her eyes and sighed. 'Oh, dear; I feel the onset of a headache. I need a doctor to check it out and make sure there's nothing sinister going on.'

Laughing loudly, Maisie ran across to her car, waving her hand in the air as she went.

Susie waved back, and then stood and watched from the veranda as the car headed along the dirt track towards the road, where it turned left.

Maisie would have to drive down Lerida Road, which meant she'd pass Pete's bungalow on her way into town, she thought as she turned to go back into the house.

Would she slow down when she drove past his house and glance towards it to see if the lights were on, she wondered.

Not that they would be—he'd been really whacked when she'd dropped him back at his place, and he'd said he was going straight to bed, ready for the early start the following day.

She went into the sitting room, stood in the middle of the room, and looked around her. She could almost hear the emptiness.

The house had felt empty since Marco had died, but this was different. After a day in and around the town, it would have been lovely to have come home and sat with a drink, talking to a man. Yes, to a man, not a woman.

For the first time since Marco's death, she felt a sudden longing for male companionship.

She'd told Pete that she wasn't ready for anyone else in her life, and she wasn't—not in the way they'd been talking about.

But something had definitely changed in the last day or two.

It must be that spending time with a man again had begun to wake up feelings that had been asleep since the terrible day on which she'd driven Marco to his death.

31

B irmingham
      February, 1971

MAKING her way awkwardly between the crowded tables, Mary followed Claire to the ward sisters' area in the far corner of the hospital canteen.

They put their drinks on one of the Formica-topped tables and sat down.

'No one's going to mind if you sit here with me, Mary,' Claire said, glancing around. 'After all, you'd be a ward sister, too, if you weren't about to be a mum.'

'Too bad if they do.' Mary gave a dismissive shrug. 'But why no cake today?' she remarked in surprise, staring at the empty patch of table in front of Claire. 'You always have cake at the end of your shift.'

'And I still do, but not today. I'm having dinner with Alex tonight and I want to be able to eat my meal. We're going to an Italian place we've been to several times, and the food's really good.'

'You're seeing quite a lot of Alex these days, aren't you? Is it serious?' Mary asked, eyeing Claire over the rim of her cup.

'You make it sound as if we're dating, and we're not. We're just friends. Going on a date is altogether different.'

Mary looked at her doubtfully. 'I'm not certain that Alex would see it as different.'

Claire hesitated. 'I'm sure he does. He probably still feels guilty about Peter going, and is trying to make up for it. He's never made a pass at me or anything.'

'He'd know you weren't ready for anything like that. But think about it, Claire. He's been taking you out for a number of weeks now—on your own, not in a group. That sounds pretty much like dating to me.'

'God, I hope you're wrong! I've never thought about him in that way. Obviously, I like him a lot—he's great company and he's been really kind and helpful—but that's all it is.'

'Then maybe it's time you tried to think about him differently. From where I'm sitting, he's earned that at least. If I'm right and he's nuts about you, look how patient he's been.'

Claire shook her head. 'I'm not ready to think about anyone as more than a friend.

The trouble is,' her voice caught, 'even though Peter's been gone for almost three months, I still miss him so much that it hurts. I can't help myself.'

Blinking furiously, she looked quickly down at the table.

Mary leaned across and squeezed Claire's hand. 'If you gave Alex a chance, it might help you to get over Peter.

But only if you genuinely felt something for him. I'm not

suggesting you use him. There'd be nothing worse than you dating Alex because you thought it'd hurt Peter if he knew.'

'I wouldn't do anything so mean—I like him too much for that. And I owe him so much. Apart from everything else, I wouldn't have passed my driving test if it hadn't been for Alex. No, I'm sure what I feel for Alex is nothing to do with wanting to get back at Peter.'

'Liking someone's a good place to begin.' Mary sat back, a satisfied smile on her face. 'It must be a welcome change for a guy as handsome as Alex to have someone who's not throwing themselves at him.'

'He's not as good-looking as Peter.'

'I don't agree. I think he is, but in a different way. There are lots of nurses around here who wouldn't mind being a notch on his bedpost. You'd be the envy of them all if you ever went down that path.'

Claire sat upright and stared at her friend, mock horror on her face. 'Why, Mary! Are you encouraging me to go to bed with him, you a good Catholic girl?'

Mary smiled. 'I suppose I am, if you think you genuinely care for him.'

'Well, I certainly need to do something that'll banish Peter from my mind, and I'll think about what you've said.

Before I forget, though, are you and Keith coming to the dance in the nurses' home? It's two weeks on Saturday. You obviously won't want to dance, but it'd be great if you could come.'

'You bet! This might be the last time we're able to go out without having to get a babysitter, and I intend to make the most of it.'

'That's good. Alex will be there, too.'

'I wouldn't have thought it his thing,' Mary said in surprise.

'Nor me! I don't think I've ever actually seen him on a dance floor—not even in the days of Karen. He always used to prop up the bar with his friends on such occasions.'

'It says a lot for what he thinks of you.'

'I don't know about that. But it does show how much he's changed since we first met him. Well, you know he has, you've seen how helpful he's been. And he's not—how shall I put it—not as brash as he was.'

Mary smiled broadly. 'See, you're already thinking differently about him. I can tell from those few words. I suspect you're closer to putting a certain person behind you than you realise.

I'm looking forward to getting to know the new Alex. And Keith is, too—up to now, they've never said more than a few words to each other.'

'Thanks, Mary.' Claire sat back and smiled at Mary. 'It's so lovely you being here today. It's just like old times. I really miss you,' she added a wistful note in her voice.

'I know we still see each other, but it's not the same as working together. Between missing you and missing Peter, I've been a right mess.'

'Is there any news from the intrepid traveller?'

Claire shook her head. 'Not a word. But I didn't expect to hear from him.'

'Are you still happy about him cutting himself off in such a way? Well not happy, but you know what I mean.'

'Yes I am—it was the right thing to do, for me as well as for him. So far, there's not been an hour when I haven't thought about him, but knowing that I really can't contact him will help me forget about him. I'm sure of it.'

'But he can contact you, can't he? He knows where you live and work.'

'Not for much longer, he won't. Alex is talking about

looking for a vacancy for a GP, and I'm now ready to go after another job. After I've moved—and after Alex has moved—Peter won't know where we are or where we're working.

That'll actually be a relief. It's a bit unsettling, knowing he could contact me at any time. I'll feel better when that's no longer possible.'

'All I can say is, you're made of stronger stuff than I am,' Mary said. 'I would have at least asked him to send his address. After all, you never know.'

'But what would be the point of writing to each other? I don't need a penfriend, and he could never be any more than that. Australia's not exactly round the corner. And I'd feel awful if I heard he'd found someone else. I know he'll do so at some point, but I'd rather not know about it.'

'I'm sure that's true. By the same token, he'd feel very strange if he knew you were seeing Alex, whatever your relationship.

And he could be quite upset that you'd taken up with one of his friends. I imagine that would feel much worse than you being with a total stranger.'

Claire nodded. 'Then it's just as well that no one will be able to tell him.'

'When d'you think you're likely to leave Birmingham?'

'It won't be for a bit. I intend to be around for at least a few weeks after your baby's here.'

'I'm so glad. I want you to be one of the first people he or she sees.'

'Me, too! But I hope to be gone before the end of the year. While I hate the thought of moving away from you, I need to make a fresh start. Maybe it'll be with Alex; maybe it won't—I don't yet know.

But wherever I go, I'll make sure that it's not so far that I can't get back to see you.'

Mary put her hand on her rounded stomach. 'The baby's just jumped. It's saying it's going to hold you to that.'

They both laughed.

Claire glanced at her watch and groaned. 'I hate to say it but I must go. There're a couple of student nurses in my section who can't be trusted to do the simplest of things without someone standing over them. I've left them to it for long enough.'

She stood up.

'I'll see you at the dance, then,' Mary said, getting up. 'And Alex, too.'

32

T *wo weeks later*

CLAIRE FOLLOWED Alex into his sitting room, her high-heeled shoes dangling from her fingers.

Seeing him head for the cocktail cabinet, she went across to the armchair opposite his dark brown leather sofa and sat down. Dropping her shoes on the floor, she curled her legs under her.

Alex picked up a bottle and two glasses, moved over to the sofa, and sat down. He put the bottle and glasses on the coffee table, glanced at Claire, and gave her a wry smile.

'Why don't you come and sit next to me, Claire? If I promise not to leap on you. It feels odd, you being on the other side of the room, especially when we've had such a great evening.'

He tapped the place beside him.

Claire hesitated. Then she uncoiled her legs, and went and sat next to him.

'So you really did enjoy the dance?' she asked, leaning back against the leather and turning her head to look at him. 'I wouldn't have thought it your sort of thing.'

'To be honest, nor would I. I usually go to a dance to pick up a woman, and I do no more than it takes to catch my prey.'

He moved closer to her, slid his arm behind her shoulders and pulled her gently to him.

'But that was the old Alex, and I amazed myself by how much I did enjoy the evening.' He tightened his arm around her, bringing her closer still.

She stiffened.

Leaning down, he kissed her lightly on the top of her head. 'You've reformed me,' he murmured into her hair.

'That's good,' she said.

She heard the nervous tremor in her voice, and she sensed him glance down at her.

He pulled slightly back and relaxed his hold on her. 'But I feel I ought to warn you that we're both in danger of being sued,' he said, a trace of laughter in his voice.

She raised her head and looked at him in amused surprise. 'Sued? What d'you mean? Who might sue us?'

'The brewery. On every other occasion, my contribution alone to the night's takings ensured that the evening was in profit. I let them down tonight, and you're the reason why.'

She laughed, and again rested her head on his shoulder.

'So what did you think of Keith?' she asked. 'I saw you talking to him when Mary and I were coming back from the loo.'

'I liked him. I've seen him around over the years, of course, and we've exchanged a few words in the past, but

I've never really spoken to him, not like tonight. He seems a nice guy.'

'Good,' she said, happily. 'With Mary being my closest friend, I really hoped you'd get on with Keith.'

'You've no idea how pleased I am to hear that.' He kissed the top of her head again. 'It makes me feel as if you're starting to see us as a couple, and not just as good friends.'

A sudden stillness weighted the air.

'And is that what you want?' she asked at last. 'It doesn't feel strange to you, dating the ex of one of your best friends?'

'No, it doesn't. I think Peter would want us both to be happy, and if this makes us happy.'

He shrugged. 'And yes, it *is* what I want. At first, I felt bloody about Peter going, and about my part in it, and I was determined to help you as much as I could.

But it's a long time since guilt was my motive for wanting to see you. You've become very special to me, Claire, but I think you know that.'

He angled his head to look down at her. 'And what about you? Is this something you want?'

'I'm beginning to think it might be,' she said, resting her cheek lightly against his chest.

She felt the beat of his heart quicken.

Tensing, she inched back and straightened up.

'Don't worry,' he said with a rueful smile 'I'm not going to attempt to push you into anything. It's enough for me to know that you can see us as a couple.'

'I don't deserve you,' she said. 'You've been such a good friend.'

He stood up. 'Friendship's the best foundation of all, so that'll do me for the moment. I'll walk you home now, and then come back and have a cold shower.'

Both laughed.

Claire rose to her feet and faced him. 'Thanks, Alex,' she said quietly.

'A pleasure, lovely lady,' he murmured.

Raising his hand, he trailed his fingers down the side of her face, and then he leaned down and kissed her firmly on the lips.

After a moment's hesitation, she kissed him back.

Then she broke away from him, turned round and went across the room to her shoes, and slipped them on.

He picked his key up from the table, and held out his hand to her. With a shy smile, she took it.

33

C *obarshire*
   March, 1971

PETER SETTLED back into his seat and stared down through the cockpit window at the seemingly never-ending carpet of ochre-yellow dappled with green.

'I still can't get over how slowly it looks as if we're going,' he called across to Ned, raising his voice to be heard above the drone of the plane's engine. 'It's like we're not moving at all, but are just hovering above the ground.'

'Believe me, we're moving all right. Our cruising speed's two hundred miles per hour. Look at the dials,' Ned shouted back. He nodded towards the flight panel.

Peter gave a low whistle.

'I reckon you're getting quite dinky-di at all this, Pete. It's your twentieth call-out since you started, and that's not countin' the monthly clinics. I checked the log this morning.'

'I can well believe it. It's been non-stop since my first radio clinic, but I've loved every single minute of it.

And as I'm still missing Claire like mad, and it's at its worst when I've nothing to do, it's a relief that my days have been as full as they've been.'

They fell silent for a few minutes.

'Yup.' Ned broke into the silence. 'You've certainly had a fair number of call-outs. And at a good time of day, and there's bin nothin' too serious.

It's bin a bonzer way for you to get used to the job. And 'cos you've gone to a different station every time, you've already met a lot of the homesteaders on the outposts.'

'I was tempted to say too right, but I won't,' Peter said with a smile. 'While it might make me sound like an Aussie, it'd be cheating. If you have to think consciously about saying something the Australian way, then you're not yet a real Aussie.'

'You'll get there, cobber. How are you findin' the radio clinics?'

'Scary, but I enjoy them, if that doesn't sound contradictory. So far, I've done them all from the base station as I quite like having Susie on hand in case something technical goes wrong.'

'Susie reckons the female population is cracking up, the number of calls from women you bin getting.'

Ned glanced across at Peter and grinned.

'Tell me about it. It feels as if just about every woman in New South Wales has needed medical advice in the past couple of months. There can't be many left that I haven't met on air.'

'And soon there won't be many left you haven't met in person, either. I've never seen so many lining up at the monthly clinics to be checked over. Especially the unmarried ones,' Ned added with a laugh.

'Very funny,' Peter said with a wry smile. 'The novelty will soon wear off; you'll see.'

'I'm thinking you'd do well to have a nurse with you at all times,' Ned went on cheerfully. 'A sort of chaperone to protect you from the man-hungry, you might say.'

He burst out laughing again.

'I suggest we talk about something else. Tell me about this Will Jarvis we're off to see. He's a drover, isn't he?'

Ned nodded. 'And a fine drover at that. He's worked for the Malloys since he was a young lad. It's not like him to let his horse throw him. Let's hope his leg's not too badly injured—he'll be needed on the ranch.'

'It was the chief stockman who phoned. He said Will looked pretty bad, but pain'll do that to you. And from what he said, it may not just be his leg, but his back, too.

At least they had the good sense not to move him. The accident happened just outside the main house, and that's where we'll find him.'

'I wondered how long it'd be before we were called to the Malloys,' Ned said, shaking his head. 'I'll wager those two teenage girls of theirs will have bin bashing Ruth and Frank's ears since the moment they heard that a new doc had arrived, and even better, that he was young and unattached. They'll be keen on having a gander at you, mate.'

'Will Jarvis *must* be a loyal worker indeed if he encouraged his horse to throw him so badly that he damaged his leg and back, and all to oblige the girls.'

Ned laughed. 'You've got a point there. But I'm also surprised you've not yet bin called there on account of Ruth

Malloy. She's fair crook. She's got chronic heart disease, and the slightest excitement sets it off.

I just hope this business with Will doesn't bring on one of her attacks.'

Peter nodded. 'Thanks for the heads-up, Ned. I'll check her out while I'm there.'

'Which'll be soon. We'll be landing in a coupla minutes.' Ned peered through the window at the ground below. 'Yup, we're not far off now. Luckily, the strip's close to the homestead so they don't have to bring the ute to the plane.'

Peering down through the cockpit window, Peter saw that the earth was starting to tilt upwards towards them, and that the sparse mulga trees that dotted the sweeping landscape seemed about to topple over.

He threw a quick glance at Ned's hands as Ned put the nose of the aircraft down. To his relief, they were steady at the controls.

His ears popping, he looked back through the window at the rapidly advancing wide strip of satiny-yellow earth that stood out proud from its matt surround.

Looking back at Ned, he saw that he was trimming for the approach. Instinctively, he put his hand on the buckle of his seat belt as the yellow earth rushed up to meet them.

The Beagle's wheels brushed the earth, touched down with a bump on the hard surface, and held the ground as Ned taxied the plane and brought it to a standstill.

Peter felt himself relax, and he let his hand fall from his belt.

'Like I say, Pete,' Ned said, turning and grinning at him. 'You'll get used to it eventually.'

·   ·   ·

FEELING himself the object of a lot of curious stares, and strongly aware that he was about to be sized up as a doctor, Peter walked towards the homestead, a fairly large single-floor building that stood high off the ground on posts.

Built of wood, it had a corrugated iron roof, and a veranda that looked about twelve feet deep that ran along the front of the house, and probably round the back, too, Peter thought.

A variety of ferns and other greenery overflowed from pots that rested on stands of different heights that had been placed at the outer edges of the veranda to block the direct rays of the sun.

He went across to the group of people surrounding the man who was lying on the ground outside the white wooden fence that encircled the house. He was shaded by a large umbrella that had been opened up and positioned so as to cover him.

The man who was standing closest to the injured man, stepped forward, his face anxious.

'I'm Frank Malloy,' he said, and held out his hand to Peter.

'I'm Pete Henderson,' Peter said as they shook hands.

He knelt down next to the man on the ground and gave him a reassuring smile. 'I take it you're Will. G'day, Will.'

Will gave a slight nod.

Peter put his hand on Will's shoulder. 'If possible, try not to move. I'm going to take a look at you, and I'll do my best not to hurt you.'

'Okay, Doc,' Will said, his voice weak.

Very gently, Peter ran his hands down Will's vertebrae and across his pelvis.

'There's a break in the pelvis, Mr Malloy,' he said, getting up. 'And also in the third lumbar vertebra. I'll obviously need to get him X-rayed to be sure, but I'm pretty certain the X-rays will confirm that. And he's got a bad break in the left femur. The bone'll definitely need pinning.'

'There's coffee over here,' a woman called to them as she came out on to the veranda, carrying a tray with a coffee pot and mugs.

With a smile towards the group, she moved slightly to her right, put the tray on the veranda table, and then came down the steps towards them.

'I heard what you said,' she told Peter. 'That's bad news. I'm Ruth Malloy, by the way.'

She was looking a little blue around the lips, Peter thought.

'I'm Pete Henderson,' he said. 'If you don't mind me asking, are you feeling all right, Mrs Malloy? You're looking a little pale yourself.'

'My wife always looks pale,' Frank Malloy cut in. 'I keep telling her to take things easier and not do so much, but does she listen to me? Not a bit of it. Every day, she goes flat out from sunrise to sunset.'

He looked at his wife in exasperation.

She waved her hand dismissively. 'Ignore him, Doctor. He does like to fuss so. But you're here about Will.

He's an active man and he'll not like being laid up. In all the years he's worked for my husband, I don't think he's been ill for so much as a day. And if he has, it certainly hasn't kept him from his work. And we're talking about more than twenty years.

It's me that's kept you doctors in business, not Will.'

'Do call me Pete. I hope I'm going to be your friend as well as your doctor,' he said, and he heard some tittering.

Glancing beyond Frank Malloy, he noticed for the first time a couple of girls at the back of the group.

Inwardly groaning, he turned back to Frank. 'Did you give him the sixth of morphia I suggested on the phone, Mr Malloy?'

'It's Frank, please. Yes, and it's definitely helped, although he's obviously still in pain.'

Peter glanced down at Will. 'I'm concerned that movement may do more damage, but at the same time we must get him to hospital as soon as we can, I think our best bet is to slide a fracture board under him.' He bent down to the drover. 'Did you hear what I said, Will?'

His face contorted with pain, Will nodded.

'Don't you worry. We'll give you a further shot of morphia just before take-off, and that'll help with the pain. And you'll feel better once we get some plasma into you, which we're going to do right now. Can you wriggle your toes for me?'

Will gave a slight nod. Peter smiled encouragingly. 'That's a good sign.'

Straightening up, he looked at the Malloys. 'The plasma will help with his blood pressure, which is looking none too good—that'll be because he's in shock. While we're giving the plasma a chance to do its stuff, we'll get the stretcher ready.'

'I'm sure it wouldn't hurt if you sat down for a moment or two and had a coffee first. It's on the veranda, ready,' Ruth said. 'The biscuits were freshly made this morning. Do sit for a minute, won't you? You too, Ned. Help yourself while I go and get the coffee for the rest of the men.'

Ned shook his head. 'I'll have my coffee out here, thanks —I'd like to have a chin wag with the drovers.'

He glanced over his shoulder towards the plane, and then back at Peter. 'I'll get the plasma stand first, though.'

'Thanks, Ned.' Peter turned to Ruth as Ned headed for the plane.

'As soon as I've got the drip going, I'll have that coffee. It'll be very welcome indeed. But I'll have to make it a swift one as we want to see Will in hospital as soon as possible. Apart from anything else, I'm sure they'll want to make a start on fixing his leg early tomorrow.'

'I understand. And I'll be quick about getting the drovers' coffee so that Ned's got time to have a few words with them before you leave.' Ruth turned to go back to the house.

'Before you go, Mrs Malloy,' Peter said quickly. 'You know how easily your heart can be overtaxed, and you're definitely looking pale. I suggest I give you a quick once over while I'm here.'

'That won't be necessary, Doctor,' she said with a reassuring smile.

'I'll admit my heart bothered me a bit at first when I heard about Will being thrown, but now I know there's nothing that can't be mended, it's settled down, and I'm confident that Frank's not going to find me in a heap in front of the transceiver any time soon.'

'As long as you're sure. You know yourself better than anyone else does, and you'll be aware of any changes that ought to be looked at. If you're saying there aren't any, then I'll have to accept that.'

'There's nothing to worry about,' she repeated.

'Okay then. When I've got the plasma going, I'll be up for that coffee. Many thanks for the thought, Mrs Malloy.'

'No worries. And it's Ruth, please. Right, I'd better get the drovers' coffees. The men must be parched by now.'

And she turned and went back up the veranda steps and into the house.

Peter glanced round and saw that Ned had just pushed the plasma stand next to Will's side.

He opened his medical box, took out a bag of clear fluid, and hooked it to the metal stand. Then he slid a needle into the back of Will's hand, attached the tube from the plasma bag to the needle and checked the flow of the liquid.

Will's eyes started to close.

He made a slight adjustment to the position of the umbrella to make sure that Will remained completely in the shade, nodded towards the handful of people still clustered around Will, and then went up to the veranda and sat down at the table.

The two teenage girls broke away from the rest of the group, and followed Peter hastily up the steps.

As he sat down, they went and sat opposite him. Two faces beamed at him across the table.

'D'you need any help with the stretcher?' the taller girl asked, taking a biscuit. 'My sister and I will be stoked to help.'

She glanced at her sister and giggled.

'I'm sure Ned and I will be able to manage all right,' Peter said, his smile encompassing them both. 'But thanks for your offer.' The girls giggled again.

He finished his coffee as fast as he could, stood up, praised the biscuits, thanked the girls for their company and went back down the steps and along the path.

Walking quickly past Will, who was chatting to friends, he went across to the plane, rolled up the door and pulled out the airstair.

Then he went up the airstair to the open doorway into the plane, leaned across to the stretcher and started to drag it towards him. There was a sound of footsteps running up behind him.

Looking over his shoulder, he saw Ned at the bottom of the stairs.

'I'm guessin' you could use some help with that,' Ned called up.

'Good thinking, Ned. If you can take the stretcher, I'll bring the extra support for his back, and also the splints for his leg and pelvis, and a neck collar. We must try to stop him from moving.

It's essential he doesn't move his neck until they've X-rayed his vertebrae and pelvis, and seen the damage. With injuries like this, there's always a risk of bleeding into the pelvis.'

'Are you gonna splint him on the ground or when we've got him into the plane?'

'On the ground. I'll splint him, check the drip and then we'll load him on to the plane. We'll give him some more morphia just before lift-off. I drew it up into the syringe earlier on, ready for use.

Hopefully, he won't need oxygen, but if he does, we've a cylinder on board.'

'This is the first call-out where you've really been able to show you really know your stuff, mate,' Ned said as Peter slid the stretcher down the airstair. 'It'll make a change to hear the galahs talking about your medical skills tomorrow.'

With a loud guffaw of laughter, he pulled the stretcher clear of the airstair, hitched it under his arm, and made his way back to Will.

bove them, the endless sky was streaked with wide bands of yellow and gold that were slowly melding into a canopy of flaming crimson.

Susie leaned forward and filled their glasses with red wine as they sat on the veranda at the back of the base control station.

'Well, you've obviously impressed Ned,' she said, sitting back. 'Not just with your medical skill, but also with the way in which you handle people.

He was full of praise when he stopped by on his way home, and coming from Ned that's worth something. I don't remember him ever speaking as highly of previous doctors, and certainly not so soon after they'd arrived.'

'Good on Ned. It was well worth the money I paid him, then.'

Susie glanced at him quickly, and they both laughed.

'You had me there for a moment,' she said with a smile. 'So tell me, what did the hospital say about Will?'

'It's what I thought—they're doing an open reduction of the fractured femur in the morning. It's a bad break and there's not much else they can do. As for the fracture in the vertebra, they'll either put on a back brace for support while the bone heals, or they might inject cement into the bone. They hadn't yet decided which.'

'That sounds nasty. Hopefully, it won't need more than the brace.'

'Too right!'

She laughed. 'Hark at you!'

He grinned at her. 'It's spending time with Ned—it's kind of catching. But it's a pity Ruth Malloy wouldn't let me check her over. I didn't like her colour at all. She said she was fine, though, and I had to go with that.'

'You did a lot of surgery in England, didn't you?'

'A fair bit. But if I'd become a GP, which Claire clearly wanted, I'd have been limited to minor operations. If I'd worked in a hospital, I'd certainly have opted for the surgical side of things.'

'D'you think you'll regret not being able to do much surgery here? Obviously you'll do a bit, but nothing like you would've done if you'd been full-time in a hospital.'

'Nope. I like the variety I've got now. No two days are the same, and you never know what conditions you'll find when you answer a call. That's the sort of challenge I like.'

She gave him a broad smile. 'I'm glad you feel that way. I'm starting to get used to you and I wouldn't like to think of you leaving. Well, not yet, anyway,' she added with an awkward laugh.

'From the moment I read about the Service, I knew it was the job for me. And this is just the sort of place I wanted to live in.'

He indicated the expanse of seared red earth that lay beyond the back yard, from which rose the isolated silhouette of a eucalyptus or a mulga tree.

'Yes, this was what I wanted,' he said quietly, his eyes on the view. '*Is* what I want.'

'What made you decide to be a doctor,' she asked after a few minutes' companionable silence. 'I always wonder why people have chosen to do what they're doing.'

'If I said I wanted to help people, that'd sound saintly and do-gooding,' he said with a half-smile, 'and I'm certainly not like that.'

'But you do go out and help people, don't you? It's what doctors do. So in a way, that's saintly and do-gooding, isn't it?'

'I suppose so. Certainly at my interview for the Medical School, that was the reason I gave them, but that was only part of the truth.'

'Well, what's the rest, then?' she prompted.

'Remember, you asked for it,' he said with a grin.

And leaning back, he told her about his years in Ladakh, which had given him a love of emptiness and of feeling free, and about Kalden, his only friend, and how, when he was back in England and at school, he'd been instantly drawn to the certainty of science, which was a body of knowledge ascertained by observing, experimenting and testing.

A doctor worked with demonstrable facts, he told her, not with intangible beliefs, and he knew that he'd never be following in the footsteps of his missionary parents.

But he wasn't interested in research, he went on. Being buried in books and test tubes from morning till night held no attraction, and would be the antithesis of the freedom he wanted.

As a doctor, he'd be part of a team, but he'd also work on his own in effect, which was a sort of freedom. Although a hospital's perimeter was defined by walls, the job was far from static.

She nodded. 'I can see that.'

'But when I read about the Service...' He shook his head. 'Wow, that was an unbelievable moment. I realised I could have everything I wanted in the one job.' He paused. 'Does that answer the question to your satisfaction?'

'I'd say it was a pretty good answer.'

'So are you going to tell me something about yourself? You wanted to know me better, and I feel the same about you.'

'I'm sure I don't know why—I'm not that interesting.'

He leaned forward, rested his forearms on the table and stared at her. 'I disagree. You're English. You married an Italian. You live in Australia. All that makes you interesting.'

She met the deep blue eyes that studied her face, and she sat very still.

'Come on, Susie, you asked me why I became a doctor, and I told you,' he said with a half-smile.

'Now I'm asking to know more about you as a person. I'm breaking into the box that's holding our pasts and asking what brought you to Cobar.

There's not exactly a large Italian community here, but from what I've heard about Italians, they're very family orientated and love to be around other Italians. So why Cobar?'

She opened her mouth to answer him. Then she closed it. She stood up.

'It's getting dark. It's much too late in the day for me to start on the story of my life.'

Disappointment written on his face, he rose to his feet. 'Fair enough,' he said. 'I'd like to get to know you better, Susie, but that must be your decision.

You clearly don't want to talk about yourself at the moment, and I've no intention of trying to push you into what you don't want to do. As you say—it's late now. I'll get off home.'

He finished his wine, put down his glass and started making his way along the veranda towards the front of the bungalow.

Hurrying after him, she caught him up and walked beside him. Neither said a word.

When they reached the front of the house, Susie paused, but Peter continued on down the veranda steps. When he reached the bottom step, he stopped and looked up at her.

She inched back.

'When you go indoors now, Susie, will the emptiness in your house weigh heavily upon you?' he asked quietly.

She looked down at his face.

Moonlight glinted in eyes that were dark in their depths, eyes that were staring at her with an intensity that slid beneath her skin.

A shiver ran down her spine, and her heart started racing.

She shook her head. 'No,' she said decisively.

She took another step back and folded her arms.

'No, it won't.' She paused a moment. 'But it must do on you or you wouldn't have asked the question.'

He nodded slowly. 'Yes, it does. But that's because I'd got so used to someone waiting for me to get back home, someone I'd sit with, like you and I sat together a few minutes ago. Talking with you just now reminded me of how much I miss those evenings.'

'Was Claire beautiful?'

'Very, but in a different way from you.' He hesitated a moment. 'At times, emptiness within a house can feel oppressive. Some day you might find that, too. And if you do, you won't mind what time of day it is when you start to tell your story.'

His face broke out into a slow smile. 'Goodnight, Susie. Sleep well.'

His hand raised in a gesture of farewell, he turned away, stepped off the bottom step and walked forward, his eyes on the car.

'Goodnight, Pete,' she called after him, and she stood and watched as he reached the four-by-four, pulled open the door and put his foot on the footrest, ready to climb inside.

'No!' The word came from somewhere deep inside her.

Her arms fell to her sides and she ran down the veranda steps. 'Pete!' she called as she sped towards him.

He glanced in her direction, his hand still on the car door handle. 'What is it? Did I forget something?'

She stopped abruptly. 'I lied,' she said. 'The emptiness *does* weigh heavily on me.'

They stood and stared across the drive at each other, the air tense.

Neither moved.

Then he pushed the car door shut, took a few steps towards her and paused.

Her eyes never leaving his face, she raised her hands to the front of her cotton dress and undid the buttons slowly, one by one.

'Susie,' he whispered, a catch in his voice. 'Oh, Susie.'

And he walked across to her, to answer the invitation that shone from her eyes.

35

They lay in bed, a crumpled white sheet loosely over them, Peter's arm around Susie, holding her close. Her shallow breathing told him that she was still asleep, but that she wouldn't remain that way for much longer.

Glancing down at her tousled head, the sense of guilt he'd felt since opening his eyes that morning, deepened.

Annoyed at himself for feeling that way, he stared up at the ceiling.

His guilt wasn't about what had happened with Susie— he was genuinely fond of her. She was clever, attractive, sexy, and he was fairly sure that he was drawn to her by feelings that might well grow into something stronger than fondness.

And he knew that Susie had wanted this, just as he had, if for no other reason than that both were lonely.

Really, it had been a matter of when, not if.

No, it was guilt about Claire.

He couldn't stop feeling guilty about her, even though he'd done nothing to warrant that feeling.

He knew that a part of him would always love Claire, and what had happened with Susie last night, and hopefully would happen with her again, would never alter that.

But Claire had let him go to Australia alone, so it was her choice that she was on the other side of the world from him. There was no reason, therefore, for him to feel that he'd somehow let her down.

But he did.

In a way, his guilt must be bound up with the deep grief he still felt that Claire was no longer at his side and that they'd had such a terrible row before he'd left.

Looking back, he bitterly regretted some of the things he'd said to her.

It had been disappointment speaking: disappointment that he couldn't have both Claire and the dream that had become Australia.

And many a time since then, he'd woken in the night and found himself hoping desperately that she'd understood it had been misery and frustration speaking, and that his final words to her weren't the first things that sprang to her mind when she thought about him.

If she ever did think about him.

If she'd ever forgiven him for setting in motion the thing that had torn them apart.

Now that he'd had time to think about it, he could see how from the moment he'd said that he wanted to go to Australia, and she'd said that she didn't, the end of their relationship had been inevitable.

But not the end of him loving her.

For how much longer was he going to feel so deeply about her, he wondered in despair. His feelings should have lessened by now with the passage of time, but the guilt he felt about sleeping with Susie showed him that they hadn't.

The silly thing was, he knew Claire well enough to know that she wouldn't condemn him for sleeping with Susie.

Undoubtedly, she would have been hurt by his new relationship, but she would have understood that there really was one way only for him to get over her, and that was to find someone else with whom to enjoy his new life to the full.

She wouldn't have expected him to live the rest of his life as a monk.

And he didn't expect that of her, either.

They were both free agents now, and she might well have already found someone else herself, just as he had. In fact, being as lovely as she was in every way, she probably had.

He felt a sudden sharp stab of anguish and shifted his position.

She probably hadn't done so quite that quickly, he decided.

He could always find out from Alex, who was bound to know what she was doing, or at least where she'd gone, but he was determined not to ask him.

It was one thing to have sent Alex his address, but it would be quite another to go against everything he'd said upon leaving by opening up a dialogue about Claire.

'An Australian dollar for them.' Susie's words cut through his thoughts.

He rapidly erased the image of Claire from his mind.

'A rash offer, indeed,' he murmured, looking down at her. 'They're not worth a fraction of that.' Smiling, he leaned down, kissed the top of her head and buried his face in her long dark hair.

She snuggled up to him and yawned. 'No call-outs, then. We were lucky.' She gave him a sleepy smile.

'Not a single one. And you're right about being lucky. I feel one lucky guy.' He rolled over on top of her, and gazed down at her. 'Being with you like this.'

She trailed her fingers across his chest. 'What time did you say it was?' she asked, looking up at him from beneath long black eyelashes.

'I didn't. It's not quite six. And to answer your question, yes, we've got time.'

CURLED UP BESIDE PETER, Susie lay with her cheek on his arm, her eyes tracing his profile. She stretched out her hand, ran her palm down the side of his face, and then placed her hand lightly on his chest.

She felt him tighten his arm around her.

'I met Marco in Italy when I was on the year abroad that I had to do as part of my degree course,' she said suddenly.

She felt Peter tense, and she sensed him waiting.

Marco had been doing an engineering degree at the university where she'd been working as a language assistant, she told him.

They'd hit it off at once, and after Susie had reluctantly returned to England for her final year at the university, they'd gone backwards and forwards, visiting each other.

As soon as Susie had graduated, she'd gone to Italy, married Marco and moved in with his family.

That had been a huge mistake. She'd hated every single minute of living with Marco's family.

Repeatedly she'd asked him if they couldn't find somewhere of their own, where everyone couldn't hear what everyone else was doing, which was embarrassing and inhibiting, and where they could have some time to themselves without someone else always being around.

But Marco had turned out to be a real mother's boy—a *mammismo* was the Italian name for such a person, she said —and deliberately deaf to her entreaties, he'd refused to offend his mother by moving somewhere else.

It had been so bad that several times over the months, Susie had come close to leaving.

At the moment when things had been at the very worst, they'd received a letter from cousins of Marco's who'd gone to Australia on the assisted passage scheme.

The cousins had settled in Sydney and liked it, and they'd told him that he'd have no trouble finding work if he wanted to go out there and join them.

Not thinking that Marco would ever agree to leave his mother, she'd hesitantly suggested to him that this might be something to think about.

To her amazement, he'd jumped at the idea.

He'd actually been thinking about that very thing, he'd told her with a smile. His instant enthusiasm had shown her that, although Marco would never admit it, living with his family had finally begun to pall after the freedom he'd had at university.

But whatever the reason for his change of heart, she was overjoyed to see it, and both had agreed that a fresh start was exactly what they needed.

She hadn't been worried that her parents would make a fuss about her emigrating. She was one of four children, and the other three had all settled near her parents, and she hadn't lived in England for a while, anyway.

However, Marco's parents had been very upset, and they'd repeatedly begged him to reconsider.

But the same ears that had earlier been deaf to her pleas, were now turned towards his parents, and he'd filled in the forms regardless, paid ten pounds for each ticket, promised to work there for at least two years, packed the one suitcase that each were allowed, and led the way to the boat.

Six weeks after that, they'd been in Australia.

They'd had a great time on the journey. It had been the best six weeks since they'd married.

They'd been lucky that their ship, the *Fairsky*, had an Italian crew, as that meant that Marco, whose English was very poor, had someone he could talk to apart from her.

There'd been table tennis on the ship, deck quoits, a deep swimming pool, three dining rooms, several bars, a social hall where they held variety shows and dinner dances, a cinema and heaps of other things.

In such idyllic surroundings, it wasn't surprising that she and Marco got on so well with each other that they were like two newly-weds.

The only thing that Marco hadn't liked was the regular English lessons given on the ship—he was by nature a rotten linguist. He'd gone to the classes, however, as he'd realised that he'd have to improve if he wanted to get a good job.

They'd hoped to be able to go all the way to Sydney on the boat, and there meet up with Marco's relatives, but to their great disappointment, they'd had to disembark at Melbourne and get on a train to take them to a migrant hostel called Bonegilla, several hundred kilometres north of Melbourne.

As soon as the authorities had read the surname Lentini, Sydney had been crossed out and Bonegilla, the migrant hostel for non-English people, had been marked down as their destination.

It was the place where immigrants were sorted out with jobs and accommodation.

To his dismay, when they'd reached Bonegilla, Marco

had been faced with more English lessons. But after one month, they were able to leave for Sydney.

Once in Sydney, they'd learned that they'd been extremely lucky not to have been sent to one of the Sydney hostels.

Apparently, a lot of the Sydney hostels were really bad, and were the subject of regular health scares. And the hostel food, too, was said to be poor.

Marco didn't like non-Italian food at the best of times, and would have exploded daily if he'd been faced with meals that were inedible. Like many Mediterranean men, he could fly off the handle at next to nothing, Susie told Peter.

Not long ago, Susie added, she heard that they were closing Bonegilla, so she and Marco had been very lucky to have gone there when they did.

'Did Marco find a job in Sydney?' Peter asked.

'Yes—something in construction. It meant that we were able to rent a place in Sydney that wasn't too awful. But then I had a miscarriage—'

'Oh, Susie, I'm sorry.' He ran his hand slowly down her arm. 'How awful for you both.'

'It was. I took an age getting over it. And with me languishing, and not in the mood to go out that much, Marco started hanging around with a group of Italians he'd met and staying out later and later.

I'm sure he wasn't going with other women—it was just that he preferred being with his new friends to being with me while I was in such a state.'

'That's hardly fair. It must've been terrible, what you were going through.'

She gave a slight shrug. 'I'm not sure I entirely blame him—I must have been awful company. Anyway, by the time

I'd got over the miscarriage, he was set into that way of life, and couldn't—or wouldn't—change.

Having my husband out half the night wasn't my idea of marriage, and I finally threatened to leave. It was the job in Cobar that saved our marriage,' she told Peter.

Marco had heard that one of the mining companies there needed an engineer. It paid well, so he was keen to go after it. Because they didn't know of any Italians in Cobar, Susie, too, was anxious that he got the job, and both had been overjoyed when his application had been successful.

They'd moved to Cobar and rented a place in the centre of town. Not long after that, Susie had seen an advertisement for an assistant at the base control station, and as she'd wanted a job and it sounded interesting, she'd applied for it.

'Did Marco mind? From what I've heard about Italian men and their pride, I can't see the idea of you working going down too well.'

'It didn't. I knew it wouldn't, and I didn't tell him till I'd got the job. He was furious. Didn't I think he could support me? What would his family and friends say?

Couldn't I join the Country Women's Association and help with fund-raising activities if I was so keen to do some work outside the house? You know the sort of thing. It caused a lot of rows.'

'Did he come round in the end?'

He hadn't, she said. And things had got even worse when six months after she'd started at the station, the Base Director had retired and she'd been offered the job.

The bungalow came as part of the package as the director to be on hand for any emergencies. It would save them rent, she'd thought, so she didn't expect Marco to be opposed to her promotion.

But he was.

He'd announced that he wasn't sure that he wanted to stay in Cobar, and that if she took the post, it would tie them to the place.

Despite all the English lessons he'd had, and all the help that Susie had given him, people still found it difficult to understand what he was saying, which had made it well-nigh impossible for him to make close friends in Cobar.

He'd been certain that with the experience he now had, he'd be able to find a job in Sydney that would pay almost as well as the Cobar job, and when his contract ended, Sydney was where he wanted to go.

She'd seen the truth in what he'd said, but had ignored it, and pushed him to agree to her taking the Base Director job. In the end, he'd relented and they'd moved into the bungalow.

'About a month later, he told me that he hated living so far from the town and wanted us to move back into the town until the end of his contract,' she said, her voice flat.

'I told him he could go back if he wanted, but I was staying put. We had an almighty row and he drove off in a stinking temper, going way too fast along a dirt track that had an uneven surface.

Not surprisingly, given the state he was in, he lost control of the car. It spun round a couple of times and hit a tree. He died instantly.'

'Oh, Susie, how awful for you,' Peter said quietly.

Her eyes filled with tears.

She wiped them away. 'This is self-pity. I blame myself for the accident, and for the whole mess. Whatever they say, love isn't blind. I knew what he and his family were like before I married him, and I should never have gone to live with them.

The trouble was, I felt I'd missed out on something by not being close to my own parents, and I thought I might even enjoy being part of Marco's family.

I was wrong, though, and I realised that almost at once. Things might've been very different if we'd started married life on our own.'

'Living in a different culture isn't easy, as I know from experience.'

She nodded. 'That's right. But then,' she continued. 'After that first mistake, I made a second.

I was naïve enough to think that by moving to another country, we'd leave all our problems behind us and Marco would have changed in some material way by the time we got off the boat.

But of course that doesn't happen—you just take your problems with you, and also the way you are.'

'All that's true.'

'I could have handled things better, though. I could have tried to balance what I wanted from life with what Marco wanted. But I didn't—I was too determined to get my own way.'

'But you're entitled to a life, too. You shouldn't blame yourself for that.'

She shook her head. 'It's more than that. When I looked back after he'd died, I realised that I'd stopped loving him long before the accident. That's the truth—I just hadn't wanted to face it.

I loved him when we married, but it had already been going downhill long before we even left his family.'

'You were okay together on the boat.'

'That was more like a holiday than a marriage—we didn't have any pressure on us and we didn't have to make any decisions. That's not real life.

But once we hit Australia and didn't have his family to blame any longer, it became increasingly obvious that we were totally different as people, and I shouldn't have turned a blind eye to that.'

'It's easy to say that with hindsight.'

'Maybe. But it doesn't stop me blaming myself for not being honest enough with myself and him. I should have left him long ago. If I had, he'd still be alive, and I wouldn't have got up every day since it happened, feeling guilty.'

He looked down into her face. 'And what about now that you've talked about this? Do you feel as guilty this morning, Susie, as you did when you woke up yesterday morning?'

She met his deep blue gaze and slowly shook her head.

'No,' she said, her brow creasing in wonderment. 'No, I don't.'

36

B irmingham
April, 1971

'THAT WAS SOME PARTY ALL RIGHT,' Alex said gleefully as they came into his flat.

He kicked his front door shut behind him, pulled Claire into the centre of the sitting room, took her in his arms and spun them both in a whirl.

'What a ball we had!' he exclaimed, spinning around. 'Don't you agree? This has to have been my best birthday ever. Mike was really on form tonight—we all were.'

'It was, but you're making me dizzy,' Claire said, laughing.

He came to a stop, and both stood still a moment, panting slightly.

'I think a nightcap's in order,' he said, when he was again breathing normally. 'You'll have another glass of wine, won't you?'

'Just a small one, then.'

'Take a seat and I'll get them.'

Throwing his jacket on to the back of the nearest chair, he went over to the cocktail cabinet, picked up a bottle of red wine, and filled two glasses.

Then he went and sat next to Claire, who'd settled down on to the sofa, and gave her one of the glasses.

'Cheers,' he said, raising his glass to hers. 'So did you really enjoy the evening?' he asked, as they sat back, his arm lightly around her shoulders. 'We did get quite loud.'

'I honestly did,' she said, leaning her head against his arm. 'I loved Mike's story about when he took his three year-old nephew to church for the baptism of a friend's baby, and the boy looked up at the cross on the church wall, pointed at it and shrieked excitedly, "Worzel Gummidge!"

Wouldn't it just be the case that the little boy's words had never been easier to understand than they were at that moment? I'd have died of embarrassment, too.'

Alex grinned. 'Me, too. Yes, Mike certainly helped to make the evening swing. But the reason it was the best ever was because you were with me, lovely Claire,' he said, and he turned his head to look at her, his face suddenly serious.

'Whatever we do together, it's the best ever because we do it together.' He leaned across and kissed her lightly on the lips.

A strong tang of aftershave, tinged with the scent of his need, caught her in its embrace, and enveloped her.

She stared up into eyes that were dark with desire, and her stomach gave a sudden lurch.

'I said it was my best birthday ever,' he went on softly, gently combing her hair away from her face with his fingers.

Every time his fingertips grazed her scalp, a shiver ran down her spine.

'But the day isn't over yet,' he murmured. 'You could make it even better.'

Emptiness lodged in the pit of her stomach.

She slid out of his hold and stood up.

He rose to his feet, and faced her. His hand lightly on her shoulder, he held her still.

'Don't move away from me, Claire, not tonight, not on my birthday, not when I've waited so long. Surely, I've waited for long enough.'

Then he slid his arm to the small of her back, and with his free hand, tilted her face to look up into his.

His breath warm against her skin, he brushed his lips across her mouth.

She moved imperceptibly closer to him.

For a long moment, they stood there, his arm around her, her face against his chest.

Then she raised her hand to the back of his neck, brought his face closer to hers, and returned his kiss.

He pulled her tighter to him, deepening his kiss, pouring his need into her.

She felt his body hard against her.

A wave of hunger washed over her—hunger for the love he was offering, hunger for an end to the constant pain of loss. How else was she ever going to get over Peter, other than by letting another man take his place in every way?

It was time, she thought, and Alex, who'd shown himself to be a true friend, was the right person.

And she pressed the length of her body against his.

His shudder of delight ran through her.

Breathing heavily, he moved slightly back, and his fingers slid hesitantly across the front of her dress.

Goosebumps prickled along her arms, and she pulled back. His hands fell to his sides.

Her lips parting, they stared at each other.

'You must know how much I want you, Claire,' he said quietly. 'How much I care for you. But I'm not going to try and push you into anything. I'd never do that—you mean too much to me. But if you were beginning to feel the same way, and I think you might be...'

The tick of the clock was loud in the room.

Then she leaned forward, took his face in both of her hands, kissed him hard on the mouth and then again stepped back, a half-smile on her face.

Surprise and pleasure played across his lips. 'Does this mean what I hope it means? It would be a wonderful birthday present.'

She nodded slowly. 'I suppose it does,' she said, a tremor in her voice.

He gazed into her face. 'Don't be scared, beautiful Claire. I'd never hurt you. I've come to love you. But you know that, don't you?'

She nodded again. 'It's just that this'll be the first time.' She could hear her nervousness. She cleared her throat.

'Not the first time ever, of course, but the first time with someone who isn't Peter. It'll feel very strange, doing this with someone else.'

'Strange in the nicest possible way, I hope,' he said, his voice a smile. 'And this will be a first for me, too. It'll be my first time with someone I very much hope will ensure that I never again have another first time, and that will make it very special.'

'Oh, Alex,' she whispered.

'Now we've got a big decision to make,' he said, amusement springing into his voice.

She looked up at him questioningly.

He raised an eyebrow. 'Do we sink on to my sofa and

struggle, or do we play where the grown-ups play, in the bedroom?'

With a laugh, she glanced towards his bedroom door.

Her laughter froze on her lips.

'I can't do it,' she said, her voice a monotone, the blood draining from her face. 'I'm sorry, Alex, but I just can't.'

He frowned at her, puzzled. 'I don't get you.'

He gestured his bewilderment. 'You just said you wanted this, too, and you acted like you did. I didn't force you.'

'I know I did. And I really thought I could go through with it, and that it would help me get over Peter. But I was wrong to think I could do it—I just can't.'

'And there was I, thinking you liked me in my own right.' A faint note of bitterness crept into his voice.

'Oh, I do, you must believe that,' she cried, her eyes full of regret.

She caught his hand and clutched it tightly. 'I've liked you since the day we met in that Chinese restaurant. You're great fun to be with and you've been a terrific friend to me, just as you were to Peter.

Everything you've done for me since he left has made me like you even more, and I think that's partly the trouble.'

He shook his head. 'I don't get it. Surely liking me is a good thing?'

'It is and it isn't. I suppose it's two things really. I met you because of Peter, so whenever I see you, I think of Peter, and that keeps reminding me how much I still love him.

And the other reason is, you've been such a good friend to me since Peter left that I've come to think of you as like a brother—as someone I can lean on and trust, who'll always be there for me—rather than as someone I want to sleep with.'

She squeezed his hand, and then released it. 'I'm so

sorry, Alex—I've tried really hard, but I can't make myself feel about you in the way you want.'

'So that's it. We're not going to go any further, then?'

'I'm afraid not,' she said, her voice low.

Her eyes filled with tears.

'But I do hope we can stay good friends, even though the romance side is over.'

A WAVE of intense relief swelling inside her, she said goodbye to Alex, left his flat and walked steadily down the stairs, with each step stifling a growing urge to get to the bottom as fast as she could.

The moment she reached the street, she felt a lightness fall on her, and with a sense of joy, she started to run.

The force of her relief took her completely by surprise, and she ran till she could no longer see Alex's building, and could no longer be seen from the building, and then stopped abruptly, and stood on the pavement, stunned by the way she felt.

After the closeness between her and Alex since the day Peter left, she would've expected to feel a degree of regret that their relationship had irrevocably changed, which it would certainly have done.

But she hadn't expected to feel relief.

And certainly not overwhelming relief. And not as if a weight had been lifted, a weight she hadn't even known had been pressing on her.

She started walking along the road, her head bowed in thought.

Thinking back, from the moment Peter went out of her life, Alex had been constantly at her side.

She'd felt grief; he'd felt guilt; and together they'd

leaned on each other as they'd struggled to work through their feelings and come to terms with what had happened.

Mary had helped her as much as she could, but there'd been a limit to what she could do in her condition and living outside the city.

There'd been a limit to what anyone could do, but somehow Alex had managed to find a way of helping, whatever the problem, and had become adept at anticipating what she'd need before she'd even known it herself.

He'd been a tremendous support throughout, and without her realising it, had become virtually indispensable.

But had she really wanted that?

At first, perhaps she had.

But in a blinding flash, she realised that such a time had long since passed, and the continual presence of Alex in her life had actually started to become oppressive.

But it was only now, having freed herself from anything more than a friendship with him, that she was able to see that.

It was such a shame that she hadn't realised sooner that despite Alex's many kindnesses, she'd never be able to feel for him anything that came remotely close to the way she'd felt about Peter, and still did.

Not even though a weeny bit of her deep down, that she didn't really want to acknowledge, would have liked to do something that she knew would hurt Peter, who'd done so much to hurt her.

If she'd known months ago that she'd never be able to go through with it, it would've saved them both from wasting time, hoping for something that was never going to happen.

But it was only when she'd looked at Alex's bedroom door and imagined them naked behind it, that the truth had hit her.

She knew that the hurt and disappointment in Alex's eyes, and the deep remorse she felt for being the cause of that, were going to stay with her for a long time.

But in a funny way, she thought in a flash of sudden awareness, by finishing with Alex, she'd finally relegated Peter firmly to the past, and she was ready to begin living again.

As she speeded up her steps, she looked up at the sky and smiled.

STANDING IN THE OPEN DOORWAY, his legs planted wide, Alex listened to Claire's footsteps fade into the distance.

After all the things he'd done for her, she hadn't been able to get away from him fast enough, he thought bitterly. She'd all but run down the stairs.

Surely he deserved better than that!

He went into his flat, slammed the front door shut, went across to the coffee table, picked up their wine glasses and took them into the kitchen.

There was a slight trace of lipstick on the rim of her glass, he noticed, and he paused in front of the sink and stared at the place where her lips had been. Disappointment cut through him.

He was deeply upset by the turn of events that evening. And on his birthday, too.

No, he was more than just disappointed—he was furious, really furious by what had happened, or rather, by what hadn't happened.

All along, he'd been careful not to rush things or make any false moves.

She wasn't like his usual dates, easy to get into bed with

the minimum of persuasion—she was different, and he'd respected that difference in everything he'd said and done.

He'd known that when she was ready to sleep with him, it was going to mean something really special—both in itself, and because it would prove that her feelings for Peter had really gone—and he'd been prepared to wait patiently for as long as it took, confident that he'd get there in the end.

And he'd had every reason to think that he *would* achieve his goal.

After all, he'd done everything he could to help her since Peter had left, and he'd seen her visibly relax as the weeks had gone by, and start to look like the old Claire again. And increasingly, she'd been giving off signs that suggested she'd transferred her affections from Peter to him, and had started to care for him in the way that he craved.

Going to bed together would have set the seal on the full relationship he wanted.

And earlier that evening, as she rubbed herself against him, he'd truly thought that the time had finally come.

But how wrong he'd been!

And how wrong he'd been all along!

He'd been kidding himself that she'd ever feel for him in the way he wanted her to feel.

And all because of Peter.

A burst of hot anger shot through him.

Peter had always been there, sitting at the table with them, walking at their side, hovering above them when they relaxed on the sofa—an invisible third party who was stopping her from opening her heart to anyone else.

He may have abandoned her for a god-forsaken place on the other side of the world, and she may have tried desperately to forget him, but for all that, she still loved him as much as she ever had.

All it had taken to prove that to her, to wipe away his months of his hard work, was the thought of going with him, Alex, into his bedroom.

What was it she'd so cruelly said? She'd thought that she could go through with it.

Go through with it? Who did she think she was?

Fury burned within him.

And as if that wasn't enough, she'd made her meaning even clearer by effectively saying that if she'd been able to stomach sleeping with him, it might've helped her get over Peter!

She'd wanted to use him to help her get over someone else!

What a bloody cheek! To think of him in such terms after all the time he'd spent on her, and all the help he'd given her!

It diminished him.

White with rage, he dropped her wine glass into the sink and watched it shatter.

Just what *was* it about Peter Henderson she couldn't forget, he thought, staring with hatred at the shards of glass.

Fair enough, he could see that Peter was attractive to women, but so was he—countless conquests proved it.

And he was better in a group of people than Peter would ever be.

And Peter had proved himself to be a selfish idiot. Unlike Peter, he'd never have walked away from a woman like Claire for the sake of a stupid dream.

Yet she couldn't forget Peter.

His mouth twisted into a sneer.

Well he, Alex, had a very good memory, too.

He couldn't—and wouldn't—forget how disgracefully Claire had treated him.

And when the right situation presented itself, he'd pay her back for daring to use him so shamefully and for wasting so much of his time, time that would've been better spent looking for someone who wasn't so completely hung up on someone else.

And Peter was going to pay, too, for standing in his way and being the reason that Claire had made a fool out of him.

That was a promise to them both.

He picked up the pieces of glass from the sink, threw them into the dustbin, went back into his sitting room and crossed over to his desk.

Opening the top drawer, he pulled a thin blue air letter from under a notepad, unfolded it and glanced at the address written twice, once on the back and once under the signature.

His eyes narrowing, he fingered the letter thoughtfully.

As far as he could see, Peter's address was the sole channel through which he could exact his revenge.

It meant that it was unlikely to be nearly as dramatic as he would have liked, but in the absence of anything better, he'd make sure that he did as much harm as he could with what he'd got.

When Peter had written that one day someone might want to contact him, he would have had Claire in mind, of course. But it wouldn't be Claire who used the address—it would be him.

But not yet.

Not until the time was right.

And it would only be right when he had something of importance to tell Peter, something that was bound to hit him hard. And it would have to involve Claire.

Just as Claire couldn't forget Peter, Peter almost certainly hadn't been gone long enough to have got over Claire.

To get the ammunition he needed, he'd have to behave as if he was still a good friend of Claire's, even if it stuck in his throat to do so. But in a purely brotherly way, he thought with an inward sneer.

By doing that, he'd find out about any new men she met, and he'd keep abreast of what she intended to do in the future.

And when she moved somewhere else, which she would surely do before long, he'd deliberately bump into Mary's dull husband, Keith, from time to time, and would feign an interest in Mary and their child, and catch up with Claire's news.

Since Claire hadn't a clue about where in Australia Peter lived, she couldn't go and throw herself at his feet, were she so minded, and she'd be aware of that.

It meant that she'd have no choice but to put Peter behind her, and as soon as she moved to a new town, she'd look for someone to replace him.

She probably wouldn't be conscious of what she was doing, but she'd know subconsciously that only by entering into a full relationship with someone else—someone who had no connection with Peter—would she get Peter out of her mind.

And apart from that, in herself she was clearly ready to have a man in her bed again.

That had been obvious from the moment she'd responded physically to him that evening.

In the split second when an unmistakable sexual heat had invaded her and she'd moved closer to him, her desire for a man—but not him, she'd realised—had reawakened.

Later, looking back at that moment, she'd accept the

truth of it, and he wouldn't be at all surprised if Keith didn't tell him soon after she'd moved that she'd got engaged.

He fervently hoped Keith did.

By now, Peter would have realised from the deafening silence over the past few months that no one was going to contact him, and, if as he suspected, Peter was still as stuck on Claire as she was on him, there was a possibility that he might even throw in the towel and return to England to claim her. So the sooner Claire was tied up the better.

And there was also the likelihood of Peter returning if the new job hadn't lived up to his high expectations. That was quite possible given Peter's propensity for thinking that what he didn't have was more attractive than what he had.

Starting now to worry in earnest that Peter might be thinking about coming back, he regretted not having a photograph of Claire and him together, their arms entwined around each other in loving fashion, a photograph that hinted strongly, albeit erroneously, that he and Claire were sleeping together.

His mouth twisted into a smile. Now that would have really caused Peter pain.

Although—on second thoughts—it could have been counter-productive.

Peter would assume that Claire had stayed friends with him and the others, so confirmation of that would be unlikely to cause him to lose any sleep.

But if the photograph suggested that something stronger was going on, and Peter thought that Claire was sleeping with the very person who'd started him off on the path that had led to Australia, there was a real risk that in a fit of manic rage and jealousy, he'd jump on to the first plane bound for England and head for Birmingham.

And if that happened, Claire was certain to take him back like a shot.

So all in all, it was probably just as well that such a photograph didn't exist.

He was just going to have to be patient and bide his time until she was actually married and it was too late for Peter to do anything.

As soon as she'd tied the knot, he'd send her wedding photograph to Peter, and the moment that Peter opened the envelope and saw Claire, a blushing bride, walking down the aisle to someone else, he would feel pain like he'd never felt before.

That would be true even if Peter were in a new relationship. Of that he was sure.

The aching helplessness that Peter would feel at knowing that Claire was forever lost to him was the only payback available to him, given that there were miles of sea and land between him and Peter.

If he, Alex, couldn't have Claire—and it was clear now that he couldn't—he'd make damn sure that Peter didn't have her either, and that Peter, too, suffered the intense anguish of having to abandon all hope.

With unbidden tears rolling down his cheeks, he carefully re-folded the air letter, slid it back under the notebook, and firmly closed the drawer.

37

C obar
May, 1971

'THAT'S that done for this morning, then,' Peter said.

He turned the radio-transmitter back to receive, stretched up his arms and arched his back. 'I must've sent a record number of telegrams, and the day's not over yet. I was starting to worry that Anna would get here before I'd finished.'

Susie swivelled in her chair to face him. 'Anna Baines? She's your nurse today, is she?'

He nodded. 'That's right. And she'll be here any minute now. It's the first time she's done the clinic run with me.'

'Well, I hope she's prepared for the turnout you get. It's a large outpost and I suspect you'll have your work cut out to finish before your radio clinic this afternoon.'

He shrugged. 'Then I'll do it from the plane. That's the beauty of the job.'

'You'll like Anna,' Susie said. 'But not too much, I hope,' she added with a laugh. She stood up, moved behind his chair, wrapped her arms around his chest and hugged him.

'All that interests me is whether or not she's a good nurse.'

'She is.' She kissed the top of Peter's head, released him and sat down again. 'Assuming you're back in time, will you do the clinic from here?'

'Probably not,' he said getting up. 'I'll get Anna to drop me back here. I'll come in, say a quick hello, and then pick up the car and go home. I've one or two things to do at home so I might as well do the clinic from there. Why don't I pick you up at about seven and we'll go into town for a meal?'

'That sounds good.' She hesitated a moment. 'I've been thinking,' she went on, a trace of nervousness in her voice. 'When you come for me this evening, you could bring some of your clothes with you.'

His stomach turned over.

'Some of my clothes?' he echoed.

She shrugged, the palms of her hands gesturing upwards.

'Why not? You've stayed over every night for the past few weeks and we're still speaking to each other. It means that you wouldn't have to go backwards and forwards as much as you've been doing. I've got a wardrobe that's empty and waiting, and there's a place in the bathroom where you can leave your razor and so on.'

'Isn't that rather throwing caution to the winds?' he asked, a note of surprise in his voice. 'I thought you wanted to hide our relationship from the prying eyes and busy tongues of the town galahs.'

'Oh, come on, Pete! D'you really think they don't already know? Of course, they do; it's just they don't care. We're so far out of town that no one can accuse us of corrupting the kids, which is what they might worry about. I reckon they're happy to ignore what's going on as long as we do our jobs, which we do. Just because no one's complained to Broken Hill about our degenerate goings-on, it doesn't mean they're not talking about us.'

Suppressing a sudden formless panic, he nodded. 'All right, then. I'll bring some clothes across this evening. I'll—' The sound of a car being driven up to the house stopped him mid-sentence. 'That'll be Anna. I must go. I'll see you later.'

He leaned down and kissed her hard on the lips.

'You're going to make a lot of females very happy today,' she said, smiling up at him. 'You've got quite a tan now and you're looking pretty good, buster.'

'You're looking pretty good yourself.' He tapped her lightly on the nose.

'If you want, you can bring one or two of your new cushions tonight. As a sort of comfort blanket.' She went into peals of laughter.

'Very funny,' he said with a grin. 'If I didn't have to leave right now, we could do something better than any comfort blanket. But work calls. See you later!'

'But don't think I'll be doing your washing,' she shouted after him.

He paused halfway through the doorway, gave a slight wave and went out.

'Phew!' she said to herself.

Smiling broadly, she got up and went into the bedroom. She took a suitcase from the top of one of the two wardrobes, threw it on to the bed, opened the wardrobe door, took a deep breath and started pulling out Marco's clothes.

· · ·

SITTING BACK in the cockpit seat next to Ned, Peter idly watched the sand-coloured world slide by beneath the plane.

'You're very quiet today, mate,' Ned said after a while.

'I'm thinking.'

'Struth! If that's what thinking does to you, I wouldn't do too much of it. You've bin frowning so much I reckoned you must be crook. Maybe you should ask Anna for a pick-me-up. She's jabbed enough needles into arms this morning— one more shouldn't matter.'

'What's that about Anna and pick-me-ups?' a voice called from behind them in the airplane cabin.

Peter twisted round and saw that Anna had turned in her cabin seat and was facing them.

'It's just Ned's idea of a funny,' he told her. 'I said I was quiet because I was thinking, and he was sure you'd have a cure for that.'

'The best pick-me-up at the end of a day's work is found in a glass,' she said lightly. 'Some of the nurses occasionally pop into the hotel bar at the end of their shift. You should come along sometime.'

'I'll remember that,' Peter said with a smile.

As he turned back to the window, his smile faded, and anxiety clouded his face.

He'd been feeling unusually flat since the moment Susie suggested he leave some clothes at her place. But why should that make him feel so low, he inwardly agonised.

After all, it was the obvious thing to do. As Susie had rightly pointed out, he'd slept there almost every night since their first night together.

So what was the problem? If there *was* a problem.

It was hard to know what was bothering him. All he knew was that something was.

There was a buzz and crackle of static, and then Susie's voice sounded through the airplane radio.

'Victor Charlie Papa to Mike Delta Foxtrot. Are you receiving me? Over.'

Banishing all thoughts from his mind, he pulled on his headphones and mouthpiece as Ned responded to the call.

'Mike Delta Foxtrot to Victor Charlie Papa,' Ned said into his mouthpiece. 'Receiving you loud and clear. Go ahead, Susie.'

'We've got an emergency at the Malloy Station. Can you divert? Over.'

'Mike Delta Foxtrot to Victor Charlie Papa. We're diverting.' Ned glanced at the clock on the control panel. 'Eta is fourteen hundred hours. But we'll contact the Malloy Station ourselves. Over and out.'

'WE'LL NEED THE STRETCHER, NED,' Peter called to him as he grabbed his medical bag and ran down the airstair. He heard Anna following close behind.

Frank Malloy was standing at the front door, holding it open. His daughters hovered in the shadows behind him, their faces frightened.

'She's in the sitting room,' Frank told them. Motioning for his daughters to move aside, he led the way.

Ruth Malloy was in her armchair, her left arm pressed against her chest, her face deathly white and contorted in agony. Peter took one look at her, opened his bag, took out his nitroglycerin tablets and pushed one under her tongue.

Frank stood at the side of his wife's chair, looking down

at her, his face full ofconcern—and also real fear, Peter noticed.

'She's got tablets of her own,' Frank said, a tremor in his voice, 'but she couldn't remember where she'd put them or I'd have given her one. She should've had one sooner.'

'Not to worry.' Peter gave him a reassuring smile. Glancing down at Ruth, he saw that the tablet was starting to take effect. Her face was losing its tautness and she was beginning to relax a little. 'How long have you been having pains, Ruth?'

'On and off for a couple of days now,' she said, her voice thin and strained. 'But it's not been bad like it is now. It's not been this bad for a long time.'

'You should've called me sooner.'

'You would've sent me to hospital,' she said weakly. 'They kept me in a month last time, and that was only about six months ago. I can't afford to be spending that amount of time in hospital. I've too much to do. Much too much...' Her voice faded away.

A staring, far-away look came into her eyes, and her white face took on a bluish pallor. The acute pain had returned, Peter realised, and he swiftly pushed a second nitroglycerin tablet under her tongue.

He heard Ned come in behind him with the stretcher.

He turned slightly. 'We'll get her on to the stretcher now,' he told Ned and Anna. 'But with as little movement as possible—the less the better.'

He looked back at Ruth.

Her body was rigid and her eyes full of fright. The second pill hadn't had any effect and she was clearly still gripped by an agonising pain.

The expression on Frank's face told him that Frank, too, could see that.

'We'll give her some morphia before we attempt to move her, Frank. That'll help her,' he said, taking out a syringe and a vial of morphia.

'I'll do that, shall I?' Anna volunteered.

'Thanks, Anna.' He handed them to her. 'We'll need a sixth of morphia.'

She drew up the sixth and injected it into Ruth's arm.

'Her skin's cold and clammy,' she said, straightening up.

'And her pulse?'

Anna held Ruth's wrist a moment, and then looked at him anxiously. 'Not good.'

'At least the morphia's beginning to take effect now. You can see it making her drowsy. It'll make it easier to move her. Remember, as little movement as possible.'

'I'll help you,' Frank said quickly. 'I've done this before.'

'Thanks, Frank. If the pain comes back, we'll give her another tablet. As soon as she's on the plane, we'll start the oxygen.'

Frank nodded. 'I'm coming with you.'

'Of course.' He put his hand on Frank's shoulder. 'Try not to worry too much, Frank. We'll radio ahead from the plane and there'll be an ambulance at the airport. They were probably tuned in, anyway, and are already waiting for her. We'll have her in hospital in no time.'

Frank's eyes were bleak. 'I've seen her like this a few times before, and I know that one day it'll be for the last time,' he said, his voice low. 'But not yet, eh? I'm not ready for it yet.' He turned away. 'Not that I'll ever be,' Peter heard him add.

. . .

PETER GOT up from the seat closest to the stretcher, moved
to the cockpit and put his head between the two cockpit
seats.

'How's she doing?' Anna asked, glancing up at him.
'You'll tell me if I can help, won't you? I can easily swap seats
with Frank.'

'Thanks, but I don't think that'll be necessary. And Frank
clearly feels the need to be close to her so it's best to leave
him there if possible. The oxygen's helping, and she's easier
in herself, but I'll be glad to get her into hospital.

Will you radio Susie, Ned, and tell her I'm going to the
hospital with Ruth? I'll stay on there with Frank, and then
go back to my place. It'll be too late to do anything else by
then. I'll do the morning clinic from my house, and then go
back to the hospital to check up on Ruth. Tell Susie I'll catch
up with her later on in the day tomorrow.'

Ned nodded. 'If that's what you want, mate. It's as good
as done.' He adjusted his mouthpiece and switched the
radio to Send.

Peter turned to go back to his seat, and stopped. 'Oh, and
Ned. I feel really bad about having to change our plans for
today. You'll be sure to tell Susie that, won't you? Stress to
her that I don't have any choice.'

His face impassive, Ned glanced sharply up at Peter.

Then he nodded and turned back to the radio. 'Mike
Delta Foxtrot to Victor Charlie Papa. Are you receiving me?
Over.'

Peter heard the static on the line, followed by Susie's
voice. He turned away and moved back to his seat.

Susie wouldn't be best pleased that he wasn't going to be
turning up that evening with a suitcase of clothes, he
thought as he sat down again. But he obviously couldn't

leave Frank before they knew how things were going to turn out with Ruth.

And if the worst happened, well, Frank would need to be supported until his family got there.

Therefore, he couldn't really move his things into Susie's place until they knew the prognosis for Ruth.

After that would be the time to take their first steps towards a life together, because that's what it would be from the moment he hung his clothes in that empty wardrobe of hers.

He felt a tightening in his chest.

Why, he thought as he stared at the stretcher, when on the point of settling down should he feel as far from settled as he did.

38

Peter leaned across the stretcher, re-positioned the face mask on Ruth and checked the flow of oxygen.

'She's doing well, Frank,' he said, sitting down again. 'The oxygen's helping. Like I said, try not to worry too much. It won't be long before she's in hospital.'

He glanced at Frank, ready to give him a smile of reassurance, but Frank was staring fixedly at his wife's face.

Peter looked down at Ruth, and then back again at Frank. And at the expression in Frank's eyes. Something inside him turned over, and he found himself unable to tear his eyes from Frank's face.

'I've loved her since I first met her,' Frank said, his gaze not moving from Ruth. 'A skinny thing, she was, but I took one look at her and she became my Ruthie. And she always will be. Every minute with her has been wonderful. But there haven't been nearly enough of those minutes, and I dread the day I have to go home alone from the hospital.'

'We'll try to see that that doesn't happen any time soon,' Peter said, putting his hand on Frank's shoulder. 'We'll do our very best for her, I promise.'

His eyes rimmed with red, Frank glanced at Peter. 'Don't get me wrong, Doc. I love my home, my girls, my family, my friends. I love every inch of the ground on my station.

A man's relationship with his land is personal—a bit like a marriage, you could say. I've worked the land since I was a lad, learning from my father till the day came when I had to work it on my own.

But not alone—never alone. Whatever I had to face, I could face it 'cos it was Ruthie and me, and not just me.'

'It must be very hard on you, having to watch her when she has an attack.'

Frank nodded. 'It is. If you've ever been in love, you'll know how I feel every time I see her in pain. And how afraid. Each morning, Ruthie and I go out on the veranda and watch the daybreak together. That's how it's always been with us. If I had to watch the sun come up on my own...'

He shook his head slowly. 'Well, it wouldn't be the same.'

'Like I say, we'll do our very best. I know what you mean about the start of the day—it looks beautiful for sure, and smells it, too, with the scent of eucalyptus in the air. And the end of the day, too.'

'When Ruthie was in hospital for a month, nothing looked right. She's my life. If she loses her fight, she'll take my life with her.'

'But you love the homestead and the earth on which it stands,' Peter said gently. 'Obviously, it'll be tremendously hard at first, but you'll be in a place that you love—'

'—that means nothing to me without Ruthie,' Frank cut in. 'How could it? She's worth more to me than any piece of land.'

His voice rose and he looked at Peter, his eyes desperate.

'It doesn't matter where you live. All that matters is that you're with the person you love.

If I could get Ruthie to agree, I'd hand over the station like a shot and move the four of us into a small house in town. I'd find a house that was easy to look after and not far from the hospital. That's the truth. Nothing matters to me as much as Ruth.'

A chill spread through Peter.

'And she won't move?' he managed to ask.

Frank shook his head. 'She knows what I feel about the land, what it means to me, and she loves me. She wants to spend the years she's got in the place that I love.'

Peter opened his mouth to speak, but the expression in Frank's eyes as he looked back at Ruth, silenced him.

SUSIE SWITCHED the transceiver to Receive mode and sat back in her chair. So Peter wouldn't be bringing his clothes over that evening. It would be the next day at the earliest, and not very early at that as he'd be doing his clinic first and then going to the hospital.

She knew Ned well enough to know from his tone of voice that he'd felt uncomfortable at passing on what he believed to be excuses. And that's what they clearly were.

If Peter had wanted to see her that evening, he could have done so, no matter how late, and Ned knew that as well as she.

And if he'd genuinely thought it would be too late to turn up that evening, he could have come across early the following morning, done his clinic from the control station as he usually did, and then gone off to the hospital. The distances involved were negligible.

But what Ned couldn't possibly have known was that a

wave of relief had swept through her as she'd listened to Ned convey Peter's message. Its strength had taken her completely by surprise, and she was still reeling from it.

And she'd been thinking about it ever since.

In Peter's early days in Cobar, he'd been nothing more to her than a pleasant, very attractive man whose company she'd increasingly come to enjoy.

But his physical presence in her life day after day, his ability to make her laugh, the warmth in his smile, his enthusiasm for living life to the full—all that had aroused in her feelings that had lain dormant since long before Marco had died, and she and Peter had gradually drawn closer. The idea that he might one day move in with her had crept into the back of her mind.

And she could also see, now that she was giving the subject some thought, that she'd probably sensed subconsciously that getting together with Peter might help to overcome the feeling of guilt over Marco's death that had daily dogged her tracks.

Which is what had happened.

Peter was a terrific guy, and she didn't have a single moment's regret that they'd ended up in bed together. On the contrary—for the last few weeks, she'd felt herself come alive again.

So why was she so relieved that he wasn't bringing his clothes to her house that evening?

She stared at the radio for a moment, and then got up, crossed the room and went into her bedroom.

The first thing she saw was the suitcase she'd filled with Marco's clothes, which stood against the far wall. She sat down on the bed and faced it.

The minute she'd pulled the first of Marco's clothes out of the wardrobe, she'd known that she was truly ready to move on from the past. Her energy building, she'd pulled his clothes from the wardrobe until it was empty.

But was she actually moving on?

Her brow furrowed.

It would be Peter in her bed, not Marco, but apart from that, she'd be living in the same way that she'd done for some time now.

She'd have the same job, in the same town, with the same people around her every day. Just with a different man.

A lovely man, it was true. But did she really want to start sharing her life with another man at the very moment she'd finally freed herself from the last one, no matter how fond she was of him?

And did she really want to carry on just as before?

Was the fact that she was asking the questions an answer in itself?

She could see that Peter loved every minute of the life he'd chosen for himself, that he couldn't wait to see what challenges each new day would bring.

Having discovered where he wanted to be, he'd pursued his dream of getting there with single-mindedness and at the expense of finding happiness with the woman he'd loved—and deep down, clearly still did.

But despite his profound regret over Claire, anyone could see that he'd found fulfilment in the life that Australia had given him.

But could they say the same about her?

She'd finally been able to put behind her the guilt and grief that had overwhelmed her in the months immediately after Marco's death, and she stood on the threshold of a new life.

But was she in danger of throwing away her chance to see what that new life could offer her?

Was she playing it safe and hiding behind the feelings she had for Peter, when she should be asking herself what she really wanted to do now that Marco was gone, and then making sure that she did it?

When she looked at the months ahead, could she see herself getting the same enjoyment out of her life as Peter would be getting out of his?

And was the love she felt for Peter the sort of love she'd felt for Marco in their early days together—a love that made you feel as if you were soaring above the world?

Would such a love even be possible with a person whose heart so visibly still belonged to someone else?

Or was theirs the sort of love that had been born out of need?

Peter had walked into her life at a moment when she'd needed him much more than she'd realised. She'd been going about her work like an automaton, closing further and further in on herself.

And then Peter had arrived and breathed life into her.

In having to make the effort to teach him what he needed to know, and in responding to him, she'd got to know him as a person and had slowly begun to feel human again.

For that reason, she'd never cease to be glad that they'd grown as close as they had, so close that him moving in had seemed the inevitable next stage.

But now that she was thinking about it, did she really want that to be the next stage in her life?

And did Peter?

Wouldn't he have come over that night if he had?

Just as she'd needed help with putting Marco behind her, Peter, too, had needed help with putting the girl in England behind him?

Had he spent the day coming to the conclusion that although they loved each other in a very special way and would always feel a deep sense of friendship, things between them should go no further than that?

For that was the conclusion she knew she'd reached.

So what did she—she, and no one else—really want to do?

She stood up, walked out of the bedroom, through the sitting room and kitchen and out on to the veranda just as a flock of galahs rose in a cloud from a nearby gum tree, their pink and grey feathers vivid against the yellowing sky.

She didn't actually have to stay in Cobar, she thought, leaning against the wooden balustrade and watching the galahs wing high above the ground.

If she wanted, she could make a completely fresh start somewhere else, somewhere which held no memories of Marco. She could do a different sort of job, maybe something more nine to five, that a social life would fit around more easily.

Excitement started to well up within her.

She could move to a large town, for example. There were opportunities galore in such a town for those who wanted to grab them. She could go to Sydney, or better still, to Melbourne.

Melbourne would be completely uncharted territory for her. She'd seen nothing of the city when she and Marco had disembarked there as they'd had to go straight to Bonegilla. It would be fun to get to know a new city.

Or she could go to Adelaide.

There was so much she could do if she were free.

And in her heart she knew that if she felt the way about Peter that she'd felt about Marco when she'd first met

Marco, she wouldn't want to do any of it—it would be enough to stay in Cobar with Peter.

But she knew with sudden clarity, it wasn't.

RUST-RED DUST ROSE up the sides of the car, caking the windows each time the wheels veered off the bitumen strip and churned up the crimson sand bordering the road from Cobar Hospital to Peter's bungalow.

Reaching his drive, Peter turned sharply on to it, brought the car to a halt and jumped out into a cloud of swirling red particles. With dust stinging his eyes and settling in his throat, he slammed the car door shut.

Hurrying into his house, he threw his medical bag on to the sofa, went straight through to the kitchen, filled a glass with water and drank it thirstily.

Then he put the empty glass down on the worktop, leaned back against the fridge and closed his eyes, waiting for his heart to stop racing.

From the moment he'd learned that Ruth was stable and sleeping and would in all likelihood survive the night, and had seen Frank sink into the chair beside her bed, insisting on spending the night there, the turmoil that had been bubbling inside him all day had unleashed itself.

Images had tumbled into his mind, springing from thoughts he hadn't known he had, thoughts that must have been dormant in the back of his mind, waiting for the right moment to ambush him.

Their moment had come as he'd driven away from the hospital, and they'd broken free and flooded his mind.

As he'd driven home, he'd pictured himself getting into his car the following day, a packed suitcase in his hand, and driving the short distance to Susie's.

He could see it all so clearly.

He'd stop the car in the shade of the gum tree just outside the base control, take his suitcase from the car and walk with it to the front door. The door would open and a woman would be standing there, smiling at him. That woman would be Susie.

Susie, not Claire.

But it should be Claire.

Oh, how he ached for it to be Claire!

How could he have got everything so completely wrong? How could he have repeated the mistake he'd made in Ladakh, and let himself once again dwell on the things he didn't have, and make them into the things he wanted to have more than anything else in the world?

In doing that, he'd failed to see that what he really wanted more than anything else was right under his nose?

More than the sense of freedom, more than the emptiness offered by wide open spaces—it was Claire, he wanted. Claire, the only woman he'd ever truly love.

And he'd been too stupid to see that!

How could any dream, any country, any life—no matter how much you loved that life—compare with being with the person you loved?

Why, oh, why, had he needed Frank Malloy to show him something he'd been too blind to see for himself? He'd made a mistake that was going to hurt him for the rest of his life, and he had no one to blame but himself.

In self-accusing torment, he flung open the kitchen door and stepped out on to the veranda.

A loud chattering stirred the silence of the evening and he glanced up as a flock of galahs flew above his house, coming from the direction of the airport. Dropping to the parched red ground, they settled like petals of grey and pink blossom.

His head pounding, he ran down the veranda steps, strode across his yard and out on to the wide expanse of burnished red-gold beyond his yard.

Alone on the hard ground, surrounded by a scarlet emptiness, he stopped, threw back his head and cried up to the sky,

'Claire! Oh, Claire!'

PURPLE SHADOWS WERE LENGTHENING across the land when he parked his dust-covered car in front of the base control station.

His hands empty, he went up the steps and knocked on the front door. Footsteps sounded around the back of the house, and he turned to his right as Susie rounded the corner of the veranda and came towards him.

She hesitated a moment when she saw him standing there, and a look of surprise flickered across her face. She glanced down at his hands, and back to his face, and then she continued towards him.

Reaching him, she stood in front of him, waiting.

He looked down into the face that he'd come to know so well, the face of the woman who would always have a special place in his heart.

'We've got to talk,' he said quietly.

She nodded. 'I know.'

39

B irmingham
  May, 1971

'Telephone for you, Sister,' the young nurse called to Claire, and held out the receiver to her.

Claire took the phone. 'Hello. Sister Meredith speaking.'

Forty minutes later, she'd hastily packed a few clothes in a bag and was hurrying out of her flat and across the road to her car. She jumped into the car and drove south-west through Birmingham, heading for the County Hospital in Hereford.

'Your mother seems quite comfortable now, although she was very shaken when she was brought in,' the nurse said, leading the way to the cubicle. 'I'm afraid we've had a steady stream of people who've fallen on the ice today, and like most of the others, she looks far worse than she is.'

'Snow in May is somewhat unusual, and the overnight freeze can't have helped. I'm not surprised it took a lot of people by surprise,' Claire remarked as they walked along.

'Well, it shouldn't have done—the forecast was right for once.'

The nurse stopped in front of the curtains, put up her hand to pull them aside, and then paused. 'You'll know what to expect, being a nurse, and I'm sure you'll appreciate that it isn't as serious as it looks,' she said.

'Yes, I do. My mother's used to being as fit as a fiddle. I don't envy anyone treating her—she won't like having to obey orders. In fact, I imagine she's already tried to issue some of her own.'

The nurse gave her a quick smile and drew back the curtain.

Claire took a step forward, and stopped in sudden shock.

Her mother's wrist was black and blue and visibly swollen, despite being half-hidden by the sling which supported her arm, and her face, which looked thin and drawn, was covered in cuts and scratches, around a number of which there were traces of blood.

She turned and looked questioningly at the nurse.

'Like I said, it looks worse than it is. She's just back from having her wrist X-rayed, and there weren't any fractures. But it's always a shock when it's someone you know. She'll look better when I've cleaned her up a bit.

I was about to do her face when you arrived. I've already cleaned her knee, and put on a dry dressing so that her stockings won't stick to the grazed skin. It doesn't need anything more than that.'

'And you say her wrist isn't broken?'

'No, it's just very bruised, with a mild sprain. But it's obviously extremely painful. I'll put on a crêpe bandage for support, and she'll have to keep her arm in the sling for a couple more days, or at least until the swelling's subsided.'

Claire nodded.

'You already know all this, of course,' the nurse went on, 'but I'm being on the safe side. Sometimes it's easy to forget what we know when the patient's a person we love.'

'I heard that,' Grace cut in weakly. 'I'm not sure how much love there is. It's a long time since I've heard from my daughter, and even longer since I've seen her. It's a sad day when it takes an accident to bring a daughter to see her mother. Or to see how much longer she'll have to wait for her inheritance.'

Claire moved up to her mother's side, leaned down and kissed her on the cheek.

Her mother's skin felt dry beneath her lips.

'Hello, Mother, how are you feeling?' she asked, straightening up.

'Look at me, will you? How d'you think I'm feeling?' Grace retorted in irritation.

The nurse stepped forward and took Grace's pulse. 'You're doing very well, Grace,' she said reassuringly, her voice slightly raised.

'My name is Mrs Meredith,' Grace said sharply. 'And there's no problem with my hearing.'

With a tight smile at Grace, the nurse turned to Claire.

'Doctor Saunders prescribed a tetanus vaccination for your mother, just to be on the safe side, and a few mild analgesics which'll make her more comfortable. I'll go and get everything and be back in a minute. I might also be able to get you both a cup of tea, if you'd like one.'

Claire glanced at her mother, who gave a slight nod.

'That's very kind of you, Nurse, thank you. I didn't stop

on the journey as I was so anxious to get here, and the word tea has made me realise I'm actually quite thirsty.'

'I won't be long,' the nurse said, and she went out of the cubicle, pulling the curtains closed behind her.

'I'm sorry I've not been to see you for a while,' Claire began, sitting down on the chair next to the bed.

'I hoped you were going to bring Peter to see me,' Grace said peevishly. 'It's several months since I've seen him.'

'We work such long hours that it's difficult to make plans to go anywhere,' Claire said, struggling to push back the impulse to burst into tears at the mention of Peter.

'Well, now that you've found your way here again, I expect you to bring him to see me very soon. I'd like him to look at my wrist and tell me if they've treated it in the correct manner.'

'*I* can tell you that, Mother, just as well as Peter. They've done everything they should have done, and the nurse has gone to get the same medication that Peter would have prescribed. And as I intend to stay for a few days, I can keep an eye on your wrist for you.'

'He's a doctor. I want to hear what he has to say, and not what a nurse thinks is the right course of action. I'd like you to ask him to come and see me.'

'Thank you for that vote of confidence, Mother. I'm a ward sister now, in charge of state-registered nurses and students. But as far as you're concerned, treating a bruised wrist is beyond me. Well, thank you for that.'

'You may look at my wrist if you wish when my sling needs adjusting,' Grace said grudgingly. 'But I'd like Peter to look at it, too.'

'He can't,' Claire said bluntly. 'He's in Australia, and he's been there for a while.'

To her horror, her eyes filled with tears and she started to cry.

CLAIRE OPENED the curtains in her mother's bedroom and glanced towards the slight figure in the bed. She went over and sat down on the side of the bed.

'How are you feeling this morning, Mother?'

'Very sore, Claire, but that's only to be expected.'

'And there's nothing other than soreness? No pains in your chest or anywhere else? No difficulty with breathing?'

'No, nothing else. It's only my wrist and my knees—both are very painful. However, you'll not hear me complain. It was unwise to go out when I knew there was a risk of ice. But it was for a short distance only, and I thought that if I was extremely careful, I'd make it in safety. Unfortunately, I was wrong.'

'Where were you so keen to go?'

'To lunch with Cecilia and Jane. They live in sheltered accommodation that's attached to a residential home near here. I lunch with them there every month.

I always enjoy our lunches and I wasn't going to let a little snow stop me, particularly as we had something of importance to discuss. However, it was a mistake to have allowed my wishes to cloud my judgement.'

'It's unlike you to do anything so reckless, Mother. Unnecessarily going out when it's icy underfoot is plain stupid. It's not only the very old who have to be careful— you can break a bone at your age, too.'

'I have to agree with you, Claire.' She paused a moment and glanced around her room. 'While I enjoy living on my own in my beautiful flat, I do enjoy company at times.'

Claire opened her mouth to speak.

'No,' Grace said quickly. 'I'm not criticising you.' The trace of a smile flickered across her lips. 'Not this time, anyway. I recognise that you live at a distance and that you work difficult hours. No, I'm stating a fact, which is that I get lonely on occasions.'

'You've never told me that before,' Claire said slowly.

'Well, I'm telling you now. And what I want you to tell me now is why Peter is in Australia. But first, I'd like you to bring me a cup of tea and two slices of lightly toasted bread. Then you may sit with me and tell me why he's over there and you're over here, crying.'

'IF I UNDERSTAND YOU CORRECTLY, you've chosen to stay in England rather than go to Australia with Peter, even though that means you'll never see him again. Is that right?'

'That's it in a nutshell.'

'Well, I must say you do surprise me, Claire. But I suppose you've always been a rather determined young woman. Once you'd adopted a line, you pursued it single-mindedly, irrespective of other considerations.

I'm thinking back to the time you insisted upon becoming a nurse. Such a choice of career was totally against my wishes, but my wishes completely failed to prevail.

Nevertheless, for you to have placed more value on where you live than on the man you purport to love, does, indeed, surprise me. And it disappoints me somewhat, too.'

'Now it's your turn to surprise me, Mother. You're the biggest snob ever, and you've always valued material possessions more highly than you have inner worth, so to speak.

Think back to how you disparaged Walthamstow the first time you met Peter, and how you described the people there. You've always considered where a person lives to be very important.'

'And I still feel that way. But I like Peter and I thought you did, too.'

'Of course, I did. And I still do.' Her voice cracked. She steadied herself, and then went on. 'He's not easy to forget. I sort of went out with someone for a time after Peter left, but I finished it a while ago. I still miss Peter too much to be able to think seriously about anyone else.'

'So what do you intend to do?'

'I've started looking for another job. When I've left Birmingham, I'll stop thinking about him. At least, I hope I will.' She paused, and gave her mother a half-smile. 'You sound almost sorry I didn't go to Australia, even though you might never have seen me again. I took you into consideration when deciding whether to go or not, you know.'

'If that's true, you shouldn't have done,' Grace said bluntly. 'You've lived your life as you wanted till now, and I see no reason for you to change tack at this late stage.'

'I know you're not that old at the moment, Mother, but there'll come a time when you need more help. People change with age, and you won't always be able to do as much as you can at the moment.

Your fall yesterday, and how shaken by it you still are, proves that if nothing else. If I were in Australia, you'd be totally alone. Is that really what you want?'

Grace brushed the toast crumbs from her sheet. 'You're correct, of course—people *do* change with age. I used to think I'd never be able to contemplate leaving this flat. But in fact I've been thinking about doing so for some time now, and I'm inclined to think that this would be the right time to make such a move.'

Claire stared at her mother in amazement. 'I don't believe I'm hearing this. Where are you thinking of going?'

'I know I'm on the young side to contemplate such a move, but to the same sheltered accommodation as Cecilia and Jane. It's of the highest standard. Each unit is well appointed and fitted out in the height of luxury. I shall take my own furniture and curtains, of course.

By being there, I shall have the advantage of being alone when I wish, but also of having company when I wish. And there's medical help on hand at all times, should I need it. All I'd have to do is pull a cord and the warden would come.

Then eventually, when I can no longer manage on my own, I'd transfer to the nursing home that's part of the development.'

'But there's always a long waiting list for such places.'

'I've been on the list for several months. A unit has become available and I was planning to see it yesterday before lunching with Cecilia and Jane. At my request, the hospital contacted the home about my fall, and the room will be held for me.'

'I don't know what to say. You've taken me completely by surprise.'

'When your surprise has worn off, you'll realise that I didn't consider you at all when making my plans, any more than I expect you to consider me.'

'I don't get what you mean.'

'I'm afraid the units and nursing home are expensive, as one would expect, and this will somewhat dent your inheritance. By how much depends upon the number of years ahead of me.'

'Unlike you, Mother, material wealth doesn't mean a lot to me. I wouldn't be a nurse if it did.' She smiled warmly at her mother. 'I hope you have so many years of good health ahead of you that I don't get a penny.'

'Thank you, dear,' Grace said stiffly. 'I do believe you mean that.'

'I *do* mean it,' Claire said. 'You're my mother, aren't you?'

Grace sniffed. 'I'm not sure how much that should dictate our feelings. We feel affection for each other as a mother and daughter should, but we've never been close in the way that some parents and children are. That's the fault of my character, I'm sure, but whatever the reason, it's a fact.'

Claire made a move to speak.

Her mother raised a thin hand to stop her. 'No, Claire, let's be honest with each other. We've never had the kind of relationship whereby our lives revolve around the needs of each other.'

'But—'

'You said that if you'd gone to Australia, I would've been totally alone. You now know that this would not be the case —in fact, I suspect that I'd hardly notice your absence. After all, I've barely seen you since you started at Birmingham.

Yes, I get a letter once in a while and the occasional telephone call, but in reality, it makes no difference whether those originate from Birmingham or from somewhere further afield.'

Claire sat up straight, and frowned. 'What are you trying to say?'

'I didn't think I was trying to say anything at all—I thought I was making it very clear that neither of us is responsible for the other, and each of us must do what we want with our lives.

What I'd like now is for you to contact an agency nurse and book her for a week. By the end of that time, I'll have no more need of her.'

'But I was going to stay for the week to look after you, and longer if necessary.'

'I would prefer you to go home and look after yourself, Claire. Now that we've removed any necessity for you to consider my well-being when planning your future, you're free to consider what you truly want to do with the rest of your life.'

She paused a moment, and cleared her throat.

'There is one other thing I should tell you, however. Before I start to use up your inheritance, I intend to make you a most generous financial gift. I wouldn't want the choices you made to be limited by monetary considerations.'

'But—'

'There are no buts. I'm doing only what I want. It would give me peace of mind to know you were happy, so I need to ensure that you are in a position to go anywhere in the world that you wish. By taking the path that will make you happiest, you will have fulfilled your duty as a daughter.'

Claire stood up. Looking down into her mother's face, she took Grace's hand.

'Thank you, Mother,' she said, tears trickling down her cheeks. 'I think you might be surprised by how much I love you at this moment, and indeed, by how much I've always loved you. From the bottom of my heart, thank you.'

Her breathing laboured, Claire struggled up the track to the summit of Bilberry Hill.

Reaching the top, she paused at the edge of the ridge, at the point where the ground fell away in a steep slope lined with threadbare bilberry bushes, their small pointed leaves still clothed in autumnal red.

As she stood there, a lone figure surrounded by the enormity of the landscape, the anguish that had been swirling within her since she'd left her mother, rose up.

She put her hands to her mouth to hold it back, but it was too powerful, and raising her eyes to the pale-grey sky, she dropped her hands and let her grief break free.

How could she have been so stupid, so very, very stupid? How could she have been so blind to what really matters? How could she have got it all so wrong?

From the moment she'd left her mother and driven back to Birmingham, her mother's words had reverberated in her head—the words she'd said, and the words she hadn't.

Her eyes wide open to the truth at last, for every inch of the journey home, her inner torment had raged.

And she had only herself to blame for her misery.

No one else.

She'd let pride stand in the way of her happiness.

Without even giving it a moment's thought, she'd taken Peter's interest in Australia to be a comment on his feelings for her and, her pride wounded, she'd refused to let herself hear his words. Instead, she'd opened the door to blinkered self-righteousness.

It was hurt pride that had stopped her from reading the brochure he'd begged her to look at, and from considering whether to try out a life that was different from anything their friends would be doing.

She'd turned her back on it without even attempting to find out what it was that had fired him so.

But wanting to do something different didn't mean that he didn't love her enough—only a small-minded person, as she'd let herself become, could think that it did.

It wasn't as if he'd wanted to pursue a life in Australia without her—he hadn't. She'd always been a part of his plans. She was the one who'd drawn back—not the other way round.

And as for the pathetic reasons she'd come up with for not wanting to go!

She went red with embarrassment as she remembered the words she'd hurled at him.

She'd used her mother as an excuse. But her mother was a self-contained, independent woman with the means to secure whatever she wanted for her comfort, as Peter had rightly pointed out.

And she'd always known in her heart that her mother's happiness didn't depend upon her being physically present in her mother's life.

And yes, she loved living in England—it was where she

was born, after all—but that didn't mean she couldn't love living somewhere else, too. Of course, she could. If she was with the right person, she could live anywhere in the world.

And Peter was the right person.

From the moment she'd met him, there'd never been so much as one second in which she hadn't felt truly cherished, nor so much as one second in which she hadn't loved Peter with all her heart.

But she'd let herself lose sight of that, and now she was paying the price for her wilful blindness—she was unhappier than she'd ever been. In losing Peter, she'd lost a part of herself and she'd never feel whole again.

How she wished she could turn the clock back!

If only she'd argued when Alex had told her that it was better that Peter didn't give anyone his Australian address. She should have said that it was a bad idea, that it was all too final and she should have his address.

She should have insisted on it.

But in a state of pique, she'd accepted the decision without demur, and all she knew was that he'd flown to Sydney Airport. He wouldn't have wanted to live in a large town, so he was bound to have left Sydney, and could be anywhere in Australia.

And Australia was a huge country.

And now that she could find him if she wanted, she had no way of doing so.

From the moment she'd left her mother, beneath all the frustration and anger at herself, a kernel of hope had taken root, and had grown steadily within her—hope that it wasn't too late for her and Peter, that he might still have feelings for her, just as she had for him.

Well, she wasn't going to give up on him that easily.

She raised her head and stared towards the far hills. She didn't know how she'd find out where he was, but she *would* find out, and she'd go to him.

If he was already with someone else, she'd be forced to accept defeat, painful though it would be. But it was worth the risk.

Now that pride and stubbornness had been peeled back from her eyes, she could see with the utmost clarity that she couldn't care less whereabouts in the world she lived, so long as she lived with Peter.

'I'M REALLY HOPING you can help me, Alex,' Claire said, perching on the edge of his sofa.

Alex sat down next to her. 'You know that I will if I can. But first, are you sure you don't want a drink—wine or something else?'

'I'm fine, thanks.'

'Whatever you are, you're not fine,' Alex said. 'You've clearly been crying, and you're obviously not yourself. Whatever it is, you'll feel better when you've told Uncle Alex.'

She gave him a wan smile. 'You know me too well, Alex. The thing is, I still love Peter to bits. But you already know that, don't you? But what you don't know is that I've decided to do something about it. I'm going to find out where he is and go to him.'

'I must admit, I'm not entirely surprised,' Alex said, his smile not quite reaching his eyes. 'But are you sure? He said some pretty nasty things to you before he left. Small-minded, I think you said he called you. Don't you think it might be better to leave things as they are?'

'He might regret what he said. After all, I said some pretty strong things, too, and I now wish I hadn't. I'd like the chance to tell him so, and to find out how he's getting on. And to find out if he's with someone else. It'd really hurt if he is, but at least I'd know I had to get over him.'

'So how can I help?'

'I was wondering,' she began, clasping her hands round her knees, her heart thumping fast in anxiety, 'if Peter stuck to the agreement not to tell anyone his address. Knowing him, I thought he might have sent it to you as an afterthought.'

She drew in a deep breath and held it, staring at Alex with hope.

He shook his head slowly, an expression of deep regret on his face.

'You're not the only one who wondered if he'd weaken like that—I did, too. But he didn't.'

He gestured his helplessness. 'If he'd done so, I'd have written to him long ago. I'm really curious to know how things have turned out for him. But like you, I've no idea where he is. So although I wish I could help, unfortunately I can't.'

Her shoulders slumped, and she sighed in despair. 'You were my only hope. But I knew it was a long shot as I was sure you'd have told me if he'd written.'

He nodded. 'I would've done.' He paused. 'So what will you do now?'

'I haven't a clue,' she said flatly. 'I've been in Hereford for the last few days and I'm totally shattered. My mother had a bad fall, but she's all right now.'

She stood up and started to move towards the door.

He rose to his feet. 'Is there any other way you could get his address?'

'Not really. If he didn't send it to you, he won't have sent it to anyone else in the group—you were his closest friend.'

She gave a slight shrug. 'Maybe I'll be able to move on, now that I know it's impossible to contact him. I've applied for some jobs and I should be hearing from them soon. If I get one of those, I'll probably be too busy to think about Peter. And getting to know a new place should take my mind off him. At least, I hope it will.'

He walked to the door with her and opened it. 'I'm sure it will,' he said, his smile effusing sympathy and regret.

'Moving away is the most sensible thing to do, but don't go too far from here—Mary and I will want to keep in touch with you and meet up from time to time. As for Mary's little girl, you'll want to watch her grow up.'

'That's very true.'

'But being forced to make some new friends, too, is no bad thing. You've so much to offer that you should have a man in your life, and I'm sure you'll find that man as soon as you escape the confines of Birmingham and all of its sad memories. I certainly hope you do.

I wish you nothing but happiness, as I'm sure you know.'

AT LAST, Alex thought, his face twisting into a sneer as he sat down again on the sofa.

By denying that he had Peter's address, he had finally been able to take a step towards exacting his revenge for what they'd done to him.

If Claire *had* got in touch with Peter again and they'd resumed their life together, the anger and jealousy he'd felt since the night when Claire had rejected him, might have continued to eat away at him.

Instead of it dissolving in the satisfaction of knowing

that Peter and Claire were irrevocably lost to each other, them getting together, and his helplessness to do anything about it, could actually gnaw with greater ferocity than ever before.

So it may be a small step only, but it was a pleasing one.

In the absence of Peter's address, Claire would move away, but not too far from Mary.

With minimum effort on his part, therefore, she'd stay in his line of vision, and all he'd need to do was bide his time, wait for her to get married, snap the all-important photograph—and then, bingo!

Nothing was going to bring him greater satisfaction and pleasure than the moment he posted a photo of a married Claire to Peter.

He still wished he'd been able to think of an even more hurtful punishment, something bigger and nastier, but despite lying in bed night after night, driving himself to the verge of madness in an attempt to come up with an alternative plan, the reality was that given the distance between him and Peter, the photo was the most he could do.

He looked round the empty room, and shivered.

Definitely, the sooner he was able to send that photo to Peter the better.

It was eating him up, waiting for the moment to come, his days full of hatred for Peter, and also for Claire. He could feel its effect on him.

But somehow he couldn't take control of himself, couldn't let his anger go, couldn't go back to being the lively, outgoing Alex he used to be. A sense of oppression weighed heavily on him from morning till night, and he couldn't shake it off.

It was all Peter's fault, and he wouldn't be able to go back to his former self until he'd hurt Peter as hard as he could.

When he'd done that, he'd start living again. He was sure of that.

He just had to be patient a little longer. And he could be.

He leaned back against the sofa, and waited.

41

Claire followed Margaret Henderson into the narrow parlour. Christopher glanced up from his book, promptly pushed it to one side and rose to his feet.

'Claire!' he exclaimed, smiling broadly. 'What a pleasant surprise. But you should've let us know you were coming—we would've had something a bit more exciting in the house than our usual evening fare.'

'It was a spur of the moment thing. I knew that if you weren't here, you'd be at the Mission, so I knew I'd find you somewhere.'

She clutched the small travel bag she was holding in front of her more tightly.

'Actually, I didn't really know I was coming till I found myself in the car on the road to London.' She tried to laugh. 'But don't worry—I won't impose on you for long.'

'You won't be imposing at all,' Margaret said quickly. 'We're both delighted to see you, aren't we, Chris? There's plenty of food so you must stay for supper, and you're welcome to stay overnight if you'd like.

You've a bed here for as many nights as you want. We've rather got into the habit of storing things in the spare room these days, but Peter's room is empty. His bed is always made up and aired, you know,' she added, a catch in her voice.

Claire saw a shadow cross her face. Margaret's hair had turned very grey in the few months since she'd last seen her, she noticed.

'Thank you for such a lovely welcome   especially as I don't deserve it. I haven't been to see you since Peter left. I should've come sooner. But missing Peter like I was... well, I couldn't. But if you're sure I'm not putting you out, I'd love to stay for the night.'

Margaret's face broke into a smile of genuine pleasure. 'I'm so glad. Let me take your coat and hang it up.' She held out her hand and waited while Claire put her travel case on a nearby chair and unbuttoned her coat.

'Would you like to freshen up?' She pointed vaguely in the direction of the kitchen and bathroom.

Shaking her head, Claire gave her coat to Margaret. 'I'm fine, thanks.'

'Then sit down with Christopher, dear, while I get us all a cup of tea. You look as if you could use one. And then you must tell us what's brought you here.'

She went through to the kitchen, and Claire went over to the table and sat down opposite Christopher. A moment later, she heard the sound of cups clattering.

She saw that Christopher, too, was greyer than the last time she'd seen him, and that his face was more lined.

'How've you been?' she asked. 'You're both looking well.'

'And we are, thanks. No need for a nurse yet,' he said with a laugh. 'We're still busy at the Mission, as you'll probably have guessed. In fact, I can't see a time when the work will come to an end: people need more help these days, rather than less.

With so much to do here, I doubt we'll be sent anywhere else, and we're a bit too long in the tooth for that, anyway. And Margaret would never agree to move away. Not unless the posting was to Australia,' he added dryly.

'Here we are,' Margaret said, coming in with a tray. 'I'm afraid that the best I can do for biscuits is Rich Tea. Chris and I seldom eat biscuits so I don't bother to buy them.'

She put a cup of tea in front of each of them, the plate of biscuits in the centre of the table, rested the tray against the wall, and sat down.

'Did I hear someone say the word Australia?' she asked, glancing from one to the other as she raised her cup to her lips.

'Only in passing,' Christopher told her. 'We were making conversation until you joined us. But now that you're here, I imagine that Claire's keen to tell us what brought her to Walthamstow. I'm assuming that something did,' he added, smiling at Claire.

'You assumed right,' she said. She cleared her throat. 'I don't know if you know that Peter decided not to send his Australian address to anyone, including me?'

Margaret nodded. 'Yes, we did. He was adamant that he'd find it difficult to settle if he knew he could easily get in touch with his past, and vice versa. We didn't agree with his decision, but we understood what he was saying.'

'I really wish I had his address,' Claire blurted out.

Christopher nodded. 'I see,' he said quietly.

'I wondered if he might've sent his address to someone, after all,' she said, her words tumbling out in a rush. 'He'd have sent it to Alex, if to anyone. But I went to Alex and asked him, and Peter didn't.'

Margaret frowned. 'How strange! I know he intended to —he told us a while ago that he'd had second thoughts about being quite so out of contact, and was going to get in touch with Alex. I suppose he must have forgotten to do so.' Her frown deepened. 'But I don't think he *did* forget—I'm certain he said he'd written to Alex.'

'I don't know why I didn't think of coming to you first of all. But I've missed Peter so desperately, and been so unhappy, that it must've stopped me from thinking clearly. You know how you can't always see the most obvious things? But this morning, having been told by Alex yesterday that he didn't have Peter's address, I was at my lowest ebb, frantic that I wouldn't be able to contact Peter, when it suddenly hit me that you were bound to know where he was. I must've been mad not to have thought of you sooner. But I'm right, aren't I?'

She could hear the hope and desperation in her voice, and she put her hand to her throat to steady herself.

She saw Christopher and Margaret exchange quick glances.

'This cutting himself off,' Christopher said, leaning forward, 'I think it comes from spending so much of his time in Ladakh thinking about what he was missing in England, that he didn't appreciate what Ladakh had to offer.

I know he later very much regretted that. He wouldn't have wanted to repeat the same mistake, and I think he was afraid that if he had a lifeline to England, he'd never completely focus on his new life, and it'd be the Ladakhi situation all over again.'

She bit her lower lip. 'I can see that.'

'As Margaret said, we felt it was a mistake for him to cut himself off in quite such an extreme manner, but it was his decision and we have to respect it. We promised him that we would.'

'But I'm right—you *do* know where he is, don't you?'

'Yes,' Margaret said.

Weak with relief, Claire slumped back against the chair, breathing deeply.

'We've had regular letters from him since he left,' Margaret went on. 'He's very good that way. He uses those blue air letters, the ones that fold, and his letters are detailed and interesting so we don't feel as far from him as we obviously are.

At the last minute, he worried about leaving us alone, you know, and said he wouldn't go,' she added. 'But we urged him to leave. We'd been free to make our own choices in the past—it was his turn now. With God and our Mission, we'll never be alone, but through Peter's letters, he's still with us, too.'

'You should know that we intend to respect our promise not to give anyone his address,' Christopher said gently. 'I'm sorry, Claire, but we can't break our promise.'

Tears started rolling down her cheeks.

'I just want to get in touch with him again.' She put her hands in front of her face. 'I wish I'd gone with him. I've missed him every minute of every day since he left.'

She heard a chair being pushed back, and felt Margaret's arm around her shoulders. 'I'm sorry,' she sobbed, leaning against Margaret. 'I didn't mean to cry. It's just a relief that someone knows where he is.'

'Here, Claire, take this.' Christopher handed her a hand-kerchief and she wept silently into it.

Her tears slowing, she wiped her eyes

'Assuming you had his address, would writing to him really be a good idea?' Margaret asked, returning to her seat.

'You might completely unsettle him, and for no reason at all —he's miles away and he loves the life he's leading,'

'I don't want to write to him,' Claire said, blowing her nose. 'I want to go to him. My mother's given me some money, which means I can go to Australia. Peter's in my head every minute of the day and I can't get him out of it. Morning, noon and night, all I can think of is Peter. I love him and I know I always will, and that's all there is to it.

I should have said to hell with everything and gone with him to Australia, but I didn't. I was so, so stupid. And I want to go to him now and tell him that, but I don't know where he is.'

Her voice broke, and her eyes brimmed again.

Margaret leaned across and took Claire's hand. 'He's been in Australia for some months now, dear,' she said.

She paused, and tightened her hold on Claire's hand.

'On several occasions, he's mentioned a woman he works with. He hasn't said much about her—just that she's a widow—but reading between the lines, Christopher and I thought there might be something developing between them. I'm sure you wouldn't want to go all the way there and find Peter with someone else.'

'I'd willingly take that chance,' Claire said, choking back her tears.

She looked from one to the other. 'I know what Peter and I had, and I know it was special. I'd be really surprised if he didn't have someone else, he's such a terrific person. But he may not have found that same something special with whoever it is.'

'But what if he has?' Christopher asked.

'Then I can always treat it as a holiday, have a look round and come back. Or I might even decide to stay there if I like the look of the place.

One of the advantages of being a nurse is that I'll always find work wherever I am. Peter always used to say that. I obviously wouldn't stay in the same town as him—that'd be too painful—but I could go somewhere else.'

'You do surprise me. Peter said one of the reasons you wouldn't go with him was that you loved living in England,' Christopher remarked. 'And there was your mother to think of, too. Have you changed your mind on both counts?'

'Mother's got her life sorted out, and she's actually encouraged me to go. That's one of the reasons she gave me the money.'

'That's very good of her.'

'It is. As for living in England, if I've learnt anything at all in these last miserable months it's that nothing matters as much as being with the person you love.

I love Peter and I absolutely have to see him again, even if it's only to hear from him that he's fallen in love with someone else. I just have to see him. So, please, will you give me his address? Please.' Her voice trailed off.

'I'm afraid we gave our word to Peter,' Christopher began.

Margaret put her hand on his to stop him. 'But in a way, that promise is a little out of date, don't you think, my dear?'

Christopher raised his eyebrows enquiringly.

'Originally, Peter didn't want anyone at all, apart from us, to have his address. But once he was there, he changed his mind and sent it to Alex, and he told us he'd given Alex permission to pass it on if he thought it appropriate.'

'And you're thinking that he thought that one day Claire might ask for it, or he hoped she would,' Christopher said.

'Exactly!' Margaret exclaimed. 'So in a way, if we gave Claire his address, we'd only be doing what Peter hoped Alex would do.'

Claire saw Christopher nod imperceptibly to Margaret, who promptly got up, went to the sideboard, opened the top drawer and took out a notepad.

She returned to the table with it, wrote a few lines on the top sheet, tore off the piece of paper and put it in front of Claire.

'Here you are,' she said with a warm smile, her eyes watering. 'I've given you the address of where he lives, and also where he works. Nothing would give us greater pleasure than knowing that the two of you were back together again. May God be with you.'

Claire picked up the paper and clutched it to her chest.

Unable to put her gratitude into words through the tears that were falling again, she glanced from one to the other.

'Watch out, don't let it get wet!' Christopher exclaimed, smiling. 'The ink might run and then where would you be?'

He paused. 'Margaret's right, Claire. We would be overjoyed to know that you and Peter were reunited. But no matter where your journey ends, you have a permanent place in our hearts, and our prayers will always go with you.'

'Thank you,' she said, barely able to speak. 'Thank you, thank you.'

42

The following day

THE AFTERNOON AIR was cooling rapidly, and shadows lengthening as Claire parked her car and hurried across the road to the building where Alex lived.

She went quickly up the steps and through the main door. Minutes later, she was facing Alex's front door. Taking a deep breath to rein in her anger, she knocked at the door, and stepped back.

Alex opened the door wearing a dressing gown, and unshaven.

His surprise at seeing her gave way to wariness. 'You've caught me as I was about to take a shower,' he said, visibly disconcerted. 'I didn't go in today—I've been a bit under the weather.' He indicated his dressing gown.

'Don't worry. This won't take long.'

'Then you'd better come in. You can have a seat while I

tidy myself?' He stood aside to let her go into the flat. 'Sit, won't you?' He pointed towards the sofa. 'I won't be a minute.'

'I'd prefer to stand, thank you,' she said.

'As you wish.'

'Why did you lie to me, Alex? I thought we were friends.'

He attempted a laugh. 'I've no idea what you're talking about.'

'Then let me give you some clues. Blue air letter. Peter's address. Do you need any more than that?'

He shrugged. 'Sorry, you've lost me.'

'Then, let me make it easier for you. Peter told his parents that he'd sent you his address, and told you that you could pass it on if you felt it was the right thing to do. Is it coming back to you now?'

Alex tightened his dressing gown belt. 'So that's what you're talking about. Yes, that's true. If you're wondering why I didn't give it to you, it's because I didn't think it the right thing to do.'

'And exactly why not?' she asked, her voice ice-cold.

'Because for years you'd been telling me that you couldn't bear to live anywhere other than England, that you wanted a little house and kids. And for years, Peter had been talking about a very different dream.

I'm a friend of you both, and I wanted you both to be happy.

Having missed Peter so much, you now think you'd be happy to settle wherever he wants to live. But after the initial euphoria had worn off, you'd have struggled, and in the long run, it would've destroyed what you felt for each other. I thought it better to leave things as they were. I was only doing what I thought best for you.'

She took a step closer to him. 'Well, I don't believe you.

When I came to you a few days ago, I was desperate to contact Peter. My priorities had changed, and you knew it. Refusing to tell me his address was nothing to do with our happiness. Quite the opposite—it was about stopping us from getting back together. Why, Alex?'

He shook his head. 'You've got it all wrong, Claire.'

'And what's more,' she went on. 'I've spent the night thinking about the role you played in all this. Yes, *role*, Alex. I use that word for a reason. At some point, you stopped being our genuine friend. You feigned friendship, but acted otherwise. I don't know why you turned against us, but your actions show that you did.'

'I've always thought you had a lively mind, Claire,' he said with an attempt at a laugh, 'but I really think you've let your imagination run away with you this time.'

'Really?' She raised her eyebrow. 'A true friend would never have given Peter that brochure about Australia. You've just said yourself how much he talked to you about what he wanted from life. You knew he was restless, and that the brochure was likely to fire him up about Australia. And equally, that it was the last place I'd want to go.'

He shrugged. 'I rather think you're crediting me with too great a degree of clairvoyance. No one could have predicted that Peter would choose to fly off to that ghastly-sounding place rather than stay with the woman he was supposed to love.

And no one could've predicted that you'd be such a self-righteous bitch that you'd dismiss the idea of Australia without even reading a single word about it.

Probably, in a mischievous mood, I saw the brochure and thought I'd stir things a little. But I only set everything in motion—you two did the rest.'

'No, Alex, you did more than that. Not only did you stoke the fire in Peter, but you made sure it kept on burning. But what could you possibly hope to gain by breaking us up?'

'Nothing. Which proves you're wrong. I gave him the brochure out of a misguided sense of fun. But my responsibility stops there.'

She hesitated. 'This wasn't about me, was it? Only you were everywhere I turned after Peter left. The only explanation that seems to fit the facts is that you encouraged Peter to go to the other side of the world, feeling pretty sure I wouldn't go with him, in order to go out with me.'

'Don't flatter yourself! As if I could have foreseen that you'd let Peter go off alone! You're going down the wrong path, Claire,' he said, his voice softening and taking on a placatory tone.

'I've always seen myself as your friend. That's why I tried to help you. It's what friends do for each other. Given the circumstances, it's not surprising that we grew closer. But when you said the romantic side of things was over, I accepted that.

I didn't think you meant our friendship was over, though, and I was acting as your friend when I didn't own up to having Peter's address. I was trying to be instrumental to your happiness.' He attempted to smile.

'And that's just what you *have* been, Alex,' she said steadily. 'So I'm sure you'll be delighted for us.'

His brow creased. 'What d'you mean?'

'If it hadn't been for you, Peter's parents would never have given me his address. But because they knew you could pass it on if you thought fit, they felt able to break their promise to Peter and do what you clearly should have done, but didn't.

So indirectly, it's thanks to you that I've now got Peter's address. There's a pleasing irony about that, don't you think?'

She started to walk towards the door, and then paused and glanced at him over her shoulder. 'You can tear up Peter's address—you won't be hearing from either of us again, and we'll never want to hear from you.'

He took a step forward. 'Come on, Claire, you've got this all wrong.'

'I don't think so.' Reaching the door, she stood still and looked back at him. 'I feel sorry for you, Alex. The old Alex had so much going for him by way of personality and looks, and was such fun to be with.

But that Alex has completely disappeared, and a very nasty, very unattractive person has taken his place. For your sake, I hope you can ditch the substitute before it's too late.

As far as I'm concerned, however, this is the last time I shall ever see you, and I couldn't be more pleased about that.'

Turning her back on him, she walked out of the flat and slammed the door shut behind her.

For a long moment, Alex stood and stared at the open doorway.

He heard her bound down the stairs, and he heard the door close behind her as she went out on to the pavement.

And then there was silence.

Trembling uncontrollably, he spun round and ran to the window just as her car was starting to pull away from the kerb on the opposite side of the road.

Leaning forward, he pressed his face against the glass, and watched her car until it disappeared from sight.

Motionless, he continued to stare along the road in the direction she'd taken as she'd driven out of his life.

Finally, the low light of day starting to drain away, he turned and looked around his sitting room.

Desolation weighted the air.

Shaking himself, he went across to his full-length mirror and stared at his reflection. As if seeing himself for the first time for a long time, he saw what Claire had seen—a man in the process of disintegration.

What was he doing to himself, he thought in sudden shock, and he stepped back.

He must pull himself together. This wasn't him.

Fortunately, it wasn't too late.

He just had to accept that Claire and Peter were going to get together, and there was nothing he could do to stop it. They belonged to his past. He must now forget about them, and face his future.

His future, not theirs.

Over the past few months, he'd expended all his time and energy on how to avenge himself on the two of them, and he hadn't given any thought at all as to what he was going to do with his life.

Well, it was time he did.

And thinking about it, in a way he was making the same mistake as Peter—dwelling so much on the future that he wasn't enjoying the present.

Well, things had to change, and they were going to.

He must decide what he wanted to do, and pursue that single-mindedly.

When he'd told Claire he was thinking about being a GP, he'd told her what he knew she wanted to hear, and then he'd kidded himself that this was what he truly wanted.

But in reality, he'd hate the closeness that a GP had with his patients, and he was going to look for a job in a hospital, but not in Birmingham.

There was nothing to keep him there.

Most of his friends had moved away. Mike was about the only one who'd decided to stay in Birmingham. But as he'd got into the habit of coming straight home at the end of his shift, he'd rather lost contact with Mike.

And while he could always get in touch with him again, he didn't know that he could be bothered to try to explain why he'd been shunning the bar, parties, clubs and social gatherings for some time now—or even to understand it himself, for that matter. So it was probably better it leave things as they were.

What he needed was a completely fresh start, and that's what he'd have.

He'd shave, and then he'd have that shower he'd told Claire he was about to take. After that, he'd put on some-thing smart, go up to the hospital, work through every vacancy advertised, and then apply for at least one job.

Taking such immediate, positive action would bring him closer to the end of what seemed to have been a very long tunnel.

Turning away from his reflection, he started towards his bathroom. Then he paused.

It was possibly a little late in the day to be starting on such a venture.

As he had the seven thirty shift the following morning, it would be more sensible to stay on after that and check the list of vacancies, so he might as well leave tidying himself and going to the hospital till the morning.

He poured himself a glass of wine, sank back down on the sofa and put his feet on the coffee table.

He wouldn't lose a job by not going out that evening, he thought. Tomorrow was soon enough.

43

Cobar

CAUGHT in the rays of the morning sunlight as it stood on the dark grey tarmac, ready for take-off, the Beagle shone pristine white above its bright-yellow underbelly.

Peter paused on his way to the plane, medical bag in hand, and stared hard at it.

'My last clinic run,' he said, his voice leaden with regret. 'And my last flight ever for the Service, unless there's a call-out in the next two days.' He glanced at Susie, who'd stopped walking when he did. 'It's nice of you to see me off for this one, Susie.'

'I thought it the least I could do. As you say, it could be the last medical flight you have for a while.'

'You'll be missed, mate,' Ned said bluntly, going ahead and unlocking the door. 'We've got used to you,' he added, rolling up the cabin door.

Peter opened his mouth to comment, then closed it, not trusting himself to speak.

Susie gave him a sideways look. 'You're jumping ahead of yourself, Pete. This might not be your last flight. You've got a month back home in which to decide what to do.'

He turned to her in surprise. 'What do'you mean? I quit the Service, didn't I?'

She grinned at him. 'Not exactly.'

His forehead creased in bewilderment 'What are you talking about. I gave in my notice, and I know you passed it on as they're sending a relief doctor rather than asking Brian to stand in. So what's this about a month?'

'Actually, I only sort of passed your notice on,' Susie said. 'There'll be a relief doctor all right, but they're not looking for an actual replacement for you—not yet, anyway.'

'Sort of passed it on? Surely, you either pass something on or you don't?'

'Oh, oh! I can see someone's on the way to gettin' as mad as a cut snake,' Ned cut in. 'Take my advice, Pete mate,' he said, tapping the side of his nose. 'Don't try to understand what a woman means. It's never worth it.'

'Actually, I told the Service you needed some time off as you'd got ailing oldies in England,' Susie said. 'And why not? They might be ailing and not have wanted to tell you so in a letter. I said you were an only child and had to go back to sort things out, and that you'd need about a month to sort things.'

'Why, you little bottler, Susie,' Ned said with a broad smile. He glanced at Peter. 'She's done you a favour, mate. And maybe the Service, too.'

He threw his bag on to the floor of the cabin, pulled out the airstair and went up into the plane, whistling.

Peter gazed at Susie in amazement. 'What d'you do that

for? You know I won't be returning if Claire's willing to take me back. I know it's a big if after all this time, and after the things I said before I left, but if there's the slightest chance of that happening, I'm going to take it.'

'As you said, it's a big if. She might have found someone else by now and not want to pack him in for you. And even if she hasn't, she might figure that you've already let her down once, as she sees it, and you could do so again.'

'Which'd be a fair comment. Though I wouldn't.'

'And you might find that you'd built her into something she isn't. Absence, rose-coloured glasses, and all that.'

He shook his head. 'I don't think so.'

'On the other hand,' Susie went on, 'you might find that she really does mean more to you than a job you clearly love and are great at. If so, write to the Service and tell them you're not coming back.'

She put her hand on his arm. 'Personally, I think you belong here, Pete, and I've left the door open for you to return if you want. Don't dismiss the possibility that Claire might be willing to come back here with you. If she's missed you as much as you've missed her, it's possible.'

'I wouldn't even hint at it! I don't care where I live, as long as I'm with Claire. She made it very clear that she wanted to stay in England, and I'm going to prove to her that she's more important than any place. If I get the chance to, that is.

I'm willing to live wherever she wants. I've got a lot to prove to her, and banging on about how much I love it here and love the work would not be the way to go about things.'

'Well, just know that the Service door will be open for a month,' she repeated.

He nodded. 'Thanks, Susie. It means a lot to me that you feel so strongly about it. I appreciate it.'

'Forget it; I did what any mate would've done. And I owe you a lot. You got me through a difficult time.'

'I could say the same to you.'

'Like we said before, we were both in the right place at the right time for each other, but it's run its course. It was a ripper of a course while it lasted, though,' she added, smiling at him with open affection.

He grinned at her. 'To quote Ned, ain't that the truth?' He hesitated. 'I'd like to think we'll always be friends, Susie, even with me back in England.'

She shrugged. 'It's a nice idea, but we both know it won't happen. We'll move on and lose touch. That's life. And anyway, when you come back from England—*if* you come back—I won't be here.'

He stared at her is surprise. 'What d'you mean?'

She lowered her voice. 'I've handed in my notice. They radioed me this morning that they're sending a permanent replacement in a couple of weeks, and when I've inducted whoever it is, I'll be off. No one in Cobar knows that yet, and that includes Ned.'

'I'd no idea you were thinking of leaving! How come?'

'If it wasn't for you, I'd probably still be stuck in my guilt about Marco, unable to leave the scene of the crime, so to speak. But thanks to you, I'm not. I'm ready for pastures new. I want to go somewhere that doesn't hold any memories of Marco, and do something entirely different.'

'Where will you go?'

'I'm going to see what I think of Adelaide. Maybe I'll stay there; maybe I won't. I've no ties so I can go wherever I want.'

Peter shook his head in admiration. 'You're something else, Susie Lentini. You've got guts, I'll say that for you.'

'You can say it again after the clinic run,' she said, laughing. 'But we've both got a few more days here, so why are we talking as if it's goodbye now.'

'Perhaps because it feels like it.' He smiled warmly down at her. 'I'll see you when I get back. You can tell me your plans in more detail then.'

He turned from her and walked across to the airstair. Pausing a moment at the foot of the stairs, he gazed up at the plane's fuselage, and then, taking a deep breath, he walked slowly up the stairs and into the cabin.

'Bye, Pete,' he heard Susie call after him.

He raised his free hand in the air and waved it, his eyes fixed firmly in front of him.

THE MINUTE the plane came to a halt, Peter undid his safety belt and got up from his seat in the cockpit.

Pausing a moment, he rested his hand lightly on Ned's shoulder, and then he walked through the cabin, picked up his medical bag, rolled up the cabin door and left the plane.

As he stepped on to the Cobar runway, the finality of what he was doing hit him hard, and he stopped.

Taking a deep breath, he turned back and ran his fingers lovingly along the plane's yellow underbelly.

That might have been the last time he walked down the airstair, he thought, and the last time he would feel as one with a pilot and plane.

Inwardly choking, he slung his medical bag over his shoulder, dragged his eyes from the fuselage and started walking towards the airport building.

His vision blurring, he took his hands from his pockets and wiped his eyes.

He must pull himself together, he told himself firmly. As

Susie said, that might not have been his last flight. He could be called out several times in the next few days, and he'd soon be a total wreck if he went through the same emotional upheaval at the end of every flight.

His vision clearing, he glanced over his shoulder for a last look at the Beagle, and then turned back to face the way he was going.

A figure was standing in front of the airport building, staring in his direction. A slim figure with startling red hair.

The heat must be playing tricks with his eyes, he thought. His steps slowed. He rubbed his eyes with the back of his forearm, blinked a couple of times and looked back at the building.

The figure was still there. It took a step towards him.

He felt a sudden tightening in his chest, a sense that he was going to explode. His bag slipped from his shoulder to the ground. He put his hands to his head in disbelief and stood still.

The figure started to run towards him.

A name sprang to his lips. He wanted to call that name, but he couldn't. He just couldn't. He took a step towards the running figure, and another, and another and he found that he, too, was running.

They reached each other, and stopped, inches apart.

He stared down into her face, his eyes full of disbelief, full of wonder.

'Claire,' he breathed, her name a heartfelt outpouring of love. 'My Claire.'

She nodded. 'I've come home, Peter. Being with you is being home.' Her voice shook. 'I love you with all my heart. I'm here to stay, if you still want me.'

'If I still want you?' he echoed. 'Oh, Claire.'

He held out his arms to her.

With sheer joy on her face, she stepped into his waiting arms. He pulled her close to him, and buried his face in her hair.

Unmoving they stood on the tarmac, their two hearts beating as one.

'THE SUNSET'S never looked more beautiful,' Peter said as they stood on the veranda at the back of his bungalow, staring out at the night, his arm around Claire's shoulders, her arm around his back.

'The sky's never been a more glorious orange, and the streaks of pink and gold have never been richer and deeper. And that's because you're here with me.'

'It's really stunning in a wild, empty sort of way. I can see what you like about the place, Peter.'

'But what I said earlier holds. I was going back to England, anyway, to find you, and if you want to return to England, then that's what we'll do. And I wouldn't look back —not ever.

No matter what I feel about living here, the last few months have shown me that I can never be truly happy unless I'm with you.'

'The same goes for me,' she said, nestling closer to him. 'But you obviously love it here, so I want to give Australia a try. And I've a feeling I'm going to like it, too.'

'There's a locum coming in a few days' time, which means we could go off for a couple of weeks, see a bit of the area, do some exploring.' He glanced down at her. 'And if you still want to stay on when we get back, there's a change I'm going to make.'

'And there are some things *I* want to suggest, too, but you go first.'

'I want us to have a normal life together, and that would be difficult if I stayed a Flying Doctor. The unpredictability of the job makes it incompatible with family life, so I'm going to give up the job.'

She dropped her arm and drew slightly back from him. 'But you love it; that's obvious. It's in everything you say, and in the confidence you've gained. It's in how relaxed and happy you look. I don't want you to give up the job—I want you to do what you're happiest doing. We can work around the hours thing. And anyway, if I get a job as a nurse, I'll have irregular hours, too.'

He started to speak, but she raised her finger to his lips to stop him.

He took her hand, gently moved it aside, then he kissed each finger, one by one.

'Believe me, a nurse's hours are more regular than mine,' he said, putting his arm around her again. 'No, I'm definitely going to do something different, but if what I'm hoping to do works out, I'll enjoy doing it.'

She glanced up at him. 'What've you got in mind?'

'I think I might be able to come to an arrangement with both Cobar Hospital and the local doctor, Brian Bailey. Brian's said several times that he wants to slow down a bit, and I've a feeling he'd be open to a partnership.

And I might be able to get some regular hospital hours, too—maybe a couple of days a week. They need another surgeon. It means moving into town, but we'd have to move, anyway, as the bungalow belongs to the Service.'

She reached across and hugged him. 'That's a great plan to have in reserve, but there's no need to jump into anything.

We've no kids yet so we can take the time to get it right. You don't have to give up flying for me, Peter.'

'I'd be doing it for myself, as much as for you,' he said. 'I want us to come home to each other at the end of the day and spend the evening together, just us and our children, assuming children come along. If I can make the arrangement that I think I can, I'll have you, a family life, and an interesting balance of jobs.'

She reached up and kissed him lightly on the lips. 'It's great to know that there's a good alternative if it doesn't work out, you being a Flying Doctor now that we're together. But let's wait and see what happens.' She paused. 'Thank you for being prepared to give up something you love for me—it means a lot.'

'I'm the one who should be thanking you.' He raised his hand to her head and ran his fingers slowly through her hair. 'I can't believe you're here... you're really here.' His voice broke. 'I can't put into words how happy I am.'

'Me, too, Peter. I was mad to have thought I could ever be happy away from you.'

'And was mad to think of trying to live without you,' he said quietly. 'You mean everything to me, Claire, and you always will.'

She reached up and kissed his cheek. 'And now for my suggestions,' she said. 'It's very simple. I'd like us to fly your parents out for a visit—I owe them so much. And that means we'll need three more chairs for the veranda, and a table. We'll need that for here or wherever we finish up. I want to start and end each day, sitting out here with you as the sun goes down, knowing that there's nowhere in the world that either of us would rather be.'

'Oh, Claire.'

For a long moment, each stared into the face of the other, their eyes filled with love.

All around them, twilight deepened into night, and a multitude of glittering stars shone out of the indigo sky, a canopy of silver splinters that lay above them, illuminating the future.

Their hearts full, hand in hand they turned to face the light.

IF YOU ENJOYED IN A FAR PLACE

...it would be really kind if you could take a few minutes to leave a review of the book.

Reviews give welcome feedback to the author, and they help to make the novel visible to other readers, both through the review and because a number of promotional platforms today require a minimum number of reviews before they'll accept any publicity for that book.

Your words, therefore, really do matter.

Thank you!

LIZ'S NEWSLETTER

Every month, Liz sends out a newsletter that tells you about her work in progress, and any travelling and interesting things she's done in the past month.

You'll be the first to see the cover of the next book to be published, and you'll also receive information about forthcoming promotions and special offers.

You can sign up to Liz's newsletter through her website – www.lizharrisauthor.com

As a thank you for signing up, you'll get a free download of her light almost-contemporary novel, *Word Perfect*, which was inspired by Liz's six years in California.

THE ROAD BACK

In a Far Place is a standalone novel and is complete in itself. However, it tells the story of Peter Henderson, one of the characters in the earlier novel, *The Road Back*.

If you enjoyed *In a Far Place* – and hopefully you did – and haven't yet read *The Road Back,* which came out in a second edition in August 2022, you might be interested in reading the Prologue to *The Road Back,* which you will find in the next few pages.

THE ROAD BACK: THE PROLOGUE

London, early August, 1995

Amy stood under a large black umbrella and stared at the tall Victorian semi-detached house on the opposite side of the road, the house where she'd begun her life, where she'd been cast off by the woman who'd given birth to her.

She put her hand into her pocket and pulled out a yellowing piece of paper.

Holding the crumpled paper close to her chest to protect it from the rain, she read again the first of the words printed on it: her birth name, Nima Carstairs; the name of her birth mother, Patricia Carstairs.

She looked back at the tall house. She'd lived in that house for almost six weeks. Six weeks was no time at all compared with her years in Primrose Hill, where she'd lived before and after she'd married Andrew, but it was an important part of her life

She'd been someone else when she'd lived in that house: she'd been a Nima. And she hadn't been wanted.

Nima. What sort of name was that? Who would call their daughter Nima?

Her eyes were the eyes of a Nima; people were always remarking upon her eyes. But apart from her eyes, would she have looked different, or liked different things, if she'd stayed a Nima?

She'd not been able to stop asking herself those questions since the moment that morning when she'd first opened the letter that her father – her real father, the one who'd brought her up and loved her - had left for her to read after his death.

In his letter he'd written down the name of the home for unmarried mothers where she'd been handed over to him and his wife.

Her eyes had filled with tears as she'd read that that day, thirty-two years ago, had been the happiest day of their lives. He'd gone on to say that he felt she ought to have a way of tracing her birth parents in case she ever wanted to do so, and he'd tucked her Adoption Order into his letter.

She'd felt very strange as she'd unfolded the order and seen the name that her birth mother had given her.

She'd always known she was adopted, but she'd had a happy childhood, loved and protected by her adoptive parents and loving them back in return, and she'd never felt any need, nor any desire, to find out about the people who'd given her away.

Instinctively, she'd known that looking for her birth parents would hurt her mum and dad, and she wasn't going to do anything that would cause them unhappiness. Her birth parents had never been interested in her, and she wasn't interested in them.

So the thrill she'd felt when she'd first read her name

and that of her birth mother had taken her completely by surprise. She'd had to sit down.

For the first time ever, a powerful wave of curiosity had swept through her.

Why had her birth parents given her away like that? Her mother had carried her for nine whole months – how could she have parted with her?

She had carried her own baby for fewer than three months before her miscarriage earlier that year, but she'd been overwhelmed by grief, and so had Andrew, and they were still grieving. What kind of woman could ever give her baby away?

What kind of man could let her?

She'd read her father's letter again, her vision blurred.

He'd known her so much better than she'd known herself, and he'd wanted to help her do something he believed that one day she would want to do.

And her mum must have agreed. The letter was dated two years earlier, just before her mother died. Her father must have asked for it to be given to her after they'd both died. It had been their final act of kindness to her.

She'd read his words again, and had known instantly that she had to go at once to the house where she was born, no matter how bad the weather.

She folded the Adoption Order, put it back in her pocket and stared again at the house in front of her.

The rain was bouncing off the grey tiles of the pitched roof, cascading in sheets over the edge of the eaves and falling on to the sloping roof of the bay window that flanked the heavy dark blue door.

Her eyes on the house, she gripped her umbrella tightly, stepped into the road and walked across to the other side. Her boot hit the kerb and she looked down. The broken reflection of the house swirled in an oily puddle that had pooled in the gutter. A black sump reflecting another world.

She stared back up at the house.

Day was fading fast, but there was no electric light in any of the rooms; the place looked deserted. She probably shouldn't have come on such a dismal day as this, but she had, and she wasn't going to stop now.

She stepped on to the pavement and made her way between the moss-stained brick gateposts, past the squat stump of a tree that lay behind one of the gateposts, to the stone steps that led to the front door.

A shiver of nervous excitement ran through her as she went up the steps: her pregnant birth mother had walked up those same steps almost thirty-two years earlier. And she'd walked back down them again a few weeks later, leaving her baby behind, leaving Nima.

Why?

Reaching the narrow porch, she glanced at the tarnished bronze plaque next to the door. The house was clearly being used for offices. She put her ear against the door and listened hard, but she couldn't hear anyone moving around. Her heart sank: they must have left for the day.

She took a step back and looked along the front of the house to the sash bay window surrounded by chipped white masonry, but she couldn't see into the room.

Large droplets of rain hit her forehead and she moved back under the porch.

A button on an intercom next to the plaque told visitors to press for assistance, so she pressed the button and waited.

The buzzer reverberated in the silent interior of the house. Reluctantly, she turned to leave. She'd have to come back another day, and make it earlier in the day.

Then she heard a sound behind her.

She spun round and saw that the front door was open and that a young woman in jeans and a cream polo-necked jumper was standing in the doorway.

'Can I help you?' the woman asked.

'Gosh, you made me jump!' Amy exclaimed. 'I thought that everyone had gone home.'

'There's only me at the moment, I'm afraid, and I'll be off shortly. But if I can help you at all, I'd be happy to do so.'

'I don't know that I need actual help. To be honest. I just wanted to see inside the house. I don't even really know why.

My name's Amy Stevens and I've just found out that my birth mother stayed here when it was a home for unmarried mothers. I badly wanted to see where I started life. I don't suppose I could have a quick look round?'

Seeing the woman hesitate, Amy took the Adoption Order from her pocket and handed it to her. The woman ran her eyes over it and returned it.

'Come on in,' she said, opening the door wider.

Amy walked into the house.

A long, dimly lit hallway stretched out in front of her. Octagonal marble tiles, inset with small black squares, covered the length of the floor.

At the far end of the hall, a greyish-white staircase led to a shadowy landing. The dark green walls of the hall were broken up by modern, semi-glazed doors, each with a plaque on the front. A large, gilt-edged mirror was fixed on the wall to the right of the front door.

Damp hung in the air.

Amy shivered.

The woman laughed. 'I agree; it's not the most cheerful of buildings. But it's a job, and the people who work here are a great bunch, and that's all that matters. I expect you'd like to wander around on your own. You can go anywhere that's not locked. Let me know when you're ready to leave, will you? I'll be in the room here.'

'Of course, I will. Thank you,' she called after her.

She looked around her, a sense of depression creeping over her at the thought of having started life in such a cold, bleak place, and a lump came to her throat.

She swallowed hard and took a step further into the hall. Her foot slid on the tiled floor. Glancing down, she saw that water was dripping on to the floor from her damp umbrella. There was a metal rack under the mirror, so she went and slotted her umbrella into it.

Straightening up, she caught sight of her pale reflection in the mirror.

Turning back to the hall, her eyes wandered from one door to another. All were closed. Despite the woman's words, she had an uneasy sense of being an unwanted intruder. Her eyes strayed back to the mirror.

The person staring back at her was interesting, rather than pretty. To Andrew, she was beautiful, she knew; but really her face was a little too round, a little too wide. Her long, dark brown hair hung straight, and that narrowed her face a little, but she couldn't disguise her wide mouth.

Andrew always said that when she was happy, her smile took over her whole face.

At the moment, though, she wasn't smiling; her eyes were glistening with unshed tears.

Narrow, almond-shaped and heavy lidded, they were the eyes of a Nima, not of an Amy. Did they come from her natural father, whose name she didn't know, or could they have come from her birth mother, the woman called Patricia Carstairs?

She walked slowly to the foot of the staircase and looked

up at the dark landing. She was probably born in one of the rooms up there and then handed over to someone else.

Why, oh why, had her mother given her away, and why hadn't her father stopped her mother?

What were they like, her birth parents?

ACKNOWLEDGEMENTS

When my debut novel, *The Road Back,* was first published in 2012, I received a large number of letters from readers, many of them asking what happened to Peter Henderson, the missionaries' son.

I decided to tell them, and the result is *In a Far Place*. So my first thank you is to all of the readers who gave me the idea of writing Peter's story, which soon became the story of Peter and Claire.

Once again, I must thank the brilliant cover designer, Jane Dixon-Smith, for a striking cover that perfectly captures the tone of the novel, and to my eagle-eyed editor, Jane Eastgate. I'm tremendously lucky to have both of them in my writing life.

As ever, I must also thank my friend in the north, Stella, who is always the first person to see what I've written and who never fails to be honest about it. Her critical comments are invaluable.

Much of *In A Far Place* is set in Cobar, New South Wales, 1971, at a time when Cobar had a population of about 3000.

I had learnt through my research that NSW was one of only two Australian states at that time where a Flying Doctor didn't have a local medical practice, didn't work in a hospital, and wasn't one of a pool to be called upon in an emergency.

Cobar, a town in NSW, had an airstrip, but it had never

had a Royal Flying Doctor Service, which is why I chose to set the novel there.

Inevitably, research doesn't always come up with everything one needs to know, and I'm very grateful to Peter Morgan, Works Manager for Cobar Shire Council, for his helpful response when I wrote with queries about the Australian setting.

He was kind enough to pass me on to Gary Woodman, General Manager, Cobar Shire Council, and Stewart McLeod Director of Technical Services, Dubbo City Council, both of whom took the time to answer all of my questions. I'm very grateful to them.

Indeed, the prompt response from everyone to whom my requests were passed, and the friendliness with which this was done, made the book a pleasure to research.

I also had excellent help when researching the part of the story that takes place in England.

In researching the geography and curriculum of the medical school and hospital in Birmingham, I was greatly aided by Professor Jonathan Reinarz, Director of the History of Medical Unit, University of Birmingham.

Professor Reinarz was extremely helpful, and I'm enormously grateful for the time and trouble he took to advise me, and to help me with the places to go in order to find the information I needed.

Finally, I should like to thank Dr Anthony Solomon, whom I interviewed about his years as a student in the medical school in Birmingham in the 1960s. By his detailed replies to my questions, Dr Solomon furthered my understanding of the geography of the area, and the relationship between the medical school and the hospital.

Through my membership of the Romantic Novelists' Association and of the Historical Novel Society, I've made some wonderful friends – I won't list them as they know who they are - and my writing is better for our conversation and writerly discussion, frequently over a lunch. I owe a huge debt to them all.

Finally, I'd like to thank my husband, Richard, for being the support that he is, and for putting up with me sitting in front of the computer, lost in my fictional world, hour after hour, day after day.

ABOUT THE AUTHOR

Born in London, Liz Harris graduated from university with a Law degree, and then moved to California, where she led a varied life, from waitressing on Sunset Strip to working as secretary to the CEO of a large Japanese trading company.

Six years later, she returned to London and completed a degree in English, after which she taught secondary school pupils, first in Berkshire and then in Cheshire.

In addition to the fourteen novels she's had published, she's had several short stories in anthologies and magazines.

Liz now lives in Berkshire. An active member of the Romantic Novelists' Association and the Historical Novel Society, her interests are travel, the theatre, reading and cryptic crosswords.

To find out more about Liz, visit her website at:

www.lizharrisauthor.com

ALSO BY LIZ HARRIS

HISTORICAL NOVELS

The Colonials

Darjeeling Inheritance

Cochin Fall

Hanoi Spring

The Linford Series

A sweeping saga set between the wars

The Dark Horizon

The Flame Within

The Lengthening Shadow

General historical novels

The Road Back

In a Far Place

The Heart of the West

A Bargain Struck

The Lost Girl (To be republished in 2023 under the title Golden Tiger)

A Western Heart

CONTEMPORARY NOVELS

The Best Friend

Evie Undercover

The Art of Deception

Word Perfect

Printed in Great Britain
by Amazon

45543279R00219